THE LAST WEEKEND OF SEPTEMBER

BECK STANLEY

ISBN: 978-1-947939-87-5
Printed in the United States of America

Published by Author Source
Kansas City, MO
www.AuthorSourced.com

DEDICATION

Thanks first and always to God for creative gifts and for always hanging on when I let go.

Thanks to my cheering section; my husband and best friend Chuck Stanley; my inspiring friend Dr. Kate Handtke, who led the way; my hero and sister Pamela Ryan; my tolerant and loving son, Dr. Robert Pippin; and my friend LeeAnn Hunter, without whom there wouldn't have been a journey to inspire a story.

A thanks to Mike Owens and the great Author Source Media creative team.

A very special and heartfelt thank you to Dr. Simon Presland, my editor, friend and I believe an earth-bound guardian angel. Your patience and kindness is inspiring.

PROLOGUE

It was late September, 1991. The Colorado landscape changed quickly in mirrored sunglasses as the driver behind them negotiated familiar turns in a sleek, black Mercedes. Hands and jaw muscles flexed and released in nervous anticipation. A rather unpleasant year had passed waiting for this reunion.

Lifting his chin, he tilted his head first one way then the other, urging tensed muscles to relax. Loose gravel sprayed over the embankment as the Mercedes slid around another curve a bit too fast, bringing Horsetooth Lake into view. He knew speed would not take away the damage a year had done. He only wished it could.

* * * * *

Lenore closed her eyes to the sun-warmed breezes of September as they teased and cooled. It wasn't unusual for the early Colorado autumn to provide such a day, but it rarely coincided with an afternoon off. She had nearly decided to just go home and catch up on sleep.

"You're smiling."

Lenore opened her eyes to watch ripples on the lake gently lift and race one another to the shore. In her present state of relaxation, it was an effort to reply to her best friend, but with a yawn she managed. "Thanks for talking me into coming here."

"It didn't take much to convince you," Leah said with just a hint of self-justification.

Lenore didn't state that it was easier to join her best friend on the present adventure than to put up with the whining. Instead, she filled her soul with the beauty surrounding their perch atop a huge boulder. The landscape towered behind them to the trail head and the highway, then receded in front to the clear mountain lake. A soft breeze whispered gently past the duo before continuing its conversation with the trees.

The lake had become a place of solace for Lenore Appleby and Leah Chase when lives became so complicated that gravity seemed to exert too much force, preventing them from soaring. They had laughed, cried, prayed and screamed atop this mass of granite anchored near the shore. They believed, with all certitude, divine hands had placed it there solely for them. It was a place where hurts healed a little faster and nerves calmed a little easier.

Lenore would soon wish she were anywhere else on earth.

The persistent breeze caught her long hair, momentarily blinding Lenore's view. She smoothed the tickling strands from her face and looked where Leah was sitting, only to find her best friend standing.

"What is it with you today?" Lenore scolded. "I'm usually the one who's never still. Sit down, you're ruining the ambiance."

Apparently satisfied for the moment all was secure, Leah obediently sat down beside Lenore. Though her smile remained, her attitude changed abruptly.

"You know, Lenore, I love you very much."

There was no doubt. Leah and her husband, J. D, were like family. A cross between parents and siblings.

"I love you, too." Lenore assured, with a little giggle.

As if disregarding the reply, Leah continued. "We've gotten through so much this past year because of that love. All I ever want for you is happiness, and if I could take all the pain away, you know I would."

Lenore looked into her friend's gray-blue eyes and tilted her head to one side. A slight frown furrowed her brow and she started to reply, but was hushed with a small shake of Leah's head.

"I would never intentionally bring any pain to you. You believe that, don't you?"

Lenore nodded. "Where are we going with this, Leah? Is this going to be like the time you told me you had advanced stages of "CRS," and I thought it was some horrible terminal illness until you said it was "Can't Remember Shit?" She laughed.

Leah did not. She glanced up the trail toward the highway, took Lenore's hand and continued. "You have to trust me now. If you love me and will trust me, you'll understand everything very soon." She looked toward the trail again and smiled as Lenore's eyes followed her gaze. "All the clouds are about to be blown away."

A black Mercedes was parked at the trail head. Lenore's smile was replaced with a whisper of "No" when the driver stepped out of the car. He stopped, looked over the hood at Lenore and Leah, closed the door and began moving toward the trail.

Lenore looked at Leah and shook her hand loose as if stung by a wasp. "What in God's name is going on here?" She stood, gesturing toward the car. "This is something you thought I wanted?"

"Well, yes Lenore. I thought—"

"After all that's happened, how could you ever be a part of this?" Lenore's voice rose as she moved to the edge of the rock. "You've been with me, for God's sake." Tears spilled down her cheeks as she scrambled to the ground.

Leah moved to follow. "Lenore, please wait. Just listen to …." She stopped as she stared into cold, wet-lashed eyes.

"Listen to what?" Lenore glared at Leah. "I can't go through all this again." Then quietly, "Damn it, Leah, you know!"

She turned to leave and heard her name called. It pierced her brain like a bullet.

* * * * *

Gregor Parishnikov stopped on the trail as he watched Lenore clamber down from the rock. Was she coming to greet him? His apprehensions had been for nothing. He smiled and called her name, but something was wrong. She had turned away from him. As if struck a blow, she stumbled slightly, then began running toward the lake.

The hurt and confusion he felt was immediately replaced with fear for Lenore's life. His expertise on mountainous terrain, though untested for nearly a year, would have to enable him to reach her before she reached the water. He passed Leah, and raced on for Lenore.

* * * * *

She knew from the sureness of the footfalls approaching, it was not Leah. Her heart pounded a deafening roar in her ears as panicked eyes looked for an escape. The icy-cold lake was rapidly becoming her only option. Grabbing onto a dead, bleached-out tree to steady herself, Lenore took a deep breath and plunged awkwardly into the water.

She gasped, as the shock of the water temperature registered throughout her body. When a strong hand suddenly seized her arm, stopping her forward momentum, a guttural cry escaped her throat and echoed off the lake surface. She thrashed and struggled against her captor as fear became anger. Years of frustrations exploded from somewhere deep within.

She reached out with her free arm to strike, but it was also quickly restrained. The cold water sapped her strength, making Nike-clad feet heavy and ineffectual as she kicked and strained against the steady force holding her in the now murky water.

Gregor held fast to both of her arms until he felt her struggling subside in the waist-deep water. His tears mingled with water sprayed from his captive's hopeless thrashing. God, what had she been through? How could he ever hope to make it up to her now? He pulled her to the shore, then let Lenore to sink to the ground.

As Gregor released her arms, Lenore felt Leah's comforting touch on her hair, smoothing the wet, tangled veil away from her face. The option of escape exhausted, she spoke between sobs.

"Why are you here? Why are you starting this again? I was getting over it. Over you." She clenched her fists and pressed them into her temples. "Just go away. Don't make me go through this again." Then in a whisper, "I won't survive it."

"I'm not here to hurt you, Lenore. After I tell you what I've come to say, if you still want me to leave, I will go and not return. Please hear my words."

The accent was there. The voice, soft and familiar, but the comfort she had once derived was now replaced by anger. She could not bring herself to look into his face. She feared the hypnotic effect would reach her very soul and destroy any chance of control or sanity.

She stared through tear-glazed eyes at the drops of water falling from her hair onto the ground, forming tiny craters as they dried in the powdery dirt. The soft manicured hand of Leah was on her left knee. The one on her right, softly tracing imaginary lines on her faded jeans, was the hand she had been so willing to place her hopes and life into at one time. The hand that had caressed. The hand that could destroy her now.

CHAPTER 1

Lenore Appleby took one last glance at the house and managed a sad smile. The locked door was symbolic of her unraveled marriage. However, for the next three days she wouldn't have to think about it. For the next three days she could be and do anything she wanted in Glenwood Springs, Colorado. Over three days maybe she would have the strength to do what was inevitable. Vacations, even little ones, were funny that way; they helped clear away the cobwebs and renew one's capacity to face problems, even solve problems.

She arranged her luggage from biggest to smallest at the curb, listening and waiting for the vehicle that would whisk her away from the realities of everyday life and unbearable situations. She couldn't wait inside the house any longer. It was the last weekend of September, 1990 … and the first day of her vacation.

Lenore pushed away thoughts of the situation she was leaving her seventeen-year-old son to face. Joel knew the routine and how to avoid confrontations with his stepfather. He had permission to stay with a friend, if things got out of hand. Yes, Lenore had taken care of everything. She could leave for a while. She had to. Just for a while.

The sound of squealing tires drew her attention to the street. A '72 Chevelle convertible, lovingly referred to as "Baby," driven by a smiling blonde with oversized sunglasses perched on her nose, passed Lenore, did a quick U-turn at the end of the cul-de-sac, and stopped in front of the house. The blonde pulled her sunglasses down and peered over the top as she addressed the laughing brunette.

"Hey, Lady, need a lift?" With that, a bubbling bundle of energy in the form of Lenore's very best friend, Leah Chase, bounded from the car.

After rousing shrieks and affirmations that the day had finally arrived, the two women busied themselves with trying to fit Lenore's luggage into the nearly filled trunk space. It would be no small task, but sheer will and laughter was a powerful force against mass and limited dimensions.

Lenore felt a trickle of perspiration slide down her forehead and onto her nose where it dangled until she wiped it with the back of her hand. She looked at Leah. Her friend seemed to be working just as hard, but there wasn't the faintest show of sweat.

"How do you do that?"

Leah glanced at Lenore, then stopped and looked at her fully. "Do what?"

"Keep from sweating."

Leah laughed and shrugged her petite shoulders. "Well, if I do, I'll have to re-do my make-up and we simply do not have time to spare."

Lenore nodded, thoughtfully. "Guess that's what I get for not wearing much make-up. I can sweat."

"No, no, no, no, no Lenore." Leah wagged a manicured finger. "You're not sweating, you're glowing."

Lenore wiped another liquid bead from the tip of her nose. "No, this is definitely sweat."

Leah laughed. "Hmmm, must be the same stuff that has my bra totally soaked right now. We'll cool off if we ever get on the road."

"Right."

They poked the last of the shoes, cameras and a stray jacket into the corners, then placed a full garment bag atop the pile. The trunk lid refused to latch.

"Okay Leah, sit on the top of the trunk," Lenore instructed, certain it was merely a matter of leverage. "Then it'll latch." She forced the trunk down to its almost closed position.

Trusting Lenore's logic, Leah stepped onto the bumper, turned and planted her rear on the freshly polished surface. She immediately slipped off and slammed into Lenore, who barely managed to keep them both from tumbling into a heap. The trunk lid sprung up in open defiance.

After laughter subsided, and Leah assured Lenore she had no desire to re-mount, they re-arranged and shifted the contents until, with some persuasion, the trunk lid closed. Then they stood back.

"Think it's going to hold?" Lenore asked.

"Maybe. Probably. Don't you?" Leah reached out and tapped the trunk lid with her palm. It didn't budge. She pushed a little harder and jumped back, throwing her arms in front of her face as if expecting an explosion. Her antics provoked more laughter from Lenore.

Convinced it would remain closed for their trip, the ladies gave a final pat to the lid and walked to their car doors. Lenore noted the parade boot covering the downed convertible top.

"I've never seen this before. It looks great!"

Leah beamed with pride. "It's such a task to put on, but J.D. helped me because he knew I wanted Baby to look her best for our trip."

"And she does. I'd say she looks really slick."

* * * * *

Leah's groan could scarcely be detected above the sound of the engine roaring to life. Laughter filled the air as they drove out of the neighborhood. Troubles, concerns and everyday life were tucked away with the luggage. With a final stop for ice to chill the rivers of Diet Coke habitually consumed, and a plenary of snacks to sustain life in the unlikely event of being stranded along a major interstate for a month or two, the two friends were finally heading out of town.

Seatbelts and sunglasses in place, and cups of Diet Coke brimming in the cup holders, Leah eased the convertible onto the interstate, then accelerated, and was rewarded with a roar from the peppy 350 small block engine. The Chevelle's custom rosy beige paint glistened in the morning sun as she conveyed her passengers toward their destination. For Lenore and Leah, it was more than a ride. It freed their souls to soar.

CHAPTER 2

John Dixon III sat across the table from the older man and sipped his coffee. Like his companion, he was an agent for the Central Intelligence Agency of the United States. His assignment was to closely monitor the activities of former Soviet citizens, who had been granted political asylum. Dixon's assignment, Gregor Parishnikov, had been a most efficacious agent for his government. It was only after months of interrogations at "The Farm" near Langley, Virginia, that the former Soviet citizen was placed in Colorado. Having been the senior agent in charge of monitoring the transition from defection to release, Dixon was offered the opportunity to continue on a permanent basis. He had eagerly accepted the assignment. Colorado was home and provided an opportunity to escape the congested lifestyle around Washington, D. C.

It wasn't a difficult assignment, though there was always suspicion that the Russian was simply making himself a comfortable front for other activities. They offered him counter-agent status, but he had wanted out of the game. No deals. A reluctance to return to the Soviet Union to face a potential bullet blasted into the base of his skull, or imprisonment that could ultimately have the same effect, seemed reason enough to let him decline the offer.

Keeping an eye on Parishnikov was not just for national security. It was necessary to maintain the Russian's health. Factions, both Soviet and American, resented him and would have no compunctions about eliminating him. The man seemed genuinely grateful for John Dixon's presence.

Parishnikov was a solitary person, more out of necessity than design. He skied Aspen and Snowmass, hiked throughout the region's back country and occasionally spent an evening satisfying his passion for dancing to American music at nearby clubs. There were no regular partners, and since his English was heavily accented, his conversations were few. His smile was genuine, his manner polite and locals were friendly, if not downright protective of him.

However, none were considered friends. It was of his own choosing. Living a lifetime without the luxury of being able to trust anyone was hard to change.

Dixon was the closest thing to a friend for Parishnikov. Gregor knew John was one person he could trust, had to trust, for that matter. He taught the American to ski black diamonds and appreciate mountain back country. John taught him the basics of American life, from grocery shopping to house purchasing. They talked and laughed easily together. John knew Gregor could lose him on a backpacking trip, or ski far from the American agent's ability to follow. He tried to avoid thoughts of more mortal consequences, though he had occasionally felt a tinge of dread when they were separated on a remote trail. Always, Gregor would be waiting around a curve or atop a fallen log for John to catch up; his mischievous grin allaying any misgiving from John. Though it was a friendship of sorts, John never forgot who he was watching; that would be as dangerous as turning his back on a bear.

Today, John would be turning his assignment over to Frank Gillespie for a week, possibly two. Frank was nine years his senior, though at forty-two, John outranked him. They had worked together for ten years on various assignments, and it was John's duty to familiarize Frank with the dossier of Gregor Parishnikov, a.k.a. Greg Parish.

John studied the man who shared the table with him. Frank was a no-nonsense sort; regulation all the way. He had apparently seen little joy in life, evidenced by the creases in his face. They represented tough assignments and short nights sleeping on lousy pillows. His eyes were quick; he missed little. His idea of going casual was taking off his tie and not putting a military shine on his wing-tips. This was going to be like putting oil and water together, but Gillespie was one person John knew he could rely on to provide surveillance and protection for Parish.

"Frank, do they make wing-tipped hiking boots?" John teased.

"Christ, don't you have any little old ladies for me to watch?" The older agent cringed, shook his head and frowned. "How about a nice dull accountant?"

Although being necessarily fit and trim, Frank wasn't the athletic, outdoor type.

John laughed. "Don't panic. Parish has promised to take it easy on you. He'd love to get you onto a mountain trail because he thinks everyone should enjoy the outdoors, but he doesn't have any plans to go climbing this weekend."

"I feel a great relief," Frank muttered, opening his note pad. "Now what's his routine?"

"Usually gets here around eight on Friday night, does a little grocery shopping, then goes home. Saturday he'll pretty much stick around the house; you know, yard work, house work. Might take the dogs for a run around the property."

John was amazed that Frank was actually writing everything down.

"Sunday is another quiet day at home if he's not on a mountain, then on Monday he goes back to Denver, leaving about four in the morning. Stays in the apartment I showed you. Very routine. Back to Glenwood Friday evening."

Frank stopped writing and looked up at John. "That's almost a little too routine. This could be better than a little old lady."

"Well, there's an occasional break in that routine." John smiled and raised his eyebrows. "If the mood hits him, he might go dancing Saturday night. He loves country-western music. Says it's very American."

Frank tapped his pen on the paper. "Then he picks women up, goes home with them or takes them to his home?"

"Hardly. He dances with a few, but always goes home alone. Says he's never met one he wanted to take the time needed to explain his life. He doesn't think an American woman would accept him if he did, and he's perfectly happy with his current lifestyle."

"Or so he says." Frank frowned. "So how do I tail him?"

"You go dancing." John grinned as Frank stared at him.

"What I mean is, you don't tail him. You simply go where he's going. He'll probably even ask you to join him for breakfast Sunday morning. He makes a pretty good omelet."

Frank sighed, sat back in his chair and tossed the pencil down next to the notepad. "That's not regulation, Dixon."

"You're right. Regulation doesn't work with Parish. He's aware of the surveillance and accepts it. He's very suspicious of someone who's there, but pretending they're not. He was KGB, remember?"

Frank crossed his arms over his chest. "All the more reason not to fraternize."

John wondered if he would be able to get through the regulation book imprinted on Frank's brain. "It's not considered fraternization. The Company knows this is the only way to observe Parish. You have to get right in the middle of his life. He has nothing to hide and actually appreciates the companionship. He trusts me; there aren't many he does. He's an intelligent, honest man who chose to make this his country."

Frank pondered the information for a moment, then blew out a breath. "I suppose if the Company knows and accepts, then I'll have to."

John knew this wasn't easy for Gillespie, given the older agent had put in time as an operative in Europe. He had encountered more than one KGB agent, though to the best of John's knowledge there had been no deadly incidents. Just the cat and mouse games spies play in the world of espionage.

"I hope so, Frank. It's the only way."

Frank nodded. "I'll play it by your rules. Now, when do we meet?"

"This evening. Today we'll go over area maps and I'll acquaint you with his territory. We'll do a visual of his home and the surrounding property. I'll introduce you to the young couple who house-sit while Parish is gone during the week. They watch the place and care for the dogs." John picked up the check from their waitress, and Frank didn't protest. "You're going to get a crash course on this one. It's all you should need to take over so I can hop a plane for D. C. tomorrow morning."

John left a twenty-dollar bill on the table for a ten-dollar ticket and the two agents left the café.

Walking through the parking lot, Frank immediately lit a cigarette and offered one to John, who refused as usual. It was never a habit he had acquired, though he occasionally found a good cigar enjoyable.

"Frank, if this were your permanent assignment, you'd give up those things."

The older agent inhaled deeply and squinted against the morning sun, then exhaled a thick cloud of smoke. "So, you'll be gone two weeks?"

"John nodded. "At the most. You know how things go back at headquarters."

"Going to go visit your family?"

John shrugged. "The smell of old money clogs my sinuses, but I'll probably visit my grandfather. He's not doing well. When I'm not busy at Langley, I'll spend as much time as I can with John Milton Dixon, the original."

"Isn't he the source of all that old money?" Frank asked.

"Yes, but he never wallowed in it. He earned it, made himself comfortable and raised his family. My uncle is the one who took over and made it dirty. Once Grandfather was voted out, he wanted no part of it. He couldn't control how it was used."

"Guess you're a lot like him. You could be sitting back there at board meetings and fancy dinner parties. You do have the interest your father left you, right?"

John nodded. "Yes, but I'll take hiking around these beautiful mountains any day. Hell, thanks to Parish, I'm skiing black diamonds."

Frank shuddered. "Just don't forget to come back."

The two agents reached John's black Mercedes and he patted the older agent on the back.

"What's the matter Frank. Afraid you'll have to give up those wing-tips?"

"Hell no! Just hate the thought of having to get a cleated sole put on. It'll ruin the fine lines."

John laughed, more at the thought of Frank scrambling around rocks and traversing mountain streams than the picture of heavy hiking soles attached to such a classic styled shoe. As soon as Frank finished his cigarette, they climbed into the car.

CHAPTER 3

Rush hour traffic abated by the time the Chevelle convertible had maneuvered around Denver, on I-70 westbound and into the fold of mountains. They left the Front Range of Colorado, where the foothills of the Rocky Mountains tiptoe onto the plains of Eastern Colorado and the cities of Fort Collins, Denver, Colorado Springs and Pueblo clutter and crowd against the foothills from north to south. As they drove past the ordinary people going about their business, Lenore and Leah felt splendidly unplugged from routines. Though they both enjoyed driving, Lenore was a gracious, if somewhat reluctant, passenger, and a most competent driver when it was her turn. In the throes of conversation, Leah had a tendency to follow her gaze rather than the curve of the road, and had no sense of where she was when they were away from familiar territory. Lenore was a consummate driver with an uncanny knack of direction.

On this, their second trip to Glenwood Springs, familiarity heightened their excitement. Golden Oldies blared from the radio until granite and earth blocked the signal. An assortment of tapes would provide a plethora of familiar tunes until communication with local stations beyond Glenwood Canyon was possible.

The freshness of the mountain air and pine forests further lifted their spirits. The sight of two attractive women, laughing and animated in the classic convertible, provoked a few stares and a couple of outright flirtations.

"I'm old enough to be their mama." Lenore laughed as two young men cruised beside the convertible, smiling and waving, until traffic forced them to continue their journey. "If they only knew, they certainly wouldn't waste any time putting miles between us and them."

"Now Lenore, we aren't that old." Leah quickly checked her reflection in the rearview mirror. "They obviously appreciate what they see. Can you find the tape with the sixties tunes?"

Lenore opened the tape case and began the search. "Which one do you want? There are three different sixties tapes."

"I don't know. Read what's on them."

Lenore began reading the tiny print on the back of the cassettes and was relieved when Leah made her choice. She popped the tape into the player and settled back into the comfortable bucket seat.

Leah chattered above the music. "Isn't this beautiful Lenore? They say this is supposed to be the peak weekend for Aspen viewing."

Lenore nodded.

"The weather report was good, too." Leah continued. "Highs in the seventies through Monday. Perfect, huh?"

"Great."

Whether it was from reading the small print or watching the road through a windshield too close, due to the cooler's location on the floorboard behind her seat, Lenore had a headache. The accompanying nausea and dizziness signaled the onset of motion sickness. She closed her eyes, trying to will away the affliction.

Leah glanced over at her friend. "Lenore, what's wrong?"

"Can we stop?" Lenore groaned. "Don't panic, but I'm about to throw up."

Leah pulled onto the Interstate's shoulder as far as she could. As soon as the car stopped, Lenore bolted from the car and walked a few steps before the retching began.

Leah scooted across the seat and out the passenger door. She stood alongside, making sure Lenore's hair was free of the flow. When the action slowed to an occasional gag, Leah guided Lenore to an outcropping of basket-sized boulders where they both sat down.

"I didn't think that was a normal shade of green for you. Keep breathing deeply." Leah offered a tissue produced from her pocket and handed it to her friend. "Breathe in through your nose and out your mouth, slowly. In and out. That's it. Keep it up. In and out."

Lenore obeyed as Leah walked back to the car for paper towels that were lying beside the ice chest. She tore a couple of sheets from the roll, then opened the chest and dipped them in the ice water. The mountain air was tainted with exhaust fumes from the interstate traffic coursing past, oblivious to two women. When Leah handed the wet paper towels to her friend, Lenore buried her face in them and didn't bother to remove it when Leah announced that a Colorado Highway Patrol car was pulling in behind the Chevelle. Leah stood to meet the officer walking toward them.

"What seems to be the problem?"

"Well Lenore's thrown up." Leah gestured toward the brunette nestling her face in a paper towel, as if it was an obvious situation.

He looked first at the petite blonde addressing him, then where Lenore sat, still breathing slowly and deliberately. "Looks like this must be Lenore." He stood closer. "Motion sickness?"

She nodded.

"Can you help?" Leah pleaded.

The officer looked over at her. "I can only suggest you get to a drug store and buy medication, if you're going to continue your trip. Where ya heading?"

Lenore looked up from the paper towels and managed a weak reply. "Glenwood Springs."

The patrolman offered her a soft smile. Lenore didn't know if it was because of the green of her eyes or the green of her complexion.

"It's just not a good idea to stop on the highway. Do you think you can make it to Idaho Springs? You're not far."

Lenore nodded. She accepted his hand to stand up, and accepted his assistance back to the convertible. She sat down, resting her head on the back of the seat. Leah climbed in behind the wheel and secured both their seat belts, which produce a smile and a tip of the hat from the officer.

"I'll be right behind you until we get to Idaho Springs, then I'll lead you to a drug store."

"Officer, you might not want to follow too closely in case she throws up again, you know." Leah offered the advice with the utmost sincerity.

"You're probably right, Ma'am." The officer returned to his patrol car as Lenore shook her head slowly. Leah maneuvered the convertible back into the flow of traffic.

"Lenore, wasn't he handsome?"

"I didn't notice," she replied, with closed eyes. "How much further?"

"He said it wasn't far. Wasn't that nice of him to stop?" Lenore didn't reply, but Leah continued. "You should have seen his eyes. Beautiful blue. Bet he has a hairy chest."

"Leah, Robert Redford himself wouldn't interest me right now. Let's just find the drug store."

"Oh, okay." Leah pouted for a moment. "But you know, one of these days you'll appreciate good looking guys again. Here's our exit."

It was the only thing Lenore wanted to hear. The patrol car passed, then led them into the pharmacy's parking lot. The patrolman lowered his window when the two women got out of their car.

"They should have what you need in there. You might want to let the medication take effect before you get back on your way. If you follow the walk there," he gestured, "you can go under the interstate and see the falls." His smile and manner were sincere. "Have a safe trip, ladies."

Lenore nodded and smiled weakly as Leah attempted to continue the conversation.

"Thank you so much for your help." She walked beside the patrol car as it was slowly pulling away. Lenore turned toward the store as Leah posed another question. "Are there any road reports you could give us?"

"The roads are clear. May be a few flurries on Vail pass, but nothing major. Probably not even enough to put the top up on your convertible. You'll encounter a delay in Glenwood Canyon where they're working on the road."

Lenore was at the door when Leah relented, thanked the patrolman and sprinted to catch up with her. Inside, while Lenore found the Dramamine, Leah was de.ep in conversation with employees and customers at the pharmacy desk. She could find common ground with a total stranger. The naïve individual would find themselves hopelessly drawn into Leah's web of words, and open up the way a tightly closed bud responds to warm sunlight. Lenore marveled at how Leah never seemed to meet strangers. She always walked away knowing things about people most ministers never learn about the most faithful of their flock. It was a common occurrence and never inspired gossip from the two women.

Leah collected people. She was hard to resist. Her smiling blue-gray eyes peeked out from the blonde fringe atop her five-foot petite frame. She was a beautiful woman both physically and spiritually. A gentle kindness surrounded her like an aura. Her stylish locks were always in place; nails and make-up done to perfection. Her laughter and sincerity put the most troubled soul at peace. Lenore loved her best friend.

Lenore's physical assets were, in her own mind, a little less discernible. Long, dark, straight hair, neatly trimmed to just below her shoulder blades, was always shiny and full, and usually the first thing most people noticed about her. Though initially shy, her reserved demeanor never affected her professionalism at work. That, she reasoned, was different than personal encounters. She was five inches taller than Leah, and though never considered petite, she had an attractive figure. It took restraint and exercise for Lenore to maintain it, while Leah's figure was as perky as her personality. She exercised for the sheer enjoyment of it.

Those who knew Lenore well would agree that her eyes were a secret weapon. She could hold someone's attention with a full gaze from dark brown eyes framed in black lashes. Leah called them Lenore's barometers. Tiny specks of green became startlingly dominant when she was angered, sad or ill. Truly the mirrors of her soul, they evoked the honest, trusting spirit dwelling within. Few were privileged enough to look long into the mirror.

With a glass of water secured by Leah from her newfound friends, Lenore took the motion sickness medication before leaving the building. Following the suggestion of the officer, the ladies crossed the street to walk along Clear Creek, a river from which the town had once managed to dredge a successful economy. There were dark weathered timbers from a long-abandoned mill on the opposite shore, vestiges of a time when the town's economy depended on something other than the many travelers on Interstate 70.

The timbre of a waterfall soon lured Lenore and Leah through a walkway under the interstate to an observation area. There, cooling mist floated from a tall cascade of water to kiss their faces, then drift away, allowing the dry mountain air to soothe and warm their skin.

Lenore's nausea and headache gradually faded, and Leah knew things were back to normal when she began having to pace alongside Lenore to carry on a conversation.

"Guess you're ready to go."

Lenore looked at her watch. "We've been here nearly an hour. We should get back on the road. We've still got a lot of miles to go."

"I need to find a place to whiz." A very normal announcement for Leah.

"We'll go back in the drug store. They won't mind." Lenore grinned. "Heck, they'll probably send you Christmas cards this year, if you leave your address."

Lenore had made the remark in jest, but when they entered the drug store, employees greeted Leah by name. Lenore was perfectly content to be the anonymous friend of Leah Chase.

Before resuming their westward journey, Lenore moved the cooler to the driver's side of the back floorboard, allowing the seat and her nose to ride further away from the windshield. The air was noticeably cooler with higher elevations near the Eisenhower Tunnel, but warmed again when they descended the mountain and drove into Silverthorne, where the Golden Arches of McDonald's promised a quick lunch. They entertained one another and the workers by speaking in their version of a proper British accent.

After lunch, Leah tossed the keys to Lenore as they approached the convertible. "Your turn to drive."

"I thought you wanted to drive all the way," Lenore remarked, not unhappy with receiving the new duties.

Leah took a panoramic view of their surroundings. "I thought I did too, but it'll be safer if you drive. I'm doing too much looking." She stopped and regarded Lenore. "Unless you're sleepy from the medication."

"I feel fine since we ate." She took a deep cleansing breath and surveyed the mountains surrounding them. "I sure don't remember the trees being this brilliant last year. Why don't you take some pictures along the way?"

With Leah's help, she moved the cooler back over to the passenger side, then reached down beside the driver's seat and pushed the lever to slide the seat a little further from the windshield.

"Excellent idea!" Leah agreed as they walked to the back of the car. "I don't think the colors had reached peak last year."

Lenore inserted the key into the trunk, then hesitated for a second or two, wondering if there would be a problem closing it again. She gave the key a turn and the trunk lid opened normally. "Imagine how spectacular the scrub oak will be around Glenwood Springs?" She smiled, visualizing their destination.

"It's not far now." Leah assured, as they retrieved cameras, jackets, gloves and earmuffs. The lid offered no resistance when it closed.

* * * * *

Nearing the top of Vail Pass, Lenore and Leah donned foul weather gear, along with their sunglasses, determined to take the pass with the top down. Snow flurries on the pass necessitated using the wipers, and the heater was on high, but the ladies never felt the slightest discomfort. Occupants of passing vehicles would alternately shake their heads and smile or wave with a thumbs-up.

After descending the pass and driving past Vail, the weather allowed them to shed jackets and accessories. The heater was turned off as brilliant sunshine and seventy-four-degree air warmed them nicely.

Lenore was glad to be driving. Leah admitted she would have driven them, quite literally, into some of the most beautiful sights on earth. The shimmering gold Aspen trees tucked and nestled among the dense forest evergreens of the mountains and valleys provided one spectacular view after another. Lenore finally stopped to let Leah take pictures. She was tired of trying to drive and hang onto Leah's shirt tail as the free-spirited blonde stood up in the car to snap a view.

Conversation quieted upon entering Glenwood Canyon. They marveled at the beauty and differences from the eastern slope of Colorado. The canyon was dark and narrow, with stratified rock buckled from the earth's formation, and deepened by erosion of the river flowing through. It allowed only narrow glimpses of the clear blue sky above.

"We've certainly seen changes just since last year," Leah remarked.

"Yes, but as nice as it is to have a four-lane highway, I still miss the old road. It made me feel nestled down into the earth."

"Well, Lenore, there are the tunnels. How much more nestled down in the earth can you get than inside a tunnel? You even get to beep the horn!"

Lenore laughed. "Silly me, what was I thinking?" She checked her watch. "I wonder if we'll get there by 2:30? The construction delays weren't too long."

"Probably, but I wasn't aware of a deadline."

"Sorry. I'm just used to meeting schedules and moving all day long." She stretched and arched her back against the plush seat. "How 'bout I put my watch away when we get to the lodge and leave it in my purse for the entire weekend?"

"You'd do that for me?"

Lenore smiled and patted her best friend on the arm. "Leah, I think I'll do it for myself."

Glenwood Springs, Colorado was less than a half hour away.

―

CHAPTER 4

South of Glenwood Springs, three men sat in a comfortable living room. The host was gracious and animated, anxious to put his guests at ease. John knew Greg Parish as well as anyone was allowed and felt secure in turning his assignment over to Frank. The flow of conversation seemed to indicate Frank and Greg were compatible. They talked of Greg's enjoyment of the outdoors. Sensing Frank's uneasiness, the Russian wanted to assure the older agent.

"There are many things I need to do here at my home in preparation for winter. I will not be doing any hiking this weekend."

"I can't say I'm disappointed, but don't change your routine for me."

"I assure you I will not, Frank."

There was only a slight edge to their voices. John knew Greg was sincere, though he suspected the household chores were more of an invention than a necessity, out of respect for his new comrade. He would not test abilities as he had with John. It was the Russian, not particularly the Soviet, way to respect elders. He looked at John, giving a slight nod. Yes, it would be safe to leave for a while.

"Great! If you two have worked out your plans, we need to be leaving." John stood and shook hands with Greg. "I appreciate your coming home early tonight for the meeting. I can get back to Denver earlier and get some rest before I hop the plane to D.C. tomorrow morning. I'll be as close as a phone call, if there's a problem."

"It is never an inconvenience to come to my home earlier than planned, and there will be no problems in your absence." Greg smiled at Frank, then spoke again to John. "You will return in one week, correct?"

"One week at the least, two at the most."

"Are you sure you do not have time for eating?" Greg asked. "I would be pleased to prepare dinner. It would be enjoyable to have company."

"Another time, Greg. Thanks." John walked toward the door.

Frank shook hands with the Russian though he didn't offer comment on the dinner invitation. The two agents were escorted to the black Mercedes. As they pulled away from the house and onto the road, Gregor Parishnikov stood near his house flanked on either side by two Great White Pyrenees dogs.

He was not a tall man, by some standards. At five feet nine with the physique of a well-trained athlete, his height was never a detriment. He was tanned from the many outdoor activities he enjoyed, and the dark hair falling in natural waves to his collar was beginning to show a few strands of white at the temples. He wore a well-trimmed beard and mustache of thick black hair, devoid of the influx of white.

His eyes were dark and behind them was a lifetime of learning to read people quickly and accurately. Trust was rarely an option. This Frank Gillespie would be no challenge. Gregor would follow a routine for a few days, just to make him comfortable. He smiled. It would be a game. A game that would result in fulfilling a promise he had made himself when he left the Soviet Union. John would no doubt be angry with him. He would understand at a later time.

Gregor Parishnikov startled the dogs as he turned and mounted the steps to his house, laughing and clapping in a most unfamiliar way. There were plans to make.

* * * * *

A few miles down the road the two agents discussed plans of their own.

"You seem comfortable with the situation, Frank."

The older agent popped a piece of gum into his mouth, knowing he couldn't smoke in the Mercedes. "Yes, if Parish is all he appears to be."

"Well, in two years he hasn't given me any reason to think otherwise."

Frank was quiet for a minute. "Why'd he leave the Soviet Union? I figured once KGB, always KGB."

"He says he wanted something else." John negotiated the turn into a motel parking lot, pulling up next to Frank's truck. "It nearly cost him his life to leave. He took out one of their agents."

Frank looked at John with raised eyebrows. "He killed someone?"

"No, he blew away both of his kneecaps. Poor bastard probably wished he would have killed him." John shut off the engine and turned to face Frank. "No way Greg could ever go back. He'd be dead in a heartbeat. There's always the chance they could make a hit on him here, too."

"Likelihood?"

"Low."

"Great. Maybe I can catch up on some of my reading this week." Frank looked relieved, almost relaxed.

"Better than a little old lady?"

"Infinitely!"

Frank climbed out of the car, immediately lighting a cigarette and spitting his wad of chewing gum to the middle of the parking lot. John wondered what lucky citizen was going to enjoy scraping the mess off a shoe at some point. He stood beside the car and surveyed the cheap motel Frank had chosen.

"You know, Frank, the Company would pay for the best room in town for you."

Frank shrugged his shoulders. "Why? This is closest to the subject, and all I need is sleep and a shower."

"Your choice. Give me a call if there's a problem."

Frank tipped his fingers to his forehead in a slight salute and walked to his room. John got back in the car and began his trip to Denver. He was going to miss Colorado. Little did he know he was going to miss the beginning of a great adventure.

CHAPTER 5

The eastern city limits of Glenwood Springs would have been evident to the blind, but the assaulting odor produced by natural hot sulfur springs produced cheers and laughter from Lenore and Leah. A familiar route soon deposited them at their favorite lodge, where the older gentleman behind the desk seemed genuinely glad to see them, greeting Leah by name, of course.

After receiving a key to the same room they had shared on their previous visit, collecting an assortment of brochures and the local paper, they turned toward the door. The large, stuffed black bear standing alongside the exit appeared to salute, and as they had done on their previous visit, they simultaneously saluted in return. Their silliness caused the clerk to laugh, and knowing smiles from the departing duo.

It took several trips from the car to their room on the second floor before they kicked off shoes, opened fresh cans of Diet Coke and toasted their arrival. Their home for the next few days closely resembled a rummage sale with clothes, jackets, shoes and cameras scattered from the front door to the bathroom. It didn't matter. They had a lifetime to put everything in some semblance of order, or at least if felt that way for the moment. They were away from normal routines and normal lives. Until they returned home on Monday, there would be no schedule to keep and no one to please but themselves. Lenore struggled with the obvious.

"We should get things in order."

"No," Leah corrected. "We should put it off and go have some fun. We're finally here! We have to clean up and organize all the time. Be a rebel, Lenore. Walk around it and let's go to the pool."

Relenting, she looked down at her wrist. "I guess if I'm going to be a rebel, I'd better ditch this thing right now." She unfastened and deposited the offensive timepiece on top of the television. "I'm on 'Quality Time.' The rebel is ready to howl." And she did.

"That's the spirit, Lenore. I swear that watch is around your neck instead of your wrist."

"It's the only way I know how to function these days. Without time and routines, I'd never survive."

"Not this weekend!"

"No, not this weekend. Routines be damned!" She began digging through the piles until a suitcase surfaced. "Let's go to the pool!"

"The big stinky one?" Leah asked, opening her own suitcase.

"No let's save that for tomorrow. How about the motel pool tonight? We can sit in the hot tub for a while, too."

"Good thinking, you little rebel."

After a quick change, and checking to make sure nothing showed that shouldn't show, they grabbed towels and walked to the pool. Lenore was the first to get into the clear blue water. Although a chill was enveloping her, she managed to lure the dainty blonde into the water.

"This is wonderfully refreshing. Hop in."

Leah, determined to keep her hair dry, sat on the edge and eased slowly into the water, shrieking as the cold penetrated her bathing suit.

"Lenore Appleby, this is freezing! How can you stand it?"

"The key is to keep moving. You'll get used to it. This is a heated pool."

"They need to turn up the thermostat for me. I'll just stand here until someone arrives with an ice pick to get me out."

Lenore left Leah dipping herself shoulder deep in the water and swam underwater to the opposite end of the pool, then surfaced to swim two laps before stopping near Leah.

"Ready to go to the hot tub?"

Leah's nod and chattering teeth were answer enough. She accepted Lenore's hand as they took the shortest route, over the side of the pool instead of the steps.

"I'm frozen to the core!"

"I feel absolutely marvelous! Invigorated! Alive!" Lenore teased as she grabbed their towels.

"The word 'insane' comes to my mind," Leah called over her shoulder as she led the way through the door to the hot tub.

Humid air and the odor of chlorine greeted their senses as they draped their towels on white plastic deck chairs, then eased slowly into the water.

"This water is really hot!"

"It's supposed to be. That's how this large, lovely tiled unit gets its name." Leah sank down into the agitating water, serenity easing across her face.

Lenore scrunched her nose against the splatter of bubbles. "I meant it felt overly hot."

"That's because you froze your tight little butt off and didn't realize it until now. Relax and let the bubbles soothe you."

Though Leah stayed far enough above the water to ensure her hair would remain dry, Lenore sank to neck level and blinked against the popping bubbles. She allowed her arms to rise and float in the water, imagining herself a rigid noodle, succumbing to the effects of boiling water. She relaxed and soon her face was bathed in serenity as well.

"You know Leah, there were a lot of times when I didn't think we'd make it back this year. I really needed this. It's worlds away from reality and I love it."

"Do you think we'd appreciate it as much if things were better back home?" Leah asked.

"Maybe not. Probably not."

Their voices echoed off the tiled walls. A couple who had been nuzzling one another on the other side of the pool got out and left. Leah seized the moment to breach a subject Lenore wanted to forget.

"Lenore, I don't have any choices right now. I have to help Shelly with the boys until she finishes school, but then they'll be out on their own. In the interim, I have a loving husband to take some of the stress away. You're doing the right thing, getting away from Nick. When are you going to file for divorce?"

The dark-haired lady looked at the steam covered windows, knowing she couldn't ignore the question. "I don't know, Leah. This is such a scary situation. You just don't understand."

"Tell me what's so scary."

"Fear of the unknown, or maybe just knowing what's coming. I've been through one divorce. I remember what it was like trying to raise my two little boys alone. I wanted to hang on long enough to get Joel out of high school. Have I the right to disrupt his senior year of high school like this because I'm unhappy?" She stared at the bubbles. "I haven't exactly given him a stable life anyway. I keep thinking Nick will go back to the way he was in the beginning. It was good in the beginning." She let the bubbles tickle the palms of her hands. "Besides, I really hate being a two-time loser."

Leah sat up straight and stared at Lenore. "Do you want me to address those individually or all at once?"

Lenore shifted in the water and let her head sink beneath the surface. Leah watched the long dark hair dancing with the bubbles, knowing Lenore would come up eventually. It didn't take very long. She surfaced with a gasp and immediately pushed the hair back from her face.

"Whew! Don't ever try that! I think you could boil your brain."

"I don't think I'd ever consider it. Now, let's talk."

Lenore groaned. "You're ruining the moment here. This is our weekend and I resent thoughts of Nick intruding for even a minute. Let's decide where to eat. My McLunch ran out a long time ago."

"Lenore, what better place to clear your thoughts than here, where he can't touch you? You need to make changes. Make serious decisions."

"You're going after this like a pit bull on a boney leg." She studied her toes as they peeked above the bubbling water. "You're just not going to let this go, are you?"

Leah ignored the remark and maneuvered in the water to connect with Lenore's eyes.

"What makes you think it's going to get better? He's always been an alcoholic. That's not going to change just because you want it to. He's getting more volatile toward you and Joel. I don't want you to become a statistic. I realize it may be less than a year now until Joel is out of school, but what kind of damage is it doing to keep him in that situation?" She let the statement sink in. "Don't you think knowing he and his Mom are safe would be far better?"

Lenore studied the effervescent water a full minute before replying.

"Leah, you don't know what it's like to raise children alone. I don't have parents to help. They died before I even found out how to be a parent myself. I don't make enough to support Joel and myself. His dad, Craig, sends child support, but it's scarcely enough to pay for school supplies and some clothes. The only alternative would be to send him to live with his dad." Lenore gazed into Leah's eyes. "That would kill me. At least with Nick, we have a home and food to eat and we're together."

The green in Lenore's eyes had totally eclipsed the brown pigment. Leah was connected and wasn't doing to let go.

"Joel isn't a child anymore. Grant is grown now and has his career and I'm sure he would help out, maybe even move back here from Chicago. You're not alone with two babies this time. You have two grown sons. Joel may have to work to help out, but I'll bet he would in a minute to get out of there. Don't you think so? Really, don't you?"

"I just don't want him to. This is Joel's senior year. He should be having fun, not working to buy food and clothes."

"Just answer one question for me." Leah tenderly pushed a strand of dark wet hair from Lenore's face. "Do you really think Nick could change and make it all better again?"

"No, it could never be the same. He's hurt us too much and too deeply." The tears flowed down already wet cheeks. "I told him it had to stop. I told him I couldn't be put in a position to choose, because I had made that decision when Joel was born."

"What did he say to that?"

"He just grabbed another beer and told me I was too soft on Joel. Leah, I'm not one of those blindly devoted moms who think their child is perfect. I know he's not, but he doesn't give us any trouble. He gets good grades and helps around the house, even though his room can be a disaster at times. I feel really blessed to have him. There are so many his age giving their parents nothing but grief."

"Now, there's the best reason to get out." Leah stared into Lenore's eyes. "How are you going to feel when you wake one day to see Joel has turned into a version of Nick; bitter and cruel and unable to love anyone?"

Lenore frowned at the thought of her laughing, talented son changing. "I can't do that, can I?"

"No, as hard as it's going to be, you have to get out of there and get some peace back into your life."

"You certainly know what buttons to push. I know you're right, but I'm still scared."

Leah gave Lenore a quick hug, then looked into her green eyes again. "I know it's scary. You aren't alone this time though. J.D. and I are your family now. We'll be here for you and you've got so many friends who care. Your two grown up sons will help, too."

Leah's logic didn't lessen the fear. What if Nick wouldn't let her leave? She shook off the thought and managed a smile.

"You've given me a lot to think about and I promise to file for divorce. Could we please get out of here now and get something to eat? I'm not only pruned, I'm absolutely starving!"

They both climbed out of the hot tub. "Come to think of it, I'm starved too. Where do we eat?"

* * * * *

The cool evening breeze did nothing to slow the return to their room as they discussed dinner plans. In less than an hour, they were seated at a Chinese restaurant on the south end of town.

"We have to have a Chinese beer after dinner, Lenore."

Though she had grown up eating the normal meat and potatoes diet of most mid-western girls, Lenore had accepted the introduction of a variety of new foods since moving to Colorado, including the Oriental fare Leah was passionate about.

"Okay," She replied with a shrug.

The willow-thin, young woman taking the order spoke little English, but managed to communicate with smiles and slight bows as the ladies pointed to items on the menu. The food was delicious and the service very efficient. The beers arrived as the last of the table service was cleared.

Lenore sipped from the bottle after wiping the top with her napkin, foregoing the available glass.

"Not bad. Wonder what it would taste like with pizza?"

Beer dribbled down Leah's chin and onto her sweater as words erupted. "Pizza? I can't believe you can even think of pizza after the meal we just finished. Darn it!" She carefully dabbed with her napkin and noticed Lenore suppressing a giggle. "What?"

"You seem to have a drinking problem." Lenore couldn't suppress her giggling.

"You're enjoying this entirely too much."

The waitress brought the check and the usual fortune cookies. She looked puzzled as Leah blotted and dabbed at her sweater, frowning at Lenore, who continued to giggle.

"Beer not good for you?" She asked Leah.

"Oh yes, it's very good. The entire meal was perfect. My friend was just teasing me because I dribbled. I love Oriental food. I really do!" She smiled and tried to explain her passion as only Leah could. "I couldn't tell you the first time I had it. Sometimes I think I must be part Chinese, or else I had an ancestor frightened by a Chinaman."

Lenore stopped giggling and stared at Leah. The young lady smiled and nodded, then quietly laid the check on the table and walked away. Leah smiled with satisfaction and sipped her beer.

When Lenore finally found her voice, she wasn't sure just how she was going to get through to the innocent diner.

"Leah, do you have any idea what just came out of your mouth?"

"You mean besides the beer? What?" She laughed. "I told her how much I love Chinese food."

"I'm sure you meant well, but don't you think telling an Oriental person your ancestors were frightened by a Chinaman could possibly be taken as an insult? I know you didn't mean it that way, but I can't say they would feel the same. She's probably asking someone what the round-eye meant. I think it's time to go."

Clouds of confusion were clearing from Leah's mind and the impact of what she had said was reaching the top floor.

Lenore couldn't resist saying, "Ding!"

"Oh, my God, Lenore! Do you really think she was insulted? I was just trying to explain ... it's just something my Dad used to ... Oh no. I'd better go back there and clear this up."

She started to get up and Lenore stood, gently took her arm, grabbed both their purses and steered her to the cash register, whispering on the way.

"I really think we should just go. Don't worry, we can always come back for dinner sometime, say fifteen years from now."

When asked if they enjoyed their meal at the register, Lenore assured the gentleman everything was excellent. Leah stood close to the door and only smiled. When Lenore had driven out of the parking lot and onto the street, Leah hit her brunette friend on the arm.

"Why are you laughing?"

"I just didn't know after-dinner mints came in a size five and were shaped like a foot." A moment later, Leah started laughing, too.

"Why don't you stop me when I start saying things like that?"

"Leah, those little pearls fly out of your mouth like speeding bullets. No one's that fast. Let's go back to the room and give your mouth a rest. My sides ache from laughing."

The mirth and Lenore's teasing continued on the way back to the lodge. They entered the room, kicking off shoes and dropping clothes. By the time they found nightgowns and put the room in some semblance of order, they were very ready to relax. Soft music from the radio/alarm clock and a gentle hum from the air conditioner provided soothing background for talking from separate beds.

It wasn't long before Leah realized the conversation had become entirely one-sided. Lenore was sound asleep. Fresh linens, a full day and the comforting sound of Leah's voice was stronger than a sedative. Leah turned the light off and nestled down into her own bed. They were an hour into Saturday, the last weekend of September.

CHAPTER 6

A sliver of light visible through thick dark lashes, winked and lured her to participate in a brand-new day. The enticement was irresistible. Lenore loved mornings, especially in Glenwood Springs. She threw the covers back and slipped out of bed as quietly as possible, allowing the satiny nightgown spiraled around her to fall into place as she stood. Light flooded the room as she opened the curtain enough to peek outside. A bright, cloudless sky replaced any remnants of sleep with a giddy excitement.

It took a few seconds for her eyes to adjust back to the darkness when she closed the curtains. Quietly searching through her suitcase, she managed to find white shorts, a colorful hooded sweatshirt and sandals. A quick version of her morning routine was completed, and as she reached the door Leah's sleepy voice stopped her.

"Where ya going?"

Looking over at Leah's bed, she knew the voice had originated from somewhere in the pile of covers. Speaking softly, she answered. "Sorry to wake you. I'm going to the office for coffee. Want some?"

"Mmph, cream 'n sugar," Leah mumbled.

Stuffing the room key into her back pocket, Lenore opened the door and stepped into the crisp Colorado morning chill. As soon as she left the shadow of the walkway, sunlight warmed her long, tanned legs and she squinted against the brightness, grinning with a freshly brushed smile.

Lenore felt sorry for the numerous travelers loading cars to leave. She had two nights and two and a half days in Glenwood Springs and she wasn't going to waste a minute. The friendly clerk from the previous night greeted her when she entered the lobby.

"Good morning, Ms. Appleby. You're up bright and early this morning."

"Good morning yourself," She replied with a smile. She squinted at his name tag. "How do you remember names so well, Bart?"

"Oh, I've been doing this for so long, it just sort of becomes second nature. Keeps my brain from seizing up." He chuckled.

"Besides, you're easy to remember. You and Ms. Chase have been here two years in a row. You're both just as friendly as two people can be, and that makes it nice to remember as well. Got big plans for today?"

Lenore poured hazelnut flavored coffee into large Styrofoam containers and looked around for packets of sugar and creamer. With only a glass container filled with sugar and half and half in a tall thermal carafe, Lenore poured equal amounts into Leah's cup. Lenore drank hers black.

"No real plans, I suppose. The big pool, of course, but otherwise just relaxing. Maybe a shopping spree. It's good to be away from routines for a while. That's what makes this time so special; no schedules to keep!"

The innkeeper chuckled, then turned his attention to a man who had entered, greeting him by name and smiling. The departing traveler wasn't about to be cajoled from his crabby morning attitude so easily. Lenore stirred the contents of Leah's cup and looked at the silent stuffed bear, as if asking for approval on the mixture. His glassy-eyed stare gave no indications or criticism, so she shrugged her shoulders and left the lobby, coffee brimming in two cups.

Lenore pondered the man in the motel office and wondered how anyone could not revel in a new day. How could it be anything but a good morning when it was too early for anything to have made it otherwise?

She watched her shadow proceed her down the drive, as memories of childhood days in a Kansas refinery town floated through her thoughts. She remembered hot, humid days when she would chase her shadow from one soothing patch of shaded sidewalk to another before the sun-scorched pavement could blister dirty, bare feet. The shadow of a grown-up lady led the way now, and the bare feet were soft, clean and covered by expensive leather sandals. The memory wasn't painful, but reflective. Those days were carefree.

"Ow-ie shit! Hot-hot-hot!" was Lenore's startled response when hot coffee dribbled onto her hand as she turned the corner to climb the stairs. It was from Leah's cup, mostly because it was so full, but also, Lenore thought, because it was the one that would make her hand sticky. She rolled her eyes and continued, carefully, up the stairs, then sat down the offending cup to open the door.

Leah had not stirred. Lenore sat the cups on a table near the window and slipped over to the sink to wash her hands. Walking back by the bed, she spoke softly to a mound of sheets and blankets, certain there had to be a body in there somewhere.

"Your coffee is on the table. Come out when you're ready."

A mumble emanated, assuring Lenore her friend was indeed there. Grabbing her coffee and a pillow from the bed to guard against the chill of the metal chair, Lenore went back outside and sat down at the little patio table to enjoy the morning air and her hot coffee.

The immediate view from the protruding area of balcony on the walkway was of a parking area and tasteful landscaping. The busy street, nearby motels and other businesses geared toward the traveling public were occupying the area beyond the lodge. Lenore barely noticed any of it. Her focus was on the rise of mountains beyond the occupied civilian area of Glenwood Springs. Sunlight cascaded down the face of the slope, as the morning sun rose above the mountain behind her, setting the scrub oak aflame with colors of orange and red and gold. It looked like a magnificent sculptured carpet carefully fitted into the mounds and folds of the mountain.

The beautiful valley was originally a summer gathering place for Ute Indians before the white man discovered it in the mid-1800s. The Utes had fought Comanche and Arapaho to retain the rights of the "Yampa," the big medicine of their Manitou, believing the healing powers of the mineral waters and vapor caves made them superior warriors and hunters. It was a sacred place, yet they had welcomed and shared with the white man. After the Meeker Massacre in 1860, the white man drove them from their sacred valley.

Originally named Grand Springs by the first white men, with the establishment of Fort Defiance, six miles east, the two incorporated and the townsite was renamed Defiance. In 1885 the town was plotted and renamed Glenwood Springs to honor an early resident's hometown of Glenwood, Iowa. Lenore hoped the native Utes had been right, and the healing aura would touch her soul.

The sound of an opening door and a sleepy, "Hello," broke into her thoughts. Leah came to the table with a blanket wrapped around her and the cup of coffee in hand.

"Well, good-morning bright eyes," Lenore teased. "Guess this proves the dead can come back to life after all."

A smile crept across the face of her friend, who ignored the taunting. "Let me drink my coffee and get my eyes completely opened. You've got a head-start on me."

"Okay, but we're burning daylight here, you know. There's so many things we could do today." She leaned back in the chair and stretched as Leah sat in the chair next to her and adjusted the blanket around her shoulders. "The first thing, of course, is to eat. I'm starved! I think I could go all day without eating if I didn't eat so close to bedtime the night before. How about you?" She paused and waited for a reply, as Leah brought the now less than hot liquid to her lips for a first sip.

"Wow!"

Lenore raised her brows and looked at her friend. "I didn't think the coffee was that strong. I know it can't still be hot."

Leah shook her head. "It's not hot or strong; it's sweet! How much sugar did you put in this stuff anyway?"

"I don't know. I didn't measure. Want me to go get another cup for you?" She stood reaching for the offending cup. "I'll be glad to."

"No, it's okay. It was just a shock." She took another sip. "Maybe all this sugar will give me the energy I need to catch up with you." She finally turned and looked at Lenore. "How can you be this alert so early in the morning and so dead at night?"

"It's just the way God made me." She shrugged. "I've been this way from the start. My folks called me "baby doll," because when they picked me up in the morning my eyes would open and I was ready for anything. They never fought me to go to bed, either. Said when they would lay me down, I was out like a light." She thought for a second or two. "Maybe that's why I don't get sleepy when I drive; the eyes just won't close."

Leah stared at Lenore while she talked, trying to keep up with the conversation. She visualized a cheerful little doll, with winky-blinky eyes, being laid down and stood up, eyes opening and shutting with the flow of gravity. She smiled and listened until Lenore stopped talking long enough to take another sip of coffee.

"I'm glad they didn't find it necessary to name you Betsey Wetsy."

Laughter punctuated the crisp morning air as they continued to sip coffee and make plans for breakfast. Having a destination in mind and the coffee depleted, they returned to the room and dressed in blue jeans and sweaters. With the majority of the day being planned for soaking in the mineral hot springs, they used minimal effort on getting ready. Not even the meticulous Leah delayed their departure by primping.

The breeze from the topless Chevelle was fresh and a little cool, but with the heater on high and a radio station out of Aspen providing background music for their journey, it was hardly noticed. Driving south, over a bridge spanning Interstate 70, the railroad and the Colorado River, brought them to the central business district. Lenore parked the car and they waited patiently outside a highly recommended café to be seated.

"I hope it's not much longer. The yummy smells are just about to drive me crazy."

"We can go somewhere else, Lenore. We don't have to eat here."

"Oh, we'd have to wait anywhere we go. This is supposed to be worth the wait."

"Oh, that's right. A shoe representative recommended it."

"A very rotund gentleman. The man obviously knows his food."

"Right! We'll wait."

Talking and people watching occupied ten more minutes. Rewards of gourmet coffee and miniature fresh biscotti appeased them after they ordered breakfast and waited for their omelets.

Leah reached for the creamer and packets of artificial sweetener.

"Want me to do that for you?" Lenore teased.

With a comical grimace and a shudder, Leah declined. "I think I'll buy small packets of creamer and sweetener for the remainder of our stay. How about a coffee maker for the room?"

"That's up to you," Lenore said, knowing it was not a matter of expense for Leah. "I'll probably still want to get up and walk down to the office. I love getting up and out, you know."

Leah rolled her eyes and chuckled. "Oh, I know alright. It would still be nice to have coffee in the room for refills, wouldn't it?"

"Sure. They sell the freshly ground coffee here. Maybe we could get a bag of these little biscotti as well. We can split the cost."

"We can split the cost of the coffee and the biscotti, but I'm fronting the cost of the coffee maker. I can always give it to Shelly, or keep it for our trip next year."

Lenore nodded her agreement as their breakfasts were served. They ate with un-ceremonial frenzy at first, satisfying their hunger, then managed to slow down and converse between bites.

"I nearly ordered two omelets when we first came in." Lenore said. "I was so hungry! I'm sure this is plenty now. I'm really full."

Leah finished chewing the mouthful of food and swallowed before attempting more than "Mmmmm." Nodding, she added, "It's terrific! Are they open tomorrow?"

"Let's see." Lenore took the menu from between a vase of fresh flowers and a napkin holder. Frowning, she shook her head. "Nope, closed Sunday. They're open Monday. We can come back before our trip home."

"Great. Where do we eat breakfast tomorrow?"

Lenore paused with her fork at her mouth. "Well, we have 24 hours or so to decide. Let's figure out what we're going to do for a while before we go to the pool."

Leah grinned. "Why, shop of course."

Lenore tapped her forehead with the heel of her hand. "Silly me, why didn't I think of that?"

It was two hours before the ladies returned to the lodge to change for the big hot pool. The treasures were worth the effort. Leah had managed to seek out the very best bargains Glenwood Springs had to offer for them both. Her own budget allowed a multitude of outfits and souvenirs. Lenore was delighted with a half-priced jacket and earrings, which Leah had discovered and talked her into buying. She had found a nice black dress shirt for her son to wear to his concerts. She found nothing, nor bothered to look for anything, to take back to Nick.

While changing into bathing suits, Lenore tried on her new jacket in various stages of dress and undress. Both shoppers agreed it looked good with everything and nothing at all.

I've never seen you so tickled over clothing. You're positively glowing!"

"Oh Leah, I've never had anything like this. I feel so special in it. I've also never spent so much money on one article of clothing. Will I wake up tomorrow and regret the extravagance?"

"I'll make sure you don't. You deserve it. You saved the money in a very separate place to be used on something very special. You did it without dipping into the trip budget as well."

"Nick will poop when he sees what I paid."

"Here, give me the ticket and the price tag. He doesn't need to know. Tell him it was forty dollars. He might still poop, but only half as much." She smiled and wagged her eyebrows.

Lenore laughed as Leah tore the paper into tiny pieces and dribbled them into the waste basket. "If anyone can reconstruct those and show Nick, God bless 'em." She turned to Lenore, who was admiring her reflection in the mirror, still wearing the beautiful jacket.

"Lenore, are you going to wear it to the pool, or will you opt for a bathing suit?"

The jacket was hung carefully among ordinary clothes and the ladies gathered necessities for their trip to the pool. It was a warm, lovely autumn day as they left the lodge and drove to the outdoor hot springs pool.

* * * * *

Gregor glanced over his shoulder. The truck was still there and, no doubt, Frank was intent on watching his every move. What fun he could have, if he were not trying to put the agent at ease.

The late September day was warm and sunny. He suppressed a smile as he wiped a trickle of perspiration from his brow, then shook his head, forcing a spray of wetness from the ends of his dark, wavy hair. With the yard work finished, he had run out of chores.

The shirt he had abandoned earlier was laying on the porch steps. He picked it up and walked toward the truck sitting just outside the driveway. Frank got out of his truck and met him at the front of the vehicle.

"Is there a problem Parish?"

Gregor stopped and leaned against the hood, using the shirt to wipe dirt and perspiration from his face. He swiped at perspiration glistening on the thick, black hair covering his chest and trailing down the center of his chiseled stomach.

"Not at all, Frank. I was just letting you know I will be going inside the house now. I will shower and prepare to go out for the evening. Perhaps you would care to join me for dinner?"

Frank looked away for a moment, searching for the proper answer. "I don't know if that's such a good idea. I realize John socializes with you on occasion, but it's not regulation."

"Surely you must eat. How better to watch me than to join me?" It was said in such a matter of fact way, Frank couldn't see a reason to argue.

"Good point. Where do you plan to eat?"

"It is a local steak house. I will buy you a wonderful Colorado steak dinner." A mischievous grin flashed on the bearded face. "Then we will go listen to country music and perhaps dance with lovely ladies."

Frank missed the grin. "Well, I'll give in to dinner, but don't expect me to do any dancing." He shook his head. "Country music. How'd you ever acquire a taste for that?"

"It is so American." He grinned. "How could one not love it?"

"Trust me, it isn't difficult. I'll go change suits and put a fresh shine on the wing tips." He said, looking down at the already shiny black shoes.

Gregor looked down at Frank's shoes. "Do you not have any western wear or boots?"

"Western wear? Afraid not." He shrugged. "Guess I'll stick out like a sore thumb."

Gregor frowned and tilted his head with confusion. "You are afraid this will be painful?"

"No." Frank replied, laughing. "It just means I won't look like everyone else in the place. It's an expression."

The Russian smiled and nodded. He had made the serious man laugh. This was good.

"Look, I'll be back here at seven." Frank said, looking at his watch. He walked to the truck door, opened it and slid in.

Gregor watched as the truck turned around in the drive and back out onto the road toward Glenwood Springs. He would show the agent a very good time. This man worried far too much about these regulations, and it could get in the way of important plans. Gregor shook off the thought and walked into the house. He would not think more about it tonight. Tonight, was a time for pleasure.

* * * * *

The famous Hot Springs Pool in Glenwood Springs was crowded, but it didn't concern the two women laying on their rented lounges near the water. They were relaxed and doing a little people watching between conversations. There were all shapes and sizes enjoying the odorous waters, with only an occasional snicker erupting from the duo.

The original red sandstone building, though modernized and expanded throughout the years, stood on the south side of the waters, providing shade from the still hot September sun for those needing it. Lenore and Leah had worked throughout the summer to build up tans and tolerance to the sun's rays, and though an occasional dip in the warm water cooled them temporarily after getting out, the dry September air and crystal blue skies allowed the sun to further darken their sun screen protected skin.

A haven for the elite and affluent, Presidents and world travelers, the pools were originally constructed at a cost of over $100,000 in the late 1800s. The pools sat at the foot of the Hotel Colorado, which, upon its completion, rivaled the most elegant hotels in the world. They were now a pleasure for even the most ordinary of people to enjoy, and the beauty had not diminished.

"Can you imagine being able to stay here for a month? Or living here, year-round?" Lenore asked her equally relaxed friend.

"Mmmm, I'd love to be here when it snows, steam rising off the water. I'll bet it's great."

Their sighs were barely audible above the din of the crowd.

"Unfortunately, there are no plans to move the business here, and neither of us is financially independent, so this will have to do."

"Oh, I suppose you're right." Lenore giggled and stretched. "Besides, after a few years of lounging and relaxing, we'd probably get bored, right?"

"Most certainly. Maybe twenty or thirty years down the road."

"It would be a life without Nick in it at all," Lenore added.

"I hope you can end that miserable relationship as soon as we get back. At least start ending it." Leah turned over to her stomach and continued. "You're so peaceful here and so horribly stressed at home."

Lenore turned to her stomach and rested her chin on folded hands. "When I consistently have to wonder what sort of attitude Nick will greet me with when I come home from work, and have to worry whether or not Nick is going to hurt Joel, emotionally or even physically, then yes, I do stress. What a fool I was to think I could have Happily Ever After. If I can get out of this marriage, I'll forget men for the rest of my life. I'll just raise cats or something; and they'll be female cats only. I'd rather live alone than go through this again!"

A skinny woman in a brightly flowered, modest bathing suit muttered, "Amen sister!" as she passed. Behind her trailed a grumpy looking man in camouflage swim trunks with a massive belly looking as though it should be thumped to check for ripeness. "Over dare, over dare," he yelled, pointing at a vacant area to lay their towels.

Lenore snickered. "I rest my case."

"Lenore, you're just being silly now. You're a loving, intelligent, beautiful human being. You weren't meant to live alone. There's someone out there who needs to love you as much as you need to be loved. I just know it."

"I don't believe it, Leah. When you and J.D. met and fell in love, it was a forever time. People knew it was for always. You're lucky. Today, love is as deep and true as the next one coming down the street." Lenore wiped a bead of perspiration from the end of her nose. "Nick has said from day one, if I ever left, he could have another one in his bed by the end of the day. It's no big deal to men these days, or women either, I suppose. I want that old-fashioned commitment and it's not out there anymore."

"I'd argue with you, but I don't think you would be very receptive in your present state of relationship. I understand, but I just know you are wrong."

Lenore raised up and flicked another bead of perspiration from her nose. "Why my nose? Why does it always trickle off my nose?" She didn't expect and answer. "Let's take another dip the pool before we go. I need a nap today, if I plan to stay up past ten, you know."

As they eased into the warm mineral water, Leah teased, "Let's see ... if you manage to take a two-hour nap, maybe I can keep you going until eleven, as long as you don't lay your head down on the table or something."

"Hey, I'll bet I can make it until midnight!"

"Only if you take No-Doze and tank up on coffee all night."

"I could do that."

"Maybe we'll be having so much fun, you'll stay awake until one!"

"Leah, I don't think they make that much fun." Lenore laughed as she pushed away from the edge and swam underwater to the middle of the pool, where she surfaced and moved through the water with well-timed strokes, only having to stop three times in her two laps to avoid collisions with other bathers.

* * * * *

They were both ready for naps when they returned to their air-conditioned room. True to form, Lenore slept immediately. Leah read the paper until she grew sleepy.

CHAPTER 7

Leah sat on the counter cross-legged in front of the mirror as Lenore stepped into the dressing area from the shower. It was Leah's normal position for putting on makeup; she was too short to see closely, otherwise. Her hair was already dried and styled with practiced perfection, after her own shower. The style of Lenore's long tresses made it easy, but drying took time.

"Lenore, how do you wake up without an alarm?"

Lenore rubbed her hair vigorously between folds of the white towel and stepped to the mirror beside Leah.

"I could probably convince you it's my natural clock. Truth is, I usually have to pee."

"That solves the mystery alright."

"What woke you?" Lenore asked. "The toilet flushing?"

"Yes, made me have to whiz."

Lenore stopped combing her hair and looked at Leah's reflection. "How come I pee and you whiz?"

Leah continued to stroke eye shadow onto the lids of blue-gray eyes. "It's all in how bad you have to go. The more you have to go, the stronger the flow, thus producing the whizzing sound." She shrugged. "I always have to go pretty bad."

Lenore smiled and nodded, then went back to combing through long wet hair. "Now where do you want to have dinner?"

"The nice restaurant we passed on the way to the mall is one you said was recommended. Was it from the rotund sales rep?"

"No, actually it was a very lovely lady customer when she learned of my vacation plans. She said it's quite elegant—white tablecloths and all, but not horribly expensive."

"Great. Then what?"

Lenore plugged in the hair dryer. "We'll just play it by ear. Maybe ask a local." The 1500 watts of drying power temporarily ceased communication.

* * * * *

They were at the restaurant by seven, a quiet local steak house that hosted two very unlikely dinner partners. Gregor watched the man setting across the table enjoying food and forgetting, for a time, regulations.

"It is good, yes?" he asked.

"Parish, I can't remember having a better steak. Glad I took you up on your offer."

"I am pleased to have the company." Gregor said as he took a bite of his pan seared trout.

Frank cut into his rare steak and dipped a generous piece into dark brown sauce, pausing before shoving it into his mouth. "How late do you make these Saturday nights?"

"It depends very much on the band and the number of ladies willing to dance with me." He watched Frank chew the tender meat, and wondered if this man had ever dared to dance. Perhaps it was not regulation.

Frank swallowed his mouthful of steak, then took a sip of coffee. Then he looked squarely into Gregor's eyes. "John tells me you never take anyone home with you. Is that true?"

Gregor did not avoid the piercing eyes of the agent. "It is true."

"Not because you haven't had the opportunity, I trust. Are you a queer?"

"No, I am not homosexual, Frank." The Russian smiled and lifted his eyes to the ceiling, where cut crystal lamps cast a soft glow throughout the otherwise rustic room. "I have had many opportunities." He looked back into the agent's eyes. "The women who would come with me are not looking for anything other than physical satisfaction. Perhaps I am old-fashioned in your country, but I do not believe it is the proper way. I am waiting for a time when I can share a good life with someone very special. I will know her and know when it is right."

"Well, you have your reasons."

Both men reached for the dinner check, but the Russian was quicker.

"You are here by my invitation, Frank. On this I must insist." The smile disarmed any argument from the CIA agent.

"Okay, but the next one's on me." He put his wallet back into the inside pocket of his suit coat. "In fact, I insist on buying the first-round tonight."

Gregor liked the fact Frank seemed to be relaxing. "It will be my pleasure to accept your generosity."

It wasn't far to the dance hall. The music was loud, but the table selection was still fairly open. They chose a table in the corner on an elevated section of the room. From there, they were able to see the band, the dancers and anyone coming into the room.

Frank spoke loudly to make himself heard over the band. "Parish, this is a western bar, you wear western clothes and boots, but instead of a cowboy hat, you wear a baseball cap. Why?"

"It is my favorite hat." Gregor answered, matter-of-factly. He adjusted the dark blue cap emblazoned with a "Ford" logo.

"Good enough answer for me."

Frank sat back in his chair and watched the Russian scope the room. It was a familiar maneuver for someone in their line of work, or former line, in Gregor's case.

"What are you looking for?"

The Russian turned and smiled at Frank. "I am trying to see if there are any lovely ladies who would be able to dance with you and not step on your wing-tipped shoes."

Frank put a hand up and protested. "I think I'd better leave the dancing to you."

"It is your choice. The ladies here, however, may not be so willing to leave you alone."

Frank rolled his eyes as Gregor smiled. It was an amicable situation. Regulations were not going to interfere.

* * * * *

The wait for a table was over half an hour, but as the waiter poured water into crystal glasses and introduced himself, the interval vanished.

Lenore studied the menu as Leah scanned their surroundings. "Lenore, ask that lady what she's eating. It looks wonderful."

Before Lenore could comply, the lady at the next table graciously gave Leah the information she requested. Leah and Lenore closed their menus with a decision to try the hazelnut encrusted halibut for themselves.

The young waiter returned, taking their orders and suggested a Chardonnay to accompany their meals. The wine was brought to the table, sampled and poured. With a toast to Glenwood Springs and their special weekend, the ladies savored the taste and took a moment to smile at one another. It was Leah who spoke what they both were thinking.

"We should dine like this every day. Elegant surroundings. Attentive waiters. Delicious wines and well-prepared meals."

Absolutely." Lenore reached over and squeezed her friend's hand. "Shall we just stay on here in Glenwood Springs and inform our families we intend to stay until our money runs out?"

Leah sighed. "No need, dear. We'd be home on Tuesday anyway."

"True. Sad, but true." Lenore giggled.

The waiter returned with salads and refilled their water glasses. When the last bite of salad was consumed, the plates were promptly removed, their dinners served and more wine poured into the crystal glasses.

"You ladies seem to be having a nice time. Where are you from?"

Leah, always the first to make new acquaintances, informed him of their Front Range origin of Fort Collins and their inevitable return to reality.

"I will do my best to make this portion of your stay as pleasant as possible," the waiter replied.

When the meal was nearly finished, the waiter returned, offering coffee and dessert. Though the desserts were turned down, freshly brewed coffee was poured into delicate china cups.

"Kevin, this has been delightful." Leah said to their waiter, and it took only a second for Lenore to realize she'd read his name tag.

"I'm so glad you've enjoyed it. Could I offer anything more?"

Lenore shook her head and smiled. Leah smiled and nodded, then raised one little manicured finger.

"Actually, you might be able to help us. Could you suggest a local spot where two women our age could go listen to a band and not look too out of place and still have fun?"

"Let me make a phone call and see who's playing at a little saloon/dance hall outside of town. Do you like country/western music?"

Both ladies nodded and Lenore added, "That'll work, but remember we're old enough to be your mother."

"Ma'am, there's no way." He smiled and gave a wink. "You couldn't be anywhere near my mother's age."

As he left, Lenore laughed. "He just got himself an extra couple of dollars on his tip."

"Please, have another cup of coffee," Leah urged.

With directions to the saloon and a generous tip left on the table, the two ladies left the restaurant fully satiated. They walked to the convertible, a little sad that the top had to be put up for their great adventure this night, but given the hoped-for late evening and unknown destinations, they had agreed it would be best.

"This will be fun," Leah said as she buckled herself into the passenger seat.

"Well, let's hope so."

"Oh Lenore, he was such a nice young man. I think we can trust him on this."

"Okay. I guess we're off." She grinned as she started the car.

"And we're leaving, too!" Leah added the expected silly response.

CHAPTER 8

They were nearing their destination, according to the directions given, when Leah pointed at lights ahead on the right.

"There it is. Over dare, over dare," which produced a hoot from Lenore as they remembered the guy from the pool.

After parking and getting out of the car, they both stood in front of the building.

"Where's the front door?" Lenore asked.

"Hmmm, can't tell. Let's just stand here for a minute. Surely someone will go in or leave pretty soon so we can proceed without looking totally lost."

"But we are lost, Leah."

Before Leah could protest, a voice from behind startled them both.

"I believe you gals could use an escort. Grab a hold of these old arms of mine and we'll head inside."

Lenore turned to find an ancient, leathery-faced cowboy standing at the rear of their car. He smiled and tipped his hat to each of them. He looked harmless enough, and obviously knew where the entrance was. Lenore was sure Leah, in her five-foot glory, could wrestle him to the ground and escape if need be. The twinkle in his eyes assured her it would not be necessary. Leah had already made up her mind, stepping to his side and accepting an arm. Lenore shrugged and accepted the remaining arm, and they were properly escorted to the door.

"Thank you, sir." Leah patted his arm and Lenore smiled.

"Name's Gus. You ladies like to dance?"

His attention was focused on Lenore, though Leah was the one conversing with him. She was trying to stifle a giggle, knowing Lenore was uncomfortable.

"We love to dance, don't we Lenore?" Leah grinned as Lenore gave her a dirty look. "My name is Leah."

"Well, if you ladies would honor an old man with a dance or two tonight, I'd be honored to pay your way in the door."

"Oh, we couldn't do—"

"Why thank you kind sir," said Leah. "We would love to dance with you."

With thanks and assurance they would see him on the dance floor, the ladies waved their farewell, and headed for the restroom.

"Great Leah. Now we're going to be stuck with that old geezer all night."

Leah answered from within the echoing confines of her own stall. "Oh Lenore, he's nice. He won't bug you too much." She giggled. "Maybe." She giggled again. "He was sure taken with you."

"All I want to do is melt into the crowd and listen to music. I don't want to dance with anyone." She walked to the sink and washed her hands. Leah joined her.

"Well, you're going to have trouble staying invisible tonight, Lenore. Between your new jacket and those eyes of yours, you'll be a target."

Lenore gazed into the mirror and ran her fingers through her satiny hair, then stood back and unzipped the new jacket. She scrutinized the black jeans and lacy edged, black tank top.

"I won't be a target if you don't try to collect anyone." She eyed Leah. "What's the smile for?"

"You look incredible."

Lenore crossed her eyes and shook her head. "I won't look anyone in the eye tonight and you just have to promise you won't talk to strangers, or I may burn this jacket!"

"I'll make a concerted effort."

Lenore cocked one brow and looked at the sincere smile on Leah's face. She started to ask for a blood oath, but knew even with that, it would be an impossible request. She shook her head again and opened the door.

* * * * *

The carved wooden doors with oval panes of etched glass opened into a huge room decorated with carved wood and old-fashioned chandeliers. Lively country/western music moved dancers on the crowded floor in a rhythmic circular pattern, as the ladies scanned the room for empty tables.

* * * * *

The first thing Gregor noticed was her smile. Then he watched the way she talked and laughed with her friend, and the way the light shone on her long, dark hair. He would most certainly ask her to dance.

* * * * *

It wasn't long before Leah noticed a couple leaving and she grabbed Lenore's sleeve, half pulling her up the steps to out-maneuver another couple heading for the same table. From their elevated seats, they had a great view of the dance floor and congratulated one another.

* * * * *

They were so close. He could see her clearly now and hear their conversation. Such a beautiful woman. Did she really say she would not dance with anyone? This could not be!

Frank was ready to leave, saying something about his age and lack of interest. Gregor made no attempt to dissuade him. Apparently, Frank did not notice Gregor's distraction as he turned to leave. Perhaps he did and was sure the Russian would not be changing any plans at this point. He was correct, for the time being.

* * * * *

Lenore ordered a scotch and water and waited for Leah to decide what she would drink. After a lengthy discussion with their waitress, her choice was gin and tonic with a twist of lime. They sat back in their chairs and watched the crowd.

"Leah, check out the guy leaving. He has on wing-tips, for crying out loud."

Their giggling was interrupted by a voice from a nearby table.

"I'm sorry, but you cannot sit at that table."

Lenore shot a warning look at Leah, but knew it was of no use. The statement could have easily been ignored, but the accent was an irresistible force. Before Lenore could get up to leave, Leah had turned in her chair to address the person speaking.

"Now just why can we not sit at this table tonight, sir?"

"It is because you are far too beautiful. You will drive me crazy, unless you agree to dance with me."

Original, Lenore thought, and rolled her eyes. Leah laughed and was led to the dance floor, leaving Lenore to pay for the drinks when they arrived. She sipped her scotch and water, content to be an observer. She scoped the dance floor until she saw Leah dancing with the stranger. They laughed and talked as he twirled her around the floor. He was a good dancer and Leah was having a great time. Lenore loved to dance, but Nick refused. He said it was sissy stuff. She closed her eyes trying to erase the thought of Nick. Opening her eyes, she found the stranger once more and knew nothing could be further from "sissy" than what she was watching.

After two songs and Lenore's refusal to dance with two different guys, Leah returned to the table. Her dance partner returned to his own just long enough to grab his drink and join them. His vacated table was filled before he had sat his drink down.

Lenore half-listened to the conversation flow between her table partners, partly out of curiosity, but mostly out of self-defense. Leah had found a new friend where Lenore saw only a stranger. She tried to identify his accent, but it eluded her. Living in Fort Collins, where so many foreign students attend Colorado State University, she had thought herself adept at accents. It was an asset of her job, and she could tell Leah was trying to identify it as well.

"Greg, where are you from?"

"I am from here."

Evasive, Lenore thought.

"You are most certainly not a native Coloradan, Greg." Leah laughed. "Before this, what country were you from? Your accent is interesting."

"Why is it important to know this? I am an American."

"I just figured it out. You're uncomfortable with letting people know much about you. You're afraid it would make them uncomfortable."

Just then, both ladies figured it out.

"You're Russian ... am I right?" Lenore turned to and stared into the eyes of the dark-haired man. Her gaze was captured by dark eyes, warm and powerful.

"I am Russian by birth. I choose to be an American now."

Lenore knew if she didn't break the connection soon, she wouldn't want to. Her heart was beating quickly, and she felt the sting of tears as she realized her control was slipping into the depths of his eyes. A loud "whoop" from somewhere close startled her and she looked toward the sound, grateful for the interruption. It was the elderly cowboy, Gus.

"There's the little filly I've been lookin' for. Come on down here and give this old cowboy a thrill by dancin' with him."

"I'd love to, Gus." Lenore said as she stood and headed for the dance floor, glancing at an open-mouthed Leah. She was escaping, and Leah knew it.

The ancient wrangler was a great dancer and Lenore was actually enjoying herself. She glanced toward the table more than once and saw Leah and the stranger deep in conversation, though his eyes followed her. She wondered how long she could keep this old fellow dancing before he collapsed?

"You sure ain't from around here."

Her attention was drawn back to her partner. He was looking into her face, smiling with dentured perfection and beer breath.

"No Gus, we're actually from the Front Range; just visiting for a few days. Have you always lived around here?"

"Yep, never wanted to be anywhere else. You sure are a purty woman." He gave her a little wink. "You should consider movin' here so's I could dance with you all the time."

"Oh, I could never do that. I'm married and have six kids waiting for me at home. You wouldn't want me to abandon them, would you?" She assumed he would be properly discouraged. He wasn't.

"You get rid of that man of yours and bring them kids. I'll help you raise 'em. Raised eight of my own."

"Gus, if I ever decide to do it, I'll look you up. You're a sweetie and I feel very complimented by your offer."

"Ain't no compliment. I'm serious." He twirled her around and back to face him. "You and them kids would want for nothin'."

"You talk a powerful argument, Gus. I'll keep it in mind." She giggled and patted his back as they danced.

At the end of the song, he wasn't about to let her go and she was glad. A slow song started and he began singing. It was horribly off key, but she just smiled and let her partner lead her around the floor. After a third song, he led her back to the table.

"You keep that offer in mind," He said to Lenore with a wink.

With assurances and thanks, she sat back in her chair and sipped a much-diluted scotch and water, pleased when the waitress delivered a fresh one. One sip and she knew it was not the usual bar scotch, but a deliciously smooth single malt.

"Lenore Appleby, this is Greg Parish. He's from Russia ... Isn't that neat?"

"Neat." Lenore said, flatly.

"I am very pleased to meet you, Lenore. Your friend has told me a great deal about you."

Lenore looked toward him, focusing on his mouth rather than the eyes. Soft lips parted to reveal even white teeth and an infectious smile, surrounded by the blackness of a neatly groomed beard and mustache. Her eyes lowered to the tufts of dark hair peeking from the top of his shirt. As if teasing, he opened another snap, exposing more of his chest and the dark curls covering it. Lenore quickly looked away and shifted in her chair to look out onto the dance floor.

"Careful Greg. Lenore will lose all control." Leah laughed. "She can't resist a hairy chest."

Lenore could feel the warmth of a blush flooding her face as she tried to mentally fade into the woodwork. His hand was touching hers; lifting it. She didn't fight it as he stood.

"You will dance with me, please?"

There was nothing in her entire being strong enough to say no to him. She stood and walked to the dance floor. She fit comfortably in his arms as they began to move with the beat of a two-step. He would twirl her, but never completely severed their touch. She found herself smiling.

After a second lively two-step, the music slowed and he pulled her closer. They moved easily together, talking about the music and the band.

"I like what you are doing," he said as he pulled back and smiled at her.

It wasn't the dancing he referred to.

Realizing that she was stroking the soft curls of hair at his collar on the back of his neck, she stopped immediately and dropped her hand back to his shoulder, heat flooding through her face.

"I'm so sorry. I didn't think about ... I was just so—"

"No, I did not want you to stop. You were only doing what you wanted to do. You should relax and enjoy yourself. Your mind needs to allow your body to have a good time."

His smile disarmed her and she smiled back. He turned his hat around and pulled her closer, humming along with the song. Unlike her previous partner, Greg's voice was soothing and in tune. She smiled, thinking it seemed somehow odd, he didn't hum with an accent. When the song ended, he held Lenore for a moment in a soft embrace, then took her hand.

"I think you are a very special lady. You have beautiful eyes. They speak what your mind will not let it say."

Lenore frowned and turned away, then as if to prove a point, she turned back.

"Don't try to read more than is there. You've quite an imagination and some very polished lines." She looked directly into his eyes. "Very few people can read my eyes. I don't allow it."

She turned and walked back to the table, muttering under her breath, "What is it with the guys in this place?"

Greg caught up, putting his hand on the back of her waist, escorting her to their table. Leah joined them after having danced with Gus.

Sensing a need to talk, Leah announced her intent to go after fresh drinks, though the ones on the table were far from empty or unpalatable, knowing Greg would offer to perform the task. She was right.

"Lenore, he's wonderful! Aren't you excited? He's quite enamored with you."

Lenore simply stared at Leah, not knowing where to begin.

"What is it?" Leah urged. "Aren't you having fun?"

Finally, Lenore spoke. "Leah, do you recall the conversations we've had since being in Glenwood Springs about my situation and my desire to be alone?"

"Well, we knew that last part wasn't going to fly when you said it." Leah laughed, then stopped when she noticed Lenore wasn't joining in.

"I have been propositioned by an ancient old cowboy and I'm not sure what just happened with your Russian friend." Lenore pointed a thumb toward the bar. "We've not even been here two hours!"

"What happened? Talk to me!" Leah was absolutely delighted with Lenore's dilemma.

Lenore searched for the right answer. "He makes me uncomfortable." It sounded silly when she said it, but hoped Leah would understand.

"What makes you uncomfortable? Did he get fresh? He really didn't seem the type."

Lenore frowned and bit her bottom lip. *Maybe I'm making myself uncomfortable*, she thought.

"I don't know. Why'd you have to talk to him in the first place?"

"He spoke first! He told us we couldn't sit here." Her defensive tone softened. "Then there's that wonderful accent. We get to meet a real live Russian. I think it's neat."

"You said that before. He wasn't actually challenging us you know. This whole table thing was a "come-on" and a pretty bad one, too."

"Oh Lenore, he's harmless, funny, fascinating and absolutely infatuated with you." Leah grinned and fluttered her eyelashes.

Lenore rolled her eyes and shook her head. "I don't want him to be infatuated with me."

Seeing her friend so serious, Leah got a little more serious. "Lenore, he's from a totally different culture. Some foreign people aren't afraid to express themselves. I'm a good judge of character, aren't I? He doesn't scare me in the least."

"Maybe I'm just paranoid. It's not as if it will go any further than tonight. Right?" She smiled at Leah, who smiled and wagged her eyebrows.

"Stop that!"

"Just try to relax and enjoy yourself. You're being far too intense about this."

Lenore sipped the smooth scotch in front of her and nodded. "Intense, huh?"

"Yes," Leah said, touching her friend's arm. "I've been intense. And I'm far more comfortable in hotels or motels."

It took a second for Lenore to catch the pun. She laughed and patted Leah on the shoulder. "Good one."

"Thanks. Now, listen to his accent so we can imitate it later. It's a neat opportunity. I wonder how he wound up in Colorado?"

Lenore was sure Leah would have the answer before the evening was over. She tried to bury her cautions, assuring herself Leah was indeed a good judge of character. When he returned, she joined in the conversation, but avoided looking in his eyes and at his chest. She tried to keep the conversation light as they danced again.

"Greg, why do you turn your cap around when we dance? You don't when you dance with Leah."

He turned the cap around to the correct position. Lenore understood as the bill touched her hair when he looked down toward her face. She laughed, which seemed to delight her partner. He turned it back around and hugged her.

"I enjoy your laugh. It makes me want to laugh as well."

"Well, thanks. I'm going to enjoy telling Leah you turn your cap around with me and not her because she's short."

"Yes, this is true, but there is one thing more." He flashed his most mischievous smile. "I do not dance as closely to her."

Lenore stiffened, suddenly very aware of just how close they were.

"It bothers you because I find you attractive." It was a statement, rather than a question.

Grateful the song ended; Lenore walked off the dance floor to join Leah. When Greg sat down, she excused herself, heading for the sanctity of the ladies' room. She lingered, even allowing others to go ahead, before slowly walking back to the table. Greg was absent and she had no intention of waiting for his return.

"Leah, it's time to go."

"I guess so. I can't believe you've managed to stay awake this long. It's after one-thirty." Leah stood and smiled. "Just let me go whiz and I'll be ready to go."

"Great. I'll go on out and warm Baby."

"Don't you want to wait and say good-bye to Greg?"

"Not especially." Lenore smiled. "I'll meet you at the car."

The fresh air tasted wonderful and she drank it in. The quiet was as refreshing as the air after the din of the saloon.

"Could I walk you to your car?"

Lenore was startled to hear Greg beside her.

"Not necessary. We're parked at the north end of the lot." Deciding against going alone to warm the car, she added. "I'm waiting here for Leah."

Greg leaned against a rare 1969 Ford Mustang Boss 429. "I am parked here. I arrived early tonight."

"Wow, nice car!"

"It is a very American car." He spoke proudly. "Mr. Henry Ford was a genius, you know."

"I won't argue with you about that." She walked around the car, admiring the highly polished surface. "Mr. Henry Ford would have hated this beauty, though. It isn't black." She laughed, and wondered if he understood. When she turned to explain, words would not form. Their eyes met, he touched her cheek, then gently tilted her chin upward to meet his lips in a soft kiss.

Lenore felt all sensations at once. It was frightening and wonderful. His gentle hands were softly caressing her hair and her neck. She found herself kissing him back. He kissed her eyes and her forehead, then stepped back and looked again into her eyes.

Lenore put her hand on the car to keep from collapsing. She shook her head, trying to clear her mind enough to talk.

"You shouldn't have done that." She blinked tears away. "Greg, why did you?"

"I apologize if I have offended you."

It wasn't offensive in any way, but she wouldn't let him know.

"Leah will be here in a second. You just get in your car and leave and we'll do the same."

He took her hand. "Lenore, speak the truth to me. Did I offend you?"

She refused to look at him. "Offend me? Yes. No. I just ... it was a surprise."

"You are a very passionate woman. Why do you fight it? Look into my eyes and tell me it was not enjoyable and you feel nothing for me."

Lenore leveled her eyes, hoping the austere look would dissuade him.

"What I feel is none of your business. I apologize if I have given you cause to think otherwise. I am not in a position to feel anything for anyone, because I am, for the time being, a married woman. Now, I'm very tired and I want to leave without you. Do you understand what I'm saying?"

Before he could answer, Leah came out the door. Lenore immediately grabbed her arm, leading her away. The blonde lady barely had a chance to speak.

"Nice meeting you Greg, 'bye," she said over her shoulder, then turned her attention to Lenore. "What the hell is going on?"

"Just get into the car. I'll explain on the way back to the lodge."

Lenore started the car and put it in gear before Leah had closed her door. As they drove past the front of the saloon, Greg returned Leah's wave.

"Now, talk to me. What happened back there?"

Lenore pulled onto the highway and began driving toward Glenwood Springs.

"He kissed me."

"He did?" Leah turned in her seat to face Lenore, who was intent on watching her rearview mirror, making sure they weren't followed by a certain red Ford Mustang.

"Yes. He kissed me and I liked it. In fact, I don't remember ever feeling a kiss nearly as wonderful as his kiss."

"Okay, so why did we leave the way we did if you liked it?"

"Because I'm married! Even though it's a temporary situation at this point, I'm still married. I'm also not into one-night stands. Because he's some foreigner we know nothing about. Want more?"

She reached for the heater controls and turned on the defroster to clear the fog from the windshield. It was cold, and she was just beginning to feel the chill.

"Wow, you got kissed by a Russian."

Lenore groaned and looked at Leah, who was as attentive as a small child hearing her favorite bedtime story. Lenore had to laugh.

"Won't this be a story for our old age?"

"Did you give him your name and phone number?"

"No! Are you nuts?"

"Yes, but that's beside the point."

They laughed and Lenore glanced at the rearview mirror once more. Content they were not being followed, she settled back into the seat and watched the road in front of them. She wasn't getting any warmer and noticed her view was getting worse. She reached up to wipe at the fog on the inside and smeared an oily film into her line of vision.

"Oh, shit!"

She turned off the defroster and began slowing to pull over. The windshield was nearly opaque.

"Lenore, what's on the windshield?"

Lenore was frantic. "Antifreeze. The heater core must have sprung a leak. We have to clear it off."

"Baby's broken?" Leah was not going to handle it well. "Can we drive her? What are we going to do?"

"It'll be okay to drive on into Glenwood Springs as soon as we can clear this mess off the windshield." Lenore was trying to sound calmer than she felt. "I don't like sitting here on the side of the road. Look for a rag or napkins or something."

They began searching compartments and under seats, producing two small napkins and a ketchup packet. Leah even offered her mysterious tissue that was always handy for some reason. As they worked to clean the windshield, Lenore noticed headlights pulling in behind them.

"Leah, we have company. Sit down and close your door. We have to go."

"Lenore, you can't see to drive. Maybe it's someone who can help."

"It's not your friendly Highway Patrolman. It's him."

"Him?" She turned around to see Greg's car. "Oh, thank God! You had me worried there for a minute."

"Oh, shit!"

"You know Lenore, you're really wearing that one out."

Leah bounded out of the car just as Lenore put Baby in gear. She slammed it back into park and yelled, "Leah, get back here!"

Frantically, she began looking for a weapon as she heard a car door open and close. Leah, however, was very animated.

"Greg, we're so glad it's you. It was scary out here on this empty highway alone. Our Baby is having problems."

Lenore muttered as she got out of the car, and looked under the driver's seat. "Great, why not just point out the fact we're also defenseless and incredibly stupid. Then he can rape and murder us at will."

"What is the problem? I will help if I can."

"Antifreeze is all over the windshield and Lenore is absolutely having a shit fit!"

"She is needing a restroom? I could drive her to one."

Lenore raised her head, hitting it on the steering wheel as she did so. The only weapon she had managed to find was a rusty shoe horn. Leah was laughing and Lenore could contain her own laughter no longer.

"This can't be happening. I must be having my nervous breakdown. I might as well enjoy it." She sat down in the seat and turned off the engine.

The two women continued to laugh, while the Russian was totally confused.

"I do not understand. It is funny to be having this shit fit?"

Lenore's head was resting on the steering wheel as she laughed to the point of having to wipe tears from her eyes. It was Leah who eventually managed to explain the situation to the bewildered man.

"I'm sorry. Lenore does not have to go to the restroom. She was just upset about the car and saying, "Oh shit!" so much. It's also used as a word of profanity, you see."

"Ah, I understand. I feel this way when there are problems with my vehicles. It is good I have made you laugh. What can I do to help with your car problem?"

Lenore walked back to where Leah and Greg stood, suppressed a spastic giggle and explained what was needed. He quickly walked back to his car, and a minute later came back with a clean rag.

"I will do this for you. It is not good for you to get this substance on your beautiful clothes."

Leah smiled as they watched Greg wipe and clean the windshield to a point of having visibility. Lenore was not yet comfortable with the situation.

"This is very kind of you, but why did you follow us?"

"It could not be helped. This is the way to my home. Also, I would have followed anyway. I was concerned for your safety. Leah told me you are not accustomed to late hours."

Lenore glared at Leah, who continued to smile. She wondered what else her best friend had told.

"Well, I'm sure we could have handled it ourselves. You frighten me, Greg. I don't even know if that's your real name. It doesn't sound very Russian to me."

He stopped wiping and turned to look at Lenore.

"I would never try to frighten you. My name is Gregor Parishnikov. Do you not prefer the Americanized version? I am told "Greg Parish" is far easier to pronounce."

"Oh, I like Gregor better," Leah piped in. "You should go by your real name. It's nice."

"Nice to you, perhaps. There are many Americans who do not appreciate my origins. You are unusual."

With a final swipe on the windshield, he turned to Lenore. "It is far too cold to drive with no heater. Allow me to take you to your destination. I can return you here in the morning."

Lenore smiled her friendliest smile, knowing she would not have to be the one to turn him down.

"No!" Leah squealed. "That's just out of the question. Someone could steal her or hurt her. I'll risk freezing before I'll allow Baby to stay here all night."

Lenore shrugged. "Thanks for the offer. I think we'll make it just fine. Probably just be a pinhole leak."

"Very well. I will follow to be sure you do not have further problems."

"We would appreciate it, Gregor. Wouldn't we, Lenore?"

Lenore sat down behind the steering wheel. "Somehow I don't think it matters what I think." Lenore put the car in gear amid Leah's good-byes and settling into her own seat. In a few seconds the lights from Greg's Mustang were following.

"Is he back there?"

"Yes, Leah." Irritation punctuated her words. "I absolutely don't know what's gotten into you tonight. Do you realize what he's told you could be the greatest pile of crap ever muttered? Now he'll know where we're staying. He could be a mass murderer or rapist or someone very dangerous."

"He could also just be one of the nicest people we've ever met. Can't that be a possibility?"

Lenore drove, teeth chattering, too mad to reply.

"I tell you he's not dangerous. He likes you, Lenore. Plain and simple. I just know it's okay. I can't explain it. I think if you listened to your heart and what your eyes were telling you instead of what your defensive mind was saying, you'd know it was alright, too."

"Leah, I have to listen to my defensive mind. I'm a married woman."

"If you were planning on staying married, then I would agree. You've already decided to leave Nick. Gregor had nothing to do with that. You're just uncomfortable because he got to you, and he got to you because he was supposed to. You needed it."

"What do you mean by that?" Lenore glanced at Leah, then back to the road. "Do you think I need any more frustrations and problems in my life? You think I need to start feeling something for a stranger I'll never see again after tonight?" She shook her head and glanced at Leah. "Do you?"

"You don't know that, Lenore."

"I'm trying to figure a way out of a marriage to a cruel, hurtful jerk who's tearing me and my son apart. I don't have time or energy left for dreams, Leah."

"Who says it all has to be a dream? Who says you'll never see him again? I tell you; this is supposed to happen."

"You scare me when you talk that way."

"How, with my teeth chattering?"

It brought the intended chuckle from Lenore and lightened the mood. The cheerful little blonde lady began speaking in her version of a Russian accent, her teeth chattering, knowing her partner could not refuse the challenge.

"Perhaps we will take him to our room and pry secrets from him."

"Be very careful, my little cohort." Lenore mimicked with chattering teeth. "He may have hidden a microphone in our vehicle. We cannot let him know of our intentions."

Leah turned to face Lenore, startling her with an outburst. "What if he's a spy? What if he's a double agent or something?"

"Oh, that's just what I wanted to hear. I can see the headlines now: 'Idiot American women arrested for fraternizing with known Russian agent. Film at eleven.'"

They howled with laughter.

Leah added her own comments. "Honestly officer, Lenore was only checking his mouth for hidden microchips."

"Yes, and that bulge could have been a pipe bomb. I was only trying to diffuse it before he turned it one an unsuspecting crowd."

"Did he have one?" Leah asked.

"What?" Lenore replied with a glance.

"Did he have a bulge?"

"Oh, for cryin' out loud, I have no idea." She laughed. "I honestly did not check."

"Is he still back there?" Leah asked.

"Yes, which has me convinced he's either a serial killer and we're his intended victims, he thinks he's going to get lucky tonight or he's hopelessly insane. I think Baby could lose him."

"Or, he's a caring individual who's interested in your safety, like he said."

"My theories are more realistic."

"No, they're paranoid. He's interesting. I want to talk to him more, don't you?"

Lenore checked the rear-view mirror and glanced at Leah. She didn't doubt her motives or her interest. "No Leah, I don't."

"I've got to whiz!"

Lenore knew she needed to hurry. She also fervently believed her friend knew every public rest area between Glenwood Springs and home and ninety eight percent of the public restrooms at home, by personal experience. When she squeaked through a yellow light and left the Mustang stopped at the red, she increased her speed. Leah, preoccupied with her bladder's indelicate condition, didn't notice. They crossed the bridge and turned left. When they pulled into the parking lot of the lodge, Leah had already found her room key. She was out of the car, racing for the stairs before Lenore had put the car in park.

Lenore started to move the car to the other side of the lodge, then decided to make a run for the room instead. In her effort to hurry, she dropped the keys and kicked them under the front of the car.

"This can't be happening," she grumbled.

After groping several seconds on hands and knees, she found the keys. She was tempted to stay in position when she saw the lights of a car pull in the drive, then park beside Baby. Deciding it was too cold to play hide-and-seek, she stood.

Gregor was out of his car. "Is there another problem with your car?"

Lenore was confused for a moment, then realized he was wondering about her crawling around under the front of the car.

"Oh, no. I dropped the keys and couldn't reach them." She jingled the keys and smiled.

"You are very cold, Lenore." He said, stepping to her side.

The nearer he got, the less she thought about being cold. She moved onto the sidewalk.

"Look, Leah wants to talk to you and it's too cold to talk out here. I guess if you want to come up to the room, it's okay. You have to promise you will leave when we tell you to go. Is that clear?"

"Absolutely. However, I will warm you and you will ask me to stay."

"Not likely."

He laughed a warm and genuine laugh that made her smile. Warm was good. She started for the room and he took her hand as they ascended the stairs. It felt like a very natural thing to do.

Leah emerged from the bathroom when they entered the room. Two queen sized beds loomed larger than life and Lenore felt awkward. She excused herself and went into the bathroom. After the necessary part was over, she washed her hands and stared at her reflection, wondering where she had left her common sense. Though what she needed was sleep, she knew it would not come soon and a headache was nagging her about it. She brushed her hair and shook three ibuprofen from a bottle, swallowing them with a glass of room temperature bathroom water. It was not her beverage of choice, ever.

"Blah, bathroom water." She whispered and shook with a shiver.

Leah and Gregor were sitting on the floor between the beds, engrossed in conversation. Lenore stretched out on the bed behind Leah and rested her chin on her hands. She watched the Russian and tried to listen. She enjoyed watching him talk. His lips were soft and sensual. He smiled easily. Her mind wandered back to the kiss and she closed her eyes.

"Come, I will do that for you."

Lenore opened her eyes and realized Gregor was addressing her. Had he read her thoughts?

"I beg your pardon?"

"You are rubbing your neck. Sit here and I will do that for you. I can make your headache leave."

Sitting on the floor facing Leah, Lenore moved her hair aside as Gregor moved up to the bed behind her and began to massage her neck and shoulders. His hands were incredibly strong, but gentle. She closed her eyes, enjoying the pampering.

The conversation continued between Leah and Gregor, the sound of their voices lulling Lenore. She was sure Leah was learning things about the Russian few had ever known. She smiled at the thought of her petite friend becoming the CIA's most effective interrogator. No secret would be too deep for to uncover.

Gregor kissed the top of Lenore's head, bringing the drowsy brunette back to the real world as Leah spoke.

"Doesn't it sound like fun?" What do you think?"

"Sure. What?"

"I told you she wasn't listening." She addressed Gregor, then back to Lenore. "Gregor has offered to take us for a drive. Doesn't it sound like fun?"

"When? I think I'm too sleepy."

"Not now. Tomorrow. Well, today actually."

Lenore checked the clock radio and groaned. "Four-fifteen? I can't believe I'm still awake. I have to get some sleep."

"We're all sleepy. Gregor, we'll let you sleep in Lenore's bed and we'll sleep in mine."

"In my country everyone sleeps in one great bed." He teased. "Then they do not get lonesome."

Leah laughed, and Lenore turned to look at the Russian. His smile was sincere, but the twinkle in his eyes belied his words.

"You aren't in Russia! Unless you want to simply leave now, which is probably the best idea, or go sleep in your Mustang, you'll do it our way." She stood and stretched. "This is nuts. I must be nuts to agree to this. No one would ever believe there hasn't been some sort of perverse orgy going on in here."

"Orgy?" He questioned.

"Never mind. Look it up later." She pulled the covers back from the bed she had slept in the night before and retrieved her pillow, tossing it onto Leah's bed. She took the spare from the closet shelf, fluffing it as she ignored his smile.

"I'll only be in the bathroom for five minutes, you two. Don't start anything you can't finish." Leah giggled as she left the room.

"Leah!" Lenore felt a blush warm her face. She was not surprised when Gregor's arms slid around her.

"I ask only for a goodnight kiss."

She shuddered, despite the warmth building inside her. She looked up, accepting his lips. His hands were feather-soft as they moved to touch her face and hair, as if caressing a work of art. Her arms returned his embrace. She opened her eyes when the kiss ended and looked into his face.

He looked deeply into her eyes. "Goodnight, my precious lady." He kissed her forehead and her eyes, then held her face as he kissed her lips again. He stroked her hair and traced a line around her lips. She had never felt such gentle caresses. She was aroused, though he had not touched her anywhere beyond her face and hair, and had difficulty finding her voice.

"Goodnight, my Russian Bear." She whispered with a smile.

He smiled and pulled her to him in a comforting hug.

"Yoo-hoo! I'm coming out."

Lenore stepped from Gregor's side and crossed paths with Leah. She could feel the blush of his kiss still on her face.

Behind the closed door, Lenore looked in the mirror and touched the lips he had kissed so gently. There was a soft smile in place. She couldn't suppress it. She didn't try very hard.

With teeth brushed, face washed and hair brushed, she left the room and carefully hung her elegant jacket among ordinary clothes, smoothing out the wrinkles from laying on the bed.

"Hope I didn't take too long. Your turn."

Gregor put his finger to his lips and pointed to Leah, her even breathing indicated she was sound asleep. He touched Lenore's cheek as he passed and gave her a quick kiss.

"You look beautiful even without your jacket."

She smiled and watched the door close. She slipped into the bed as quietly as possible and fully dressed. Leah didn't stir. Lenore couldn't wait to tease her about staying awake the longest. When Gregor returned, she was under the covers, trying to make her breathing sound as even as Leah's.

Through nearly closed eyes, she watched as he removed his shirt and hung it carefully on a chair. The sight of his chest made Lenore's heart beat faster. She concentrated on the rhythm of her breathing. He stepped between the two beds and she closed her eyes. She could hear him remove his boots and his belt, then empty his pockets onto the night stand. She was glad he didn't remove his pants.

Before he turned off the light, she felt the gentle caress of his hand on her hair. She ached to return his touch. With the light off, she opened her eyes fully. He was looking toward her though she knew his eyes couldn't have yet adjusted to the darkness. She wasn't surprised when he held his hand out to her.

CHAPTER 9

The strong steady heartbeat filtered through layers of bone and muscle and the tickle of hair under Lenore's cheek. It was morning, but she wasn't anxious to stir. Instead, she flexed her fingers into the mass of hair covering Gregor's chest. She wondered if she had snored or drooled in her sleep. Fighting an urge to giggle, she smiled. Immediately Gregor's hand caressed her hair. He kissed the top of her head and hugged her closer to him. She felt safe, warm and protected. He made her feel truly precious, and it was a pleasant new experience.

She remembered laying down with Gregor. He had kissed her once, then settled her into her present position, never asking more. She stretched a little and looked up at Gregor's face smiling back at her. She liked his face, his smile. She reached up and stroked his soft beard, then touched the smiling lips. He kissed her fingertips and continued stroking her hair. She felt like she belonged there, and no guilt entered into her thoughts. She would question herself later.

"I hope your friend was not too lonesome," he whispered with a smile.

Lenore smiled and then turned when they heard movement from the other bed. Leah had turned to face them and one eye was partly open. It was like watching the dawn break. The eye opened wider, then the other peeked from its nestled place in the pillow. She sat bolt upright and looked at them. They had to laugh at the look on her face.

"I didn't dream it, did I?" She pointed at Gregor. "You're a Russian, right?"

"Leah, I am a former Russian. I am an American now," he said with a chuckle.

"Wow, that's right," she said, then noted the obvious. "Hey, you two slept together. Did you ... never mind, it's none of my business." She held her hand out in front of her as if to protest any information being offered, while she unwrapped herself from the covers and climbed out of bed.

"No, Leah, we didn't." Lenore was trying to sit up and get her own feet on the floor.

Gregor laughed.

"You didn't?" Leah sounded disappointed, which made the handsome Russian man feel the need to explain.

"I assure you Lenore's virtue is still very much intact. I will admit she might not be so fortunate the next time we lay together."

Lenore's eyes met Leah's and they smiled at one another. He had said, "next time." Leah turned and left the room.

Gregor pulled Lenore back onto the bed. She put a hand on his chest, curling her fingers into the thick black hair. His arms cradled her and he caressed her hair. Lenore felt control ebbing as she pressed her body against him. His breathing quickened and he wrapped his arms around her, holding her close. He released her and looked into her eyes.

"My precious lady, you are making me want to do more than lay with you."

"No kissing!" She said firmly through her fingers as she held her hand over her mouth. "Morning breath."

He laughed. "Very well. We will work around this problem."

The sound of the shower being turned on let Lenore know there would be ample time for making love, but not like this.

"Gregor, I don't think I've ever been so aroused, but it's just not right. You make me lose control far too easily."

He kissed her again on the forehead, then kissed her neck, just below her ear. It made Lenore arch her back and moan softly.

"You are a passionate lady. When it is right, I will make love to you. It is what we both need." He kissed her forehead and her eyes. "I will be patient." He laughed again. "Perhaps we will have mouthwash on the night stand next time."

Lenore knew she had nothing to fear from this sensual man. She also knew, when they did make love, it was going to be like nothing she had ever imagined. She needed to believe it and before she could begin to think of reasons why she shouldn't, the shower stopped.

"I'd better go make some coffee." She gave Gregor a hug and got up from the bed. He got out of bed and stretched.

"Better cage your little Russian bear, Gregor," Lenore advised.

He laughed and looked down. "I believe this is going to be a very difficult thing to do today."

The coffee was nearly brewed when Leah came out of the shower area. Her hair was still wet, but she was dressed in stylish jeans and a tunic of deep burgundy raw silk. Around her small waist was a denim sash and her shoes were matching denim flats. Always the picture of style, she was perplexed when Gregor shook his head.

"This will never work. You must have clothes which will be better for hiking and not for being beautiful. Do you have sweat clothes?"

Lenore smiled, knowing her friend's version of "sweat clothes" would be every bit as stylish.

"I'll see what I can come up with."

Leah began searching through the hanging clothes and suitcases. As she changed, Lenore poured herself and Gregor cups of coffee.

"I do not normally drink coffee. I prefer tea. Green tea in particular." He took a sip. "This is very good. I will not have trouble drinking such good coffee."

"Why do you not normally drink coffee?" Lenore asked.

"I believe the tea is healthier for my body."

"I would have to agree." She raised her eyebrows. "It's certainly done a beautiful job." She touched his chest. "Just beautiful."

Gregor took her hand and kissed her fingertips lightly, smiling. Leah reappeared in a coordinated outfit of sea green fleece wear, the jacket embellished with royal blue and mauve insets of satin cascading over one shoulder and down the opposite sleeve. She wore the latest style of Nike running shoes which looked as though they had never seen pavement, let alone a hiking trail. She smiled and struck a pose.

Lenore gestured toward Leah with a bit of a flourish. "Gregor, I present the "casual" Ms. Chase. If she needs more casual than this, we have to go shopping."

"I'm always up for shopping, but I'd rather take the drive as planned," Leah said with a smile.

"Then this will be most appropriate," Gregor assured.

"Did you want to shower next?" Lenore asked.

"I will need to make a trip to my home for another vehicle. Our vehicles will not be comfortable for this journey. I will shower there and change into other clothing and my hiking boots. This will give you time for your own shower."

A twinge of disappointment shot through Lenore like an electric jolt. This was his opportunity to make a run for it.

"Sure. Whatever." She marched into the bathroom and closed the door. Tears were welling up in her eyes when she heard the tap on the door.

"What is it?" She asked, irritated.

The door opened and Gregor stepped in. "You did not give me a kiss. I never want to leave you without one."

As she started to protest, he touched her lips first with his fingertip, then with his lips. It was soft and gentle.

"I hope coffee breath was better tolerated than morning breath." He grinned. "I will return, and we will have a wonderful day, my precious lady."

When the tears came to her eyes this time, it was for a far different reason. Gregor left the room and she heard Leah telling him goodbye. She wanted to hold onto the illusion a bit longer, and hoped the everyday routine of a warm shower would not wash it away.

* * * * *

"Dixon here."

"This is Frank. We might have a problem."

John could detect tension in the agent's voice.

"A problem with Parish? Like what?"

"I drove to the house this morning and his car isn't in the garage, the one he was driving last night. I could see where it should have been with the binoculars. Before you ask, no I didn't go to the door because of those damned dogs of his. Any ideas?"

John tapped the tip of his pen on a stack of files in front of him. He frowned and then laid the pen down. He glanced at the clock. It was nine-thirty in Langley, Virginia, seven-thirty in Colorado. He had only been in his office for a half hour.

"What time did you go out there?"

"Six."

"You tried to call?"

"Yes. Just keep getting the damned answering machine. I'm calling from a pay phone back at the saloon right now. Thought maybe he had car trouble or something. The lot's empty."

"Well, don't panic. I'm sure there's a logical explanation." John smiled. "So, you went out with him last night?"

"Against my better judgement, but he offered to buy me a steak."

John grinned. The Russian had managed to get Frank Gillespie to break a rule. "Well, how was the steak?"

"Great. What about him not being around?"

There was a little edge in Frank's voice, so John decided against any teasing.

"Drive around Glenwood Springs. His car's not hard to spot. Maybe he went to the store or out for breakfast." He could visualize Frank writing down every word. "You might also check with the police. Don't give them any details, just see if there were any wrecks or arrests last night."

"If I don't find a body, then what?"

John shook his head and frowned. "Just look for the car. Check Aspen, too."

"Okay, that'll keep me busy for most of the day. What if I find the car?"

"Surveillance, Frank. Remember surveillance?"

"Don't be a smart ass, Dixon. I'll call if I have any news."

"Sorry about the remark. Call even if you don't have any news. Especially if you don't have any news."

"Got it."

John sat the phone down and stared at it for a minute. He was going to have to talk to Parish about dropping out. It just wasn't a good idea to push someone who loved the rules as much as Frank Gillespie. In fact, it could be downright dangerous. He picked up his pen and tried to get back to work, but he knew he was going to have a hard time concentrating.

CHAPTER 10

Gregor listened to the dead air on the answering machine. He knew it was Frank and he also knew the agent was probably looking for him now. He would make his change quickly and hopefully avoid the agent altogether. Though he wanted to spend the day with his lovely Lenore, he would not risk being followed by Frank.

Within twenty minutes he had showered and fed his large dogs. By driving the back road, and leaving his Mustang parked conspicuously outside the garage, Gregor hoped to avoid the agent. Though Frank could possibly determine Gregor's Nissan Pathfinder was missing, he hoped it could be avoided. Being followed was most unwelcome today. Before leaving the house, he left a message on the answering machine.

"You have reached Parish. If it is you, Frank, I am sorry to have missed you for breakfast. I will be resting the remainder of the day and prepare for work tomorrow. I am afraid my night was far too late."

A lie, most definitely. One which could cause problems with later plans. He only knew he wanted to be with Lenore, and the cost did not matter. He would deal with it when it was necessary.

* * * * *

"He's back," Leah announced from her station at the window.

"He is?" She turned the television off in the middle of the weather forecast, which had repeated several times in her quest for distraction. Then she checked her reflection in the full-length mirror of the closet; satisfied her choice of blue jeans and a lavender V-neck sweater would do for the outing. Her Nike running shoes were worn, but not shabby.

"He's driving a black Nissan Pathfinder … very nice."

Leah pulled the curtains closed and grabbed her jacket. Lenore took her well-loved denim jacket and a camera, though she had been doubting the need for either until Leah announced Gregor's arrival.

Lenore opened the door just as Gregor started to knock, startling him.

"It looks like you are ready. Did I take too long?"

"Not at all." She lied. "We've just finished getting ready ourselves, right Leah?"

"That sounds good," Leah teased. "Where are we going to eat? I'm starved!"

"I know of a breakfast location not far from here. It will be quick so we can begin our journey. There is much I wish to show you today."

* * * * *

Healthy choices were made from a huge array of well-prepared foods. Both ladies moaned at passing up freshly baked cinnamon rolls, choosing instead the servings of fresh fruit. They were introduced to jasmine green tea and water with wedges of fresh lemon. Lenore tried to mask the pain of freshly squeezed lemon in her eye, but the ever-observant Gregor dabbed her eye with his napkin and kissed her cheek. Her eye still burned, but she didn't mind nearly as much. They talked easily with one another and the ladies proudly shared pictures of grandsons and sons with their new friend.

Within a half hour they were driving south out of Glenwood Springs. In Aspen, they made necessary stops and bought bottles of water and apples. The ladies decided to forego the Diet Coke normally consumed. They questioned Gregor about celebrities living in Aspen, and he assured them of many, though it was not to be the object of their journey. Both tourists scanned pedestrians and other drivers, certain they would find at least one famous person.

With the windows down and the sunroof opened, the warm autumn air was refreshing as they left civilization and began gaining altitude. Lenore had opted for the window seat, leaving a shorter Leah to deal with the confines of the center seat. The dark-haired lady soon tuned out her traveling companions, awed instead by the landscape.

"This is fantastic."

The ensuing silence let Lenore know they were as impressed as she. Brilliant aspen leaves sprinkled like golden confetti from the trees lining the highway, occasionally drifting through the open windows. This, the last day of September, was Colorado at her best. The deep blue sky was cloudless and provided the perfect canvas for the masterpiece of mountains and trees.

At the top of Independence pass, Gregor parked the Nissan. Soon, they were walking trails provided to explore the bird's eye view of the surrounding mountains and valleys. Leah and Lenore were amazed with Gregor's agility as he sprang from one precarious rock outcropping to another, then returned to their side.

"How do you do that?" Leah asked. "I'm a good climber, but you so go fast and never miss a step."

"It comes with many years of training. This is not difficult terrain."

Lenore wondered what his training had been in ... *Mountain Goat Patrol?* A quick smile creased her lips. Finding a slab of rock to sit on, she watched her companions continue down the trail, immersed in conversation. She was content to sit and admire the surroundings with her artist's eye. The air was cool, but the sun at this altitude warmed her. She closed her eyes against the brightness and turned her face toward it, listening to silence and drinking in fresh mountain air. This was as far away from Nick and her misery as she could get. The peacefulness she felt nearly put her to sleep.

The need for a bathroom stirred her from the roost and she walked back toward the car. A functional, though odorous, privy was nearby. Once the necessary was taken care of, she stood outside the facility and noticed a small lake on the other side of the road. It was begging her to explore, so she obliged it. With camera aimed, Lenore took pictures of the surrounding vistas and mirrored reflections of clouds and sky in the calm, crystal waters. She stood on tiptoe, climbed rocks and finally got down on her stomach to photograph from different angles. Standing up, she brushed the sand from the front of her clothes and noticed the Pathfinder was the only car left in the parking lot. She suddenly felt very alone.

Lenore took a different path when she crossed the road. Following to its end, she stood on a ledge overlooking a valley and took pictures of the road far below. It looked like a thin gray ribbon strewn haphazardly among the dark green and golds of the mountain folds. She sat down on a ledge, letting her feet dangle into a juniper bush. Solitude. All of the problems in her little world came to mind, as if carried on the breeze ascending the slope below.

She thought about her son and her crumbling marriage. It was so unfair to Joel. Lenore had begged and finally warned Nick about forcing her to choose. That choice was made the day she gave birth to Joel. Now, time and circumstance were closing in.

Lenore gazed around at the majestic views, then up to the cloudless sky. This was probably as close to God as she could get.

"I really don't need any more confusion in my life right now, God. What I need is some serious direction. Why do you bring someone like Gregor into my life when we both know I can't have him? I don't even know him, and yet me makes me feel loved and safe and happy. Why can't it be like this with my husband instead of with a man I'll never see again after this weekend? It just isn't fair!"

Tears slipped down her cheeks.

Just then, she heard her name called, Lenore stood on the ledge and wiped tears from her cheeks. The trail was a bit more challenging going up and she slid several times before making it to the top. She saw Leah and Gregor walking toward her.

"Howdy! You two must be ready to leave."

Leah wasn't smiling as she got closer.

"Lenore, I thought you were napping on the rock behind us. You were gone and we've been calling you for fifteen minutes. We were scared to death! Have you been crying?"

The trio walked toward the black Nissan. Lenore sidestepped Gregor's attempt to take her hand and avoided eye contact.

"I'm fine. Had a sneezing fit from all this fresh air." She smiled. "That's probably why my eyes look green. I did some exploring and took pictures. Sorry to worry you."

Gregor opened the passenger door, allowing Leah to enter first, then stopped Lenore.

"I was hoping to spend time with you here on top of the mountain." He started to take her hand, but she patted his instead.

"It's okay, Gregor. We'll check it out together next time, okay?" She hoped the sarcasm was noted as she sat down and closed the door.

"That was rude!" Leah scolded, as Gregor walked around to the driver's side. "Are you mad because we were talking so long?"

"Absolutely not, Leah." It was true.

Gregor sat down in the driver's seat and started the engine. He was quiet as Lenore continued.

"This was just the first time I've actually been alone in a while. At least alone enough to think with no distractions. Reality just sort of smacked me directly in the face." She took a deep breath and blew the air out noisily. "What a mess."

Leah gave her best friend a hug, then said in a low voice. "It'll be okay. I'm not going to tell you it isn't going to be difficult, but you're tough. You'll get through just fine and you won't be alone."

"I get so weary of having to be tough," Lenore replied in almost a whisper. "When does the easy time come for me?" She stared out the passenger window at the changing scenery. "I'm confused about this whole situation as well. I just don't know what's come over me. I really don't need someone stepping in here and giving me something else to have to deal with and get over."

"Lenore, how do you think Gregor feels about what you're saying?"

"Don't know," she mumbled. "Don't really care. Maybe he's relieved he won't have to lose any sleep over me. I'm tough, you know. I'll get over him easily."

Leah addressed Gregor. "I think it's time for you to have a little conversation with her, don't you?"

Lenore didn't want any more encouragement from him.

"Gregor, I'm sorry. I apologize if I've offended you. Let's just drive and look at all this gorgeous scenery."

"There is a place I want to show you. We will talk, Lenore."

When the car stopped, the stubborn brunette was out and walking toward a bubbling stream before Gregor could come around to open her door.

"Lenore, you give him a chance," Leah called out to her. "He really doesn't deserve your attitude."

The Russian caught up with Lenore as she slowed. He pointed to an outcropping of rocks that overlooked the clear stream and offered her a hand up as he climbed. She ignored his offer.

"You are a very independent woman. Sometimes it is not good."

"It's called survival. It's the only way I know how to get through my life."

Leah called out, letting them know she would be walking near the water. Lenore sat at the edge of the outcropping and let her legs dangle. The altitude was lower and the air a bit warmer. She watched Leah wander away along the water's edge.

Gregor sat down and let his legs dangle beside hers. He took her hand and she didn't pull away from him.

"Lenore, since I have come to this country I have not been with any woman until you. If you will look in my eyes, you will see I am speaking the truth. You have touched my heart, precious lady. I did not think it was possible."

When Lenore looked at Gregor, she saw sincere truth in his eyes. He touched her cheek and smiled.

"Why me?" She bit her lip. "Can't you see what an impossible situation this is?"

"Why do you say impossible?"

"We're from two different worlds, you and I. I have two sons. My oldest son, Grant, lives in Chicago, and my younger son is still at home, a senior in high school. He deserves as normal a life as I can provide. I've done a pretty poor job of late. I've got to work very hard to get out of my marriage and let his last year of high school be somewhat peaceful and normal. Maybe then it will be my turn, but this is going to be the hardest year of my life."

"Lenore, I can make it better for you, if you would let me."

"No, don't you see? What I have to do, you can't help me with. I have to get out of a very destructive marriage. I'd love to believe you, but right now, I can't afford to. I can't afford to be hurt anymore. I have to stay focused. No one knows how really close I am to the edge."

She was speaking metaphorically and she wondered if he was listening literally. She let it drop when he sat back further from the edge, pulling her back into his arms. He held her and rocked back and forth, smoothing her hair in a gentle, nurturing way.

"It is hard for you, but you must try to believe in me. Leah has told me of the situation with your husband."

Lenore frowned. She would question Leah's decision to provide him with her personal information later.

"I am prepared to help; with the hope you will learn to believe in me. It will not be easy. My life is complicated with situations from my past. We must both learn to trust. We must learn to be strong together."

"How can you say these things to me? How can you feel this way?" She frowned and spoke almost to herself. "This sort of thing just doesn't happen to a little girl from Kansas."

He laughed and kissed her lightly on the cheek. "I do not know about this Kansas girl. I only know the precious lady I hold in my arms."

"What are your complications, Gregor? What did you do in Russia? Why are you here? Do you have a family there?"

"There are many things to tell. Perhaps some things you will not wish to hear, but you will know all of my past. This is because I believe we will have the future together. We will not talk of these things now. It is getting late and we must leave."

"When Gregor? When will we talk?"

"It will happen. This is not the time. We must find our friend."

The handsome Russian stood and helped Lenore to her feet. They scanned the banks of the stream until they saw Leah, walking carefully with hands full of rocks and driftwood. She smiled, unable to wave at her companions.

* * * * *

The trip back to Glenwood Springs was interrupted with occasional stops for picture taking. It was dark by the time they reached the lodge. A serious lack of sleep and the day's activities had the ladies dragging, but the Russian looked unaffected. He walked with them to their room.

"Will you be staying again, Gregor?" Leah asked.

Lenore knew what the answer had to be, but didn't like hearing it any better.

"Though I would enjoy doing this, I must leave. I drive to Denver tomorrow for work and the hour will be very early. I must take care of a few things before then. He stepped to Lenore's side and took her hand. Please do not be sad. I will be calling you before you leave tomorrow."

"I understand." She didn't feel anywhere near as reasonable as she sounded. "We are all tired and need to rest."

"I will be keeping in touch with you through Leah until your situation is changed. Trust I will do this."

She nodded, feeling a lump forming in her throat. He best friend walked over to Gregor and gave him a hug and a kiss on the cheek.

"We will never forget this trip."

"For each of us, I assure you," he replied.

Leah walked to the bathroom and closed the door. Gregor pulled Lenore into his arms and kissed her deeply, caressing and holding her close. It was not sexual, but comforting and loving. When the kiss ended, she looked at him through a mist of tears.

"You must trust in me, Lenore," he whispered.

"I will try very hard, Gregor."

After a gentle caress of her hair and a kiss for both of her eyes, he turned and walked to the door. She didn't follow. She could not bear to watch him drive away.

Hearing the door close, Leah emerged from the bathroom in time to gather Lenore into her arms as the tears began to fall.

* * * * *

Gregor drove away, his mind on the woman he had just left, the one he had waited for all his life. He would do all he could to make her happy. Soon, he would have the life he had dreamed about. Only one very important task must be completed.

If he hadn't had so much to think about, perhaps he would have noticed Frank's truck across the street in the shadows. As he turned out of the parking lot and started toward home, he didn't pay attention to the other vehicles on the street. He was trying to focus through the mist in his eyes.

Frank was able to stay a reasonable distance behind and follow the Russian all the way home. When he pulled into the drive, Gregor finally noticed lights behind him. He got out of the Pathfinder as the garage door was raising and walked to the truck. Frank turned off his car's engine and got out to meet him, aware of the two large white dogs coming toward them.

"Hello, Frank."

"Where the hell have you been? I'm supposed to keep track of you, and you're not making it easy. I don't like it. I don't like it one little bit."

He knew exactly where the Russian had just been, but he was going to see what sort of answer he would get.

"I apologize for causing you concern. I needed to take a drive today. It is the last weekend to see the aspens in such glorious color.

Had I been able to find you, we could have enjoyed the drive together." Gregor smiled. "I hope you were not inconvenienced."

"No, Greg. No inconvenience at all. I'd just appreciate it if you'd keep me informed when you plan to be out of touch. Just as a matter of consideration, if you please."

The Russian could sense the sarcasm in Frank's voice. His jaws tightened as he turned toward the house, calling out over his shoulder, "Understood. I will be much more considerate from now on, Frank. Good night. I must feed my dogs."

"I'll be ready to roll at 4 am. Try to be on time."

He watched the Russian drive the Nissan into the garage, flanked by the dogs. As the garage door closed, Frank started his truck, turned around and headed back to Glenwood Springs.

Twenty minutes later he pulled into the parking lot of the lodge, driving slowly past the cars in front of the building. Two Colorado cars, one from Nebraska, one from Ohio and two trucks each from Kansas and Arizona. He parked and wrote down each number, prepared to run them through the system.

* * * * *

"Lenore, wake up. I'm starved! Lenore!" Leah shook the sleeping lady gently at first, then with a little more vigor.

It took genuine effort to be called from the depths of sleep Lenore was enjoying.

"What? It can't be morning. Is it morning, Leah?"

"No, it's only ten-thirty at night. I got up to go to the bathroom and realized I'm starved. Aren't you?"

"Actually, sleepy would best describe me." Her eyes remained closed.

"Here's a Diet Coke. Come on, Lenore. Just sit up and you'll be fine."

"Leah, if I sit up my eyes will open and I won't be sleeping any longer. Why are you doing this to me?"

"Because I'm starved. I'm positively famished!" She shook Lenore again. "Look how gaunt I've become. I may fade away entirely before morning."

She had the sleepy brunette smiling and she knew her eyes would soon open, then they could begin foraging.

77

* * * * *

Frank watched the two ladies walk down the stairs and get into the Chevelle convertible. They had come out of the room he had seen Greg leaving earlier. He followed. What at first appeared to be evasive driving, turned out to be a quest for food. They circled several closed fast food restaurants before giving up and pulling into a convenience store. Sunday night in Glenwood Springs did not provide a variety of dining experiences. He followed them back to the lodge and parked across the street in the shadows. They apparently had no idea they were being observed.

* * * * *

Back in their room, Lenore and Leah emptied the bag from the convenience store. There were prepackaged sandwiches, chips, cookies and more Diet Coke. Lenore opened her sandwich to squirt mustard from a packet and stopped.

"Look, part of my ham is green."

Leah looked with concern and agreed, then opened her package.

"I have a rainbow on my roast beef."

Lenore frowned. They looked at one another, grabbed another packet of mustard each and covered the offending colorful meats with the cheerful yellow condiment. They took their first bites.

"Mine tastes okay, how about yours?" Leah asked.

"Actually, it tastes a lot like mustard. Suppose they're okay?"

"Well, I look at it this way." Leah made a face and crossed her eyes, causing Lenore to laugh. "If it's poisonous, we will at least have full bellies for a while and we'll be able to get some much-needed sleep before the effect of food poisoning hits us."

"Sounds good to me."

"Also, if we get food poisoning, we'll get to stay a few more days in Glenwood Springs. That would be good, wouldn't it?"

"I don't know how good it would be if we were in the hospital."

They both fell silent, eating and considering their chance of survival. After consuming half of her sandwich, Lenore pushed it aside and grabbed the package of cookies. Leah swallowed one more bite of her own sandwich.

"Giving up?" Leah asked.

"Just doesn't taste good and I can't see eating it just for the sake of a full belly. I think I should enjoy the taste a little, too."

"Cookies taste good." Leah wrapped the remainder of her sandwich in a napkin and reached for a cookie.

"Exactly." Lenore bit into a chocolate chip cookie. "Tastes just like your mother made when you were a child."

"Really?"

"Sure, if your mom was an elf and did all her baking in a tree." She smiled.

"So, you knew my mother, did you?" Leah fell into her British accent.

Lenore replied in her own British accent. "Of course. Lovely lady. Rather short and had a penchant for green, if I remember correctly."

"Oh, that's Mother alright."

They laughed and continued eating cookies and chips, and drinking Diet Coke. With half the package of cookies consumed, they stopped.

"I feel better. How about you?" Leah asked.

"I'd say we could survive a few more hours. Maybe now you'll let me get some sleep."

Leah pointed to the clock. "Look, it's after midnight. You're turning into a real night owl, Lenore."

The sleepy brunette yawned. "I'm so proud."

"How are you feeling about Gregor?"

Lenore shrugged. "I'm trying to not think about him. Let's just table the subject for tonight and see what tomorrow brings."

"You don't want to talk about him?"

Lenore cocked one eyebrow and looked at the little blonde, who was perky and far from sleepy. Leah was determined, but so was Lenore.

"No, I don't. I gave in about eating. Now be fair and let me go back to sleep."

"I can't see how you could sleep when you've finally met the love of your life."

"You're really reading a lot into this," Lenore said, irritated, as she pulled her sweater off and removed her bra.

"All I know is what I saw and what he's told me."

She looked at Leah with raised eyebrows. "And, there's the fact you've told him everything about me except my bra size."

Lenore found her nightgown, tossed it onto the bed and pulled her jeans off. She was not going to take the bait.

"C'mon, Lenore. He wanted to know. Aren't you curious about what he's told me?"

"No Leah. Not tonight." She walked to the bathroom in her blue bikini panties.

Leah had cleaned the mess from their feeding frenzy by the time Lenore came out of the bathroom, with her face was washed, hair brushed and a freshly brushed smile in place.

"Hope that Diet Coke doesn't keep me awake. As tired as I am, I don't know how it could."

"I hope it does so we can talk more about Gregor. You need to you know." Leah grabbed her own nightgown and slipped to the bathroom. Once out of the bathroom and her own cleaning routine completed, Leah resumed her attempts to lure the brunette into conversation. Lenore was sitting on the bed, massaging lotion onto her tanned legs.

"Gregor said you make him believe in forever. Wasn't it a wonderful thing to say?"

"Wonderful." Lenore muttered.

"Do you believe him, Lenore?"

Lenore blew out a breath. "Leah, I am going to try really hard to believe him, but it is going to be a terrific challenge." She knew there was no sleep coming anyway, due to the two Diet Cokes she had consumed.

Leah sat down on her bed and crossed legs, Indian style, delighted to have won.

"You just concentrate on the happy part. You need to find out what it's like to be loved like you're the most precious woman in the world. You've never had it and it's scaring you. I believe Gregor is God's way of letting you know how you're supposed to be treated. It's going to give you the strength you need to get away from Nick. I know you waffle back and forth about leaving him. Maybe Gregor is the catalyst you need to get it over with."

Lenore absorbed what her best friend was saying, then said, "He really does make a believer out of me when we're together." She shrugged. "When he's out of sight, I start questioning the sanity of what I'm feeling. Am I so desperate for affection, I'm making something out of nothing?"

"If it's nothing, then we're both fools."

"If we're both fooled, then what?"

"You will be out of the miserable marriage to Nick. You will have some peace of mind knowing you are providing a safe, secure place to finish raising Joel. I wouldn't call any of that foolish. Would you?"

"Just hang on to me with both hands. If I go for this and it turns out to be nothing, it's going to hurt awfully bad."

"Just think about what it will feel like when it's true, Lenore. Finally, true." She patted Lenore's hand. "No more dark clouds."

"He said he'll call later this morning. I suppose there's the first test." Lenore stood up and stretched. She picked up her nightgown and just as she slipped it over her head, the hair on the back of her neck stood up. She turned away from the window and toward Leah, letting the nightgown settle around her, her eyes wide.

"Leah... would you go check in the bathroom and see if I left my black onyx earrings on the back of the toilet?"

Leah looked at her friend quizzically, then lifted herself off her bed, and walked into the bathroom.

Lenore marched to the other side of her bed, pretending to straighten the covers. Her heart skipped a beat when she noticed the safety chain off the door and the dead bolt not turned. She stretched again and casually moved closer to the door. She took a deep breath, hoping she had the nerve to deal with the possibility of someone looking back at her as she looked out the tiny peep hole. A wide-angle view of the walkway in front of their room revealed the shadowy figure of a man moving quickly away. She could feel her heart pounding against her chest. Trembling fingers secured the safety chain and dead bolt. She grabbed a chair and jammed it under the door knob, just as Leah came out of the bathroom.

"Lenore, I sure don't see them. When was the last ... hey, what are you doing? Scared of the boogie man all of a sudden? You look like you've seen a ghost."

"We had a visitor. Thankfully he didn't want to come in." She pulled at the gap in the curtains, but it simply wouldn't close all the way. "I think I have some hairpins in my makeup bag. Let's get this thing closed."

"We had a window-peeker? Did you actually see someone? Don't you think we should call the police or the office at the very least?"

Leah ran to the dressing area and dug into Lenore's small bag, coming up with three long hair pins and one huge safety pin.

"We'll be fine. He took off at a pretty fast pace when he realized I knew he was there. I doubt he'll be back, but let's not give him, or anyone else, such a good view, just in case."

Both ladies were shaking hard enough to make the task of closing the curtains more difficult. They finished and stood back, glancing at the window, then the door.

"Who do you suppose it was?"

"Probably one of the hunters. There are lots of them staying here right now."

"Hunters have guns, Lenore."

Lenore hugged her trembling friend. "Silly girl, hunters wouldn't waste their ammo on us. Besides, look at that door. No one is going to get in here. They were probably just taking a walk and saw our light. I was stupid enough to be running around in little more than my smile. He got quite a show."

"You can say that again."

"He got quite a show." She laughed, hoping to calm Leah a little more.

"I knew you'd say that." Leah laughed, too. "If you feel secure, then I feel secure. Let's try to get some sleep. Today is our last day in Glenwood Springs."

They hugged, then crawled beneath the covers of their respective beds. As soon as Lenore could hear Leah's even breathing, she got out of bed and searched the darkened room for a weapon. Finding only an umbrella and a huge assortment of shoes, she tucked the umbrella in bed with her, whispering, "I guess if this doesn't work, we'll have to shoe him." She smiled at her pun, knowing Leah would have appreciated it.

Snuggling up to the umbrella, it was mere seconds before Lenore fell asleep.

CHAPTER 11

John Dixon let the hot shower water flow over him, trying to wake up. He had worked late and what little sleep he had gotten was anything but restful. He could hear the phone ringing in the next room and cursed as he turned off the water, grabbed a towed and sprinted for the phone.

"Dixon here."

"Did I wake you?"

"No, you got me out of the shower. I sincerely hope you have good news for me."

"Well, if finding your Russian is good news, then yes it's good. He's safely back in his house. I had a little talk with him about disappearing. I think I convinced him it wasn't a good idea."

"Diplomatically, I trust?"

"Dixon, I'm hurt. Have you ever known me to be otherwise?"

They both knew John could site a plethora of examples, but he opted for details.

"Where did you find him?"

"Far as he knows, I found him pulling into his driveway last night. Truth is, I found him at a lodge where I spotted the Nissan. I hung around and followed him back home. He must have had a pretty good time, because he didn't have any idea I was around."

John managed to dry most of his body while he stood near the bed, then sat down and began to towel his hair while he talked.

"Lodge huh? That's unusual." John dropped the towel on the bed. "So, he was with a woman, huh?"

"No, he was with two women."

John nearly dropped the phone as he juggled to hang onto it and stood again. "What did you just say?"

"I said he was with two women. I went back to the lodge and checked tags. Saw them come out of the room, so I tailed them around town. They bought food at a convenience store and went back to the room."

"Two women."

"That's what I said. Not bad lookers, either. I ran the tag. Car's owned by JD and Leah Chase of Fort Collins, Colorado. I don't think the other woman was JD."

"Strange. First time he's with a woman and he's with two? At least one of them is married? Are you sure you saw the right women?"

"Absolutely. Got a good close look at them, too."

"How'd you do that, Frank?"

"Surveillance, Dixon. Remember surveillance." He didn't mention he was window peeking and nearly got caught.

"I guess I deserved that. Did they look suspicious?"

"I wouldn't describe them in those terms."

"Okay, use your own terms." He cringed, knowing Frank Gillespie's lack of finesse in such matters.

"One was a petite little blonde. Late thirties, early forties. Trim, sexy. Nice dresser. Same age group for the other one. Five-five or six, long dark hair, good-looking and built like a brick shit-house. They both had wedding rings."

"My, my … Aren't we graphic. I wanted to know if you thought they could be a threat to our national security, and you just described two candidates for a fold-out."

"Hazards of surveillance. They didn't look like a threat to security, but I plan to follow-up and find out all I can."

"Well, we know who the car belongs to, and it must be one of them. I'd prefer you stick like glue to Greg. He's the assignment, you know."

"If he tries to contact them again?"

"We'll follow up if necessary. Now, if you don't mind, I'm freezing my ass off in this air-conditioned room and I can't reach my robe from here."

"Understood. Parish will be here any minute to head for Denver. At least that's the plan."

"Great. Call if anything comes up."

John replaced the phone receiver and grabbed his robe. He talked to his reflection as he ran an electric shaver over the stubble on his face.

"Two women. Two married women, at that. Greg old buddy, you amaze me. Not so much as a serious flirtation in all this time and you get tied up with married women. Two of them! I can't wait to hear your version of this little encounter."

* * * * *

A couple of time zones west of John, a former Soviet spy was driving away from a home he would not see for a very long time.

A seasoned government agent paced restlessly, ready to follow the former spy to the front range of Colorado. He would soon be put to tests he would fail.

Lenore Appleby and Leah Chase slept peacefully on their last morning in Glenwood Springs, Colorado. For Lenore, the world as she knew it had changed. Peaceful sleep would become a rarity.

CHAPTER 12

The knocking drifted from her dreams to wakefulness. As the fog of sleep lifted, Lenore realized the knocking was at their door. She sprang from the bed and looked through the peep hole to see a smiling housekeeper with towels in hand.

Lenore moved the chair, released the safety chain and opened the door. She informed the housekeeper of their planned departure, and would accept the towels. The housekeeper assured her it would be no problem to return.

Leah was sitting up in bed when Lenore closed the door with the fresh towels in hand.

"Leah, I'm beginning to think I'm no longer a morning person. We have to check-out in an hour and a half. We'll never make it."

"You make coffee. I'll call the front desk."

Lenore began her task as she listened to Leah talk to the friendly gentleman at the office.

"Bart has no problem with our departure time, whenever it is. No extra charges." She smiled.

"He's very kind. I was hoping to get a wake-up call from Gregor."

"He'll call, Lenore. How 'bout a dip in the pool before we have to pack up and try to fit it all back into Baby?"

"Only if he calls first. I wouldn't want to miss it." She frowned, the feeling in her stomach telling her she might as well go to the pool, but trying to ignore it.

They busied themselves getting organized for packing, both glancing at the phone as if it would light up instead of ring. They drank their coffee on the balcony with the door to the room left open, waiting for the phone to ring.

When the car was nearly loaded, Lenore grabbed her purse and the room key. There was nothing left to take from the room.

"Leah, we'd better get going. We have a long drive ahead of us."

"We haven't left yet. We can wait a little longer."

"He knows there is a check out time, which was an hour ago, and that we will be heading home. He just isn't going to call. I was right and you were wrong." Lenore shrugged. "Let's go."

Her voice was emotionless, but Leah knew there was plenty building in there somewhere. They walked to the office and turned in the key. After paying and thanking Bart, the stuffed bear seemed to bid them farewell. Leah patted it on the head. Lenore fought the urge to stick her tongue out.

After checking the coolant level and deciding it was safe, Lenore sat behind the wheel of the car making sure her seat belt was fastened and adjusted the mirror, while Leah settled into the passenger seat.

"Lenore, we need to talk about it."

"Don't be silly. I'm fine. It was an interesting experience and that's how I have to look at it for the time being. If I try to do more, I'll fall apart. Let's go somewhere and eat. It's too late for breakfast."

Leah blew out a breath. "Okay. You know, I'll bet we're the first women to actually lose weight on a vacation. Last year I put on four pounds. I think I must have lost five this year."

Lenore smile at her friend as she drove out of the parking lot.

The ate at a small café downtown, sidestepping any discussion of Gregor. Leah flinched when the waitress offered Lenore's sandwich on white, wheat or Russian rye bread. The brunette's jaw muscle tightened as she selected wheat bread.

With snacks and Diet Coke handy and winter gear in the back seat, Lenore settled behind the wheel of Baby. They crossed the bridge heading north, giving them a view of the Colorado River and the Hot Springs pool, took three left turns and merged onto the interstate highway that had all too recently brought them to Glenwood Springs.

* * * * *

It was just before noon when Gregor finally shed the hovering agent by sending him for lunch, and found a private moment at his desk. He sat quietly, staring at the phone. He had missed them by only ten minutes. When the clerk said there was a possibility of their returning for a pair of sunglasses, Gregor left a message.

＊＊＊＊＊

"Lenore, we have to turn around!"

Leah's outburst startled the brunette. "What? Why?"

"I left my sunglasses lying on the desk at the lodge office. They're my favorite sunglasses. Can't we please go back for them?"

"But we've gone twenty miles! Do you realize how long it will take?" She looked at Leah. "Are they really so very special?"

"Honest Lenore. You know I've had those sunglasses for years. I have plenty of others, but those are my very most favorite. Please, please, please? Let's turn around."

With a groan and a heavy sigh, Lenore found the first available exit and headed back to Glenwood Springs. The sulfurous odor of the pools wasn't nearly as wonderful as when they had arrived on Friday.

"Don't you wish we were just starting our weekend again, instead of ending it?"

"Yes!" Lenore replied with feigned enthusiasm. "We'd spend Saturday evening eating pizza and swimming instead of dancing."

"Oh Lenore." Leah punched her on the arm. "You don't mean it."

"Owie! Yes, I do."

"You're being silly."

"No, I'm being honest."

Lenore pulled into the lodge drive and parked under the awning at the office. Leah went inside to retrieve her sunglasses, and as usual, took far longer than Lenore assumed it should. She tapped the steering wheel to the beat of an unheard tune, then finally turned off the car. She was ready to go drag Leah out, when the cheerful, smiling blonde came bounding out the door, waving her sunglasses.

"You are going to be so glad we came back for these."

"Why, is Bart going to give us a frequent flyer bonus of a free room next year?" Leah settled into the passenger seat, then Lenore started the car and turned back toward the street. "You know, I think we should go somewhere else next year."

"Lenore, he called."

Traffic was clear, but instead of pulling out onto the street, Lenore put the car in reverse and backed into the first space available.

"Say that again." She looked at Leah as if her friend was speaking a foreign language.

"You heard me. He called and left a message. We're to meet him at Mile High Stadium at 7:30 this evening. Can we make it?"

Lenore didn't answer. She put the car in gear, pulled out of the parking space and after carefully checking traffic, entered the street and drove to the entrance of the interstate. She accelerated and merged into the flow of traffic heading east. Both women were silent for the first ten miles. Leah fed a tape into the player and the music drifted in and out of Lenore's consciousness. As a raspy voice began singing about first encounters and love, she remembered how the Russian had first sat at their table, smiling and teasing. She smiled, remembering how he had laughed and held her close when they danced, turning his hat backward. She had laughed in spite of herself.

She remembered their first kiss and how it had taken her by surprise, and how he had held her when they slept, never asking more than she was willing to give. She remembered the words he spoke atop the rocks beside the stream, telling her he wanted to share future time with her, and not just the night. Could it really be happening? She glanced at Leah as tears spilled down her cheeks.

"Oh, Lenore, I'll turn it off."

"No, don't."

"Why are you crying?"

Lenore shrugged. "Don't know."

Leah patted her arm. "It's hard, isn't it? You've tried to be so strong and tough. Here this handsome fellow has the nerve to just burst right through all your barriers and offer you a life you've always wanted. One with love and happiness."

The brunette nodded, wiping away her tears.

"It's really okay to cry, you know," Leah assured her. "I understand what you're struggling with and you don't have to be strong with me."

"I want him more than I've ever wanted anything in my life. How did he capture my heart so easily?"

Leah used her rendition of Gregor's accent. "He has his ways, you know, and I'd never say it was easy."

Lenore smiled.

"Will we make it in time?"

"Easily," Lenore assured, accelerating for effect.

"I wish Nick would just disappear from your life. It would be easier than all the crap you're going to go through."

"I know." Lenore took a deep breath and calmed her breathing. "If it wasn't for Joel, I think I would have simply stayed in Glenwood Springs and lived on the streets until I could afford housing. It would have been better than dealing with Nick."

"I wish you didn't have to go home to him. I'm so afraid of what he's going to do to you or Joel in one of his drunken rampages. I couldn't handle it if anything were to happen to you, Lenore."

Lenore kept her eyes on the traffic ahead, while appreciating her friend's concern. "Don't worry about me. I can take care of myself. I just worry about Joel. I'll kill Nick if he ever hurts my son. I swear I will."

"You're telling me you could kill someone and it would be no big loss to the world, right?"

"That's an odd question." Lenore glanced at Leah.

"Don't you remember Gregor saying hit men were just providing a service, eliminating those who don't deserve to live?" She sipped her Diet Coke. "He said it was no big loss to the world."

Lenore stared open-mouthed at Leah, until the blonde grabbed the steering wheel and shrieked, bringing the brunettes attention back to her driving.

"Why on earth were you talking about hit men?"

"Do I need to drive?"

"No. I'm fine. Talk!"

"Well, if you had been listening instead of drifting into your private little world like you do, you'd have heard him."

"Is he a hit man?"

"No, or at least I don't think so." Leah grinned, teasing Lenore. "He was just reluctant to discuss his former line of work in the Soviet Union. When I said I hoped he wasn't a hit man, he asked why. When I said I wouldn't want to meet one, he said the part about them just having a job to do like anyone else. There are good people and bad people in the world, and when the bad ones are eliminated, it's no big loss to the world."

Lenore took a sip from her Diet Coke and thought about what Leah had said. Gregor … a hit man?

"Maybe he's just known a few hit men in his life. There's no way he could be one. It's not in his soul. He couldn't kill."

"I don't think so either," Leah said.

They drove in silence for a few miles before Leah spoke again.

"Has to be a spy."

"Why does he have to be a spy?"

"He's in fantastic shape. He's been trained to survive. He said he could be dropped anywhere on the planet and figure out how to survive."

"Maybe he's just a former Olympic athlete or something," Lenore mused. "They're in good shape. He might have learned the survival stuff in school. Maybe it's required." She raised her eyebrows and glanced at Leah, thinking that her logic was more plausible.

"That's possible, I suppose." Leah pulled the cassette from the player and placed it back into the protective case. "I just think it's so sad, the way he was raised and all."

"How's that?"

"He told me on the mountain about being raised by grandparents until his dad sent him to a boarding school. He was trained to be a tool and not show emotions or have feelings. He hated it. That's why he came to the United States and asked for political asylum."

"Phenomenal!"

"I know. How could he be such a nice person after such a life?"

"No! I mean it's phenomenal how you glean information from people and actually retain it. I truly admire you."

Leah fluttered her eyelashes when Lenore glanced at her and smiled. "It's a gift, you know."

Lenore laughed at her talented travel companion. "Yes, it is. How 'bout we talk about something else for a while? I've got a stomach ache."

"Do we need to stop?"

"No, not that kind of stomach ache. It's the kind you get when you're really nervous about something."

"I understand."

They traveled east, engaging in benign conversation and enjoying the remarkable scenery. They had truly relished the peak viewing time for the golden, fluttering aspen leaves. The sun seemed to set the mountains ablaze where clusters of aspens nestled among the dark green firs and pines.

Even with the top up, and plenty of solar energy, the lack of heat was noticeable as they neared the top of Vail Pass. Leah grabbed coats from the back seat and managed to put on her own, but Lenore decided to stop. Leah assured her it was possible to put a coat on while driving seventy miles an hour and not lose the time required for stopping. The patient brunette smiled and nodded, knowing Leah had doubtless managed such a feat more than once in her life.

"I wish we had hot cocoa instead of icy Diet Coke right now." Lenore shivered and yawned. "Can you reach my earmuffs and gloves?" she asked as she merged back into the flow of traffic.

Leah released her seat belt and turned in the seat to fetch more cold weather gear. She wound a knitted scarf around Lenore's neck, as the brunette ducked and dodged to maintain a view of the road. Lenore managed her own gloves and earmuffs. Leah layered on her own survival gear, though hers was color coordinated.

By the time they reached Dillon, it was time for a break. A warm cup of anything was what they both desired. Leah had not once asked for a bathroom break, which was certainly curious. Lenore pulled into the fast-food restaurant and turned to ask her best friend about her dry spell.

"Don't you need to go—"

Leah jumped out of the car and yelled over her shoulder. "I may absolutely burst all over the place, if anyone gets in my way."

Lenore muttered, "Well, that answers my question in no uncertain terms." She locked the car and walked inside, heading for the bathroom. Seeing no puddles, she smiled. Leah had held it like a trooper. "Glad you made it," she said, her voice echoing off the ceramic tiled room.

"I may never stop peeing!" Leah replied within her stall. "I can't remember ever feeling anything so absolutely wonderful as emptying my bladder. Poor thing must have been stretched to the size of a basketball."

"Why didn't you tell me to stop earlier?" Lenore asked from the next stall. "I would have, you know."

"I know you would have, dear Lenore, but I wanted to get as far as we could as quickly as possible. I didn't want to impede progress."

"You might have peed in the car, you silly girl." Lenore laughed. "Next time say something!"

"I suppose it might have gotten a bit frosty if I'd watered down the upholstery," Leah replied, laughing.

"Not to mention you could have been frozen in place." Lenore giggled.

"Would you have chipped me loose, Lenore?"

"What are best friends for?"

Their laughter was echoing off the walls as Lenore finished her necessary task and was washing her hands. An older woman in an expensive black wool dress coat and sensible shoes came out of a stall and walked to the sink next to Lenore. She slammed her purse down on the counter and glowered at the startled Lenore from a pinched little face, even as Lenore smiled at her.

"You ladies, and I doubt either of you are, should consider who might be listening when you talk of such vulgar things."

Any other time, Lenore would have smiled sweetly and offered a sincere apology for offending anyone. It was how she was raised and part of working with the public. But she wasn't at work. She was cold and tired. She had been in an emotional whirlwind for months and the last two days had taken their toll, as well. She spoke quietly at first, ignoring the "Ah-oh" from Leah.

"Ma'am, we were talking about peeing. I wasn't describing sexual encounters in front of a ten-year-old." Her voice was getting louder and she flung her arms open wide for emphasis, making the woman flinch. "We're in a bathroom for crying out loud! I'm sorry you can't have as much fun talking about peeing as we can. Your very existence must be horribly mundane!"

The woman escaped the bathroom as Lenore continued her verbal rampage at the closing door. "You didn't wash your hands!"

The sudden silence echoed as loudly as her voice.

Uproarious laughter erupted from the stall where Leah was finishing her task with a flush.

"I can't believe I did that." Lenore put her head into her hands. "I'm probably going to go to hell for yelling at an old lady."

Leah washed her hands and stopped laughing long enough to reassure Lenore. "I'm pretty sure it wasn't a go-directly-to-hell offense. I'm sure she will simply think twice about trying to instill her version of manners on total strangers. You may have actually done the world an invaluable service."

"I'm not cold anymore. Maybe we should make a run for it."

"No, I'm sure you're warmed up," Leah said with a laugh, "but let's get the coffee or cocoa or something."

They strolled to the counter and ordered hot cocoa and coffee. Lenore was relieved to see her victim had left the building. They were two hours from their meeting and the daylight was beginning to fade. It was going to be a cold ride. The had yet to go through the Eisenhower Tunnel and dreaded the descent to the Front Range of Colorado. However, given no problems, they would make the appointment with time to spare.

After spending ten minutes at a booth drinking both cocoa and coffee, the friends headed out, and Lenore made a cautious check of the coolant level, adding a bit from the jug of coolant JD had insisted be carried on their journey.

"Would you like for me to drive a while?" Leah asked while they retrieved more sweaters from the trunk and a wool blanket kept for emergencies. "I'll be glad to."

"I don't think I could even sit still if I wasn't driving. I'm wired on caffeine now."

With sweaters layered beneath their coats and a wool blanket tucked across their laps, the drive was miserably cold, but lively conversation helped distract them. When they saw the glow of lights from Denver, their spirits glowed as well.

"How are we doing on time?" Leah asked as she saw Lenore sneak a peek at the watch she had managed to return to its familiar position on her wrist.

"Pretty funny, you being so concerned with time." Lenore teased. "We're doing fine."

Theirs was the only car in the parking lot as the Chevelle came to a stop and Lenore turned off the engine. The friends looked at each other, and Lenore asked, "Now what?"

CHAPTER 13

Gregor paced at the mechanic's shop. He looked again at the agent who sat in the waiting area and wondered how he was going to manage the meeting with Lenore. Maybe the mechanic was just a little hungry. He went to the shop area and smiled at the young man.

"Excuse me, will this be taking very much longer?"

"No sir. In fact, I'm just about finished."

"I do not think you are." Gregor took two one-hundred-dollar bills from his pocket and handed them to the mechanic, who looked from the money to Gregor. "I believe it will take you at least an hour and a half to repair the problem. Then you will give the keys to the gentleman in the other room. I will pay tomorrow and you may add the additional time to the bill."

"I understand Mr. Parish. I certainly do." The mechanic stuffed the money in his pants pocket and grinned.

Gregor returned to the waiting area, obviously irritated.

"I do not believe this! There are further problems with my car and I need to go back to my office. There is paperwork I had hoped to finish tonight, but forgot to put it into my briefcase." He paced for effect. "I am happy to have a mechanic to work after hours, but it will make a very late night for me. I will simply have to wait until he finishes."

The agent watched Gregor pace, fully believing the irritation was caused by the missing paperwork. He took keys from his pocket and looked at them for a moment as Gregor held his breath.

"Tell you what, take my truck and I'll wait for the car. You do what you need to do, and I'll meet you back at your place. We'll trade vehicles there." He tossed the keys to Gregor. "Will that work for you?"

"I could not inconvenience you, Frank. It will make your evening much too late."

"I insist." He chuckled. "Those foreign cars. They're always a pain in the ass when it comes to problems. That's why I drive that old Ford truck. It's reliable and when things need fixing, I can do it myself."

"I believe I will be thinking of trading for just such a truck. I appreciate your help."

Frank smiled and patted Gregor's shoulder. "No problem. Just let that mechanic know I'll be taking care of it."

Gregor went to the mechanic. "If this works, you may have an additional reward. Mr. Gillespie will be driving my car when you are finished in one-and one-half hours."

"Got it!" The mechanic winked.

Gregor retrieved his briefcase from the trunk and walked back through the waiting area, shook hands with Frank and left in the truck. He would be only a few minutes late.

At seven-fifty Lenore had checked the coolant level again and paced around the car many times. Conversation had been limited to observations of their surroundings. Leaning on the trunk of the car, Lenore announced it was time to head north, and turned toward the driver's side of the Chevelle. Leah grabbed her arm, pointing toward the entrance. A 1965 Ford pickup was rumbling into the parking lot and heading straight for them. They stood side-by-side at the rear of the car.

"Could it be him?"

"We've seen the Mustang and the Pathfinder. I have no earthly idea what else he drives. Anything is possible I suppose." Lenore shrugged.

The truck stopped and a handsome, smiling man got out. He went first to Leah and gave her a hug, then took the surprised Lenore in his arms and kissed her.

"Why do you look so surprised? Have you forgotten me so soon?" he teased.

"Gregor, it would take a lobotomy for me to forget you at this point. I'm just surprised you're actually here, I guess." She laughed. "I'm also surprised at the truck. How many vehicles do you own?"

"My precious lady, you must learn to trust me. Though my plans may become altered by time and circumstance on occasion, I will always try to be with you when I say I will. If plans change, I will contact you. There was no opportunity to contact you today." He hugged Lenore and kissed her again.

"That's true. I'm awfully glad to be in your arms right now." She smiled up at him.

"The truck looks pretty good for as old as it is," Leah observed.

"The truck belongs to an associate. I am having problems with my Saab and he will drive it when the repair is finished. The offer of his truck was greatly appreciated."

"Greatly!" Lenore agreed.

Gregor opened the convertible door for Lenore. "Please follow me now. There is a warm place not far."

"How far?"

She sat down and he closed the door, then ran to Leah's door.

"It is close. You will follow me." He ran back to the truck and motioned for them to follow as he turned the truck around, heading back toward the entrance.

"Leah, this is nuts! I have to work tomorrow. We still have an hour drive before we're home."

"Follow him, Lenore. Last year it was nearly midnight when we got home from our trip, remember? No one knows when we left Glenwood Springs or how much stopping we did on the way home. This will be fun, I'm sure."

"I wonder where we're going?"

The answer came soon when Gregor pulled into the parking lot of an upscale motel. The two women exchanged looks as they parked next to the truck.

"Leah, I don't think this—"

The petite blonde jumped out of the car and pointed. "Look! A coffee shop. I'm dying for a cup of coffee. Maybe a piece of pie, too. Absolutely a bathroom." She sprinted away. "See you later."

Lenore sat in the car, drumming her fingers on the steering wheel as she watched her best friend abandon her for the warmth and lights of a coffee shop and a bathroom. Gregor opened her door.

"Is there a problem?"

"Well, as a matter of fact, there is." She gestured toward the building. "A motel?"

He took her hand, while watching Leah sprint to the coffee shop. "Lenore, I only wanted both of you to come inside and be warm. But it seems like Leah has other plans."

She got out of the car, muttering. "I'll bet."

Gregor opened the door to the room and kissed Lenore before they entered. The room was clean and smelled of fresh linen. It was well-furnished and clearly designed with extended stays in mind. There was a small kitchenette with a counter separating the kitchen from the combination living and dining room. The bedroom was a separate room, which Lenore could see from the front door.

"You stay here?" She asked, as he closed the door behind her.

"Yes, I will eventually purchase an apartment, if I continue to work in Denver. This place is a little expensive, but it is kept clean and is convenient to my work."

He helped Lenore remove her coat and a couple of layers of sweaters.

"My precious Lenore, you must have gotten so cold. If you could stay with me, you would never be cold again." He smiled his most mischievous smile. Which made Lenore blush and smile, too.

"I have no doubt."

Her coat and sweaters were hung carefully in a closet. Gregor led her to a small sofa in the living room and when she sat down, he tucked a blanket around her.

"You will start warming as I make you a cup of good tea."

To say she was surprised was an understatement. In minutes, a steaming cup of tea was brought. Gregor sat next to Lenore, rubbing her back while she sipped.

"This is wonderful. Thank you."

"I must be truthful to you. I would prefer to warm you in other ways, but you and I both want it to be special and right when we make love for the first time. I will be patient tonight." He smiled and kissed her lightly on the temple. "We will work on making this soon, I hope." He laughed, which delighted Lenore.

"We will most certainly work on it, Gregor."

She sat the cup of tea on the end table and snuggled into Gregor's arms. She opened his shirt and nestled her cheek into the warmth of his chest. He continued to soothe and caress. When she lifted her face to his, he first kissed her forehead, then her eyes and finally her lips. There was no urgency in his kiss. It was soft and slow, teasing with his tongue, savoring the taste; the feel of her lips on his.

Gregor's hands began to explore Lenore's body. He was tender and careful as he slid his hands down to the fullness of her breasts. He gently caressed, finding hard nipples pushing against her sweater and the lace of her bra. He softly rubbed them with his thumb, producing a moan from Lenore. He moved his hands away. He stroked her hair and caressed her neck, all the while continuing the feather soft kisses.

Lenore moved back from Gregor and slid the shirt from his shoulders. She lifted her sweater and removed it. His breath caught for only a second. Lenore began kissing his shoulder and neck, then lightly traced the outline of his ear with kisses and tongue. She kissed his lips, and let tongues dance as kisses deepened. His hands remained gentle as he released her breasts from the lacy confines and Lenore arched her back, pressing against his firm chest.

"Lenore, I do not think we are going to be able to stop." His voice was hoarse and quiet as he kissed her neck and throat, caressing and exploring.

"I don't want to stop." She moaned softly, responding to his touch and his kisses.

"Not here." Gregor stood and led Lenore to the bedroom, where he pulled the covers back on the bed and turned to Lenore. "Are you very sure, my precious lady?"

Lenore's fingers raked gently through the mass of thick black hair on his chest. "Absolutely sure," she whispered. She traced the line of hair down to the top of his jeans and unbuttoned them before sliding her hands around to his back. She kissed his lips softly, still teasing with her tongue. She massaged his lower back and slid her hands inside the back of his jeans to press his hardness against her. There would be no turning back.

She stepped out of her shoes and removed her jeans, watching Gregor remove his boots and jeans. With only her lacy panties between them, they moved toward one another and into bed, where fevered bodies responded to desire. They explored and kissed, each urgent to satisfy the other. Lenore's orgasms mounted in intensity until Gregor could no longer control his release. Hot fluids of lovemaking mixed with the strong pulsing of their orgasms and produced uncontrolled moans of pleasure.

As breathing returned to normal and heartbeats slowed, they remained entwined. Gregor lifted a tendril of hair from Lenore's face and kissed her. She smiled and nestled against his chest, comforted for a while by the sound of a steady heartbeat.

With a deep sigh, Lenore raised herself on one elbow and looked at the smiling Russian. She touched his lips, tracing their softness. He kissed her fingertips.

"I really must go. This wasn't how I wanted it to be, but it was wonderful."

"I cannot wait until the time you will not leave our bed after lovemaking."

"It may be a long time, Gregor. You really need to think this situation over very carefully. I have two sons, one of which is still at home. There is more to me than what you have here tonight."

"Lenore, what we have here tonight is a very small part of you. I am in love with you and the whole of you is what I love. Your children are an extension of you. I will love them as well."

"Your words amaze me."

"You mean the way I speak the language?" He smiled.

"No." Lenore giggled. "I mean what you say. You speak from the heart, don't you?"

"That is the only way I know how to speak to you. You captured my heart when I first looked into your eyes."

Lenore knew her heart was his at the same moment, but she would not say those things to him. There were too many complications to overcome before she would feel secure enough in her life to allow her heart to have control.

"I have to go." She got out of bed and carried her clothes to the bathroom where she washed traces of their lovemaking away before dressing. A shower at home would remove the lingering traces of his touch. She wasn't afraid of Nick being able to detect anything. More than likely, he would be in a drunken slumber by the time she got home.

When she came back to the living room and put on her bra and sweater, only seconds before there was a knock at the door. She was startled and Gregor glanced nervously at the time before walking to the door. Lenore thought it curious, but let it pass as Leah was invited into the room.

"I can't drink any more coffee and I think we probably need to head home, don't you Lenore?"

"Yes." She took her other sweaters and coat from the closet and began layering for the ride home.

Gregor helped and gave tender kisses and hugs while doing so. They were both smiling and relaxed.

"I think you will be warm enough for your drive. Perhaps you will let Leah drive the car. I think you should rest." He suggested with a tender caress of her hair.

Leah agreed. "I'm so wired on caffeine I could drive back to Glenwood Springs!"

Gregor walked them to the car and hugged Leah. He opened the door on the passenger side for Lenore and took her into his arms for a long, tender kiss and assurances.

"I will be in touch with you the day after tomorrow. Be safe and be patient my precious lady. We will survive the tasks ahead of us and be together. Trust this, Lenore."

She smiled and only nodded. A lump in her throat prevented speaking and tears were welling up in her eyes. He kissed her forehead and her eyes, and with one soft kiss on the lips, he settled her into the car and closed the door.

Leah respected Lenore's need to be silent, sensing things the way best friends often do. The lights of Denver became more infrequent as they drove north, and Lenore's thoughts collided and confused her.

* * * * *

Gregor glanced around the room, making sure all was in order before he opened the door to Frank.

"I appreciate your help with this matter, Frank. I was able to work on my project and will perhaps not lose nearly so much sleep."

The agent surveyed the room, noting the paperwork scattered around a briefcase at the table. He looked relieved.

"Not a problem, Parish." He tossed the keys to Gregor's Saab on the table. "I think I'd be finding a new mechanic, though."

A tiny electric jolt registered throughout the Russian's body. "Why is that, Frank?"

"I just got the feeling they weren't being totally honest, maybe taking advantage of you. You know, you're being not as familiar with such things. The mechanic said there was an electrical problem and he fiddled with gauges and tested everything. After an hour, I stepped in and started watching him. Funny how the problem just seemed to disappear. I took the car and went on my way. Hope you don't mind, but I stopped for a burger on the way here. Didn't want to eat in your car and figured the food would stink up the car if I did, so I ate in a fast food joint. Looks like you kept busy enough."

"That was most considerate of you." Had Frank not stopped for food, Gregor would have been introducing Lenore and Leah to the agent. That was something he did not want to do at this point. "Was my vehicle running properly?"

"Seems fine to me. Used the lights and radio. I think if there was a problem, it would have shown up."

Gregor retrieved Franks keys from his jacket pocket. "Perhaps you are right. I will look for another mechanic. The afterhours convenience is not worth it if they are dishonest." He handed the Ford keys to Frank. "I thank you for the use of your truck. It was different to me, but an interesting experience."

Frank laughed. Gregor looked surprised.

"I don't think I've ever heard anyone call driving my truck an interesting experience before. Glad you could use it." He slapped Gregor on the back in a friendly gesture. "I'm beat. I'm heading to my motel to get some sleep. Give me a call in the morning, would you?"

"Of course. Again, thank you for your help."

Frank left and Gregor stretched out on the sofa, smiling. He had managed to win back Frank's confidence. It would be needed in the next two days. He had arrangements to make, and somehow find a way to see his beautiful Lenore, all without Frank. It would take some careful maneuvering.

The people who cared for his dogs and watched his home were always prepared for Gregor's possible absence, given the potential for foul weather between Denver and Glenwood Springs. All bills were paid through automatic withdrawals from his bank account. He was financially secure and most of his assets were unknown and untouchable to the Americans. The loss of his job, due to an extended absence, would be of no concern.

The thing he needed most was sleep. He would have dreams of his beautiful Lenore. What better motivation could he have for solving problems? He would find a way to see her again and hope the short absence from her life would not be discouraging. He would make it up to her when he returned.

The introduction of love into the Russian's life had already compromised him. He had begun to think with his heart. That was dangerous.

* * * * *

"Want to talk yet?" Leah asked, patting her friend on the arm.

"Uh-huh." Lenore took a deep breath and exhaled slowly. "Leah, we made love."

"Silly girl, that was fairly obvious when I walked into the room. What I want to know is how it happened and if you liked it."

"I don't know and absolutely," Lenore teased.

"You're just being mean-hearted now." Leah pouted.

"It's true. He sat me on the sofa and tucked a blanket around me. Then he prepared a cup of hot tea for me. I honestly don't think either of us planned on anything intimate at all."

"He made you tea? What a wonderful and nurturing gesture."

"Yes, that was a first in my life."

"So how did you go from drinking tea to making love?"

"Kisses, Leah. The most wonderful kisses. They were feathery soft and sweet. I was so aroused I thought I would explode."

"Wow!"

"Wow, indeed!"

"So, was the rest of it as good? You don't need to give details."

"I won't. It was like nothing I have ever experienced in my life. It was beyond anything I've ever dreamed it could be."

They drove in silence for a while.

"Leah, even if this is all there ever is, I don't think I could ever regret making love with this man. This is how it's supposed to feel, isn't it?"

"Yes! Now you should be even more motivated to get away from Nick."

The mention of Nick made Lenore shudder.

"I feel like I could get through anything right now. I wish I'd met him long ago instead of now when things are complicated."

"I think you met him at just the right time in your life. You've endured so much. It's your turn now and I think you will appreciate it more by having gone through your trials. There are things you have to do, like get out of your lousy marriage and get Joel raised and out on his own. Gregor will help all he can, I'm sure."

"I know what I have to do. I just can't involve him. I have to be careful with Nick. He could complicate things if he knows about Gregor."

"I guess I hadn't thought about it that way."

They drove a few more miles in silence.

"You know, Leah, I've never made plans beyond getting Joel out of school and into college. Now I feel like there may be something after that. I've never been afraid to be alone, but in the sense of solitude, not loneliness. Does that make sense to you?"

"Sure, no one wants to be lonely, but sometimes it's good to be alone. It'll never feel lonely when you're loved like Gregor loves you." She glanced at Lenore. "You're part of my family now, too. We'll always be there for you."

"I want to know all about him. I want to know the good and the bad, whatever it might be. I know so little about him, and yet I love him. I've never been so sure of anything in my life, and yet I was not about to tell him."

Leah put her hand on Lenore's. "You don't have to right now. You have to get used to what your heart is telling you. This is what I've been trying to tell you about for so long. This is the real meaning of it all; the tenderness, sensitivity, nurturing. This is what makes the surf crashing on the rocks a reality and not the theatrical segue most people think. All these things you feel are real. The uplifting rush of birds, the fireworks, the euphemisms for the moment of climax are real when you've got what's always been missing in your life."

Leah glanced at her friend and smiled. "All these people wandering around wondering what all the fuss is about, well, that's it. Now you know first-hand, those things aren't theatrics. You've found it exists, and you can't continue in the dead-end, abusive relationship with Nick. It's your turn to soar. Don't question it. Just enjoy it."

Lenore nodded and squeezed Leah's hand. She had actually listened to every word.

"I plan to enjoy it for the rest of my life if possible. It's going to be an eternity before I hear his voice again or see him. Do you think Nick is going to notice?"

"If he's sober or awake enough to notice anything, it'll be that you're tired from a long weekend and a long drive home. I wouldn't worry about it. By tomorrow, he'll be back to true form. He wouldn't notice if you had a third eye!"

"You're right. I just feel like it's written all over me in neon paint."

"You're certainly glowing, but you and I are the only ones who could know it's anything other than driving without a heater. Don't worry."

"Funny, I hadn't noticed the cold until you said that."

The convertible eased around exit 269-B, taking them off the interstate toward the city. They would be home in ten minutes and Lenore felt especially weary.

* * * * *

"We're already here."

Leah slowed a little. "It's going to be hard to go back to everyday and ordinary, isn't it?"

Lenore nodded.

They returned to where the adventure had begun. The house was dark and Lenore was relieved. Leah assisted with luggage and made her bathroom stop before they hugged each other and whispered good-bye.

Lenore undressed and slipped into a familiar nightgown. She brushed her teeth and then brushed her hair. She stared into the mirror for a moment before switching off the light and going to the bedroom she still shared with Nick. She did not take a shower, hoping to hold onto the image of Gregor a little longer. Before she opened her door, she paused and opened the door to Joel's room. She could see him sleeping peacefully in the moonlight as it filtered through his window. She wished his life was always so serene.

When she opened the other bedroom door, the smell of stale beer reeked from Nick's exhaled breath. She wasn't afraid of waking him. Sleep came quickly, numbing her mind to thoughts of tomorrow.

CHAPTER 14

The sound of chirping birds called Lenore from her dreams. She knew she was home in bed, but had to struggle to bring her soul back from Glenwood Springs. Nick was beginning to stir. The thought of him reaching out to touch her, or as was his usual morning gesture, poking her with a urine-produced erection, made her quickly and quietly get out of bed.

She started coffee, then went to the bathroom to begin her workday routine. The shower felt good. As she towel-dried and combed through her long, dark hair, the lady in the mirror was smiling. Memories of a magical weekend would cheer her through the first day back at work. Thankfully it wasn't a Monday.

Lenore closed the front of her short terrycloth robe when Nick walked into the bathroom and stood in front of the toilet. As his noisy flow bubbled into the water, Lenore offered a cheery good morning, and headed to the kitchen for her coffee. A resounding fart was his only reply. She heard the shower running and turned on the radio for the day's forecast and music to get her moving. When Nick had exited the bathroom, Lenore reentered and began drying her hair. She noticed Nick standing at the doorway, dressed for work, drinking his coffee. She turned the dryer off and looked at him, knowing he had something on his mind.

"You better talk to that fuckin' kid of yours and get him straightened out."

She turned back to the mirror and brushed through her hair, perhaps a little too vigorously. "It's so nice to be home." Her sarcasm was dangerous, but she didn't care.

"Yeah, while you're out having a good time, I had to tell your kid to mow the lawn three times before he did it. That's bullshit!"

She stopped brushing and turned to look at him. "What was he doing when you asked?"

"Readin' the fuckin' funny papers."

Lenore turned back to the mirror and continued to brush her hair to avoid looking at him.

"Tell me, Nick, did you get to read the paper?"

"Yeah, I read it while he fixed breakfast and cleaned up the kitchen after."

"Did he get the lawn mowed?"

"Eventually, when I threatened to beat his lazy ass." His voice was getting loud and sharp and Lenore knew she was pushing, but anger was overriding common sense.

"Nick, he gets up and follows a routine every day just like we do." She sat the hairbrush down and turned to face him. "He goes to school and gets good grades. He's a good kid. Why can't you see that? He isn't disrespectful, at least not when he's treated with respect. Don't you think it's okay sometimes that he doesn't jump the minute you think he should? Shouldn't he be able to sit down and relax like you do?"

She wasn't going to wait for a reply to her question.

"What could it have hurt if he had read the paper before he mowed? It was Sunday, for God's sake!"

Lenore was shaking and Nick glared at her as he slurped loudly on his coffee, a known annoyance to Lenore.

"Nick, I get so tired of being caught in the middle here. I don't have trouble getting him to help out. He does it because I ask, not demand. I also respect him, which you don't. He's got feelings and intelligence and a neat personality, but all you can do is point out imaginary faults and tell him he's stupid."

Nick glared at Lenore. "I refuse to kiss any kid's ass! He's gotta toe the fuckin' line." He pointed toward Lenore with the cup and dribbled coffee on the floor. "You're too soft on him."

Lenore took a deep breath, trying to calm her nerves. "You won't even try it my way, will you, Nick?"

"Aw, you're both a couple of fuckin' morons. I'm going to work."

The house shuddered as Nick slammed the door on his way out.

Lenore pulled toilet paper from the roll and cleaned the spilled coffee. She flushed the paper away and stared out the bathroom window. There were no tears this time. A resolve to escape was overtaking any sadness.

She heard the door to Joel's room open and turned to see him standing in the hall.

"Good morning, Sweetie." She walked to the doorway and gave her son a hug and kiss.

"Mom, I'm so sorry. What a welcome home."

"Joel, I know the routine. It isn't your fault. Was he out late on Saturday night?"

"He didn't get home until after three. He woke me when he was running into things, before he went to bed and passed out."

They walked together to the kitchen where Lenore warmed her coffee and poured a fresh cup for Joel.

"His late night didn't help his personality any." She pointed to a pot of oatmeal and Joel nodded. "He had to pick a fight about something so he wouldn't feel guilty about being out so late."

"Mom, he only told me once. When I asked if I could finish reading the Garfield cartoon, you'd have thought I told him to go to hell or something." Joel poured creamer and sugar into his coffee, took a sip and shook his head. "He threw the paper out before I finished the lawn. I just went to my room for the day. He sat around and drank beer until he ran out, I guess. I heard him go to bed about nine." He took a bowl from the cabinet and a spoon from the drawer as Lenore buttered toast when it popped up. "I got up and fixed a sandwich and picked up all the empties." He shrugged. "Same last night. At least I had homework to do. I got up after he passed out and got the mess cleaned up so you didn't walk in to a mess when you got home."

Lenore shook her head and massaged Joel's shoulders as he sat down to eat. "Joel, we don't need to live like this. It would really be hard, but we have to get out of here and try to make it on our own. I'm so sorry I ever got us into this situation. I've got to get us out of it now."

The tall young man stood and put his arms around Lenore, holding her tight. "Mom, it's not your fault. He didn't used to be so bad. I think all that beer is rotting his brain or something. I just worry he's going to hurt you. He gets in such a rage over the little things. What'll he do, if you try to leave?"

"Hopefully nothing. Maybe he wants me to go. I just worry you two will come to blows. You have to promise me you won't try to push him, okay? You just can't, Joel." She looked into his eyes and put her hands on his cheeks. "I couldn't handle it if he hurt you. I know it's going to take a lot of pride swallowing, but you just have to walk away and avoid confrontations. Promise me!"

"I promise, Mom, just for you. Someday I'd love to beat him to a pulp."

"I know, but right now we have to just get away."

Lenore had to stretch a little to give her son a kiss on his cheek. He hugged her again, smiled his little boy smile and sat back down to finish his breakfast. When he headed to the shower, Lenore prayed quietly for patience and a way out.

She was dressed in comfortable dress pants, a lavender sweater and comfortable two-inch heels, or as she referred to her ensemble, her practical work clothes. She poured her third cup of coffee as Joel came in. Lenore would feed the cat. When his ride honked, he kissed his mom and ran out the door.

Spot, the cat, ran in as Joel left and Lenore poured her food into a dish and sat fresh water beside it on the floor. She cleaned the breakfast dishes and went back into the bathroom to finish her routine.

She brushed her teeth and practiced a smile in the mirror. Smiling might be her biggest challenge of the day. Lenore grabbed her purse and jacket and left for work.

* * * * *

Parking in her usual spot behind the store, thoughts of Gregor eased back into her mind. She managed a genuine smile as she walked in the back door, ready for whatever the day would bring. JD was huddled over paperwork as Lenore peeked into his office. She tapped lightly on his office door and waited for him to find a convenient stopping place.

"Is that the traveling shoe saleslady knocking on my door?" He turned and smiled at Lenore. "I didn't think you were going to come back this year."

"It was all that whining from Leah. She refused to stay with me and I figured I'd get pretty lonely without her. Besides, how could you guys stay in business without me?"

"I was going to close the doors today if you didn't come back." He chuckled. "Sounds like you two had a good time."

"We managed somehow." She laughed. "Did she tell you what a wonderful conversationalist I am around midnight?"

"She said you last about three seconds after your head hits the pillow, but you make up for it when the sun comes up. Leah has never been too keen on mornings." He smiled. Lenore knew he meant it in the most endearing of terms.

JD Chase was a man in love with his wife, and it was a love fully returned by Leah. They were not only ardent lovers, but the best of friends and high school sweethearts, who made it work all these years. Lenore had so often envied their relationship, wondering if she would ever find such a love.

"Some are meant to crow at dawn, others are born to howl at the moon," She replied. "By the way, I got used to lounging, so be patient. You may even have to retrain me."

"I think we can do that. Glad you're back."

The phone rang and Lenore walked out of the office as JD picked up the receiver. She walked to the front office behind the register, hung her coat on a hook and slipped her purse into a drawer. She went about her duties and settled into a familiar routine. The cash drawer was filled and lights turned on. Then the back door opened.

Royce was taking off a light jacket as he crossed the floor to Lenore and gave her a welcome back hug. A former native of the Maine woods, he thrived in the cold weather and the jacket was more of an appeasement to his wife than a necessity.

Royce was in his early thirties. He was a mixture of old hippy and young politician with a dose of Catholic guilt thrown in. He had hitchhiked to Colorado in his early twenties and fell in love with the land. He had badgered for a job at the store until, with the promise to cut his ponytail, he won a position.

He appeared complaisant, but a maniacal look from pale blue eyes could dispel any thoughts of weakness. He was slight of build with thinning hair, which Lenore assure him was a sign of virility. He smiled easily and had a strong clientele, encompassing those from similar lifestyles to retirees. Although occasionally a little too outspoken for Lenore, she found him to be a good friend.

"Lenore, we were taking bets you wouldn't come back this year."

"Hope you didn't lose much. I couldn't survive without all these feet every day. Must be in my blood."

"Yeah, if they cut us, they'd get toe jam!" He laughed.

Lenore groaned and wrinkled her nose.

"Really, I hope it was a magical weekend. You needed a good peaceful break. Speaking of smelly appendages, how was Nick when you got home?"

"Fortunately, asleep. He made up for it this morning. Couldn't even say welcome home. Just the normal routine about Joel. It doesn't make any difference if I'm there or not. Things are going downhill at twice the speed of light."

Lenore followed Royce to the front office where he hung his jacket on a hook. "We can all see it's getting worse. The stress is tearing you apart, Lenore."

They walked back to the sales floor and leaned against the backs of chairs.

"I did a lot of thinking this weekend. I'm so tired of this existence with Nick. He picks fights with Joel and calls him names. Joel is not that hard to get along with."

"I know. He's a rarity these days. He's respectful and polite. Who couldn't get along with him? He takes after his mom."

"That was a sweet thing to say, Royce. Thanks!" She smiled. "Anyway, something has to change. I felt like I was walking into the bowels of hell when I opened the bedroom door last night. Do you think Joel and I could make it on our own?"

"I know you're one bright lady. If anyone could do it, you could." He put a hand on her shoulder. "Have you talked to Nick? I mean does he know how determined you are to have peace?"

"As much as I can, Royce. He frightens me anymore. It's hard to find him sober enough to talk about anything. He's changed so much. I don't even know him."

Before the conversation could continue, Rusty walked in the back door.

"There's my girl! You'd better get back here and give this old man a hug." Lenore giggled and walked briskly back to be totally enveloped in his fatherly affection. "Did you have a good time?"

"Yes, I did Rusty."

"That's good! You needed your time away. I hope you never thought about home the whole time you were gone. You look like you might have gotten some rest, too."

"Yep." It was hard for Lenore to keep a straight face as she agreed. "Just bummed and lounged around the pools and got lots of sleep."

"You ready to get back to work?"

"Of course not! I already warned JD."

They all laughed, and JD walked out of his office to unlock the doors. "Well, aren't you a cheerful crew. How come you guys can't be like this when she isn't around?"

"If you guys were as pretty and sweet as Lenore, I'd probably be more cheerful when she's gone," replied Rusty, "but you aren't!"

Lenore blushed a little and gave Rusty another hug. He was another unique individual. Lenore knew he was most comfortable on the back of a good horse, traversing a mountain trail. The store was, more than anything, a social outlet to stay in touch with lifelong friends in town. He and his wife, Gertie, had a successful horse ranch in the foothills. After working all week in town, they retreated to their sanctuary and reveled in the sunsets and serenity of the Rocky Mountains.

Russell, or "Rusty" as he was known to all, was tall and well-built for his age; he had just crept over the mid-sixties several months earlier. He had a full head of curly hair and a full mustache, which were both streaked generously with silver. The western clothing and boots he chose to wear were never challenged. He was too good at what he did for the head office to ask him to change to the latest style proffered. Older ladies often giggled or blushed with a wink from the handsome man, and the gentlemen he assisted were assured of knowledgeable experience.

Lenore had learned a great deal from Rusty about selling shoes and other merchandise offered at the store. It was a tough business to break into for a woman. Unlike so many shoe stores, this was still a full-service operation. They possessed the perceptive skills of knowing when to offer alternatives, proper fitting and adjustments. It had taken time, but Lenore had a loyal following of her own. Many of Rusty's customers came to her for assistance in his absence.

The leader of the group was Lenore's best friend's husband, JD Chase. Although he had grown up in a Texas college town, his accent was nearly imperceptible. Lenore often teased him when they all went out, that the more he drank, the further south his accent drifted.

He was six feet tall, which put a foot between him and Leah. It never seemed a hindrance. He didn't mind having to stoop a little and Leah was very accustomed to stretching up for most everything. His blond, wavy hair was growing lighter at the temples with the influx of silver weaving its way through. He was in his mid-forties and although his shoulders drooped a little, either from genetics, or years on a fitting stool, he was in good shape. He exercised regularly and played golf, which had netted him countless business contacts.

JD had been in the company for twenty years and was a good businessman. He was always at ease having to leave town on buying trips, shoe shows, meetings or vacations. He had a competent crew. They were all loyal and hard-working. He was easy to work for.

They talked and teased Lenore about her weekend, wanting to know all about the pools and the views. Lenore talked easily among them and they were laughing over the vision of Leah turned around in her seat, trying to stand and take pictures from a moving convertible with Lenore desperately hanging onto her shirt tail. JD simply put a hand over his eyes and shook his head.

A rattle of the still-locked doors interrupted the assembly. JD ran to unlock them.

"Ma'am, I'm really sorry we didn't have the door open for you. How can we help this morning?"

The lady sniffed indignantly and strode past him toward Rusty, who guided her skillfully toward the display of sensible walking shoes.

The group proceeded to assigned duties and soon they were all busy with customers of their own. Sales tallied up and JD spoke to Lenore as they both wrapped up purchases at the register.

"Looks like it's going to be a good day. We were sure slow yesterday."

"Of course! They were waiting for me." She laughed.

"Lenore, you'd best be careful. It might be your last vacation."

It was busy and Lenore loved it. Each new face through the door brought a challenge. It wasn't many years earlier she had been so shy, ordering pizza over the phone was enough to make her break out in a nervous sweat. Her confidence and graceful manner in the store had made her a success, and the shy little girl from Kansas was but an occasional painful memory. At work, Lenore was in control of her life and her eyes sparked with knowledge. Only after the doors closed for the evening and she was on her way home, would the helpless feeling of being totally out of control seep in.

She sat on a fitting stool and was vaguely aware of the nasal drone of conversation between the couple she was with. Her mind was in Glenwood Springs and she smiled at the empty seat in front of her. The gentleman paraded and turned like a model on a runway for his wife. A warmth washed over her and she wondered why she didn't feel guilty. She would get to hear Gregor's voice tomorrow and this day was passing swiftly. It was nearly lunch time.

Her thoughts were brought back to the business at foot when her customer plopped down in her line of vision and announced his desire to try a different style. She smiled and excused herself to retrieve the size eleven, kiltie-tassel loafer in cordovan. She could get through the rest of her workday, and somehow through the night at home. The wall of shoe boxes yielded its treasure. She returned to the customer, carefully slipping the fine leather onto his foot with the aid of her personally engraved stainless shoe horn.

* * * * *

It was a half-hour past the posted closing time when Royce locked the door and called to Lenore, "Hey lady, let's go home. I didn't think those people would ever leave. Don't they realize we have a life beyond this place and it would be nice to get at it?"

As long as there were customers in the store, no one stayed alone. Lenore usually volunteered to remain.

"They've obviously never worked in a retail environment. I'll bet they squeal when they have to stay late at their jobs." She closed the door to the safe and gave the dial a spin. "I guess this means I have to go home now."

"Maybe he'll be sober tonight and you can talk to him. If not, well, I guess you've gotten good at that scenario." Royce carried his jacket over his shoulder to the back door, while Lenore was slipping hers on.

"Unfortunately, yes." She turned off the lights and locked the door behind them. "Joel is there and I missed him this weekend. Maybe we can spend some time together."

"There's my Lenore. Find the positive. I'm proud of you." He grinned and gave Lenore a hug.

She waved to Royce as he rode away on his bicycle, ever the environmentalist. Lenore let her car warm a bit before she backed out of her parking spot and headed for the street. She seldom hurried to get home. Today it was especially difficult. She wondered what sort of mood Nick was going to be in tonight, given the argument they had that morning. The thought of Joel home alone with Nick hurried her along.

When Lenore pulled into the drive, Nick was standing at the front door wearing only his worn jogging shorts and holding a beer in his hand. She was aware of a growing pain in her left temple. She wasn't surprised at the headache; she was looking at the source of her stress.

Nick held the door open as she walked up to the house. A resounding belch blew the odor of beer past her nose as she entered.

"I thought you could make Italian sausage for dinner. I don't know want you're going to eat since you don't like it." He walked to his recliner and resumed watching the television. "Bring me another beer."

Lenore felt the throb in her head increase as she sat her purse down and kicked off her shoes. She started for the kitchen.

"What took you so fuckin' long to get home?"

"Late customers, as usual." It really didn't matter what she said, it would have produced an argument.

"How come you're the only one who stays late? Don't any of them other bastards ever stay?"

"Nick, we all stay when we have to. I get paid for it anyway, and I wish you wouldn't refer to my co-workers as bastards." She could have let the comment pass, but she wasn't feeling submissive at the moment. She hated his outlook on life.

"Just get my fuckin' beer and fix supper. I'm hungry!"

As Lenore opened the refrigerator door to retrieve Nick's beer, she noticed the four empties on the counter. He had just finished his fifth and she was holding the sixth. It was going to be a very long night. She walked into the living room and sat the beer down on the table beside Nick, ignoring the empty he held out to her, which he consequently crushed and threw on the floor. She walked down the hall to Joel's room and quietly opened the door. He was busy working at his desk and looked up with a smile when he heard his mom's voice.

"Hi Joel. Got a lot of homework?"

"Not any more. I'm just finishing algebra. How was your day?"

"Good for being the first day after a vacation. I think I was number one in sales. How was your day?"

"As usual, fine until I got home. He's been here since about four. I was really glad I had homework to do. Weird, huh?" He smiled, making his mom smile, too. "Do you need help with dinner?"

Lenore hugged her son. "No, I'm fixing Italian sausage. Finish your homework."

"What are you going to eat? You hate the stuff."

"I'm not especially hungry. Got another headache. I'll just fix dinner and go to bed early."

"I'll take care of the dishes. I know he won't."

"Baby boy, you can count on that. I appreciate your help. I'll talk to you after bit." She hugged him and smoothed his hair. "I missed you."

"I missed you too, Mom. I'm glad you got to go with Leah though, you needed to have some fun."

Lenore returned to the kitchen and washed her hands thoroughly. She went about her preparations and ignored Nick's request for another beer. He managed to find his way to the refrigerator and get his own, adding his empties to the growing pile on the counter. When he left the kitchen, Lenore carried them to the recycle container three feet away.

* * * * *

An hour later, hot Italian sausage, pasta, salad and hot Italian bread were ready and set on the dining room table. She could think of nothing more than getting out of her work clothes and into bed. Her head was pounding, and three ibuprofen tablets had given no relief. She called Nick from the living room and Joel from his bedroom. As she turned to leave the dining room, Nick stopped her.

"I've got a trip. I'll be leaving about four in the morning, so you'd better get my clothes washed and packed. I'm going to bed as soon as I'm finished eating."

Lenore turned to face him and stared for a minute before she could speak.

"Why didn't you tell me this an hour ago, or when I walked in the door tonight? I have a headache and wanted to go to bed myself. You could have at least started the wash when you got home."

He looked at her blankly and started to eat. Lenore walked out of the room and down the hall to get his clothes from the hamper. Gathering the bundle into her arms, Lenore noticed an unfamiliar scent. As she sorted the clothes in the laundry room, she found the source of the musky perfume. It was on one of Nick's favorite shirts. She grimaced and threw it into the washer with his work clothes. As the water level raised, she added his underwear to the load and bumped the wash temperature to warm, knowing fading and shrinkage could result. She didn't care if his tidy-whities were white or not; a small, but pleasurable gesture of revenge on her part.

Lenore washed her hands in scalding water. It made her feel dirty knowing Nick had been with someone else. She had seen him in action when he had too much to drink. He groped every woman within reach, gesturing and grabbing his crotch and generally making an ass of himself. Maybe this time some bimbo had taken advantage of her absence and his style. If it was true, maybe he would leave her alone and not cause problems when she left.

She did not feel the slightest twinge of guilt about Gregor. It was the first time she had thought of him in hours. No, what she had with Gregor was different in so many ways. There was nothing vulgar about it or him. It was special and wonderful. For an instant, she wondered if it had all been a dream.

She methodically dried her hands and closed her eyes, trying to bring the vision of her smiling Russian to mind. She could not envision his face. Her mind was too clouded with the disgusting creature having dinner with her son.

It would be a long time before she got to bed tonight, but with any luck, Nick would pass out before she got there. It would be worth the effort if he would be gone for a while; she and Joel referred to his trucking runs as little reprieves.

Joel cleared the table, helped fill the dishwasher and accepted a hug and thank you before going to his room. Lenore went into her bedroom, undressed and was searching through her closet for a nightgown. Nick's sudden presence in the room felt stifling and intrusive. She took her nightgown from a hanger and started to leave the room when he reached out and grabbed her breasts. It was both repulsive and extremely painful.

"Nick, stop! That hurts! Stop it!"

"Well, quit trying to leave and it won't hurt, will it?"

Lenore freed herself and backed toward the door.

"You're drunk and I have a headache. I have a lot to do before I can go to bed tonight, so just leave me alone."

"Don't you want some of this?" He pulled down the front of his shorts and exposed his flaccid penis, shaking it at her and leering through alcohol-glazed eyes.

There had been a time in the beginning when Nick had excited her and she had enjoyed a physical relationship with him, but he had never been vulgar with her then. She looked at him now and felt her stomach lurch. She had to swallow the bile accumulating in the back of her throat.

"No, I don't want any of that. I told you I don't feel well."

He grabbed her hair, pulling her face down toward the pathetic looking organ. She twisted away from his grasp and glared into his eyes.

"Don't you ever do that again." Her voice was raspy and low. "Not ever! Go to bed and sleep it off or pull it off, I don't care. Just leave me alone." She slipped the nightgown over her head. "I'm sure there's someone out there who thinks it's really suave when you do that, but I think you're disgusting!"

His hand moved surprisingly fast, considering the amount of alcohol in his system. Lenore hadn't anticipated his move and the slap across her mouth stung sharply. She tasted blood and stood motionless, bracing for another blow.

He turned toward the bed, muttering. "Fuckin' bitch! That'll teach you."

Lenore turned off the light and eased out the door on legs threatening to collapse. She closed the door, then started down the hall and ran into Joel.

"Mom, are you okay? I thought I heard ... Jesus, what happened?"

"Nothing Joel. Go back to your room. Please!"

She grabbed his shoulders and attempted to lead him away from the door. His eyes were dark green with anger and he tried to enter the room where Nick was peacefully drifting into a drunken slumber.

"No Joel! Remember what I said about staying cool? We argued. He's drunk and I pushed too far." She stayed between Joel and the door. "I'm okay. You have to obey me on this. Please, Joel. Do as I ask."

His shoulders finally went slack against her grip.

"Mom, I'll do as you ask this time. If there is ever a next time, I won't stop. I'll beat his brains out." He sighed as he looked at his mom. "Let's go get your lip taken care of."

He led her to the bathroom and Lenore looked in the mirror. Her lip was beginning to swell and blood had made a path from her lip to her gown. Joel took a washcloth and ran cold water on it. He squeezed out the excess and dabbed carefully at her mouth. Lenore winced.

"I'm sorry, Mom. It looks pretty awful."

His jaw muscles flexed as he dabbed gently at the blood. Lenore let her son do what she could have easily done for herself, knowing he needed to feel helpful.

"I never thought he would hit me, Joel."

"Mom, he's losing it. Next time it could be a lot worse. He's got that gun and ... who knows?"

"I don't want to think about the gun." She took the cloth from Joel and pressed it to her eyes for a minute. "We have to make plans to get out while we can. I just don't know which is more frightening: dealing with him or trying to make it on our own. I don't make very good money at the store."

"Mom, I can get a job. We can do it together. I know we can make it. We're a team." He hugged Lenore. "I'd rather be a little hungry than dead."

"That's not funny, Joel. Let's just get through the next few days and let me see what I can figure out. You have to go to bed and I have to finish his laundry and pack." She stared at the wall and shook her head. "Where do we begin to pack for ourselves?"

"Bring home boxes from the store and we'll just do one room at a time." He tilted her chin to get a look at her lip. "Are you sure I can't stay up and help you with something? I don't feel very sleepy."

"No, Son. There's nothing you can do. Try to go to bed; you need your sleep."

With a hug, he started down the hall to his room and then came back, poking his head in the doorway. "I love you, Mom."

"I love you, Joel."

When the laundry was put into the dryer, Lenore didn't hesitate before turning the temperature to the highest heat. She looked down the front of her gown to spots of blood mingling with petite roses and delicate lace. She was too tired to rinse it out. The stains would be left as a reminder of her now violent spouse.

Lenore walked to the guest room. It was always kept clean in the event her son Grant could take time off for a visit from his life in Chicago. She would sleep there tonight at the risk of angering Nick further. She couldn't bear the thought of being touched.

Another hour, and one suitcase was packed and sitting in the hall for Nick's trip. She returned to the guest room that was filled with memories of Grant. Her gentle giant of a son had sent many of his drawings to her; they were framed and displayed with a mother's pride.

Although his communication skills had vastly improved since getting out of school and living on his own, Lenore missed seeing him. He was busy building a career as an illustrator in Chicago and visits were rare. Unlike Joel and Lenore, Grants eyes were blue, and became a darker shade of blue when he was angry or ill. When the boys were young, a look in their eyes confirmed an illness before a thermometer. They had inherited their mother's variant eye color. To their disdain, they had also discovered it prevented faking an illness to get out of school.

Grant was six-foot three and weighed two hundred-twenty pounds. He had come into the world at a robust nine pounds, one ounce. He was a handsome man who loved his mom. Though his career was sedentary, he led an active life, and she made a mental note to ask Joel to not tell him about her injury. He had sworn vengeance if Nick ever hurt her or Joel when he had witnessed the increased drinking and verbal abuse on his last visit. She was glad he wasn't there to see what she was putting his brother through, but she ached for his smile and assuaged presence.

She switched off the light and sank into the softness of the small bed. Sleep came between fitful dreams.

CHAPTER 15

Gregor was ready to leave when he made the wake-up call.

"Good morning, Frank. Are you awake?"

"Awake and wishing I was dead. I've been up half the night in the bathroom."

Gregor smiled. "Are you ill?"

"Not just ill. Hell, I'm sick as a dog. Either got the flu or food poisoning."

"We had the same food last night, Frank. I am okay. Is there something I can do for you? Shall I come to your motel?"

"No, I might be contagious. The motel office is bringing some bottled water and medicine to stop the diarrhea. Got aspirin here, just can't keep it down. The headache is the worst part."

"Would it be better if I did not go to work today? It will be a long one. I have several meetings to attend and one is in Colorado Springs."

"Colorado Springs, huh?" Frank figured his meeting was probably in Fort Collins and had little to do with work, but he really didn't care. "Go ahead to your meetings. I gotta trust you today, cause I sure as hell can't follow you."

"Perhaps you should call another agent to take your place for the day." It was a suggestion he knew Frank would refuse.

"Just call me if you're going to be especially late, okay?"

"Of course. Anything else?"

There was a hesitation. "Parish, just don't let me down."

"Let you down?"

"Don't pull anything like you did in Glenwood Springs on Sunday."

"You are speaking of my drive to look at the trees?"

"Right. No sight-seeing today."

"Frank, there are no beautiful trees to see here."

"I hope not."

"Have a good day and rest. I will check with you when I return."

Gregor hung up the phone and put on his tie. He would to go to work, but he would not be there long. After he saw Lenore, he would not be back for a very long time.

He threw an empty vial and needle into his briefcase, to be disposed of later. Effects of the food poisoning from last night's meatloaf dinner would wear off, eventually. Most importantly, Frank would be out of the way and Gregor's plans could begin.

* * * * *

Lenore could hear Nick as he prepared to leave. She feigned sleep when she was aware of him standing in the doorway of the guest room. She wondered if he realized why she was there or if he felt any remorse if he did. The slam of the front door on his way out answered her question. If he remembered, he wasn't sorry. That frightened her even more.

Unable to stay in bed any longer, Lenore got up and walked to the kitchen. It would be a while before sunrise. She turned on the light and made coffee, hoping the sound of the brew gurgling to completion would not disturb Joel.

She poured herself a cup, and with the first sip was painfully reminded of her lip. A few more careful sips and she was feeling revived enough to walk into the bathroom and look into the mirror. What she saw produced a groan. The bruise and swelling were very evident. She dug into the back of the medicine cabinet and produced a sample of liquid foundation. She tested it and was satisfied it would conceal a bit of the bruise. The swelling was another matter; there was no concealing it. She went back into the kitchen and topped off her cup of coffee, then walked into the living room and opened the drapes. There was not even the faintest glow on the horizon. She stood in the darkness, wondering what she was going to tell everyone. The cat had stirred from her lair and rubbed affectionately against Lenore's legs.

"You aren't fooling me, Spot. You just love me for my ability to open a can." The large, long-haired Calico voiced objections to her motives. Lenore smiled and turned toward the kitchen, stumbling to avoid falling over the hungry feline's herding technique. "Damn it, Spot!" she whispered. "I'm going to break my neck one of these days because of you."

Spot raced ahead to the kitchen and watched intently for her owner to meet her at the cabinet, wherein the little cans of love were kept. Lenore had come to love Spot in spite of herself. Joel had introduced the fragile bundle of fur at Christmas three years ago. When she had held it against her neck and heard the faint purring, a bond had formed.

Joel and Grant had picked the unlikely name because of the freckles of color on Spot's nose. Nick had tolerated the cat. Lenore remembered Nick being far more tolerant of everything in those days.

Spot watched Lenore's every move as the cabinet was opened and a can retrieved. She stood on her back legs and stretched to sneak a furry paw over the edge of the counter.

"Hey, I don't need your help. Hands off, you little fur ball." She laughed.

Spot obeyed and Lenore scraped the odorous contents onto the dish. She sat it on the floor and filled a second dish with fresh water. Spot mewed a grateful sound between bites and Lenore gave her an affectionate rub down the back to her tail, where Spot's rear-end lifted right on cue.

"You silly old cat, you may have helped me out this morning."

Lenore returned to the living room. She would tell the guys at work she had finally fell victim to Spot's presence underfoot and fell against something. She scanned the room for likely obstacles. In an attempt to test her theory, she faked a stumble and veered toward the arm of the sofa. She was confident she could very well have hit her mouth on the wooden trim and smiled at her resourcefulness. She didn't want to alarm her friends with the truth, and given the many times she had complained of near-misses with Spot, she was confident her story would be believable.

Soon the sky became inflamed with hues of pink and lavender, the wispy clouds outlined in a luminescence of gold. It was then Lenore remembered Gregor would be calling her at work.

A spasm of pain shot through her intestines in anticipatory nervousness. She clutched her arms around her waist and cursed. She always got a stomach ache when faced with uncertainty and fear. Was she afraid he would not call, or was she afraid he would? She decided it wasn't too early to begin her morning routine and meandered to the shower, hoping the normalcy of ritualistic movements would ease the discomfort.

* * * * *

The morning was going well at work. Lenore had warned Joel against relating the details of their previous night to anyone. She told him he was also not to phone his brother, Grant. The guys at work appeared to buy the story of her encounter with Spot. It was a slow business day and Lenore stood near the front counter arranging a display of snow boots. She talked with JD, discussing the seasonal weather ahead. JD focused on her lip, changing the subject.

"That's sure a bad looking lip. Bet it hurt, didn't it?"

"Sure did." She chuckled. "If I didn't love Spot so much, I'd have thrown her out."

"You'd better hope Leah doesn't see your lip. She isn't going to buy the story of the cat any more than I do."

Lenore turned away from JD and busied herself with the placement of treated leather footwear.

"Why did he hit you, Lenore?"

She started to protest, but when she looked into the gentle eyes of her boss, she knew it was useless. JD took her arm and sat the boot she was holding back on the display.

"Come on. Let's go get a cup of coffee."

He steered Lenore out the front door with a nod to Rusty, who nodded back. Had none of them believed her? They sat down at a table away from others in the coffee shop and she allowed tears to fall silently as JD ordered their coffee. She was sure the waitress could be imagining all sorts of things.

"Okay, now tell me what really happened."

Lenore took a folded napkin from the shiny stainless-steel dispenser and dabbed at her eyes, then blew her nose, wadded the tissue into a ball and took another from the dispenser. JD waited patiently.

"I was tired and had a headache."

"Like every night with him," JD interjected.

"Well, yes. He was pretty drunk and wanted to have sex, I guess. I was just repulsed, the way he grabbed me and everything. Then he pulled my hair and wanted me to, well ... he wanted me to—"

"I think I get the idea." JD said, rescuing Lenore from having to say more. "He got mad because you said no."

"Maybe if that's all I would have said, he wouldn't have hit me. I'm afraid I was pretty vocal about it."

"That's not it, and you know it. It was coming to this no matter what you said or did."

Lenore stared earnestly into her boss's eyes. "He's never struck me before. It really scared me." She started to shred a napkin. "What if he tries to hurt Joel? I had to physically restrain Joel to keep him from going after Nick."

"I think it's time to just get you two out of the situation before anything gets worse." He took the pieces of used napkin from her shaking hands and replaced them with a fresh one. "How long is he going to be gone this time?"

"He didn't say." She shook her head. "This is exactly why I didn't want any of you to know what happened. I know we have to get out, but I can't. Not just yet."

"Why?"

She blew her nose again. "Economics. Plain and simple. I don't make enough money to support us. This is Joel's senior year. I can't expect him to get a job paying enough to actually help. For now, we're stuck."

"You just start getting things packed. You can put it all in the basement of the store until we can find you a place to move. I'm going to check with some people and see about getting you into the management program. You'll be working more hours, but you'll also make a lot more money. I've been wanting to offer it to you for a long time, but I didn't suppose Nick would allow you to work the extra hours it takes." He took a pen from his pocket and wrote on a napkin. "Do you think you could make it on this?"

Lenore looked at the figure he had written on the napkin and nodded, too surprised to speak.

"Okay, that takes care of the long-term problem. Right now, we have to get you out of there. You could move in with us until you get on your feet—"

"Positively not!" Lenore sat back in her chair. I won't take a chance of endangering anyone, if Nick tries anything. I have no idea what his reaction will be." She shook her head. "Besides, you have your house full already with Shelly and the two grandsons. I'll figure something out."

"You know there's always room for you and Joel, but I won't force you into anything." He frowned and then smiled. "You could get a loan. We could co-sign for you at the bank."

"Let me think about it. I appreciate your ideas, but I don't know if I want to go into debt before I even start out. There has to be another answer. I can always go to a safe-house in an emergency."

"You do realize everyone wants you safe and we'll do anything it takes? We could make a personal loan and you wouldn't have to pay us back until it was easier."

"I know, and I thank you for the offer. Let me see what I can figure out. I'm just a jumbled-up mess right now." She dabbed her eyes. "We'd better get back."

"I wish all my employees were as anxious to get back to work." He smiled and they stood to leave. She hugged her boss, disregarding the stares from patrons and the nosy waitress.

Lenore dashed through the doors of the store and checked her make-up, doing minor repairs at the bathroom mirror. They were busy and Lenore was relieved, sticking to her cat story when customers questioned about her lip.

It was an hour before closing when she was called to the phone. "Hello, this is Lenore Appleby."

"How are you, my precious lady?"

"I'm especially well now. How are you, Gregor?" Lenore asked as she nudged the door closed to the front office with the toe of her shoe. Rusty was deep in conversation with a customer at the counter a few feet away.

"I am pleased you remember who I am."

She could tell he was teasing. "I've thought of little else." She chose the lie over explanations of the truth. "It's wonderful to hear your voice."

"Can I see you?"

"Of course. When? Where? I wish I was wherever you are, right now."

"I am not far. Would it be possible to see you when you get finished with your work?"

"Yes. It shouldn't be a problem. Nick is gone and I'll tell Joel I'm going shopping; he won't mind." She wondered if the smile on her face could be felt through a telephone line. "I won't have the whole night. Am I worth a couple of hours?"

"Yes. You are worth every wonderful moment you will give me."

They made plans to meet at six, though Lenore told him there was always the possibility of her having to stay later than planned. He assured her that waiting would be no problem.

"I can't wait to see you, Gregor."

"I will be there."

Lenore hung up the receiver and the phone rang immediately, startling her. She had to ask the caller to repeat their question twice.

* * * * *

Lenore was able to leave at closing time, since Royce and JD were both with late customers. Joel made plans to have a friend come to the house for a study session and assured his mom they could fend for themselves for dinner. Company was not an option when Nick was home, so Joel was glad for the opportunity.

Traffic was heavy, but moving. She reached the mall with seven minutes to spare. She took the time to purchase a box of stationery for proof of her shopping trip. Lies bothered Lenore. Even the little ones.

She exited the opposite side of the mall from where she was parked, then realized she didn't really know what vehicle to be looking for. She scanned the parking lot, pretending to check the contents of her package. When she heard the car horn beep, she looked where the sound had originated and saw the smiling Russian standing beside a silvery-brown Saab. She walked with a deliberate gait toward the car, her normal stride. She always walked with the assertive posture of a woman who knew where she was going, whether she really did or not. Leah said Lenore was able to get lost and no one ever knew.

When she reached the car, Gregor was inside and had unlocked her door. She slid into the seat beside him and tossed her package into the back. She looked straight ahead as he backed out of the parking space.

"You look very beautiful. Where can we go to be alone and perhaps walk?"

"Turn left at the light, then right at the next. We'll go to the lake; there shouldn't be many people around this time of year, especially this late in the day. Follow the road west. You'll see signs from there."

Lenore finally turned to look at Gregor. He was as handsome as she remembered. His appeal had not changed with the geography, and she felt a tingling very deep inside.

She studied his profile as he drove, trying to burn the image into her mind. She was smiling and Gregor glanced her way, smiling back. He took her hand, raised it to his lips, caressing it with feather-light kisses.

"Gregor, you'd better hurry. I want to kiss you and hold you and my self-control is stretched to its limits."

The Russian laughed and accelerated a bit. How she loved his wonderful laugh. She eased toward him and rested her head on his shoulder. She studied his hand as he held hers, the nails were trimmed and clean. She traced the blue lines under the black hair on the back of his hand. She moved her hand to his shirt, unbuttoned it and slid her fingers into the thick, black chest hair. An uncontrolled moan escaped her lips.

Gregor eased the car around the curves of the lake road and finally pulled over. "Will this be a good place to walk?"

Lenore looked at the surroundings and nodded. Gregor turned off the engine, got out and walked around to her door. The air was crisp and clean near the lake, but their light jackets would provide adequate warmth. Gregor took her hand as they descended the steep trail. Her two-inch heels were comfortable in the store, but not practical for rugged terrain. He guided her carefully over rocks and around bushes until they were at the water's edge.

The lake had receded to expose smooth driftwood. Choosing a suitable spot, they sat down and Gregor turned Lenore toward him, enveloping her in a warm hug. He smoothed her hair and kissed her temple, then tilted her chin to kiss her lips.

Lenore winced from the pain and Gregor moved back to look at her. A frown took the place of his smile as his fingers gently touched the bruise. Lenore lowered her eyes. She had forgotten.

"How did this happen?"

She considered the cat story for only a moment. When she looked into his eyes, she knew she would not lie to Gregor.

"Did your husband do this to you? You must tell me, Lenore."

"Yes," she replied, flatly.

"Has he hurt your son as well? Was this because of me?"

"No Gregor, only me." She looked away from him and watched the waves of the lake gently buffet the shore. "He hit me because I refused to have sex with him. I didn't expect him to hit me. I suppose I asked for it because I wasn't very polite in my refusal."

Gregor touched her cheek and turned her face toward his. "There is never a reason for a man to hit a woman. He is a coward. He has also made a very big mistake."

The look in Gregor's eyes shifted from glaring anger to tenderness again as he encircled Lenore with his arms and pulled her to him. He kissed her forehead and her nose and both of her eyes, then held her away from him and looked again at the bruise.

"He will not get away with this. He has hurt you and he should be hurt. He will not hurt you again, I will make sure of this. You must not stay there."

Lenore gently soothed his frown with her fingertips. "Yes, Gregor, I know that. I'm making plans. My boss is putting me in the management program, which will mean more money. I just have to wait a little longer."

"Wait? Why must you wait?" He looked into her eyes as if she had lost all sense of reason. "It is not safe for you there!"

"I have to be able to afford the move for Joel and me. We have a little time before Nick comes back from his trip. We'll be okay."

He shook his head. "I will help. Come back to my home in Glenwood Springs. You would be very comfortable and he will never know you are there. There is room for your son, as well. There are schools for him. Please, say you will let me do this for you."

Lenore had no way to know how huge his offer was; he was willing to forego plans he had made for a very long time in order to secure her safety.

"Gregor, I appreciate your offer. I know you're sincere, but I can't just disappear." She touched his cheek, stroking the soft, black beard. "Joel has to finish high school and it wouldn't be fair to make him leave in his senior year. I want you two to get acquainted on the very best of terms. If it was just me, I would leave right now and not give it another thought." She shook her head. "I would never have come back here at all. Please, understand."

Lenore saw the hurt and concern in his eyes. She put her head on his chest and her arms around his waist.

"Oh, please don't be angry with me. I just couldn't handle that. I need you, Gregor. I need you so much. Hold me."

He took her into his arms and rocked gently. "Lenore, I could not be angry with you. I am very concerned for you. I must protect you from this animal; it is he who angers me."

Fleeting thoughts of his conversation with Leah about hit men entered her thoughts. "You must believe me when I tell you we will get out. I want my life to be free of him and full of you. It just has to be right." She hugged him and rubbed his back. "You make me feel so safe and happy when we're together. Can we not talk of it anymore right now? I just need you to hold me."

"I will make you feel better." He kissed her very lightly on the lips, then turned her away from him. He massaged her shoulders and neck. His strong hands knew where to touch and she felt herself relax. He kissed the back and side of her neck and she giggled.

"What is funny?"

"Look!" She pulled up the sleeve of her jacket and showed Gregor her arm.

"I have given you turkey skin!" He smiled.

Lenore laughed. "We call them goose bumps."

"I do not know the name perhaps, but I am glad I have made it happen."

"I am glad you have made it happen, too. You are wonderful, Gregor." She turned back to face him. "I want to know all there is to know about you. I want to know how to give you goose bumps and how to make you laugh and what makes you sad and how you feel about broccoli."

"What is the significance of this vegetable?"

"It's just an example. I want to know everything that makes you who you are."

"You will know all you want. I like broccoli."

Lenore laughed and hugged him. "That's great! That's a start. I like it too, even though our President Bush has banned it from the White House because he hates it. Tell me about your house."

He caressed her hair as he spoke. "My house is in the country. It is not huge, but there is room for myself and two roommates."

"You have two roommates?"

"Yes. One is female and one is male. They sometimes sleep with me." He laughed when Lenore's eyebrows shot up.

"They are my Great White Pyrenees dogs. One is Marushka and the other is Nicolai. You will love them, but you will not love to bathe them."

"They must be beautiful. I hope I can meet them one day."

"You will know them very well." He pulled her close. "I do not think I have told you I wish for you to spend your life with me."

The statement took Lenore by surprise and she didn't know what to say.

"I have not spoken these words to another woman. You are very special. Would this arrangement be alright with you?"

"Gregor, there is so much for you to know about me. There is so much for me to know about you. What about Joel and Grant? How can you be so certain of what you want?"

"I am in love with you, Lenore Appleby. I am in love with your heart and your wonderful mind. I am in love with the way you can be so stubborn and the way you laugh and the fact broccoli is a concern to you. I am in love with the way you are so loyal to your sons and the way you dance and the way you try to hide it when lemon is squirted into your eye. I am in love with the way you look into my soul with your beautiful eyes and know what my heart is telling you. I love all that is you."

Lenore's tears were wiped with a gentle touch from Gregor's fingertips.

"I look forward to meeting Grant and Joel. It angers me to think of your husband being cruel to your younger son. Children are to be cherished and loved, even if your son is nearly grown. It will be enjoyable to teach him about this beautiful land and how to take care of it. He must learn how to survive in it as well. He is at a very impressionable age. It is necessary for him to learn of the good things in his country."

Lenore smiled at the thought of Joel and Gregor. Her intelligent son would absorb his teachings like a sponge.

"Your son Grant is already a man. I will make sure he is comfortable with me. He will know how much I am in love with his mother and he will never have to worry about you or his brother as long as I am alive."

Lenore ran her fingers through the hair at Gregor's temple. She wondered how this man had seen through all her defenses. She smiled, realizing he had seen into her soul the first time they met.

131

"Gregor, there are a million reasons why I shouldn't, but if you will give me a chance to get out of this situation I'm in, I will give you the rest of my life. I love you, Gregor. With all my heart and soul, I love you."

"I want to make love to you right now, but here is no time. Our lovemaking is to be special, always. You must be pampered and properly aroused. We will take care of that one day soon, my precious lady. Tonight, there is much I need to tell you." He smiled, but his eyes held concern.

"What is it, Gregor?"

"This is a difficult situation. I must leave."

"What do you mean?" Lenore frowned. "Right now?"

"No, I will try to explain. I must leave tonight. There is business I must take care of, but it not a good time for me to be leaving you. If there were another way, I would not go."

"Go where? For how long?"

"I cannot tell you where. Sometime I will, but not yet. The less you know, the better it will be for you. I will be gone for two weeks, possibly three. No longer. You must trust I will return. You must be strong and do what you have to do."

Lenore felt a chill and shuddered. "You have me worried. Will you be in danger?"

The Russian set his jaw and stared out over the lake. His hands were softly caressing her hair. "It is something I must do. I cannot tell you more. I do not plan to be in any danger." He looked into her eyes. "For now, you must not ask more."

"But, Gregor—"

He hushed her with a gentle touch on her lips. "Lenore, there is very little time. I ask you to be cautious always about talking to strangers."

"I'm not the one with that particular habit, if you remember correctly," she teased, then realized his seriousness. "Why?"

"I am saying from now on to be cautious. Not everyone is who they pretend to be."

"I have a feeling there's a whole lot more to that statement than I'm going to hear tonight."

"I will give you a number to reach me in two weeks and leave a number for me to return your call. Do not call me from your home. I would also prefer you did not call from your work."

"That sounds a little suspicious, Gregor. Are you afraid of someone finding out about me?" She moved back from him. "Like, a wife?"

"No, I am not married," he said with a chuckle. "I was married once in Russia. It was arranged. Neither of us were in love. We divorced. There is not another woman in my life."

"Then, why all the mystery?"

"There are those who want to know every move I make because I am Russian born. I do not wish for them to know of you and possibly try to keep track of you as well. It could disrupt your life, and until you are safely out of your situation and I return, this is not good."

Somewhat pacified, she sighed. "Okay. What about the phone number?"

"In two weeks, you must call my service and leave a number for a public phone and a time for me to call. It is safer this way." He smiled and softly touched the tip of her nose. "If I would be you, I would listen to what I am saying."

She let him pull her close again. "Two weeks will pass quickly. Perhaps you will be safely out of your situation by that time."

"I don't see how, but it's a lovely thought. Just hold me as if you'll never let me go."

He held her and slowly rocked. Gentle hands massaged her back and smoothed her hair. In the fading twilight near the water, he tilted her chin to softly kiss lips that parted slightly to receive his. He held her back and traced each feature of her face, studying, memorizing. Eyes met, moist and full of love for one another, and souls merged. She was not afraid of what she had to face, and she knew Gregor was a part of her future.

His quiet voice broke the silence. "We must be going back to the city."

"I know." She sighed and gave him a hug. "Just when I find you and need you most, I can't have you … it isn't fair."

Gregor stood and assisted Lenore to her feet.

"Our time apart will only serve to make our future together more precious." He kissed her again and led her back up the hill to the waiting Saab.

The parking lot was nearly empty when they returned to the mall. Lenore asked Gregor to take her directly to the car; she did not care who saw them.

As he stopped the car, they both unlatched their seat belts, then Lenore took Gregor's hand. She kissed the palm and closed his fingers, encasing the kiss in his hand. She caressed his cheek and stroked the softness of his black beard. Her fingertips traced his lips and he kissed them.

"Come back to me, my Russian bear."

"I will return, my precious lady. I have found what I've needed all my life. I will not give it up now."

"The number, Gregor. I need the number of your phone service." She got her address book and opened it. She had a pen and was ready to write.

"You should be careful where you write this number."

He recited the number and Lenore wrote. When she finished, she showed her work.

"See, this looks like a zip code and that looks like someone's shoe size. I'm the only one who could figure this out." She smiled, proudly.

"Very good, my clever one. Now, let me hold you for a moment longer, then you must go."

He held her as if drawing part of her into him, to keep until they next met.

"Wait for me, Lenore. I will return."

"I will always wait for you, Gregor." Tears stung her eyes as she kissed him on the cheek and got out of the car. An overwhelming emptiness enveloped her as she watched the taillights recede. She wanted to follow, to run away from the task she had now to begin. Knowing it was impossible, she quietly prayed for his safety, as tears ran freely from dark, green eyes.

* * * * *

At a secluded phone booth near the interstate, Gregor pushed numbers into the system, waiting for a series of clicks to connect him to the motel where a CIA agent was waiting.

"Frank, I thought I should be calling. I am leaving Colorado Springs now. I will stop for dinner and I did not want to cause you concern with my lateness. Will there be anything I can do for you when I arrive?"

Frank sounded relieved to get the call. "No, just glad you decided to check-in, Parish."

"You are feeling better?"

"Not particularly, but hearing from you helps."

"Then I will talk to you in the morning."

"Great. Have a safe trip."

Frank had no way of knowing what Gregor's good-bye meant. When phone records were checked, it would appear the call had, indeed, come from Colorado Springs, instead of sixty miles north of Denver. In fact, it would appear all Frank's calls had come from Colorado Springs that day. Gregor's electronic communications expertise was something the agency had been aware of, but hadn't planned on him using it to create a diversion.

* * * * *

Lenore walked into the house to find Joel laying on the sofa, watching television.

"Hi Joel, how was your day? Did you and Eric get your homework finished?"

"Didn't have much homework, but we practiced for the holiday concert. You're coming, aren't you?"

"Of course. I have to go to all these free concerts while I can. They'll charge me to see you play your trombone at Carnegie Hall."

Joel beamed, knowing his mom was his biggest fan.

"We fixed home-made pizza. Eric thinks I should open a restaurant. I even got him to help me clean up the mess. I thought you'd appreciate that."

"I sure do. Thanks!" She started for the hallway. "I'm kind of tired. I think I'll take a long, hot, soaking bath and go to bed."

"We left a piece of pizza for you. What'd you buy at the mall?"

Lenore hesitated for a minute. "Oh, I bought some stationary, but I guess I left it somewhere." She knew exactly where she left it.

"Tomorrow you should call the mall and have them look for it. Someone might turn it in."

When did he get so practical? Why hadn't she simply said she'd bought nothing?

"It's no big deal, Joel. I'll call and try to find it though. I guess I will have that piece of pizza before I take a bath."

Joel followed her to the kitchen and they talked while she ate. Sitting at the table, Lenore kicked off her shoes and glanced down, surprised to find their condition wasn't too bad, considering her trek at the lake. She slid them under her chair, hoping Joel wouldn't notice.

With pizza consumed and the dishes cleaned, they both started down the hallway.

"I'm going to bed." He hugged Lenore. "See ya in the morning. Love you, Mom." He took a few steps and turned back. "Almost forgot. Nick called."

Lenore felt her stomach tighten and begin to cramp. "Oh?"

"Yeah, and I think he was sober, too. He wasn't being an asshole or anything. He just wanted a number he had left on his dresser. I gave it to him. He even said thanks."

"Did he say how long he's going to be gone this time?"

"That's the best part. He's going to be gone at least two weeks. Said they have him running from one coast to another and not anywhere close to home." He smiled. "Pretty great, huh? Maybe we can be gone before he gets back."

"I wish we could, Joel. I just don't know how to swing it. JD wants to put me in the management program, and it will mean more money, but we won't feel the effects for a while. We don't have the money for deposits and such, not to mention first and last month's rent. It's going to take a while, or a miracle." She put her hands on his shoulders when they slumped with disappointment. "Can't you hang in here with me for a while longer, Joel?"

"I can handle it, Mom, but if he hits you again, I won't promise anything. Sorry, I won't let him get away with it twice." He shook his head. "But, I'm with you all the way, Mom."

"Okay sweetheart. Now go to bed and don't worry."

With another hug, Joel went to his room and Lenore returned to the living room to turn off the television and lights. In the bathroom, she filled the tub with steaming water and foamy, white bubbles. The room was scented with the aroma of Mountain Springtime, which Lenore thought smelled nothing like an actual mountain springtime. What little makeup she wore was removed and she tuned the radio to soft music. She pinned up her long hair and stepped into the tub.

The water was a little hotter than she liked it, but she eased slowly down until only her head was above the water. She loved the luxury of bubble baths. It was a bit of selfish pampering she rarely allowed herself.

With closed eyes, she filled her mind with visions of Gregor, recalling every detail of his face. His eyes were dark and deep, so full of sweet mischief and tenderness. There were tiny lines at the outer corners, Lenore assumed, from years of squinting rather than laughter. He had a tiny scar near his right eye, perhaps from a childhood injury. His nose was straight and just right for the handsome face. Lenore smiled at the vision of Gregor she was able to bring to mind so clearly. Two weeks would be bearable if she could do this. She thought of his lips and the soft sensual kisses they produced and felt a tingling sensation throughout her body. Two weeks was going to be an eternity!

When the water began to cool. Lenore got out and dried herself. She brushed her teeth, then padded to the guestroom and slipped under the covers in a long, satin nightgown. Tonight, she would dream of her handsome Gregor. With Nick away for at least two weeks, she drifted quickly into a peaceful slumber.

CHAPTER 16

The next two days at work were horribly normal. Lenore managed to pacify Leah's request for details by promising to tell her everything on their afternoon together. She didn't have to wait long for her best friend to show up on Friday. Leah was there a half hour early.

"Let's go now! I can't wait any longer, Lenore."

JD came around the corner, and hearing his wife's pleading with Lenore, had to laugh.

"You two beat anything I've ever seen. You go away and spend a long weekend together, and four days later, you'd think you hadn't seen one another in years. Royce will be back from lunch in about ten minutes. Go ahead and get out of here." He accepted a hug from his wife as he continued. "Lenore, you'd better explain to Leah this might not happen too many more times."

Leah looked at JD, then at Lenore and back again to her husband. "What's that supposed to mean? Lenore, what does he mean?"

"I think he just got off the phone with some very important people, and it may have just changed my life. Am I right?" she asked her smiling boss.

"Yes, you are. I'll fill you in on the details tomorrow. Now get going."

Though she was anxious to know the details, she was more anxious to share other details with her best friend on their afternoon together. Leah had the convertible top down on Baby for their drive.

"I decided it was nice enough for the lid to be down. It won't happen too many more times this year. Where shall we go, Ms. Appleby?"

"The lake."

"The lake?"

"The lake. I have to eat something first. You pick lunch since I picked our destination."

"We'll just grab burgers. I want to get settled so we can talk. Obviously, there's a lot to talk about today."

Leah tossed the keys to Lenore, who soon had the Chevelle maneuvering through town, with a brief stop at Wendy's. A few minutes later, she parked the car at the spot where Gregor had parked the Saab only two days before. She turned off the engine and turned in the seat to accept her cheeseburger and fries from Leah.

"Thanks, where do you want me to start?"

"With the phone call."

"Well, I had actually been busy enough to forget he was going to call. It was a good thing we were only an hour from closing time when he did. I was a mess. I couldn't wait to see him."

Leah giggled, urging Lenore to continue.

"I picked the mall for us to meet. It was the only place I could think of at the moment." She took a bite of her sandwich and ate a fry.

"Was he still driving the truck?"

"No. In fact, I wasn't sure what to look for. He finally beeped his horn and I saw him standing beside a silvery-brown Saab. We drove right up here to this very spot and walked down to that group of dead trees." She pointed toward the lake.

Leah looked. "Okay, then what?"

Lenore talked and Leah listened with very few interruptions. When Lenore paused to take another bite from her less than warm sandwich, her blonde friend shook her head.

"I just don't believe it."

"What part?" Lenore asked, trying to speak with her mouth still full of food, too hungry to be polite in their private Chevelle restaurant.

"Not what you've told me; the fact you've actually listened and remembered."

"Pretty good, aren't I."

"Truly amazing!"

They finished their burgers and let packs of fries grow cold.

"Have you picked your phone booth?" asked Leah.

"No, any ideas?"

"We'll pick it out on the way home. Let's go explore now."

They walked down the path Lenore had followed with Gregor. They carried the bright yellow cups of Diet Coke and tossed the remaining fries to the woods for whatever creature would be hungry enough for the offering. The paper was stuffed into Lenore's pocket.

"Look at this rock, Lenore! I'm climbing it."

Lenore watched while the petite blonde scurried to the top and then turned to look down at the brunette.

"Come on up. You'll get a really good view from here."

Lenore handed the two drinks up to Leah and began climbing. She was neither as fast nor as graceful as Leah, but managed to join her best friend.

"You're right. This is great!"

"Lenore!" Leah grabbed her startled friend. "This is it!"

"Geez, why do you do that to me? I thought you saw a snake or something. This is what?"

"Sorry, but this could be our special place. Great view. Peaceful." She turned and surveyed their surroundings. "It's not Glenwood Springs, but it's only ten minutes from home. Whatcha think?"

Lenore looked around then walked from one end of the rock to the other. "Plenty of room to sit; even lay down on top."

Leah sat down, then laid down to test the dimensions of their new found haven. "Oh Lenore, I see picnics and sunbathing. This will be our little refuge on your afternoons off."

Lenore sat down next to her prone companion. "There may not be many of those left."

"What do you mean?" Leah sat up, turning to her friend. "Does this have to do with what JD was saying before we left the store?"

"Yes. Hasn't he told you he's been trying to get me into the management program?"

"Of course not. He never talks business with me. He probably figures I'll hear it from you anyway if it has to do with you or me. When does this start?"

"I don't know right now. He'll tell me all the details when we get a chance." Lenore sipped her drink. "We'd better enjoy our Friday afternoons and Mondays while we can."

"I know it's a good move and the right move for you. It'll at least double your income, and that will secure your escape from Mr. Sunshine!"

"Yes, but I don't want to get too excited about it until I know I can afford it. Then, color me gone!"

"When will Nick be back?"

"At least two weeks. I want to have all my ducks in a huddle and get the flock out of there in one big move. I'd give anything if I could go back to Glenwood Springs with Gregor. I just have to get Joel out of school first."

"I'll bet he would understand and go with you."

"I won't ask him to understand. This is his senior year and he's going to have a couple of scholarships if we're lucky. We can't screw it up now. It'll be his only chance to go to college." Lenore laid back on the rock and looked at the blue Colorado sky. "Besides, I don't know how he would react if he knew about how I met Gregor and all. I'm afraid he would think I was a whore or something."

"Lenore, shame on you. Don't ever say that! He loves you and knows what you've gone through with Nick. He knows there's no love there and he'd understand if there was someone who was going to make you happy."

"Well, let's not chance it now. I'll introduce Gregor into his life when the time is right. It's not right, right now."

"Whatever you think."

"He's going to be going through a lot of adjustments in his young life anyway. I don't want to add to it until I have us safely out of the house and out on our own. Then he may accept it and really be happy for me. I just have to make things as easy for him as I can."

Leah smoothed Lenore's hair as it fanned out across the rock. "Okay, I know you think it's right in your heart, and that's what you have to go with. I just know they're going to make a real team, don't you?"

"I hope so. I can't think about it right now. It's giving me a stomach ache."

"Does that mean you want to change the subject?"

"Yes. Please."

"Got it. When are you going to move?"

"That's not changing the subject and I don't know." Lenore sat up. "I have to have enough money for deposits and things."

"You can just move in with us for a while."

"No. JD already offered. You don't have room and I wouldn't want to endanger you or your family."

Leah held her two little manicured fists in front of her narrowed eyes and feigned a snarl.

"Nick would have to get thorough me first! I'd sock him right in the kneecaps. Maybe a little higher!"

She did her version of shadow boxing, much to the delight of Lenore. The mood was lightened. They stayed a while on the rock, then climbed down and went to the water's edge before ascending the steep terrain back to the Chevelle.

After driving for a few minutes, they spotted a public phone away from traffic noise. Though there was not an actual booth around the phone, Leah assured Lenore it was inconsequential. Lenore parked Baby beside the phone booth, got out, then wrote the number down in her little book and handed it to Leah.

"Okay, see if you can tell me the number."

Leah looked and handed the book back to Lenore. "If I can't figure it out, and I know what the number is, I think your formula is safe. I won't give the formula to anyone. They could pull my fingernails off and I wouldn't tell!"

"Leah, your nails aren't real. I don't think that's considered a life-threatening torture."

"Maybe not, but it would hurt my feelings."

"That certainly makes me feel better." Lenore laughed and gave Leah a pat on the back.

"No sacrifice too great for you, Lenore."

As they drove back to the store, Leah told of the horrors she was willing to endure, strapped into a straight-backed chair, getting her nails removed, one by one.

"Okay, Leah, I'm confident you could withstand the torture of having your nails removed, but what if they threaten to mess up your hair and make you wear uncoordinated outfits?"

"Now you're talking life threatening." Leah seemed to ponder the situation. "I would probably die of shame, but I would not talk!"

"My secrets are safe. I'll sleep well tonight." She laughed.

Lenore pulled Baby into the parking space behind the store, just as JD and Rusty were locking the door. Lenore got out of the car and JD took her place. Rusty waited as they said goodbyes and she walked to her car. He put a fatherly arm around Lenore's shoulders and gave her a big hug.

"Lenore, you know I have plenty of money. Me and Gertie have been talking and we want to give you what you need to get you and Joel out of that place and on your own. You don't even have to pay it back. We just think the world of you and we want you safely out as soon as possible. Hell, you could live at the ranch if you want. It's a big ol' place, you know. Me and Gertie never had kids of our own and you're just what we'd want if we did. I could even teach Joel to ride and shovel horse shit!" He chuckled. "It'd be good for him and I could use the help."

Lenore hugged Rusty back and knew he was sincere in his offer. Her own parents had been gone for so long, it brought tears to her eyes to feel so loved.

"Rusty, you're the sweetest thing in the world. I wish you were my daddy, but I really can't accept your offer. I guess it's a stubborn streak, but I have to do it on my own. I'll get it done, really. I just couldn't involve you and Gertie. I care too much for you both. I wouldn't want Nick to try to get revenge or anything."

"I'd take care of him, and with pleasure, too. That guy's gonna get his due someday. I hope I'm around to see it. I want you to consider the money at least."

"I'll give it serious thought. I have to get home. Joel's fixing dinner tonight, so I'd better not be late." She hugged him again. "Give my love to Gertie, okay?"

Lenore pulled out of the parking lot and drove home aware she didn't have a headache for a change. She was going to have a relaxed evening with her son, and her smile felt comfortable.

Joel waited at the front door with a tall glass of iced tea for his Mom. She hugged and thanked him as he took her jacket. The smell of spaghetti and hot bread stimulated Lenore's appetite. She was suddenly very hungry. He had set the table; even lighting a candle for atmosphere.

"Are you sure you have to grow up and leave home? Can't you just be one of those guys who lives with his mom forever?"

"Sorry, Mom. I love you, but let's face it; fame and fortune await me and my trombone. The world wouldn't understand if I lived with my mother, even if she is the greatest mom in the world."

"Okay, okay. Will you at least invite me to dinner once in a while?"

"Absolutely. Now let's eat."

They talked and laughed as they consumed the flavorful fare. Lenore's eyes were filled with pride and love as she listened to Joel relate his day's activities and plans for the evening. How could Nick be so cruel to this child?

"Is it okay with you then?"

"What?" She had forgotten to listen. Again.

"Is it okay if I borrow the car to take Eric and Liz with Kim and me to the dance tonight? We won't be late and I'll be careful. Promise!"

"I guess so. I won't need the car. Midnight!"

"One?"

"Twelve-thirty. No grace-period."

"Deal. Thanks, Mom. You're the best!"

"No, you just softened me up with your pasta."

They laughed and he hugged her before sprinting for the phone to call his friends. Lenore was drying her hands when Joel came into the kitchen.

"Sorry to leave the mess. How do I look?"

"You look very handsome, of course." She gave him a kiss on the cheek. "Don't worry about the mess. It's gone now and was well worth it. You're a good cook. I won't ever have to worry about you starving when you get out on your own."

"I've had the best teacher." He gave her a peck on the cheek. "See ya at twelve-thirty."

Lenore caught him before he was out the door and pressed a ten-dollar bill into his hand. He smiled and hugged her, walked out the door and came back in and hugged her a second time.

"What was that for?" She laughed.

"Just felt like it. Bye."

Lenore watched him pull out of the drive and down the street. A sadness filled her as she thought of him growing up and leaving home. It could be measured in months now, instead of years. She hadn't felt the empty nest syndrome when Grant had graduated from high school. He had lived with his dad at the time, and though the separation had its own place in her heart, it was different.

Lenore closed the door, walked into the living room and turned on the radio. After listening to a few seconds of rock and roll, she tuned in an easy listening station, then went to the bedroom to change into sweats and a baggy T-shirt. She finally opened the suitcase from her trip to Glenwood Springs and began unpacking.

Unworn clothing was placed into the drawers of the guest room or hung in the empty closet. She held up her new jacket for a minute before carefully hanging it and smoothing out the wrinkles. Then she carried a bundle of dirty clothes to the laundry room and started a cycle of delicates. When the phone rang, she was prepared to relate to one of Joel's friends his itinerary for the evening.

"Hello," she answered, cheerfully.

"It's me."

She hadn't expected to hear Nick's voice and didn't answer.

"Are you there? Did you hear me?"

"Yes. I was just expecting one of Joel's friends."

"Why? Isn't he there?"

"No, he went out with Kim and some friends."

"Where'd he get money for that? I suppose he's using your car, too."

Lenore's grip on the phone tightened and she thought of hanging up. "Why did you call, Nick?"

"I thought you might like to know I won't be back as soon as I thought I would. They've got me running everywhere but home."

"Joel told me it could be a couple of weeks."

"Well, the way return loads are, it could be even longer. I wasn't fuckin' expecting it."

"Okay." Her voice was flat.

"Okay? What's that supposed to mean?"

"What do you want me to say, Nick? I'll miss you, Darling? Can't wait for you to come home and slug me again? Tell me Nick, what do you want me to say?"

"Yeah, well, you asked for it."

"I asked for it?" She spat the words into the phone. "How Nick? How did I ask for it? I really need to know so I won't ask for it again!" She was shaking and tears were stinging her eyes.

"Just like this. You pushed too far! When I want you to suck my dick, you'd better pucker up and be glad there's one for you to suck. There's plenty out here who want it. Don't forget it either!"

Lenore cringed against the receiver, wondering what kept her from throwing it on the floor like repulsive vermin. The lack of Nick's physical presence fueled her courage.

"Like the one you had last weekend? Tell me Nick, was she blonde? I found blonde hair on your clothes." She lied. More than likely he had been too drunk to remember anything, but she was baiting him.

The phone was silent for a full minute and Lenore's heart was pounding. The reply came hissing through the phone.

"Yeah, she was blonde. She was the sweetest little cunt I've ever had. She sucked my big dick real good and I fucked her 'til she was about to split open. I filled her pussy with my hot juice, then I fucked her in the ass and filled that up, too. She likes it that way." His voice had gotten steadily louder. "You satisfied now, Bitch? I'm going to do that to you when I get home. You just get ready for it. I'm gonna fuck you right in the ass!"

Lenore slammed down the receiver and screamed. The phone rang again and she backed away from it. It rang, and rang, and rang. She held her hands to her ears and closed her eyes, counting the rings... six, seven, eight. She reached for the phone cord and gave it a jerk. It resisted, and the incessant ringing continued. With shaking hands, she grasped the plug correctly and released the cord from the wall.

The silence was profound.

Lenore went to the closet and reached for her coat before remembering Joel had the car. She wanted to call Leah, but she didn't want to reconnect the phone. She paced through the house as if trying to escape her fear. She wished she could go to Gregor, but then wondered if meeting him had brought this about in the first place. Besides, she had no idea where he was going or how to get in touch, at least until his return. Return from where? Why all the mystery? She felt dizzy and nauseated.

"Stop this!" she scolded herself. "Let's get some logic back in here."

She went to the refrigerator and found a can of Diet Coke behind Nick's beer. She popped the top, took a long drink and felt the scouring effect of carbonation on her throat. As her stomach resisted the influx of bubbles, a burp erupted.

Lenore sniffed and wiped the tears from her cheeks. Another drink produced another burp. When she finished the can of Diet Coke, a resounding belch echoed off the kitchen walls and she laughed.

"Great! I'm losing my mind." She rinsed the empty can and put it into the recycle box before walking back into the living room. She sat on the sofa, rocked herself and talked, trying to produce a state of calm.

"I'm safe right now. Nick's far away from here. He can't touch me or Joel right now. I absolutely have to calm down."

The pain in her abdomen was subsiding, "Relax Lenore. Breathe." Somehow it didn't have the same soothing effect as when Leah said it to her, but she slowly breathed in through her nose and out through her mouth.

"I have time to think of a solution," she assured herself. "I have time to get us out of here. It's going to be alright!"

She stood and looked at the phone. "Let's see how persistent you are."

She plugged the phone back into the wall. It didn't ring. She picked up the receiver and then sat it back down.

"No, I'm not going to upset Leah. I'm okay." She ran her fingers through her hair. "No, I'm not. I'm arguing with myself."

Lenore walked to the radio and tuned in a country music station and sang along with a familiar tune. She went to the master bedroom and began taking her belongings to the guest room. It took a couple of hours before she was out of one room and settled into the other. She smiled at her minor effort toward independence. She need never enter that room again.

It was just before midnight when Lenore heard a car in the drive. She was relieved to see Joel walk in the front door. He smiled and gave his mom a hug.

"You're up kinda late, aren't you, Mom?"

"I finished unpacking from the trip, finally, and did a little laundry. You're home early."

"The music was too loud. Eric was fighting with Liz and Kim had stiff shoulders from helping her mom clean out flower beds or something. I massaged her shoulders, but we decided to call it a night anyway." He talked and walked to the kitchen for a Diet Coke. Lenore had to turn down the music to hear him. "I'll call her tomorrow and see how she's feeling. How was your night?"

"Just a quiet evening … I didn't mind a bit." She couldn't tell him the truth.

"Nick called and might be out longer than two weeks. It's the chance we need to get out if we can."

"Really, Mom?" He hugged her, lifting her up and making her laugh. "I thought you said we couldn't afford it."

"Well, we can't afford it, but we can't afford to stay, either. I'll get a loan or borrow the money from Rusty. We're getting out of here." She hoped he didn't quiz her about the abrupt decision.

He popped the top on his can of soda and took a lengthy drink. "We can look in the paper tomorrow and see what's available. Maybe we can go looking on Sunday. Did Rusty offer the money?"

Lenore wondered why he didn't burp. "Yes, he said he had discussed it with Gertie and they want to do it. I just feel funny about it."

"Mom, he has the money and you know they think you're the greatest. I'll help you pay it back. I can get a job after school or something."

"Let's wait and see if it's necessary." Lenore patted Joel on the back, still expecting a burp. "I'm going to make more money in the management program, but it's going to mean a lot more hours at work. What I'm going to need most from you is to help around the house. Are you willing?"

"Do you really have to ask, Mom?"

"No, I don't." She smiled. "We'll go house hunting on Sunday. Right now, I want to show you what I brought back to you from Glenwood Springs."

She showed him the handsome black dress shirt, which he said he was looking forward to wearing at the holiday concert. He took off his shirt and slipped the new one on.

"Perfect fit, too! Long enough in the arms to play the 'bone. Thank you, Mom."

"You're very welcome. I have to go to bed though or I'll never make it through Saturday."

"Okay Mom. Goodnight and thanks again. I love you." He smiled. "Don't be afraid, we can make it together."

Yes, they would make it together. Lenore smiled as she heard a burp and an "excuse me" from down the hall.

* * * * *

Saturday was a busy day at work. Lenore and JD discussed her new schedule, which would begin as soon as he received confirmation and paperwork from the home office. The final approval, which he assured her was just a formality, had to come from board members. They were scheduled to meet on the following Monday and Tuesday, so she had one more week of her regular schedule, Tuesday through Saturday with a half day on Friday.

Rusty was elated when Lenore approached him about accepting the offer of help. He agreed to wait until she did some house hunting before they settled on a figure. She left work with as many boxes as the car would hold, and spent the evening packing and sorting, with the cheerful help of her son.

Around midnight she crawled under the covers of her bed and fell into a fitful sleep. She dreamed of being chased by Nick down long, dark corridors filled with writhing snakes. She awoke full of fear, and with a shaky hand she reached over and turned on the lamp on the night stand. After what seemed like hours, she finally fell back to sleep.

* * * * *

The knocking on her door startled Lenore awake.

"What's wrong, Joel?"

"Nothing Mom. It's ten o'clock and you never sleep this late. I was getting worried about you."

"I'm okay. I'm getting up." She rubbed her eyes and yawned. Her nightgown and the covers were twirled around her, so it was a fight to get out of bed. She grabbed her robe and stumbled to the door and opened it. The smell of freshly brewed coffee and fried bacon greeted her senses.

"You made breakfast?"

"Bacon and pancakes. Sound good?" Joel called from the kitchen.

"Mmm, yes!" Lenore moaned. "Smells wonderful. Coffee!"

Joel had already poured Lenore a steaming hot cup of coffee and handed it her when she walked into the kitchen, then he laughed.

"Whoa, Mom! Have a rough night?"

"Sort of. Why?" She yawned again and sipped the coffee.

"Well, your hair is ..." He laughed again. "You'd better go take a look."

Lenore walked into the bathroom and Joel followed. They both burst into laughter when she looked into the mirror. Not only were there parts where there had never been parts, but her hair was matted and tangled and full of crimps and waves.

"Holey buckets! I should have finished my coffee first." She made futile efforts to smooth out the tangles. "I don't know whether to laugh or cry. It'll take an hour to comb."

Joel took her hand. "Forget it for now. Come eat breakfast while it's hot. I'll just keep my eyes on my plate." He snickered again. "I've never seen your hair like this."

They ate and talked about moving, with Joel breaking into uncontrolled laughter only once when he looked at his mom. They cleared the table and cleaned the kitchen, then sat in the middle of the living room floor with the Sunday paper. Joel had already folded it to the classifieds.

"I found three or four. They sound good, but I don't know what we can afford." He glanced at his mom. "How much can we afford?"

"I'm not even sure. Let's see what the prevailing prices are in the area we want to live and make a decision from there."

By noon, Joel had made their list and categorized it in order of area. Lenore had showered and added a little extra conditioner to help untangle her long tresses. When the last tangle was out, she dressed and exited the bathroom.

"Don't you want to dry your hair, Mom?"

"Let's get going. The car will be warm and I don't want to spend any more time or endure any more pain because of my hair."

* * * * *

They spent the afternoon driving through familiar and unfamiliar neighborhoods, circling and crossing off the listings. Finally, she folded the paper and tossed it onto the back seat.

"Let's talk about it later and narrow it down more. I think we have a good idea where we want to live and what we can afford."

"Sure Mom, they're all starting to look alike anyway. My bacon and pancakes have run out and I'm starved." Joel pulled into a Subway sandwich shop and produced the ten-dollar bill Lenore had given him the night before.

"May I buy you dinner?" He grinned.

"Sure. Can I have a chocolate chip cookie for dessert?"

"How 'bout we get an ice cream cone instead?"

"It's no wonder you have such a sweet girlfriend as Kim. You sure know how to treat a date."

"You're my best girl, Mom." He gave her a hug, then opened his car door.

The aroma of freshly baked bread further stimulated their appetites. When the sandwiches were eaten, they decided to forego the ice cream and went home, where Lenore collapsed on the couch amid discarded newspapers.

"Mom, you look really tired." Joel slumped into the recliner and he kicked off his shoes.

"Sweetie, I am." Lenore struggled to her feet, picking up her own discarded shoes. "If you don't mind, I think I'll just go to bed. I don't know if I'm coming down with something, or just stressed about getting us moved before Nick returns."

"Don't worry, Mom. We'll make it."

"Yes Joel, we'll make it." She smiled and began picking up and folding the papers. Her son got up from the recliner, stopped her and turned her toward the hallway.

"I can do this. You go to bed." He kissed her and gave her a hug. "I'm going to stay up a while longer."

Lenore flopped onto her bed after brushing her teeth and brushing her hair. She fell asleep almost immediately. No dreams interrupted her this night.

CHAPTER 17

It was the fifth day since Gregor Parishnikov, a.k.a., Greg Parish, had dropped out of John Dixon's sight. He had flown back to Denver on Thursday morning after receiving a call from an irate Frank Gillespie, notifying the Russian's case worker of his apparent disappearance.

As far as John was concerned, it was an incredulous situation. In less than a week, a man John felt he knew as well as anyone, had managed to poison a veteran CIA agent, electronically alter incoming calls to appear they had all come from Colorado Springs and was successfully sidestepping detection. Why? What could possibly have triggered it?

As he sipped his third cup of coffee, Frank walked in the door. The older agent poured himself a cup and slumped into a chair.

"Anything?"

"Nothing, Frank. Not a damned thing."

"What now?"

John was feeling the distraction of a tension headache. He reached into a desk drawer and found the nearly empty bottle of ibuprofen. He quickly scribbled a note to remind himself to purchase more.

"Let's go over it again."

"Christ, Dixon, I've told you everything I can remember."

"I just have to be sure we didn't miss something." John swallowed two pills and drank half a glass of water. "You have to tell me the truth, Frank. Did you offend him, or threaten him in some way that might have made him feel endangered?"

"I was professional and courteous in every way. Hell, I even loaned him my truck when they couldn't get his car fixed." He threw his hands up in the air. "I don't just loan my truck to everyone, you know."

The Russian had manipulated Frank into being far from the normal, regulation loving professional John knew.

"Tell me again about that situation."

"He had papers in his office to finish for meetings the next day." He sipped his coffee, bored with the redundant questioning.

"Did you happen to follow up on that?"

"Well, no. I—"

"I did, Frank. There were no papers to pick up. He was never at his office after hours that night. We checked security cameras. I think he was trying to keep you out of his hair for a while. Tell me about the women he was with in Glenwood Springs."

"I told you the name of the owner of the car. She lives in Fort Collins. The other woman must be a friend."

"The owner of the car is Leah Chase. Look at this picture and tell me if these are the two women."

Frank only had to glance at the surveillance photo. "That's them."

John took the photograph back, staring at the picture perhaps a little too long.

Frank smiled. "Which one is which?"

"The blonde is Leah Chase. Lenore Appleby has the long, dark hair." John continued to stare at the picture.

"Told you they were beautiful." Frank laughed and sipped his coffee.

John frowned and turned the photograph upside-down on his desk.

"We need to see if there's a connection. Both women are married. Leah Chase appears to be happily married to the Appleby woman's boss. Lenore Appleby's husband is a truck driver, who just happens to be out of town right now."

"Think she's hiding Parish?"

"That's what we're going to find out. We're going to find out everything there is to know about his woman. I want to know what time she goes to bed, when she gets up, what she eats and who she's with when she does any of it."

"Are you going to question her?"

John shook her head. "Not right now. I want to observe for a while and it would be to our advantage if they don't know they're being observed."

"Physical or electronic surveillance?"

"Both. Wire taps are in place and I've initiated round-the-clock surveillance. Agents will be rotated so she doesn't see the same face too often. There may be no connection at all, but I suspect there is."

Frank nodded in agreement. "What about the house in Glenwood Springs?"

John opened a folder in front of him on the desk. "The young couple who take care of things during the week said he left this note saying he would be away for a couple of weeks." He handed the paper to Frank. "Left extra money. They didn't seem surprised or concerned. He often did that in anticipation of bad weather during the winter. Trouble is, he was always in communication." Frank handed the paper back to John, who slipped it under a paper clip in the inside of the folder. "He's dropped off the face of the earth this time." He closed the folder and rubbed his temples. "Someone knows something, and I'm going to dig until I find out who and what."

"What about Parish?" Frank asked. "What happens when you find him?"

"First of all, he'll be spending a little time back at the Farm. It's not unusual for these defectors to have problems adjusting to a new life. There's even been an occasional suicide, but since I was assigned to Greg, there's never been any indication of any problem." Dixon leaned back in his chair and stared at the ceiling. "Maybe I was just too comfortable. Maybe there were signs I just didn't see, because I was too relaxed. Damn, I just did not see this coming."

"Hey, don't be so rough on yourself. He's pretty convincing. He played me like I had strings attached." Frank swallowed the last few drops of coffee from his cup. "I'm a little anxious to talk to him about a few things myself."

"I guess you are." John looked across his desk at the older agent. "You were pretty sick, weren't you?"

"He'll be a little sick when I'm through with him!"

John understood the hard feelings, but he had to keep Frank in control.

"Remember, he could have killed you just as easily. He just wanted you out of his way for a while."

"So, I should thank him?"

"No, I believe I would thank someone a lot higher up."

Frank thought about it for a second. "I see your point."

"Good! Now let's get back to work."

* * * * *

Gregor Parishnikov walked alone down a deserted street in Moscow. The snow fell in large, lacy flakes, building on the pristine whiteness already covering the city. It was a strange sensation to walk along familiar streets he had so desperately wanted to leave. His contact had assured him finding his brother would be accomplished without incident. He walked past a vacant store window and caught the reflection of a stranger. He smiled, and the reflection smiled back.

While the CIA had initiated their search along the southern routes in Colorado, Gregor had driven north and east, into the state of Nebraska. He had parked the Saab in an abandoned shed, and begun his transformation. Shaving his beard and mustache altered his appearance considerably. His dark hair was lightened at the temples and gray contact lenses were added behind silver framed glasses.

He had taken his passport picture by using an instant camera with a built-in developer, aimed from the hood of his car. A sheet from the motel had served as a backdrop in the shed, and the headlights provided adequate lighting for the notoriously poor photographs.

Walking to a small airfield and offering the proper monetary incentives, it wasn't hard to catch a flight to the east coast of the United States.

The man in the photograph of the passport was no longer Gregor Parishnikov. He was a respected German businessman, trying to get home for his daughter's wedding. The family pictures in his wallet were of strangers, but each had a story and background Gregor had given them. Until he reached his destination, he had spoken very little English, hoping no one could detect a Russian accent when he spoke only German, a language in which he was especially fluent.

He was committed to his task. He flew to London from New York, then took a smaller airline to Germany. He used various modes of transportation to get into the Soviet Union undetected, and was proud of his resourcefulness.

As he stood in front of a store, in the reflection from the glass he recognized an old friend standing behind him. It was the contact he was to meet. Too late, he noticed the Makarov pistol aimed at the base of his skull. It had been surprisingly easy to get into the Soviet Union. It could be impossible to leave.

* * * * *

Lenore stood in the living room listening to Leah's cheerful voice on the phone. She blinked and yawned, trying to bring the clock into focus.

"Why aren't you awake? It's almost nine-thirty! You always call me by eight on our day off together."

"I can't believe I slept so late. Joel didn't wake me."

"Are you sick?"

"No, just tired, I guess. I even went to bed early last night."

"I'll be there in twenty minutes, tops! Got any coffee made?"

"I don't know. If not, I'll make fresh." She yawned again. "Maybe a shower will wake me up before you get here."

Joel had left an insulated carafe of coffee and a smiley face on a napkin. Lenore drank a cup while pinning up her hair. She examined her puffy eyes, the result of too much sleep. She was out of the shower and dressed by the time Leah arrived.

"You sure got ready fast." Leah accepted a fresh cup of coffee from Lenore. She went to the cabinet and found the sugar and creamer kept just for her use and stirred them into the brew.

"I didn't wash my hair; I'll just wear it in a ponytail." Lenore walked back to the bathroom followed by Leah. "We don't have any big plans, do we?"

"Just the usual," replied Leah. We'll get your check, go to the bank, then get breakfast."

"Breakfast first! I think I'll open my own checking account today. What do you think?"

"Brilliant idea. I would be honored to accompany you," Leah informed her friend, in her most proper British accent.

Lenore grinned. "Let me put on a little make-up and brush my teeth, then we can be off."

"And we can leave, too." They said in unison and laughed.

Lenore transformed her face and hair into something presentable to the public. A green ribbon adorned the dark tresses, and a final check in the mirror assured her most of the puffiness was gone from her eyes. She brushed her teeth, turned off the light and they left the house.

It was too cool to have the top down on Baby, so they drove toward town bathed in warmth, thanks to a recently installed heater core.

"Did you want real breakfast," Lenore asked, "or a giant cinnamon roll?"

Leah's eyes twinkled with thoughts of the locally famous rolls, warm and dripping with butter and icing.

"Cinnamon roll!"

"You got it!" Lenore made a quick U-turn in the middle of the street and headed in the opposite direction.

They were happily in search of breakfast, completely unaware of what their change in plans did to the car following them. Unable to make the change without being noticed, the agent lost sight of the convertible. He was immediately on his radio, trying to explain to John Dixon just how it had occurred.

The two hungry women pulled into the restaurant parking lot, and were soon devouring every bite of the sweet, spicy treats.

Lenore poured coffee from the stainless-steel carafe, warming the remaining liquid in her cup. "Want more?"

Leah shook her head and pushed her coffee cup away. "If I drink any more, I'll just have to whiz all day. Let's go get your check and go to the bank. Aren't you excited about opening your own account?"

"I sure am. I feel such a surge of independence. I might just get through this whole thing intact." She took in a deep breath and exhaled quickly. "I've got another week to get some changes made before Gregor returns. I want to show him I've accomplished something."

"I'm so anxious to see you out of there I can hardly sleep. How about you?"

"I went to bed about eight-thirty and you woke me this morning. Does that answer your question?"

"That's not like you." Leah looked at Lenore's eyes. "Are you feeling okay? Your eyes are green today."

"I know. I'm just tired, but I know I'm getting enough sleep." She stifled a yawn. "I wish all this caffeine would kick-in"

"I think it's your body's way of protecting you from all the stress. You're going to take the loan from Rusty, right?"

"Yes, but I hate it. I wish there were another way, but I have to get us out of there before Nick gets back."

After a few more minutes of casual conversation, they paid their checks and walked to the car. Lenore related parts of the phone conversation with Nick as she drove toward the store.

Leah listened, openmouthed, until Lenore finished. "What's gotten into him? He's always been a little on the crude side, but never so vicious and vulgar. I'm genuinely concerned for your safety. He must be on drugs."

"I'm concerned, too. I don't know about drugs, but he was sure drunk when he hit me."

"When he hit you?" Leah shrieked. "When did he hit you? Lenore, when did this happen?"

Lenore cringed. "I forgot you didn't know."

"I can't believe you didn't tell me." Leah was shaking her head and had her arms crossed. Lenore was sure she would have been tapping her foot too, if she had been standing instead of sitting.

"It happened the night before he left. I didn't see a solution to our getting out at the time, and I didn't want to worry you."

"You didn't want to worry me?" She was still shaking her head. "That hurts my feelings. We're supposed to be there for each other, Lenore."

"I know. I'm sorry, but it made sense at the time. He just back handed me and bruised my lip a little." She touched the area, which was still a little tender. "You should have seen Gregor's face when he found out."

"Sure, you tell him and not your best friend."

Lenore patted Leah's arm. "Don't be that way. He saw the bruise and asked about it. I couldn't lie to him. It was still a little swollen on Friday, but you didn't notice, so I didn't want to point it out." She turned a corner, then continued attempts to calm her friend.

"Don't be hurt, Leah. You have enough to worry about with your extended family. I love you and just wanted to keep you from having something else to worry about. Please understand."

"You just don't worry about me and my situation. I'm here for you no matter what's going on at my house." She took Lenore's hand. "You'd better not keep anything else from me."

"I promise, Leah."

"What did Gregor do? What did he say?"

"Leah, I think if he had the chance, he'd do a lot worse to Nick than what was done to me. He had a crazed look in his eyes for an instant, then it was gone and the tenderness returned."

"Maybe Nick will have an accident."

Lenore looked in the rearview mirror before changing lanes, and glanced at the blonde beside her. "I don't want to know why you said that."

"Well, Gregor loves you … and since he's—"

"I said I don't want to know." Lenore eyed her friend. "He's not a hit man! You read too many spy novels."

"Probably, but wouldn't it be great to have Nick out of your way?"

"I'm getting out of *his* way. That's all I care about. I don't wish bad things on anyone."

"Not even Nick?"

"Okay, I wish his penis would shrivel up and fall off and he'd get a plague of pimples up his nose and ingrown hair would beset his armpits. How's that?" She raised her eyebrows and glanced at Leah, awaiting approval.

"You are a vicious woman," Leah said, laughing.

Lenore parked the car, and the friends got out, then walked in the back door of the store. Lenore was going to get her paycheck and Leah was going to get a hug from her spouse. Royce met them halfway to the front of the store.

"Hello Mrs. Chase. Hi, Lenore. We just tried to call you."

"Why?"

"Because you got some mail here. Thought you'd like to have it." He waited for a reaction.

"Royce, you know I always come in on Monday for my paycheck. You wouldn't have to call." She shrugged. "I wonder who would send me mail here?"

"I don't know, but they're postmarked New York City. That any help?" He looked disappointed as she shook her head and ducked into the office, following Leah. JD gave his wife a hug and handed four enveloped to Lenore.

"What on earth?" She turned the envelopes over in her hand, recognizing the paper. It was the stationery she had purchased the night of her meeting with Gregor. She looked at Leah and their thoughts connected.

"Lenore, we'd better get going. We just have so much to do today."

The brunette stared at the envelopes in her hands. "Huh? Oh, yeah. We have to leave."

159

She turned and followed Leah toward the back door, but Rusty stopped her before she had taken ten steps.

"Did you think about the loan?"

"Yes, I really did. We can talk about it tomorrow. We're wanting to get some things done today." She pointed toward Leah and smiled. Leah was urging her forward with a gentle tug on her sleeve.

JD tapped Lenore's shoulder. "Don't you want this?"

Lenore turned to see her paycheck in JD's hand.

"Almost forgot it, didn't I?" She laughed and hoped it sounded sincere. Royce, always the curious one, wasn't going to let it go so easily.

"Must be some pretty important mail there for you to forget your paycheck. Four letters from the same person. So, who is it, anyway?" He grinned.

JD answered for Lenore. "None of our business, Royce. If she felt like telling us, we'd already know." He frowned and crossed his arms. "Don't you have something to do?"

As Royce sulked away and Rusty laughed, Lenore gave her boss a grateful hug. "Thanks. I don't know who they're from myself. See you tomorrow."

JD and Rusty waved good-bye as Leah and Lenore walked out the back door and got into the car. The envelopes were tucked under one of Lenore's legs and she started the car, pulled out of the parking area and onto the street. Leah didn't question the delay in opening the letters.

* * * * *

A blue sedan followed, having caught up with the subjects of surveillance once again. Unfortunately, traffic on College Avenue was busy and the convertible squeaked through a yellow light, leaving the frustrated agent pounding his steering wheel.

The unsuspecting women drove toward the lake, making the necessary turns west and south. They couldn't have more successfully lost their shadow had they been trying.

Lenore parked the car and checked their surroundings. There was not another car in sight. Leah could contain her curiosity no longer.

"Are they from Gregor?"

Lenore took the envelopes from under her leg, turning each over in her hands before handing them to Leah, who examined each envelope as well.

"That's the stationery I bought the night I met Gregor at the mall and we came here. I left it in the back of his car. It's either from him, or one heck of a coincidence."

"Open one." Leah said.

"Which one?"

"It doesn't matter. They're all alike."

Leah handed the envelopes back to Lenore, who felt each one as if she could be able to discern the contents.

"They're kind of thick, and they all feel the same. What could it be?"

"I'm going to scream if you don't open one and find out."

Lenore cautiously slipped a finger under the corner of one flap and carefully tore the paper. With the top open, she looked again at Leah before reaching inside and pulling the contents out onto her lap. A sheet of the pretty stationery was folded neatly around a stack of one hundred-dollar bills.

Leah started at the money, then at her friend. "Wow!"

Lenore counted the bills and started shaking.

"Leah, there are ten, one hundred-dollar bills here. Look!"

She handed the contents to Leah, who counted them and looked back at Lenore.

"That's a thousand dollars! There's no writing on the paper. Open another."

In the third envelope there were words printed neatly on paper surrounding ten more one hundred-dollar bills.

"It says: FOR YOUR SAFETY. SEE YOU SOON. I can't believe he did this." While Lenore read the words over and over to herself through misty eyes, Leah opened the last envelope.

"Lenore, you have four thousand dollars. I think this man is serious about wanting to take care of you." She chuckled.

"I think this says it pretty clearly." She held the paper out to Leah, who read it and smiled.

"Yes, it does."

"I've never seen his handwriting before. I like it." She smiled and held the paper to her chest. Then, in a quiet voice, "Thank you, God. Thank you for Gregor."

"Thank you for four thousand dollars! Lenore, now you can get out!" Leah shook Lenore's shoulders.

"Wa-hoo!" they yelled in unison.

"Did you know that's a town in Nebraska?" Leah asked.

"What?"

"Never mind."

"Four thousand dollars. Look at it!" Lenore stared at the money her fingers were counting. "I've never seen so much money at one time. My God, what if they're counterfeit?" Lenore dropped the money into her lap and turned to Leah.

"Stop it. You know they're real." She took the money from Lenore's lap and stacked and straightened. "What are you going to do first?"

"Do? I don't know. What should I do first?"

"Well, actually first of all, you need to get rid of all the paper."

"All?" Lenore held the paper with Gregor's words.

"I know you don't want to, but I think you'd better."

Lenore handed the envelopes to Leah. "Right. Start tearing."

They tore and shredded the paper into pieces smaller than postage stamps, piling them onto Baby's console. However, a two-inch by five-inch piece of the stationery was tucked into Lenore's pocket, unobserved by Leah.

Satisfied no one would be able to reconnect the paper, they looked at the stack of bills, then to one another.

"This is a lot of money. What do I do with it?" Lenore asked.

"Stuff it in your bra. That's where my Granny always kept her mad money."

Lenore raised her sweater and began tucking the money between her breasts and the silky brassiere.

"Either your Granny had bigger boobs, or she was never this mad. Here, put some in yours."

Leah opened her blouse and began tucking bills into her own lacy apparel. When the money was all under wraps, they started laughing.

"I hope no one was watching." Lenore glanced around. "I wasn't thinking about it."

"Can't you imagine some forest ranger watching through binoculars, then trying to explain it to his buddies?" She began her rendition of an imaginary conversation, complete with antics and silly faces. "I tell ya, guys, I seen the whole thing. They stuffed a whole bunch of money in their bras then just sat there laughing about it."

Lenore laughed until her sides ached as the petite blonde pretended to look through binoculars and do double-takes, making faces in various stages of astonishment.

"Stop! My cheeks hurt from laughing." Lenore said.

When breathing returned to normal without giggles, they decided to discard the paper.

"Here, stuff some in your pocket and I'll put some in mine. We'll go to our rock."

They got out of the car, then descended the trail to the rock and climbed. From their elevated perch, they scanned their surroundings.

"I don't see anyone. Feed the wind."

Leah followed Lenore's lead and dug the pieces out of her pocket. They raised their overflowing hands above their heads, letting the breeze eat hungrily at the confetti-like offering. Pieces were deposited near the base of the rock. Others were blown to the waters of the lake, settling like snowflakes upon the ripples. The remainder was lifted into the air and sent on a journey whose destination was known only to the wind itself.

"Wasn't that pretty, Lenore? Do you think it was polluting?"

"I hate to think of it that way, but I suppose it was." She sighed.

"Maybe since they were such small pieces, it'll sort of be like fertilizer or something."

"Leah, no matter what name we give it, it's still polluting."

"Well, if we had thrown it in a dumpster, it would have ended up in a landfill. What else could we have done?"

"Geeze. Think of it as fertilizer then. If you don't, you'll never get any sleep tonight." Lenore began carefully climbing down from the rock. "If everyone was so concerned over tiny pieces of paper, there wouldn't be a pollution problem."

Leah met her at the base of the rock, having taken a different route down.

"How did you do that?" Lenore asked Leah, who just shrugged and smiled. "Let's go empty our bras."

"That sounds funny." Leah giggled.

Inside the privacy of the car, they lifted their tops and checked the cargo.

"A rapist could sure make a haul off us, couldn't he?" Leah noted.

"He'd never have a chance. I'd be fighting for four thousand dollars, as well as our virtue. Looks like none of the bills have shifted." They both settled their clothing into place. "Let's go to my house and find a place to hide them."

As they drove back toward town, Leah entertained them with further ideas of the forest ranger's observations.

"And then after they polluted the countryside, they ran back to the car and looked at each other's boobs. I tell ya guys, they gotta be nuts!"

With laughter and nerves electrified, they drove directly back to Lenore's house, then hurried inside, locking the door and pulling the curtains before emptying their bras onto the bed of the guest room.

"I only count thirty-nine." Lenore checked her bra, finding no strays. "You count them."

While Leah counted, Lenore checked the lock on the front door once again and looked out the front window. There was nothing unusual to be seen in the neighborhood, so she went back into the bedroom and knelt beside Leah.

"All there?"

"Yes. Two were stuck together."

They laid the bills side-by-side on the bed, making four rows of ten each. They were as intent as two little girls playing with new paper dolls.

"What are you going to tell Joel?"

"The truth."

"The truth?" Leah stared at her friend.

"Well, I'll tell him enough to avoid telling him a lie."

The look on Leah's face told Lenore an explanation was in order.

"I'll simply tell him someone sent money from New York and didn't put a name or return address on the envelopes. That's the truth. I don't have to tell him I know who it was."

"That's good thinking. By avoiding the truth, you aren't telling a lie."

"Exactly!" Lenore affirmed, smiling proudly. "Now I just have to decide where to keep all this money. "

"How about under the mattress?"

"That's the first place someone would look."

"Yes, but who knows to look?"

"You're right."

Lenore got an envelope from the desk and put all but five of the bills inside. They lifted the mattress, put the envelope underneath, then settled the bedding back in place.

"What's the five hundred for?"

"In case Joel and I decide on a place, we'll have money for a deposit. I need to cash my paycheck, too." She looked out the window, then turned to Leah. "Let's go buy a newspaper."

"What about opening up a checking account?"

"Might as well wait until I have an address."

"That makes sense. Let's go."

* * * * *

By four-thirty the friends were exhausted from the day's excitement. Leah deposited Lenore in front of her house with hugs and assurance she would be called if they found a place to move.

Joel was playing his trombone when Lenore opened the door, and stopped when he saw his mom.

"Did you get the loan from Rusty?"

"No, Son, I didn't get the loan and don't intend to."

Disappointment clearly registered on Joel's face and Lenore ran to hug her not-so-little son.

"Oh, Sweetheart, I mean I don't have to. Sit down and let me tell you about a Guardian Angel somewhere in New York."

The confusion on Joel's face was quickly replaced with smiles as Lenore related the story of the mysterious envelopes. The tall young man pulled his mom up from the sofa and lifted her off the floor in a hug.

"Let's go rent a house, right now!"

Lenore laughed as she was deposited back on her feet.

"Leah and I did some preliminary looking today. I picked three I want you to look at. If you like them, we'll come back here and try to get in touch with the owners."

* * * * *

By seven, they had narrowed the choice down to two. They made the necessary calls and found one already rented and the other not available for three more weeks. The gentleman at the second number gave them a number for a friend who didn't like to advertise in the paper. By eight-thirty, Lenore and Joel were standing in the house they would be moving into.

* * * * *

The urgency they felt was conveyed in their packing during the evenings that week. Personal items were packed among kitchen utensils, towels surrounded glassware and photographs were thrown in plastic bags, with a promise to organize and store properly into albums when time permitted.

Leah and JD secured friends and pickup trucks to assist in the move. On Saturday night, the third weekend of October, they had loaded the last items onto a truck belonging to Rusty. Joel hopped in the front seat with him, directing the way to their destination. Lenore and Leah sat on the front step of Nick's house, watching them drive away.

"Leah, I didn't think we'd make it. I'm so tired and I have to get the other house in some sort of order, so we can sleep tonight." She stood and gave Leah a hand up. "I guess we'd better finish here first."

"What do you mean? Let's go to the new house. You're done here."

"I want to make sure things are finished and clean here before I go. I won't have him complaining to anyone about my leaving him with a mess."

"Lenore, it isn't a mess. We've cleaned as we moved things out." She opened the door. "Let's go in and take a look."

As they walked through the house, Lenore hugged her arms around herself as if avoiding a chill. There were parts of the house that looked virtually untouched. The master bedroom was intact.

She had refused to take anything from there, feeling it would hold too many bad memories.

Joel's room and the guest room were completely vacated. There was an assortment of linens in the hall closet and a fair selection of kitchenware. Lenore had left the set of dishes they had purchased together, and the set of flatware given as a wedding gift. A fair assortment of glassware was left as well. The washer and dryer, along with kitchen appliances, the dining room table and living room furniture now fully belonged to Nick.

Lenore had been given an assortment of furniture from Rusty and Gertie, who assured they were extras from around their house. She had found a second-hand washer and dryer set from the newspaper. Kitchen appliances were included in the new place. She had also indulged herself with a new queen-sized waterbed, giving both super-single waterbeds to Joel for his room.

"You should have taken everything and left him with a vacant house," Leah said.

Lenore picked up a piece of tape and a stray dust bunny, tucking them into her pocket. "I suppose most women would, but those are his things as far as I'm concerned. I want no part of him. I wish I could forget he was ever a part of my life. The mental scars will be enough to carry without having to see his things. Besides, maybe he won't be vindictive if he still has a place to call home. He has his favorite chair, the television and a refrigerator to keep his beer cold. That's all he needs. The rest is for my peace of mind, not his."

"I understand." She patted Lenore's back.

She walked to the door, turned and tossed her house keys to the middle of the living room floor. "I'm ready to go."

Lenore hugged her best friend and thanked her for the help. They closed the door for the last time and got into Lenore's car.

* * * * *

Lenore and Leah carried coolers of beer and soft drinks to the front door, just as the pizza delivery truck pulled up in front of Lenore's new house. Joel met his mom outside to relieve her of the cooler.

"Welcome home, Mom!" He gave her a quick kiss on the cheek and one to Leah as well. "Welcome to you too, Leah." He laughed. "Welcome pizza person! We're starved!"

Lenore paid the laughing delivery man, then took four pizzas through the threshold of her new home. Inside, she found Joel, JD, Rusty and Gertie, Royce and Joel's friend Eric standing in the living room, smiling.

"What's going on?" She asked, then looked around the room. "Hey, where are all the boxes? The living room is clean!"

"We've been busy, Mom." Joel opened a pizza box. "Go check out the bedrooms."

She and Leah walked through the house finding waterbeds filled, with clean sheets and blankets on them. Very few boxes were visible.

"Looks like all you need to do tonight is go to bed," Leah said.

"Bless their hearts. I can't believe it. If I had known they were going to do this, I would have bought steaks instead of pizza."

"If you can get them to work for pizza, save the steak for something really spectacular."

They returned to the living room and Lenore hugged and thanked each one. "I truly appreciate this. Just one little question. Where are all the boxes? I know you haven't had time to empty them, too."

"Lenore, just be careful when you open closets and the laundry area," Gertie advised.

"I wouldn't plan on putting your car in the garage tonight, either," Rusty added.

"I understand completely. I can just fall into bed and worry about those things tomorrow."

"Tomorrow and Monday," JD reminded her. "Will you need more time?"

"No, it'll be plenty if I can borrow Leah on Monday."

"No problem, that's normal. You girls better enjoy it, though. This is your last Monday off for a long time." He shook her hand. "You are officially my new Assistant Manager. You've been accepted into the management program."

Lenore took a deep breath and exhaled slowly. She had enough money to hold them for a while, and with the new position, life was going to be very manageable.

"To Lenore." Royce offered a toast with his can of soft drink. "May this be the beginning of a life as sweet and happy as it can be. May all the rough roads be behind you and only gentle paths lay before you. Peace and love."

The twinkle of sincerity shone in the eyes of her co-worker, as the former hippie slipped out of his establishment-clad persona.

The group lifted their various drinks and then drank.

"Thank you, Royce. Thank you all for the support and assistance. We're going to make it. I know it won't be a breeze, but the peace of mind will make it all manageable. Now, I want everyone to get in there and eat the rest of the pizza. You've earned every bite, and come to think of it, I'm starved!"

"Any idea yet who sent you the cash from New York?" Rusty asked, as they walked to the dining room and took pieces of pizza.

"No one has ever taken credit for it. I was just about to take your offer of a loan the day I got it. I'd certainly love to thank the wonderfully generous person who sent it."

Lenore and Leah smiled at one another.

* * * * *

As the last truck pulled away from the house, Lenore stood with her arm around Joel's waist and her head on his shoulder. He hugged her after turning off the outside light and locking the front door. They were home. They were safe and determined to make it work. Together!

Lenore fought the urge to dive into unpacking. She kissed her son goodnight and went to her room. It would take a while to change the bare windows and naked walls into her own personal space, but she had time. Tonight, she only wanted to sleep. She took a shower, brushed her teeth and crawled into bed. A sleeping bag, sweatpants and a sweatshirt would defeat the chill of the unheated waterbed until it came to temperature. She could have slept on a slab of granite this night.

* * * * *

A block away from the new house, the man sitting in a dark blue car relaxed when he saw the lights go out. There were taps on a public phone where the woman was planning to receive a call Monday. She

169

had left the number with Gregor's answering service. They would locate the Russian and find just how involved the Appleby woman was in his disappearance. He sipped a cup of coffee and used the mobile radio to call John Dixon, reporting the house secured for the night.

CHAPTER 18

Lenore sat up in bed and stared at her surroundings. She knew where she was, but didn't know why she was awake. Then, with her eyes opened wide, she bounded from the bed, running to the living room. She pushed the vertical blinds aside to see the less-than-graceful landing of Canadian geese, honking their arrival.

The back yard of their new home ran adjacent to acres of open fields. Foothills of the Rocky Mountains began their gentle rise less than two miles away. It was an unobstructed view of the mountains Lenore loved.

She quietly opened the patio door and stepped into the crisp October air. The cold concrete nipped at her bare feet, and she walked quickly to the edge of the frigid slab to stand on the grass, dormant and brown from seasonal changes. Her feet were somewhat insulated from the cold earth by the grass and she walked slowly to the fence line separating her yard from the field.

The large black and white birds seemed to take little notice of the human as they searched the field for morsels of grain left from late summer harvests. They conversed and scolded one another in loud honks and Lenore smiled. This was going to be a wonderful home. Her feet were beginning to ache from the cold and she turned to sprint back to the patio. Joel stood at the door with tousled hair, hugging his burgundy robe around him. He smiled a sleepy smile as his mom walked back into the house.

"Aren't they wonderful, Joel?" I wonder how many are there?"

"Twenty-one, I think." He yawned. "They move too much to get a good count. Aren't your feet cold?"

"Yes, but it was worth it. Look at the view." She closed the heavy patio doors. "I'll bet it's going to be gorgeous when it snows. Imagine the sunsets!"

"All this and no asshole. I think it's great."

"Joel, let's avoid any references to that person when at all possible, okay? Want some coffee?"

"No, I want to go back to bed, now that I know what all the noise was about. Maybe I can go back to sleep." He yawned and stretched. "Don't you want to go back to bed? It's still early."

"Heck, no! The sun's almost all the way up. I have a million things to get done today. I'm going to work you pretty hard today, so you'd better get all the rest you can."

Lenore continued to admire the view for a few more minutes after Joel went back to his room. She left the blinds open and went to the kitchen to find the coffee pot, coffee and filters, as well as two matching coffee mugs, unpacked and ready for use sitting on the counter. Gertie's efficiency with unpacking was greatly appreciated.

With a brimming cup of steaming coffee, Lenore allowed herself time to sit in her favorite rocking chair for a while, admiring the westerly view as daylight eclipsed night. She was relaxed and happy for the first time in a very long while. She made mental notes on rearranging the furniture and getting a load of wood to use in the small, gray wood-burning stove, trimmed in shining brass, sitting in one corner of the living room. The surround was of natural native rock. The landlord had assured her it would be more than enough to heat the house in the event of a power failure, or as a preference to expensive electric heat.

The living room was large, opening into a generous dining area. The kitchen was small, but provided efficient cabinet and counter space. A pantry doubled as a broom and coat closet in the foyer by the front door. It was all bright, open and clean.

The bedrooms and bathroom were at the other end of a hallway from the front foyer. An efficient and roomy laundry area was next to the bathroom. The bath and toilet were separated by a door from the vanity. Double sinks would allow Joel and her simultaneous access.

Lenore's favorite room was her bedroom. It was nearly as large as the living room, with more than enough room for her bed, night table and chest of drawers. There would be adequate room for a desk and chair someday.

Lenore's thoughts were interrupted by the presence of Spot, as the hungry feline jumped into her lap.

"Good morning, my favorite little fur ball. Where have you been hiding? I'll bet you're hungry."

Spot bounded from her lap with enough force to make coffee splatter from a nearly full cup.

"That wasn't nice, Spot!"

An apologetic meow echoed from the kitchen as Lenore walked toward the sound. When she entered the kitchen, she had to laugh. Spot sat in the middle of the floor and looked from cabinet to cabinet and back at her human.

"Don't know where it's coming from, do you? Neither do I."

Spot yowled impatiently as she circled and rubbed against Lenore's legs. It took a few minutes to locate the little dishes and a selection of cans from an array of bags. The smelly chopped meat and fresh water were put into the dishes and set on the floor, where Spot ate hungrily.

"Poor thing, you probably had to drink from the toilet. Glad your litter box was set up." Spot glanced up as if agreeing.

Lenore surveyed the kitchen, anxious for order and normalcy. She began opening closets and dragging boxes out to discern contents. She moved each box to close proximity of the room in which it was needed. She cleaned cabinets and fit shelf paper inside. As each box was emptied, it was flattened and stacked near the front door.

By the time Joel was up for the day, she had nearly finished the kitchen and the bathroom was functional, though two boxes remained to be emptied and organized. Joel seized the opportunity to shower, pointing out paw prints in the bathtub.

"I guess Spot didn't drink toilet water. We need to keep the door closed and check into fixing the drip in the tub."

Lenore had emptied the last two boxes and straightened hand towels by the time Joel exited the bathroom.

"That was great. Plenty of hot water, too."

Lenore watched her well-scrubbed son walk toward his room, letting his terry cloth robe soak up excess moisture as he towel-dried his light brown hair.

"Why don't we just go out for breakfast? I'm not quite ready to dirty up the kitchen."

"Sounds good to me," he called from his room. "I'll be ready in a minute. We need to go to the grocery store, too."

Lenore walked into the bathroom, looked at her reflection in the mirror and shrugged her shoulders. She washed her face and ran a brush through her long hair, securing it in a ponytail. She brushed her teeth, then went to her room to change from her sweats to a clean sweater and blue jeans. She stepped into her favorite brown loafers and gathered her purse and jacket. She was ready before Joel and waited patiently at the front door.

* * * * *

By eight o'clock that night, Lenore felt settled. There were still some boxes to be emptied, but most were filled with items unnecessary to everyday life. Joel had hooked the television to cable and was thrilled to find it functioning.

"This is great! I can watch the Broncos game tomorrow night. When will the phone be connected?"

"They're a little more independent, I guess," Lenore replied from the kitchen. "We won't have it until the end of the week."

"I'll just have to talk to Kim at school and make plans ahead of time. She'll like it better anyway." He joined his mom on the kitchen. "Want to watch a movie or anything?"

"No. I want to take a bath and go to bed, after we eat a sandwich."

"Okay. I'll help fix dinner. We sure couldn't have gotten away with just a sandwich with you know who here."

"Joel, we could have ice cream sandwiches for dinner if we want. It's no one's business but our own right now." She laughed.

"Mom, you're a closet junk-food junkie, aren't you?"

"What gave me away?"

"I think it was when I had to pull you out of the cookie aisle at the grocery store and beg for fruit and vegetables."

"You didn't have to beg."

"No, but it helped."

They laughed and finished their preparations, then ate at their glass-topped rattan table, a loan from JD and Leah. The atmosphere was calm and happy as they enjoyed one another's company and discussed plans and life.

After the kitchen was cleaned, Joel retired to the living room to watch TV. Lenore retired to a bathtub full of bubbles, letting the soft scented warmth ease her tired muscles. All excess energy drained with the tub-full of water. Twenty minutes later, she dried and put on a night gown, then kissed her son good-night and closed the door to her room. Fatigue and the effects of a warm bath worked their magic. Sleep came quickly.

* * * * *

Life was taking a dramatic turn for Lenore Appleby. In the span of a few short weeks, she had escaped a crumbling, destructive marriage and had a wonderful new love taking root in her soul. She was beginning a career with the store, which included a substantial increase of her income. She was looking at life with excitement and anticipation.

Lenore greeted the Monday morning dawn, as she stood at the kitchen window, a cup of coffee poised at smiling lips. She would talk to the Russian today. He would be pleased with her progress and she couldn't wait to tell him. Ten o'clock was hours away, and Lenore knew time would pass slowly. She had tried to stay in bed and force sleep, but her eyes had refused to stay shut any longer. She hoped Leah would arrive early, to help calm and reassure her of the inevitable phone call.

As time for Joel to get up and ready for school approached, Lenore took bacon and eggs out of the refrigerator. It would make a mess and she was glad. It would also be time consuming to clean, and she wanted to stay busy. Joel was pleased with such a breakfast on a school day, normally settling for a bowl of cereal and toast.

When the kitchen was clean and Joel had left for school, Lenore took a shower, leisurely scrubbing and lathering herself. After she stepped out, she dried herself with a fresh towel and rubbed lotion into her skin, then dried her long hair and dressed with care. There was always the possibility she could not only talk to her love, but see him as well. It was exactly nine when the doorbell rang. Lenore walked to the front door and opened it to see her smiling friend.

"You look ready for a terrific day! I wonder why?" Leah teased. "The house looks great. You've really been busy." She walked through the house with Lenore following. "Still looks a little generic but you've got to add some personal touches."

"If I can't see Gregor today, maybe we can shop for pink things."

"Pink?"

"Well, not necessarily pink, but girl stuff. Just things for my room right now. I don't know what I want to do with the rest." She walked back to the kitchen and Leah followed. "How 'bout some bacon and toast?"

"Sounds great. We can take it with us. We might want to head for the phone pretty soon, in case the traffic is heavy." She smiled as Lenore put two pieces of wheat bread into the toaster and pushed down the lever. "It's nice you aren't doing anything suspicious by using the public phone."

"What if he didn't get the message or he isn't back? I won't have any way to know."

"Sure, you will. Just call the answering service and see if he picked up his messages. If he hasn't picked them up, you'll know he isn't back yet and you can leave another message. Have him call on Friday afternoon."

"I'm so glad you're here. You always jog my mind back into a logical mode." Lenore handed a plate to Leah.

"I'll just make it into a sandwich and we can be on our way." Leah grabbed a Diet Coke instead of the coffee Lenore offered. They left the house with Lenore driving and their spirits high. They arrived at the phone booth with fifteen minutes to spare.

* * * * *

The sea of cars disguised John Dixon well as he observed the phone booth. He looked like a typical bored husband waiting for a wife to finish shopping. The receiver in his ear was nearly imperceptible, and it would enable him to hear conversations from the phone booth the women now approached.

Lenore Appleby and Leah Chase had not been followed this morning. Knowing their plans, John had simply awaited their arrival. This was as close as he had been to the subjects. He watched the Appleby woman pacing near the phone booth, visibly nervous.

* * * * *

"Will you relax?" Leah scolded. "We're early. He'll call if he got your message."

"I know. I know." Lenore held her stomach as she paced near the phone. "It's just my silly stomach hasn't accepted the idea yet. I'll go nuts if he hasn't gotten the message, because that will mean he isn't back yet, and since I don't know where he went or what kind of danger he could be in—"

"Enough, Lenore! Wait until there's a problem before you start worrying about it. He's as anxious to talk to you as you are to him. He'll call."

An hour later, Lenore's stomach ache was gone, but tears were flowing down her cheeks. The phone hadn't rung.

Leah tried to offer hope. "Okay, call the service and see if he got the message."

Lenore wiped her tears with the cuff of her sleeve, then dug into her purse for a collection of coins. The voice at the answering service cheerfully greeted her.

"Yes, I would like to leave a message for Greg Parish and verify the last message was picked up, please. This is Lenore."

There was a moment of silence as Lenore listened for the answer.

"Mr. Parish picked up his messages this morning as usual. He picks them up every weekday."

"I see." Lenore bit her lower lip and looked at Leah, who's curiosity was building. "Could you have him call this number Friday afternoon? Tell him it's very important. Thank you."

She repeated the number for the pay phone and hung up. Her hand lingered as she stared at the dull black plastic. Leah was at her side.

"What did they say?"

"He picked up his messages this morning."

"Why didn't he call?"

"You tell me."

"I know how your mind works. Just wait until Friday. Maybe he had an urgent meeting or something."

"Leah, it's a little more interesting than that. She said he picks up his messages every morning. She gave no indication there was ever a break in that routine."

"But you know there had to be. He sent money from New York. Maybe he phones from wherever he is for the messages."

"Maybe, but if he's able to phone in for messages, why wasn't he able to phone me, too? I don't like the feeling I'm getting about all of this." Lenore began pacing near the phone again. "For that matter, he could have phoned me at work, like he did before."

"Lenore, there could be a million reasons. Remember when he didn't phone at the lodge until after we had left? If we had just waited a little while longer, you would have talked to him then. If I hadn't gone back for my sunglasses, you would never have known."

"So, I'm just being impatient?"

"Not exactly. I know you're upset, but let's give it another week."

"Okay." Lenore sighed. "Another very long week."

"You'll get through it just fine. Let's go shopping for pink things.

"Girl stuff."

"Right!"

The thought seemed to perk up Lenore a little as they left.

* * * * *

John watched the two women talking. He knew the Agency was responsible for picking up the messages; it had been a simple matter of using a recorded version of Parish's own voice. He was a little surprised the Appleby woman seemed upset.

It was an easy task following the women to the shopping center, where they eventually left with a collection of large bags full of goods. There were no problems following them back to Lenore's house. The women were totally unaware of his presence.

* * * * *

"I nearly choked when the total came to two hundred twelve dollars," Lenore said, juggling packages to unlock the front door.

"You can afford it." Leah relieved Lenore of a package, enabling her to open the door. "Isn't it going to be nice when you come home from work and walk into that room? Your room!"

"Oh, I know I'll enjoy it. I just don't want to get used to spending so much money. I could get into trouble quickly."

"You're in management now. It's going to be a lot easier financially."

They sat in the middle of the living room floor, amidst packages, eating burgers picked up on the way home.

"I still have to watch my money. I've spent a lot of what Gregor sent."

"Yes, but look what you've accomplished. It certainly wasn't frivolous, and neither was this." She gestured at the bags.

Lenore nodded with a sigh, and took another bite of her burger.

After food was consumed, the paper thrown out and hands washed, the women began working on Lenore's room. Lacy edged sheets replaced ordinary white muslin after a quick freshening cycle in the washer and dryer. A satiny white comforter was smoothed into place. Three satiny pillows of mauve, ivory and deep blue-gray were arranged and rearranged until Lenore was satisfied. White curtains over sheers of pale mauve were hung at the window and the blue-gray color was used for tie-backs. Finally, an ocean sunset print was hung above Lenore's bed. Shades of mauve and deep blue-grays throughout the print tied it all together.

"Now, this is the room of a lovely lady. It's beautiful, Lenore."

"I can't believe it. I just love it!" She walked around the bed, smoothing nonexistent wrinkles from the comforter and arranging the pillows one more time. "I wonder if Gregor will ever see it?"

"I'm sure he will, but I doubt if he will notice anything in it except you, Dear."

They heard the front door open and close, and Joel soon appeared at the bedroom door.

"Hey Leah. Wow Mom, you did all this today? Looks cool."

"Thanks. I wanted a totally feminine room. I think I succeeded."

"No doubt about it. When do we get to fix up my room?"

"We'll do something neat for you, but I'm all shopped out for today. Can we wait until tomorrow night?"

There was a slight evidence of disappointment in his voice, but he agreed to wait. However, Lenore knew she would take him to the department store as soon as Leah left. As Joel went to his room, the ladies walked to the front door.

"Have a good week at work and enjoy your room. It's all yours and you deserve it." She hugged Lenore and whispered, "Don't stay up too late fixing Joel's room tonight."

They laughed and said good-bye. Lenore closed the door and walked to Joel's room.

"Joel, let's go see what we can get for your room. I won't enjoy mine until we do yours."

"Really?" He put down the trombone he had been cleaning. "Aren't you too tired?"

"Well, I'm tired, but this may be the only time we have to do it for a while. I'm not saying we can put it together tonight, but we can get the things you like."

Joel jumped to his feet and hugged his mom, before grabbing his jacket. He drove as they returned to the mall and shopped for guy stuff. They chose forest green comforters for the two single waterbeds and matching curtains, with an ivory mini blind. Plaid sheets of forest green and deep burgundy on a white background were found at a second store, along with two floor pillows, one green and one burgundy. A trio of mountain scenes to grace his walls and a great brass study lamp for his desk were found after combing through two more stores. His bedroom would be as fresh and masculine as Lenore's was feminine. Proud of their creative efforts, and exhausted from shopping, they returned home and ordered pizza.

"I'll have Eric come over and help me tomorrow after school. Thanks, Mom." He hugged Lenore. "I've never had such a neat room. I guess you haven't either."

"No, I haven't. We've been spending a lot of money. We are going to have to curb spending or we'll be in trouble." The doorbell rang. "One of the first things we're going to do is stop eating out and having pizza delivered."

Lenore paid the delivery driver and brought the pizza to the dining room table, where Joel had set plates, opened two cans of Diet Coke and filled two glasses with ice.

"I can always go to work after school," he offered.

"Let's hold off on that idea for the time being. Let's set a budget and stick to it."

They ate and talked of Joel's day at school. It was something Lenore loved hearing and Joel loved relating. When the pizza was gone, they cleared the table and washed the dishes. Lenore noticed there was far more fast-food trash than any other as she carried the bag to the garage and into the large plastic trash can. She vowed to make that a most unusual occurrence in the future as she came back into the kitchen.

"I have homework. Not much, but I'd better get at it if I want to watch the game." He walked to his room. "Thanks again, Mom. I love you."

His sincerity warmed Lenore as she went to her room. She admired the transformation before starting to work on the closet. She unpacked a few boxes and put her shoes on the floor of the closet in pairs, ranging from flat to high heels, dressy to casual and boots on the end. It was nearly ten when she was ready to quit.

Joel was watching the action of the Denver Broncos football game when Lenore came in to give him a kiss. He gave her a hug and kiss in return, before focusing back on the screen. He really enjoyed watching his favorite team.

Lenore showered and slipped into a long nightgown, then pulled the covers back on her bed. It was still not quite up to temperature, so the sleeping bag would remain, but it had a whole new personality. She left the light on; if she woke in the night, she wanted to see her new room in all its splendor. The smile on her face remained long after she had fallen asleep.

* * * * *

"Help me! Don't go without me!" She struggled toward the smiling man. Over her shoulder she could see Nick closing the gap between them. The writhing mass underfoot hissed, growing deeper, making it impossible to lift her legs to run.

"He's coming! He's coming closer and they're going to pull me down." She was screaming to be heard but no one could hear her. Gregor continued to smile and hold his hand out to her, but he was drifting further away.

"Please wait! Don't go! Don't leave me here all alone. You Promised! Please!" She started to cry,

"Mom!"

My God, she had forgotten Joel. She had to find him. She looked away from Gregor and began to kick and throw snakes out of her way, no longer concerned for her own safety. She had to save her son.

"Mom, wake up! You're having a nightmare. Mom! Wake up. It's me, Joel!"

181

As Joel shook her awake, Lenore slowly began to realize she was safe in the bedroom, and not in the long, dark corridor. She looked into the concerned eyes of her youngest son and continued to cry.

"Mom, you're okay." He assured her and hugged her. "You woke me yelling. You must have been having some really awful dream."

Lenore sat up in bed. "It was horrible. I'm glad you woke me."

He sat on the edge of the bed next to her and smoothed her hair, a gesture of comfort learned from a loving parent.

"What was it about? Want to talk about it?"

Lenore rubbed both hands over her face and through her hair. "I was running away from Nick, and I had to go through this dark, wet tunnel. It was like a giant sewer or something, and it was filling up with snakes. They were slithering and writhing and hissing all around me. I could see light and was trying to get to it. There was someone ...." She stopped in mid-sentence, remembering who she was trying to reach.

"Who was there? Was there someone trying to help you?"

"I guess that's what I thought. They just kept drifting further away. I couldn't make them understand I was almost there. It was as if they couldn't hear me or didn't know I was in danger. All the time I could hear Nick getting closer and closer. The snakes were just pouring down from everywhere, getting deeper and touching my legs." She shuddered. "Then I had to find you and was digging through all the snakes. Ugh, it was horrible!"

"Sounds like it!" Joel shuddered, too. "Let's go drink a glass of milk or something. How about ice cream? That'll get your mind off it."

Lenore climbed out of bed and grabbed her robe. The lights of Lenore's house came on, one by one, as they walked into the kitchen. It was three in the morning. Joel grabbed the half gallon of Rocky Road ice cream from the freezer and two spoons. They sat at the dining room table and ate directly from the carton, a habit Lenore assured Joel, they really should not get into. Then she got up from the table and got chocolate syrup from the cabinet and whipped cream from the refrigerator. She returned to the table and proceeded to drizzle chocolate into the carton while Joel watched, amazed. She pointed the tip of the whipped cream dispenser toward Joel, who opened his mouth. Lenore filled his mouth with the sweet cream and they both started laughing.

"Now this is the way to get over a bad dream!" She informed the young man wiping whipped cream off his chin and laughing.

＊＊＊＊＊

The agent sitting in a car a block away was on alert. He had watched as all the lights had come on in Lenore Appleby's house.

＊＊＊＊＊

"Mom, are you afraid Nick is going to come after us?"

"Sometimes, I guess. I hope whomever he's been seeing will keep him occupied." She squirted whipped cream on her spoonful of ice cream. "I feel safe here. As safe as we could be, staying in town. I'd move in a heartbeat if you weren't in your senior year. We will anyway if he becomes a real threat."

"Where would we move?"

"Glenwood Springs, of course." She said it before she realized.

Joel laughed. "I should have known. I hope I can at least see the town someday. Maybe if you move there after I get out of school, I can come visit."

"You could go to college there. They have a nice school."

"I can't because I want to go to CSU. I like their music department and the people in it. If you moved there, I'd miss you, but if you were happy and safe, it would make me happy." He squirted more chocolate into the carton of ice cream. "When do you think you'll get a divorce, and do you think you'll ever get married again, Mom?"

She raised her eyebrows and looked at her son. "What makes you ask such a question?"

"I don't know. I start thinking about growing up and leaving home. I hate the thought of you being alone. You're so pretty and neat. I don't see why you can't find someone to spend the rest of your life with who can be good to you. You don't deserve to be alone."

Lenore smiled, opting to change the subject. "Spoken like the true and loyal son you are. Speaking of sons, we need to call Grant. I told him we were planning the move, but I need to let him know we're settled. I'll call from work tomorrow. Any messages?"

"Just tell him his little brother misses him. I wish he was here. It would be a whole lot easier."

"Well, Grant has his own life in Chicago. I wish he was here, too. I miss him dreadfully, but I can't ask him to move. Maybe he'll come for the holidays."

"Hope so." Joel shoved a spoon of ice cream into his mouth.

"Well, I feel a lot better," Lenore said as got up and put her spoon in the sink. "Full, but better. Let's go back to bed. Thank you, Son, for waking me and keeping me company. You're one of a kind and I love you so much."

Joel scooped the last of the ice cream into his mouth, then got up and tossed the empty container into the trash can and put his spoon in the sink. Back in her bedroom, Lenore turned off her light after tucking herself in. She was a little angry about thoughts of Nick daring to penetrate the realm of her beautiful new room. A dreamless sleep enveloped her and carried her to the light of morning.

* * * * *

When the lights went off, the agent eased back into the vinyl seat of the sedan. He could report the incident to Dixon tomorrow.

CHAPTER 19

The workday was well underway when JD called Lenore to the office.

"Have a seat. Did you enjoy your last Monday off?"

She sat in the brown leather chair on the opposite side of his cherry wood desk. "Yes, very productive. Did Leah tell you about my new room?"

"Yep. Said it was pink."

"Actually, just a little mauve here and there. Definitely a girl room."

"Lenore, it's all pink to me." He laughed. "You girls sure know how to fill up a day off together. You're going to have to condense it into Friday afternoons from now on."

"It'll just have to do."

JD took his time and explained some of her new duties. "You'll start doing the books first. I'll have you in here and watch for a couple of times, then you'll take over and I'll watch you. It's a fairly easy system and you'll catch on quickly." He sat a short stack of books in front of her. "Today, you have to read a manual or two and sign some papers."

Before explaining her new pay schedule and benefits, he walked to the door and banged it with his fist. "Ow!" could be heard from the other side of the door.

"Get away from the door, Royce."

"You could have just said it."

"Right. Go find something to do." He shook his head and laughed. "Now we can discuss your new pay and benefits."

There were papers to sign and papers to read. Lenore would be reading manuals and eventually attending management training courses given by the home office. She looked up from her reading and smiled. "I can hardly believe it. Things are turning out really good, aren't they?"

"You're sure a different lady than the one with the swollen lip a few weeks ago. Do a good job, which I know you will, and you'll have your own store in a couple of years. I'll help all I can."

"Thank you could never encompass how much I appreciate all you and Leah have done for me. I'll work hard and make you proud you gave me the opportunity."

"I know you will. That's why I did it. Now get out there and tell Royce to get away from the door again. I can't figure out why he's so nosy!"

"I heard that!" The voice said from the other side of the door and they had to laugh.

Lenore opened the door to receive a pat on the back and a handshake from Royce.

"I guess since you're formally an assistant manager, I probably shouldn't hug you."

"I don't care if she's just been declared the President, I'm still gonna hug my Lenore." Rusty ambled toward the office. "Congratulations. I know you're going to do them a fine job."

There was no jealousy from her friends. They both had different goals than a career with the store. Rusty was not far from retiring to his ranch, and Royce wanted to make his part-time disc-jockey gig a permanent career someday.

* * * * *

She told Royce to go ahead and leave at closing time because she was going to be talking to her son in Chicago. It was nearly six when Lenore walked out and locked the back door, still smiling from her conversation with Grant and knowing he was planning to come for Christmas.

In the twilight she could see someone standing near her car and realized it was Nick. She stopped dead in her tracks and considered turning back to the safety of the store.

"I'm not going to hurt you, Lenore. I just want to talk a minute."

"What do you want, Nick?" She was shaking and wishing the parking area wasn't so secluded.

He took a few steps closer, and she noticed he was wearing his work clothes. He had just gotten back from his trip, so maybe he was still sober. He stopped, leaving six feet between them, but he was still between her and the car.

"You moved out," he said, quietly.

She didn't reply.

"Are you and Joel okay? Do you need anything?"

His concern confused Lenore, and she eyed him suspiciously. He was looking down, and had his hands jammed into jacket pockets.

"I did a lot of thinking on this trip. When I called and you didn't answer, I guess I knew. There's nothing I can do to make it right again, is there?"

Lenore spoke quietly. "Nick, if I had thought there was a chance, I wouldn't have left. You made sure all the love I ever had for you was dead, then you scared the hell out of me."

"I know I fucked up big time, and you had every right to move. Just let me know if there's anything I can do for you and Joel."

"You can give me an uncontested divorce," Lenore replied. "That's all I want from you. I don't want you to bother me or my son ever again."

"I understand. Tell the boys I'm sorry I hurt you." He turned and walked toward the alley, stopped and turned back to her. "Believe it or not, Lenore, I am sorry."

Lenore got into her car and locked the doors. "Yes, right now, you're sorry," she mumbled. She turned in the opposite direction down the alley from where Nick walked. She watched headlights in her rear-view mirror as she took a long route home. One vehicle she thought was following, eventually turned off. It was after seven when she pulled into the drive.

* * * * *

"Mom, where were you?" Joel met her at the car. "I've been calling the store since six. Is everything okay?"

"Yes, everything is okay." Lenore got out and gave Joel a hug. "Sorry to worry you. Nick was waiting for me when I left work. We talked for a minute, then I took the long way home; I didn't want to take a chance he might follow. He says he's sorry, but then he was sober, too. I don't trust him."

They walked together into the house.

"He didn't try to hurt you, did he?"

"No. He was quiet and said he had done a lot of thinking."

"Well, I hope the whole situation haunts him." Joel locked the door and looked out the tiny peep hole. "I hope he doesn't find out where we live."

"If he wants to find out, I'm sure he will. I just hope he isn't interested." She held onto her son and hugged him for a long time. She could hear his heart beating, and released him only after she heard the beats slow to a normal pace.

Lenore started to relate her conversation with Grant and stopped. "You said you had tried to call the store. Does that mean our new phone service is working?"

Joel laughed. "Yes, that was what I was trying to call you about, so you could call from here. First the line was busy, then there was no answer."

"That's good news! We're connected to the rest of the world now."

Joel gave her their new number, and they both made note of who they were going to call first. Joel admitted he made one quick call to Kim before trying to call Lenore. She assured him she would have done the same thing.

She related her conversation with Grant and Joel was excited to hear he would have his big brother with them for Christmas. He was further elated when Lenore told him the details of her promotion.

"You mean you could have a store of your own, like JD, in a couple of years?"

"Yes, if I work very hard and it's what I want." She was pleased with his enthusiasm.

"Do they have a store in Glenwood Springs?"

"No." She laughed. "At least not yet. I can always hope they decide to put one there, can't I? If not, it will always be my vacation spot."

"Good attitude, Mom. I'm so proud of you."

"Today was reading manuals and signing papers. Tomorrow I start learning the books. No more Mondays off." She opened the refrigerator, looking for a quick dinner idea.

"Bummer!" Joel held onto the door, joining Lenore in the quest. "You'll miss it, but I'll bet not half as much as Leah."

"I'll still have one afternoon off, which I decided to keep on Friday." She pulled a small package of ground beef from the refrigerator and let Joel close the door. "It'll just have to be enough for both of us."

"I'll do all I can to help around the house. I promise!" They both sniffed the meat after Lenore opened the package and agreed it was still fresh.

"I know you will. Let's fix some decent dinner tonight."

They worked together in the kitchen talking and planning while they prepared dinner. Lenore knew in her heart things were getting better, but uneasiness about Nick and haunting questions about Gregor shrouded her happiness like a thick veil.

* * * * *

Between learning new duties at work, making supper at night for her son and herself, and getting busy emptying the last of the boxes, the week was a blur for Lenore. However, Friday yielded no phone call. It had been more difficult because she had been alone all afternoon. Leah's grandsons needed vaccinations, necessitating a trip to the doctor's office instead of her usual Friday afternoon with Lenore.

The new duties at work were interesting and time consuming. The small amount of time she spent on the sales floor was profitable, and an enjoyable break from sitting at a desk. JD was a patient teacher and by the end of the week felt Lenore no longer needed to have him by her side when she did the books. Figures balanced and were legibly recorded. She was getting faster with familiarity of the task and by Saturday, was able to leave by six instead of seven.

The phone was ringing when Lenore walked in the front door at home. She could hear the shower running and ran to answer the phone, kicking off her shoes on the way.

"Hello," she answered, a little winded.

Leah's voice greeted Lenore. "Hi, it's me."

"Hello, me!" She laughed. "Did JD tell you what a spectacular job I'm doing? Look how early I'm home tonight!"

"He never tells me anything." Lenore heard a sigh from her friend. "I sent him to the store when he got home, and Shelly has taken the boys to a birthday party. Now tell me about the phone call."

"You mean the lack of one? I'm horribly discouraged, but I have to think about my job too much to worry about a phone call." Lenore reached into the refrigerator and grabbed a Diet Coke.

"What about Monday?"

"I have to work." She popped the top and took a sip. "If you want to go, you can see if he calls."

"Want to make plans with him?"

"Whatever. You make the plans. Friday is best." She sat the can down on the counter and leaned on her elbow. "Leah, we both know this is a wasted effort. He won't call."

"There you go with the negative attitude again. If he doesn't call Monday, I'll leave a message for him to call on Friday. How's that?"

"I guess it's okay. Leave this number for him to call."

"Your home phone number? He said to use a public phone. He isn't going to like it."

Lenore rolled her eyes and ran her fingers through her hair.

"Leah, if it's a problem, I'll handle it. This is my own personal number. What could be wrong with that?"

"He was pretty explicit about it, Lenore."

"He didn't want to call work or the house when I was still at Nick's. I can't see why it would be a problem. Joel won't be here. It doesn't make any difference, because he just isn't going to call."

Leah started to protest further, but Lenore cut her off.

"Joel just finished his shower. Let's change the subject. Just leave this number with the service, okay?"

"Okay, but I don't feel good about it. JD just got back. Better go. Congratulations on getting through the first week of management training. I'm proud of you and so is your boss! Have a good Sunday and I'll talk to you Monday, probably."

"Okay, thanks Leah."

Lenore hung up the phone. After walking to the closet and carefully placing her jacket on a hanger, she carried her purse and shoes to the bedroom. The smell of soap and shampoo floated on humid air in the hallway.

"I'm home, Joel!"

"Who called?" He stuck his head in the door to Lenore's room on his way from the bathroom.

"It was Leah. Where are you going tonight?"

"Got a date with Kim. We're going to a movie." He was drying his hair with a towel. "Got any plans for yourself?"

"Just getting out of these clothes and into some sweats. I'll probably just vegetate in front of the television, unless I get bored enough to unpack the last few boxes."

He continued to his room. "Why don't you come with us to the movie?"

"Are you nuts?" She pulled on a pair of comfy pants and a T-shirt. "No one takes their mom on a date with them."

"We could bring you home after the movie, before we go check out the dance."

"Thanks for the thought, but I really don't want to. I'm tired and just need to put my feet up and relax." She chuckled. "Most sons would rather die than be seen socially with their mother in public."

"Most sons don't have a mom they enjoy being around. All my friends think you're the neatest mom in the world. Kim thinks so, too."

They passed in the hallway, Lenore on her way to the living room and Joel heading for the bathroom mirror.

"I'm very flattered, but I'm still going to stay home tonight. Feels like a bubble bath kind of night, too."

"Okay, want me to get you a burger or something?" Joel yelled from the bathroom.

"No thanks. I'll forage," Lenore called from the living room. "Need to take the car?"

"No, Kim's already on the way."

Lenore walked back to the door of the bathroom, and rested her head on the door frame. "Not too late, okay?"

"One?" He asked, smiling his most sincere smile.

She considered his request, then agreed. With a twenty pressed into his hand as he walked out the door, she found the ensuing quiet deafening. She tuned the radio to relaxing music and walked to the kitchen. The refrigerator yielded makings for a salad and she took time to make it look as appetizing as possible.

Lenore set the table with a nice mat and a candle. After making herself comfortable in the rattan chair, she poured a glass of Chardonnay and took a sip. It wasn't an expensive wine, but Royce's house warming gift was palatable. She sorted through mail and enjoyed the leisurely atmosphere of being home alone.

When the kitchen was once again clean, Lenore took a glass of wine to the living room. She turned off all the lights in the house and put a blanket on the floor near the patio door. The foothills were illuminated in the moon's glow, casting bluish highlights among shadowy outlines. She sat down and hugged her knees, sipped wine and stared into the night.

Spot soon appeared and curled up on a corner of the blanket, delighted with her owner's nocturnal preferences. She stared through tiny slits at the cloudless night, occasionally purring or grooming a stray whisker.

The foothills became clouded as tears filled Lenore's eyes.

"Gregor, if you're out there somewhere, come back to me. You promised. Don't hurt me this way. I need you so very much."

The words seemed consumed by the walls. Lenore stood and opened the patio doors, stepping out into the chill. Again, she spoke, certain her words could reach their destination on the winds of night, reach the ears of her love, wherever he was.

"Gregor, I'm free. I'm safe. You helped me do this. Please come back to me. We can begin our life together now. I'm waiting for you." Then in a whisper, "I'll always wait for you."

The faint hum of traffic on distant highways echoed back. It was a lonely sound, and the windless night air chilled Lenore. She stood for a while and listened to the night. It offered no comfort.

She returned to the warmth of the living room and closed the heavy glass door, then walked in darkness to the bathroom. She swallowed the last of the wine in her glass, then took a steaming shower instead of a bubble bath and went to bed, falling into a dreamless sleep until well past dawn.

* * * * *

Sunday's activities were highlighted by an afternoon with Joel and several of his friends in front of the television, noisily cheering the Denver Broncos to victory. Lenore provided refreshments and was delighted when they sat her in the living room, and four, less-than-domestic young men, washed, wiped and put things back in order.

"We're going for pizza. Come with us." Joel's friend Eric said.

"Yeah, Mom."

"Come on, Ms. Appleby. You'll have fun." The four young men smiled, waiting for an answer.

"I promise I'll go next time. I have to get some ironing done tonight." She smiled. "You guys have fun, but remember tomorrow is a school day ... no late nights!"

Noisy thanks accompanied the exit of the four high school seniors and Lenore closed the door behind them. She busied herself with ironing and organizing for the coming week. She listened to the radio, dancing and singing to familiar oldies, while pushing away thoughts of the Russian as quickly as they edged into her consciousness.

She was putting the ironing board away when Joel opened the front door. They sat up and talked until nearly ten-thirty, when Lenore's yawns began to supersede conversation. She gave him a kiss on the cheek, then stood up. "Good night Son," Lenore said, hoping that dreams of Gregor would not invade her sleep.

CHAPTER 20

"No sir, no leads. We still have the Appleby woman under surveillance," John Dixon said as sat at his desk, tapping a pen on the polished surface. He had the Director on the other end of the line and was getting pressured to get answers, answers where none were to be found. "She still calls and leaves messages. If she knows anything, she's hiding it pretty well."

John shifted in the cushioned black leather chair. "We've been the only ones picking up messages at his service. He hasn't contacted anyone we're aware of. The people at his house are concerned, but say he left them with enough money to take care of things. I'm not sure where to go from here."

"Dixon, I want you to make contact with Lenore Appleby," the Director instructed. "I want a face-to-face confrontation. Talk to her and find out what she does know. If nothing else, make her uncomfortable enough to complain to Parish, just in case she does know where he is."

"What if she's innocent? What if he simply used her?"

"Do you believe that's the case, Dixon?"

John thought about it for a few seconds. "It would be out of character, but then everything he did before his disappearance was out of character. I just don't know."

"Then find out, Dixon. Use whatever resources or tactics you think necessary. We just don't need a former KGB agent wandering around this country unchecked. He had to leave a clue somewhere; your job is to find it."

John hung up the phone and threw the pen across the room. Leah Chase had been the one at the phone booth Monday. She had called the service and left a message for Parish to call Lenore's home number. That was something new. He would wait to see what happened today, then make plans. If the Appleby woman wasn't planning to hear from him again, she wouldn't be leaving messages. Maybe.

Maybe it was the hesitation in her voice when she learned he picked up his messages on schedule. Maybe it was the tears after last Friday's call ended. She had been alone, and only after she had returned to her car had she cried.

Dixon got up from his desk and found the pen which had landed behind a chair. He thought of the way her hair moved and the long, self-assured strides she took wherever she went. He shook off the thought and went back to his desk, dropping the pen in a drawer. He opened the folder laying squarely in the middle of his desk. The smiling faces of Lenore Appleby and Leah Chase stared back at him. He sat down, took the picture in his hand and leaned back in his chair.

Maybe she was as confused and surprised with Greg's disappearance as he was. He would soon be sitting in a car, monitoring calls at Lenore's home today. If the Russian contacted her at the appointed time, John would hear it. The Agency had a bit of influence in getting the phone hooked-up as quickly as it did. In fact, the Agency did all the work, including installing listening devices. If there was no call, John would make plans to contact Lenore in person.

He placed the picture back into the folder, and closed the cover. He got up from his desk, took a sport coat off the back of his chair and put it on, then walked out the front door, ready for his drive to Fort Collins.

* * * * *

Her fellow workers attributed Lenore's subdued attitude to the pressures of her new position, and the reality of being on her own again. Lenore offered no further explanation, and accepted words of encouragement and advice without protest, assuring all she would be fine. When Friday finally arrived, Lenore was ready for a break in her routine. The hope of a phone call was not far from her thoughts as she left the store. Leah would meet her at the house to await the call, or comfort her through another disappointment.

When the phone rang at one-fifteen, Lenore jumped up from her chair and stared at it. Leah finally yelled, "Answer it, Lenore! It's not going to bite you."

"What if it isn't him?" Lenore didn't move.

"What if it is? If you don't pick up that phone, I'm going to smack you about the head and shoulders."

Lenore took the receiver in her hand and answered a cautious, "Hello."

A man's voice proceeded to launch into a sales pitch for a product Lenore would never know about. She hung the phone up and turned to Leah.

"Wasn't him." She said and sighed.

"It's still early ... he might call."

"Leah, the man knows how to tell time." She picked up lunch dishes and walked into the kitchen. "I'll wait until one-thirty, then we're out of here."

"Are you sure, Lenore?"

"I'm certainly not going to waste my half-day off sitting here waiting for a call that will never come. Want another Diet Coke?"

She didn't wait for Leah's reply and got one for her anyway. "Let's go to the lake and sit on our big rock. We can stop and get some snacks. It's warm enough, don't you think?" Her voice sounded entirely too cheerful.

Leah agreed the conditions were perfect for an autumn day at the lake, knowing Lenore was trying to bury hurt feelings, instead of voicing them. She also knew the afternoon adventure would give her opportunity to force those feeling to the surface, whether Lenore wanted to or not. There were no answers to why Gregor did not call, and the questions would be painful.

* * * * *

"Hold the sack and hand it to me when I get up top. Here, I'll wrap the blanket around my shoulders while I climb."

Leah scurried up the side of the massive stone and accepted the plastic bag from Lenore, who climbed with a little less exuberance than the petite blonde. The blanket was spread out, partially defeating the chill on their granite perch. They drank in the fresh air and basked in the warmth of sunlight, as they snacked on M&M plain candies, cheese, red licorice, pretzels and their usual Diet Coke.

"What an excellent idea," Leah said. "Not a cloud in the sky and the breeze actually feels warm. I wonder when we'll get our first measurable snow this year?"

"Mmmm, who can think of snow when it's this beautiful? I love Colorado. This is the only place I've ever been where I didn't want to be somewhere else." Lenore leaned back on her elbows, allowing the sun to warm her face. "You ever want to be somewhere else, Leah?"

Leah sat cross-legged beside Lenore, nibbling on a pretzel. "Oh, when we first moved here from Texas, I wanted to be back there. We had a pretty home and Shelly was little and innocent and happy. We moved here and she got older and her problems got older, too. Shelly managed to give birth to two problems."

"She'll get it all figured out one of these days. Sometimes it takes a while. She's a good person, just has lousy taste in mates. I can certainly see how that can happen." Lenore looked over the tops of her sunglasses at Leah. "I can also tell her she could make it without them, but I doubt she would listen to me."

"No, probably not. I have dreams of her worthless boyfriend, who keeps giving her those babies, standing over her bloody body with a knife in his hand. She's looking up at me, saying he didn't mean it and she still loves him."

Lenore sat up, frowning. "You really think she's that self-destructive?"

"Yes, I do. I'm tired of trying to make her see what she's doing to herself. Right now, I'm trying to make her see what she's doing to those two babies. They're so little and they don't understand the fighting and the disrupted lifestyle. I feel like JD and I are the only stable influences in their lives. Now she wants to move back in with him and take the boys with her. I'm so afraid they'll get hurt."

Lenore rubbed Leah's back. "You can't raise them for her. Maybe if she has the full responsibility, she'll wake up and make it work, or get away from him once and for all."

"At the cost of the boys?"

"No, we would never let it get that far. Just do a lot of praying about it. I think it'd help." Lenore looked out at the lake. "Sure couldn't hurt." She sighed. "I think He answers prayers for some people."

"Lenore, He answers all. We just don't always get the answers we think we should. You got out of Nick's house and got a promotion, didn't you?"

"Yes, I tend to forget the good parts sometimes. I apologize for being too wrapped up in my own little world, I've not been paying attention to what you're going through with Shelly." She shook her head. "That's real."

"I've got JD to soldier through it all with." She squeezed Lenore's hand. "You've got me. It hurts a lot, doesn't it? That's real, too."

Lenore looked away, surveying the landscape. She didn't want to give in to the emotions so near the surface. Leah wasn't going to drop the subject.

"Might help to talk about it, Lenore. There could be reasons why he hasn't called."

"Please don't make me face it yet," she whispered.

"There may be nothing to face other than bad timing. Maybe he won't get the message about today until next Monday."

Lenore's voice was harsh. "Can't you see it's not going to happen? He isn't going to call. He's just a memory now." She took a deep breath and spoke quietly again. "He gave me the motivation and strength to get out of the situation I was in and now it's done. I'm safe and sound and he's history."

"Then why did he send you the money to get out, if he didn't plan to see you again?"

Lenore shook her head and sighed impatiently. "Maybe he's just an incredibly rich Good Samaritan, or maybe it was motivated by guilt. We'll never know."

"I can't believe it, Lenore. Think of all he said to you. Think of his eyes."

Lenore pressed her palms to her temples, as if to prevent the vision. "I was wrong, that's all. I saw what I needed to see and he said all the right things and I was so vulnerable, it worked. He screwed me in a couple of different senses of the word!"

"Lenore!" Leah smacked her on the shoulder.

"I'm not really complaining. It was excellent." Her laugh was hollow. Then she shook her head again. "What a fool I was."

"You weren't a fool, Lenore. You just mustn't feel that way. I can't believe we could both be so wrong about a person."

They were both quiet for a while, letting the soft breeze clear the air between them.

"Maybe, if he really isn't coming back into your life, you could try to see it in a positive way. He showed you what a truly special person you are and how you should be treated. You'll never settle for someone like Nick again."

"Correction!" Lenore stabbed a finger into the air. "There will never be another chance to find out. If I could be so totally wrong about Gregor, I can never trust my instincts again." She waved her hand as if brushing away a pesky insect. "I'll never let anyone get that close again."

"Now, that's the talk of a fool. You have to let this be a growing experience for you." Leah took her friend's hand and held it, patting the clenched fist until it relaxed. "I know this hurts awfully bad and it kills me to see you hurt. I'd make it better if I could."

Lenore finally looked into the eyes of her best friend and let tears flow from her dark green eyes.

"Oh God, Leah. It hurts so bad. I wanted it to be true. I needed it to be true. How could I have been so wrong?" A sob racked through her body. "I can't even thank him for the help. I can't even say good-bye."

Leah put her hand on Lenore's chin, holding her gaze. "We may never know what happened, but we're not going to let it defeat you. You're starting out in a new direction. Joel's counting on you. JD's counting on you, too. You have too much to offer and too many good things to look forward to. Now go ahead and cry and curse or whatever you need to do, but let's get him out of your system and go on from here. If he was this big a phony, he certainly doesn't deserve any more tears from you!"

Lenore sniffled and managed a little smile. Leah handed her a tissue from her mysterious, unending supply. Lenore hugged Leah, then stood. Leah watched her stand and frowned.

"What are you doing?"

"You said to get him out of my system, didn't you?"

Leah stood and cautiously agreed.

"Well then, here's to the Russian!"

With both arms outstretched and fingers curled into an obscene gesture, Lenore slowly pirouetted on the rock necessitating a ducking action from Leah.

"I hope you're plagued with nightmares about how you broke my heart. If I ever see you again, I will pretend we never met or I'll slap your face and spit in your eye!" Lenore yelled to the wind.

Leah cupped her hands to her mouth and screamed, "And I'll sock you in the kneecap or a little higher and tell you what a mean person you really are!"

Lenore started laughing when the petite blonde began her own pirouette. "You know those tiny little fingers could never really offend anyone." She giggled.

"They may be little, but the feeling behind them is monstrously huge!"

They laughed and danced around the rock, gesturing and yelling until they collapsed on the blanket out of breath, out of energy and finally out of tears.

* * * * *

A half mile away, partially hidden by the landscape, John Dixon lowered his binoculars and stared at them as if mistrusting what they had so clearly brought into view. He put them slowly back to his eyes.

* * * * *

The two friends sat looking out at the lake until their breathing returned to normal. Lenore stared at the spot near the lake's edge where she had heard promises from Gregor. Her smile faded, and the green eyes glazed over, unblinking. Eventually, Leah's eyes focused on the same spot.

Lenore and Leah knew the pain and memories of dreams hoped for were not erased so quickly. It would be a healing process. Lenore would bury herself in work and focus on raising Joel. Leah would be there with love and encouragement.

The bouquet of dead flowers they later sent to Gregor, in care of his answering service, was an especially cleansing gesture.

CHAPTER 21

With Thanksgiving behind her and the Christmas season in full swing, Lenore was busy. Although thoughts of Gregor intruded at the most inopportune times, she never spoke of him to Leah.

John Dixon had decided to wait until after Thanksgiving and the ensuing retail rush before making contact with Lenore. It was two weeks before Christmas, when Lenore walked out of the office and was directed to the men's side of the store to assist a customer who had requested her. She nodded her acknowledgment to Rusty, and rounded the corner to see a man standing with his back to her, looking at a display of hiking boots. He didn't look like anyone she recognized, or hoped to.

She stifled a sigh and painted on a smile. "Did you need some assistance, Sir? I'm Lenore."

Her smile was immediately erased when he turned to face her. His assessing gaze made her feel uncomfortable.

"Yes, Lenore." He held the sample boot out to her. "I'd like to see these in a size ten. Could you get those for me?"

"I'll be happy to. Please have a seat and I'll bring them right out."

She was thankful the hiking boots were in the back of the store. Out of sight from the customer, Lenore leaned her head against a wall and silently cursed herself for letting thoughts of Gregor get control. She couldn't imagine why this man had requested her. Maybe he was a referral from one of her regular customers. When she returned, a smile was firmly in place. Joel called it her phony, professional smile, but it was the best she could offer.

He spoke without looking at her, examining the boots before handing them back to her.

"You must enjoy your work."

"As a matter of fact, I do." *Odd thing to say,* she thought. "I'm one of the lucky people who looks forward to getting up and going to work in the morning."

"I could tell. I'll bet you're a morning person." He smiled a phony professional smile of his own. "Am I right?"

Was he coming on to her? She frowned slightly. No, he was probably just conversing with a shoe clerk.

"Yes, I'm a morning person. Let's put the other boot on and you can walk around the store a bit." She launched into an informative and enthusiastic sales pitch as she laced the other boot.

"You'll find them a little stiff at first, but they take very little breaking-in. You'll be pleased with the stability and workmanship. Gore-Tex is not only a waterproof material, but it breathes, making the boot very comfortable and light weight."

He walked only a few paces, then sat back down in front of Lenore.

"You're quite a sales person. I'll take them." He smiled. Again. "Would you consider having a cup of coffee with me after work tonight?"

He continued to smile, but she didn't smile back. Something in his eyes belied his sincerity.

"No thank you." Lenore said as she loosened the laces on the boots. "If that's part of the deal, I guess I just lost a sale, and you're going to miss out on a terrific pair of boots."

"I'll take the boots, Lenore, but I think you should reconsider my offer. There's the matter of a certain person we're both acquainted with, and I would like to talk to you about him; a certain fellow you met in Glenwood Springs the last weekend of September. You get off at five-thirty if I'm not mistaken."

Lenore looked past the man in front of her to where Rusty was busily wrapping up a sale at the counter, out of earshot. She felt sick and a chill made her shudder. She leveled her eyes at him and spoke quietly.

"Who are you?"

"Let's just say I'm your date after work tonight. I'll be waiting at the coffee shop on College Avenue. Don't disappoint me." He tied his own shoe laces while Lenore stared at him. "I wouldn't discuss this with anyone right now, particularly your friend, Leah. We may want to talk to her, too." He stood up. "Now, shall we go to the counter and ring up the sale? That will be cash, and I need a receipt."

Lenore put the boots back into the oversized box and closed the lid as she stood. He bowed ever so slightly and allowed her to proceed him to the register. Rusty continued to converse with a longtime customer as Lenore nervously wrote up the sale. She handed the receipt and change to the man who slipped it into an inside pocket. He smiled again at her.

"I'll see you later, Lenore. Thank you very much for your help. They have quite a treasure in you. I trust they appreciate your work. By the way, my name is John."

Rusty and his customer fell silent as they caught the end of John's statement. They watched as he carried the expensive boots to the door and turned once again to smile at Lenore before exiting.

* * * * *

"What was that all about?" Rusty asked, after his satisfied customer left the store.

"He invited me for a cup of coffee after work."

"He did, huh? You aren't going, are you?"

"Sure. It's just a cup of coffee." She hoped she sounded convincing. She was shaking inside and excused herself before they could notice her hands were shaking as well. "I need to finish those reports. Call me again if you need me."

Lenore ignored Rusty's frown as she turned to walk back to the office.

Over the next hour, the numbers blurred together on the ledger and she pressed the eraser end of the pencil to her lips as thoughts raced through her mind. Finally, she gave up and looked at the phone. She wanted to call Leah, but the words John said echoed in her mind. JD returned from the bank to find his star employee in a fog.

"Having a problem?"

"No, just having a little trouble concentrating right now." She smiled at her boss. "I think I'll go to the freight room and empty a few boxes, if you don't mind."

"Sure, go ahead. I can finish up here. Now don't go lifting anything heavy. You call Rusty or me to do it. Royce is going to appreciate your help; he won't have so much to catch up on tomorrow."

JD took the seat Lenore vacated as she left the office. She found the physical labor of the freight room a much-needed distraction. It was after five when she considered the job complete and returned to the sales floor. There were no customers in the store, and JD stood at the front counter with Rusty. She tossed the wet paper towel she had used to dry her hands to Rusty, who caught and deposited it into the trash. JD was smiling.

"Rusty tells me you have a date after work tonight. Is that right?"

She forced a smile and continued toward the duo. "Just coffee. Sounded safe and he was nice."

"I didn't care for the looks of the guy myself," The older man noted.

"Rusty, you sound like a father. No one is good enough for Lenore as far as you're concerned." JD patted Rusty on the back. "I think it's a good idea. She needs to get out a little." He turned to Lenore. "Just in case though, you drive your car there and park it in front of the café. I don't want you walking down the dark alley alone later tonight."

Lenore shook her head and laughed. "You two amaze me. Here I am, forty-one years old and you two act like I'm sixteen going out on my first date. I'll be fine. I'll park in front, and if he's weirdo I'll leave and drive directly to the police station, okay? Now, can I go, Dads?"

They were laughing as the last customer of the day walked through the doors and JD greeted her. Lenore and Rusty busied themselves with checking displays and straightening boxes. At five-thirty, the doors were locked, and Lenore was able to leave. JD had offered to do the book work, and Lenore didn't argue.

A few minutes later, she parked directly in front of the small café, and waited to check out the clientele. She didn't recognize anyone but John, who sat in a far booth, watching the door. She turned off the engine and took a deep breath before leaving the car to enter the brightly lit business. He stood when she entered.

"Glad you decided to make it, Lenore. Please sit down. I took the liberty of ordering our coffee."

She sat down on the opposite side of the table, ignoring his efforts to help her with her coat, and left it on. She had no intention of staying long. When he sat down, she focused on his eyes as she spoke. She wanted his full attention.

"What's this all about?"

"Well, looks like we're going to dispense with the small talk." His smile disappeared. "We've lost track of your friend. We don't like that. You seem to be the last person to have seen him."

Lenore frowned. "Who are you, and who is the 'we' you refer to?"

John took a small leather case from an inside pocket and opened it, showing it to Lenore. "We are on your side … but he may not be. That's why it's important we locate him."

She looked at the insignia of The Central Intelligence Agency of the United States of America, and photo ID, and back into the face of John M. Dixon III, Agent. "Because he's Russian, right?" Her heartbeat quickened and pain gripped her abdomen.

He answered quietly after looking around. "It's because he's a former Soviet operative who defected a couple of years ago. We've kept close tabs on him. We thought it necessary, given his former profession."

"Damn it! Leah was right again," she mumbled.

"What was that?"

"Nothing." She shook her head, then tilted forward and frowned. "What has this to do with me? I told you at the store, I haven't seen him in quite some time and I don't expect to."

"Your phone messages would say you thought otherwise."

Lenore sat back in her seat and her eyes widened as he continued.

"We know you've left your home number for him to call, which you wouldn't do unless you expected to hear from him. I need to know, Lenore, just when you last saw him and what was said."

Lenore considered telling him it was personal, but cold blue eyes convinced her to cooperate. She sipped the tasteless coffee and looked around the room.

"Don't worry, Lenore, no one can hear us. Just smile when the waitress comes back for refills. We're on a date, remember?" His thoughts echoed what the director said and professionalism was not going to work with Lenore.

She sat her coffee cup down and glared at the man across the table from her.

"I may cooperate with you, sir, but I won't pretend to enjoy it. Look, I was taken-in by this Russian, or whatever he is. He didn't tell me about what he did or who he was. I saw him last, two days after I returned from Glenwood Springs. At that time, he said he would be gone for a couple of weeks, but if I called and left a number for him, he would call me when he returned." She shrugged her shoulders. "He hasn't returned any of my calls, but he's picked up the messages. That tells me he just isn't interested."

"Well, we're the ones who've picked up his messages."

"Great." Lenore massaged her forehead.

"Do you know where he was going?"

"I asked, but he wouldn't tell me. May I go, now?" She pushed the coffee cup away and picked up her purse.

Dixon knew he would have to keep her attention.

"You're very lucky to be getting out of your marriage to Nick Carlson. It's no good being married to an abusive alcoholic, is it?"

She didn't whisper. "What's going on here? How do you know all this?" She dropped her purse back to the seat, leaned forward and spoke quietly. "Have I been under surveillance?"

"Just as a precaution, I assure you. We like to know with whom Greg is associating. Funny, you're the first woman he's seemed serious about. You must be something special."

Lenore felt violated. She glared at her table partner and spoke between clenched teeth. "I'm not enjoying this conversation, John, if that's even your real name. I think our little date is over!"

She slid on the vinyl seat toward the aisle as John put his hand on her arm.

"Please stay, Lenore. I apologize for my rudeness. I'll try to be a bit more refined in my remarks, but it's imperative we have your cooperation."

It was not as much a request as an order. She stared at the face across from her and remained in the booth. The coffee cup shook a little as she brought it to her lips.

"Lenore, Greg could be considered a very dangerous man in some circles. He's very well-educated and speaks several languages fluently. He's been trained by the Soviet's best to do their bidding. We were quite surprised when he decided to defect. To take such a notorious adversary into this country and let him have the run of the land, so to speak, would be foolish on our part. He was free to do as he pleased, but we made sure we kept track of him. It could well have been a plot to gain our confidence and use it to destroy us."

John continued relating the facts about Greg Parish to Lenore, as if reading a well-memorized dossier.

"He convinced us he was tired of being a machine for the Communists. He wanted to be just a regular guy. He refused our offers of counter-intelligence. For the last fifteen months he's been in Colorado. He lives in Denver part of the time and works for an electronics firm. He has a home near Glenwood Springs and spends as much time as possible in that area. Says it reminds him of his childhood. His former profession was, evidently, pretty lucrative and he has a substantial savings account. Which brings me to another question: Did he assist you financially in your recent move?"

Lenore frowned and took a minute to answer. "Why do you ask?"

"Come on, Lenore. We know what your finances were and are. You dropped a couple thousand getting out. It had to come from somewhere."

She knew her attempts to evade were useless. She could feel the muscles tighten in her neck. She rubbed them and closed her eyes.

"Yes, I got help. I assume it was from Gregor. I can't say for sure. There was no return address and no words to go along with the money." She lied only a little. "I suppose I have to pay taxes on it now, right?"

He smiled. "Not my department. That's up to you. Was there a post mark?"

"New York. Four envelopes, all with New York post marks."

"We'd like to examine those envelopes."

Lenore winced. "Actually, they're in about a million pieces and hopefully bio-degrading somewhere in the world. Sorry."

"When did you get them?"

"About a week before I moved out. A week after I saw Gregor." She tapped the cup with her nail. "Is that his real name?"

"His name is Gregor Parishnikov. He goes by Greg Parish."

Lenore nodded and spoke quietly. "Easier to pronounce."

His laugh took Lenore by surprise. She didn't know if it was the fact he actually laughed, or the human quality it suddenly imparted. She smiled back.

"Lenore, I'm not here to disrupt your life. I hope you don't think I am. Maybe I was a little rude in the beginning, but I had to approach you as a hostile informant. I think Greg really cares about you. That may or may not comfort you at this point. I've kept track of him off and on for two years. You're honestly the only one he's seemed to care about. That's why we thought it important to watch you."

He genuinely smiled. "I promise we will try to stay out of your personal life, but you will be watched. Not only in the hopes of finding where our friend has gone, but for your safety as well."

Lenore raised her eyebrows. "You think Gregor would try to hurt me?"

"Far from it. Although he poisoned one of our agents in order to see you, I don't think he would—"

Lenore had a look of horror on her face. "He killed someone?"

"No, no!" John chuckled. "The agent had a dose of food poisoning and spent a couple of days in the bathroom. Our concern for you is, anyone who wanted to hurt him could do it through you, if they know about you. Our guess is they probably do. It all hinges on whether or not he's still in this country. I hope for your sake, and ours, he's just laying low for a while to get out of the spotlight."

Lenore swirled the last of the coffee in her cup. "You think they might know about me because I gave my personal number to the answering service?"

"Exactly."

It wasn't what she wanted to hear. "John, will you do me a favor?"

He answered before she made the request. "We'll be in touch. I'll personally let you know if we hear from him. I know it's useless to tell you not to talk to Leah, so if she can shed any light on this situation, give her this number to call." He handed her two business cards. "We'd appreciate anything."

"I understand. Thank you, John. The coffee was lousy but the conversation was enlightening."

When he smiled, Lenore noticed the coldness gone from his eyes. She smiled back and rose to leave. He put a ten-dollar bill on the table and walked with her to the car.

"I was sincere when I said you must be a special person. I'm glad you got away from Nick. You were justified."

She looked at his face and saw sincerity. He closed the car door for her and gave a nod as she pulled out of the parking space; she wanted to get home as fast as possible.

At the risk of hurting Leah's feelings, she decided to wait for her afternoon off to discuss the encounter. It was a subject she was sure would warrant a lengthy conversation.

A quiet dinner with Joel was relaxing and fun. She crawled into bed early and felt sleep embracing her. She muttered as she drifted off, "Leah's going to love being right … again!"

CHAPTER 22

At twelve-thirty on Friday, Leah met Lenore at the back door of the store. They had made no firm plans other than an escape from routines.

"Do you need to finish your Christmas shopping or run any errands today?"

"I probably should, but you think it's warm enough to go to the rock?" Lenore looked around the parking area. She was anxious to tell Leah everything about her encounter with the agent. "I really need to talk to you."

"We have coats and gloves, a blanket in the car and it's sunny. We can go to the lake if you want. We could also just go for a drive and talk in the car."

"We can't talk in the car."

"Talk about what? You're acting weird!"

"Not here!"

"Okay. Okay. Let's get to the lake."

Lenore took everything but a direct route. She watched her rearview mirror and changed directions twice. Leah tried to engage her in conversation several times, even questioning her driving abilities and her sanity, only to be hushed with a shake of the brunette's head. Lenore refused to talk until they were out of the car and walking down the path to their rock. She wanted to believe the rock was the one place still immune from surveillance.

* * * * *

John was on the car phone with a frustrated agent, directing him to where the two women usually spent Friday afternoons. He was trying to assure him they were not purposefully attempting evasive action, but couldn't quite convince himself. He had to smile at the idea of Lenore evading a well-trained agent, but would have to advise her against it in the future.

* * * * *

"You know, the hardest part of this conversation is going to be when I have to admit you were right."

"I love being right!" Leah laughed, then looked confused. "Right about what?"

"Remember when I used to get upset about your saying Gregor was a spy?"

"Vividly. There's a name you've not spoken for a while."

"Well, you were right."

They got to the base of the rock and Leah turned to face Lenore.

"I was right? He's a spy?" She looked as surprised as Lenore had felt upon learning the truth. "You've heard from him?"

"No, not from him, of him." She pointed up and Leah climbed to the top of the rock, followed by Lenore, whose abilities were improving with familiarity of the task. They quickly spread the blanket and sat down. Leah was quiet, and intent on listening to what Lenore was saying.

"You're not going to believe what happened."

"What happened? When? Doggon it, Lenore, you didn't tell me something again!" She was clearly going to pout.

"For good reason this time. I've been under surveillance. Maybe you, too."

Leah sat up straighter and took Lenore by the shoulders. "Okay, start at the beginning. What happened and when? Talk!"

Lenore blew out a deep breath. "Day before yesterday Rusty called me from the office to assist a customer who had requested me. When I came around the corner, there was a guy standing there. I was a little let down when I didn't recognize him. I guess I'll always hope Gregor will just show up like that."

Leah nodded. "But it wasn't him, right?"

"Right."

"Where's this heading?"

Lenore threw her hands up in the air. "You always give me a hard time for not remembering details. I've remembered them and now you're impatient."

"Sorry. Go ahead."

"When he turned around, I felt like alarms went off, but I helped him with hiking boots, which he then bought. An expensive pair, as a matter of fact, size ten. Before we went to the counter, he asked me out for a cup of coffee after work. I told him I wasn't part of the deal. Then, he told me it would probably be a good idea if I decided to go. He wanted to discuss a certain fellow I had met in Glenwood Springs the last weekend of September."

"Oh, my God! Did anyone hear you?"

"No, Rusty was at the counter, but he couldn't have heard, even if he was three feet away. He has a hearing loss, you know."

Leah waved her hand. "Okay, so go on. You went, right?"

"Right. But it wasn't exactly a social invitation—I had to!" She looked at Leah. "Didn't JD tell you about my coffee date?"

"Are you kidding? You know he doesn't tell me anything unless I choke it out of him."

They both laughed. Lenore had seen her best friend jump onto her husband's lap and pretend to throttle him, which always made JD laugh.

"You're doing great, Lenore. What happened when you got to the coffee shop?"

"He had a crappy attitude at first and had these really icy blue eyes. He said later it was because he had to treat me as a hostile informant or something. He turned out to be sort of nice."

"Details, Lenore." She hit the brunette's arm. "Remember the details."

"I was just telling you what I thought of him." She rubbed her arm and frowned. "That's a detail. He said Gregor moved to Colorado fifteen months ago after defecting from the Soviet Union. He used to be a Soviet operative, which I think is another word for spy. Anyway, he wanted out, so he came here. They've kept track of him because it could always just be a plot against our government or something. Whatever operatives do. When we came along, they started checking us out, too."

"Us?" Leah grimaced. "As in me, too?"

"Well, he knew your name and that we're close enough to discuss things. He had told me first to not talk to you about it, then later said he knew I would anyway. He knew about Nick. He said it was a good thing I was out of there."

"Weird!"

"Gets weirder." Lenore looked around the area. "It seems they've lost Gregor. They think because I left my home number for him to call, I know where he is. I told him I didn't. I don't know if he believes me or not."

"They've lost him? Can't they trace the phone where he picks up his messages?"

"No, because they're the ones picking up his messages. He just dropped out of sight. Someone is taking care of his house and dogs, and he isn't where he usually can be found. I had to tell him about the money."

"Did you tell him it came from New York?"

"Yes. That surprised him. He wanted to examine the envelopes. I guess you know what I had to tell him."

"Ah-oh." Leah cringed. "What else did he say?"

"They don't know if he's still around and just trying to avoid being watched or if he's gone back or what."

"He wouldn't have gone back to the Soviet Union." Leah shook her head.

"Why not? Maybe he got tired of living here and being followed. Maybe he found information and went back to deliver it."

"I don't think so. He still has a brother there, but he wouldn't move back. He loves the United States and the freedom he has here. He just wouldn't move back. It took too much for him to leave the Soviet Union."

"Why do you think he couldn't have lied about it?"

"The words came too easy … from his heart. Besides, there's you."

"I'm not a factor here." Lenore shook her head. "When did he tell you this stuff about coming here?"

"When we were at the top of Independence Pass and you were exploring, getting depressed."

Lenore frowned. "Maybe you should talk to John."

"Who's John?"

"He's the agent I talked to."

"An actual agent. Wow! We're right in the thick of it all, aren't we?" Leah smiled and raised her brows up and down.

"Leah, this isn't fun and games. I or we could be in danger."

Leah's attitude subdued as she looked at Lenore. "Danger? Do they think Gregor would try to hurt us?"

"No, but they think someone could try to hurt him by hurting me, or us. He did give a dose of food poisoning to the agent watching him so he could come see me. It was also the last time anyone has heard from him. He's dropped out of sight. Since they don't know where he is, there's a lot of questions."

"Maybe there are Soviet spies after him. I think I'm glad to have our guys watching you. Since Gregor is so much in love with you, bad guys cold hold you for ransom or something. He'd do anything to protect you."

Lenore looked at Leah and shook her head. "You're getting carried away."

"Did the agent say anything else?"

Lenore took a deep breath and blew it out. "He said I'm the only one Gregor's been interested in since coming to the United States." She knew what would follow.

Leah rolled back on the blanket shrieking with laughter, waving and kicking arms and legs.

"I told you! Everything he said was right. He wasn't making it up. Ha! Ha! Lenore, I was right!"

"It would seem so." Lenore conceded. "It's not exactly a comfort right now. He's still missing and we could be in danger."

The mention of danger brought Leah back to a sitting position. They looked at each other, then simultaneously at the surrounding countryside. There was not a soul in sight, so they resumed their conversation, quietly.

"Do you think they've tapped your phone?" Leah asked.

"Mine, probably yours and the stores. Who know how far this thing goes? I wish I would have heeded Gregor's warning about using personal numbers, and I don't want to hear another, I-told-you-so."

Leah was quiet for only a second or two. "But I did!"

Lenore looked at the sky and ran her fingers through her hair from temple to ends. "I know."

"So, what do we do now?"

"I've no idea."

"Do you think they've bugged our cars?"

Lenore stood and paced around the top of the rock, looking for anything that might look out of place. "I'd say we need to be cautious everywhere." Her near-sightedness was only a frustration. She sat back down next to Leah. "I think you should talk to John. You know things about Gregor. It could be important."

Leah smiled. "You want him found?"

Lenore frowned. "Leah, he could be in danger. Maybe he needs to be found."

"True. How do we call if we can't use the phone?"

"We can use the phones. We just have to watch what we say on them. Right now, we can use a pay phone."

"Sure, now you want to use a pay phone. Isn't that like closing the barn door after the cows are missing?"

"Horse! It's after the horse is gone." Lenore rolled her eyes. "I just think there could be someone listening other than our side. Want to call now?"

"You mean bad spies?"

"Leah, I don't know what to think. Part of me worries and the other part is just wary. Maybe Gregor will just drop into my life again and all this will be okay. Maybe he's gone for good."

She took a deep breath, regaining control of the emotions edging into her voice. "He could have had an accident or something. He could even be dead and no one would know who to contact. I guess we may never know."

They quietly pondered the situation as they climbed down from the rock and walked to the car. They found a pay phone at a gas station near the mouth of the canyon. Lenore talked first, then handed the phone to Leah.

After a brief discussion she turned to Lenore. "He's on his car phone just south of Fort Collins. Where should we meet?"

"Tell him he has a coffee date at our usual spot whenever he can get there."

Leah relayed the message and turned to Lenore as she hung up the phone.

"He laughed and said he'll see us in twenty minutes. What was so funny?"

"He referred to our first meeting as a date, and I assured him it wasn't. Let's go. We'll get there about the same time."

* * * * *

The agent, who had finally found his way to the lake, took a call from his car phone. He turned south as the ladies turned north. Dixon was taking over.

CHAPTER 23

The downtown coffee shop was a clutter of plastic holly garlands and paper Santa faces proclaiming a redundant Merry X-Mas. Shoppers juggled packages and coats to take a break from holiday shopping. John walked in as the two ladies were seated. He gave Lenore a quick peck on the cheek when he sat down beside her in the booth. He was determined to keep her off guard.

"Nice to see you, Lenore. This must be Leah, whom you've told me so much about."

Leah giggled and Lenore frowned at her best friend. "Don't encourage him."

"Sorry, I thought it important to keep up appearances. Shall we order some of that delicious coffee?"

Lenore wrinkled her nose. "No, I'll have iced tea."

"Me, too," Leah agreed.

"It's a consensus. Let's wait until we're served, before we begin our discussion," added Dixon.

"I thought G-men were supposed to wear trench coats," Leah noted. "I like your jacket and sweater."

The agent didn't blink an eye as he responded. "My trench coat is at the cleaners, and thank you; I like my sweater, too."

"Sorry John, you'll get used to her." Lenore looked at Leah. "He doesn't need a fashion critique. He wants information."

John smiled. "Leah, I assume Lenore has told you everything. I need to make you aware of the importance of anything you may be able to tell us about Greg."

John and Lenore watched as Leah stirred the contents of a packet of sweetener into her tea. She took a sip, then folded her hands on the table. "First of all, I want to see your badge"

After close examination of the folded leather case and the information it held, she handed it back, satisfied he was who he said he was.

"Okay. Did you know he has a brother in Russia?"

"As a matter of fact, we didn't." He began writing in a small notebook with a silver Cross pen. "How do you know this?"

"He told me. His brother's name is Alexander. He also said his mother was dead and his father, who was a ranking officer in the Russian army, was also dead. His brother is all the family he has left."

John wrote quickly as Lenore looked at Leah, wondering how she was able to retain so much information.

Leah continued. "They really didn't know their dad, because they were raised by grandparents until being sent off to school. I think that's where he got all the special training."

"Special training?"

"Survival stuff. He knows what plants to eat and how to protect himself. He's also a good climber and loves the mountains because it reminds him of his childhood home. His grandparents were religious, so he knows about God. He just wasn't allowed to act like he did."

John continued to jot down words and Lenore peeked. The only word she could decipher was God.

"The schools taught him all the rest. He said they made him into a machine and he didn't like it. He wants to be an American." She sipped her tea, then continued. "He also says the government over there is going to fall, and if we allow gun control here, we'll end up like Nazi Germany."

Lenore and John stared at Leah, who was busy stirring more sweetener into her tea.

"Do you believe Greg is going to help with the fall of his former government?" John asked.

"Oh, no! He just says it's going to happen soon because the people are hungry for democracy. He doesn't think our government is going to have anything to do with it either. It'll come from within. Something about, the hearts will cry out and the wall will not withstand the sound. He's hoping his brother will be able to join him here."

The waitress returned to the table long enough to slap down the check, ignoring Lenore's request for more tea. She took a piece of ice into her mouth and let it melt.

John scratched an imaginary itch on his cheek with the end of his pen. "You've had some very interesting conversations with Greg. Anything else?"

Leah thought for a moment as John sipped his tea. "He knows about hit men."

John choked on his tea, and Lenore frantically patted him on the back. Leah looked concerned and offered a napkin from the dispenser. It took a moment for John to speak. His voice was raspy.

"What did he tell you about hit men?"

"He says they're people who have a job to do, and if a bad person dies, it's no big loss to the world. Is he a Soviet hit man?"

"To the best of our knowledge, no." He wiped the dribbles off the table with another napkin. "He would certainly have the capabilities, but his expertise was more along the lines of gathering and passing information electronically. When he defected, he had the opportunity and justification to kill a man who was trying to prevent his apostasy, but let him live. I hope he hasn't changed careers on us."

"John, what do you really think has happened to him?" Lenore asked.

"Honestly?"

"As honest as you can be with us."

"I wish I knew." He shook his head and wadded the flimsy napkin into a ball. "I like Greg. He seemed to be settled into his life. I was happy to hear he was interested in you. It seemed like a sign of stability."

Lenore looked at Leah and back at John, who were both looking at her. "Sorry, I don't know the answer you need."

"Maybe some of what Leah told me today will be useful. Don't give up hope, Lenore. If I can find anything at all, I'll tell you ... unless I can't. I hope you understand."

"Spoken like a true government agent."

"I wish I could be more reassuring. I think he'll be back. He'd be a fool to walk away from you." He knew he was absolutely blurring the professional line.

Lenore blushed and looked at the few remaining pieces of ice she swirled around the bottom of her glass.

"Ladies, I have to go now. It's been a pleasure." He slipped the notebook and pen into an inside pocket of his jacket. "Oh, Lenore, I don't think you'll have to worry about Nick contesting the divorce. It seems the woman he'd been seeing before you left, by the name of

Hope, appears to be expecting a baby. I imagine he'll be quite anxious to get the divorce finalized."

Lenore let out a slow breath. "Is there anything you *don't* know, John?"

He laughed and patted Lenore's hand. "Yes. When I'll see you again. I'd like to take you out to dinner sometime and have a real date."

Before Lenore could refuse, Leah accepted. "She would be delighted." John and Lenore both looked at Leah. "What could it hurt?" She smiled.

"I'll think about it, John. There's a lot going on in my life right now."

"I'll take that as a definite maybe." He smiled, stood and picked up the check. "Take care of yourselves. We'll be in touch and you have my number if you think of anything else."

He left the two women sitting in the booth.

"He's cute and he likes you."

Lenore groaned. "I don't think he's cute, and I don't care if he likes me."

"If Gregor doesn't come back, he'd be fun just to date."

Lenore ignored the remark and slid out of the booth. "It's nearly four-thirty. We'll have to go home pretty soon."

The small amount of time they had left would not be enough to satisfy their friendship needs. They drove around, savoring each minute.

"When will Grant be here?"

"Sometime Christmas Eve. He'll fly into Denver and rent a car from there. I can't wait to see him. Joel is just beside himself. He misses his big brother."

"I wish he would move out here. You and Joel would love it."

"It's just not feasible. His career is in Chicago. We just have to enjoy being together when we can. It's not been easy to accept, but I've learned to."

"What do you think about ...."

Lenore glanced at Leah, who had her hand over her mouth and motioned for Lenore to pull over. Fearful her friend was about to throw up, she quickly obliged. Leah exited the car and walked several yards away from it, followed by Lenore.

"Leah, are you okay?"

"Yes, I just didn't want to say anything in the car, if you know what I mean."

Lenore laughed. "I thought you were about to be sick."

"If you thought I was going to throw up, why did you follow? You'd have thrown up, too."

Lenore shrugged. "I don't know. Am I going to have to pull over every time we have something sensitive to say?"

"Don't you think we should be cautious? I mean, they could have little teeny, tiny microphones hidden all over the cars."

Lenore frowned and looked back at Baby, wondering where they would hide such a piece of equipment, or what it looked like for that matter.

"That's a creepy thought. What were you going to say?"

"I wanted to ask what you thought about the information he gave you regarding Nick. Do you feel bad?"

"We could have talked about that in the car." She shrugged. "If I had any feelings left for him, it would. It just confirms the fact he's been playing his little games a lot longer than I thought. Maybe he was trying to be mean so I would be the one to break things off. All he had to do was ask. I would have gracefully accepted the fact he found someone else. He didn't have to try to destroy Joel and me to get us out of his life."

"Gracefully, my Aunt Polly's petunias!" Leah yelled. "We would have taken the washer and dryer, too! I'm glad he did it the way he did. If you still loved him and found this out, it would have torn you apart, and you know it."

"You're probably right, but does it justify my encounter with Gregor?" Lenore paced and Leah followed. "I mean, I didn't know about her when it happened. As far as I knew, I was still married. Maybe not happily, but married nonetheless."

"I don't see the need to go over it again." Leah stopped Lenore with her hands on the brunette's shoulders. "You knew it was over in your heart. You didn't know about the other woman, but you knew you were hurting and miserable. I think God knew it was over and brought Gregor to you. He wanted to give you something to hang onto when you found out."

"That's absurd. If God brought him into my life, why would He take him away again?" Lenore started walking again.

219

"Maybe he hasn't." Leah caught up and walked alongside her friend, giving up on trying to stop the pacing brunette. "We don't know, yet. At least you had him when you needed the strength to get out. You have to be thankful."

"I suppose. Let's get back in the car. I'm cold!"

"Okay, I've had my walk for the day." Leah laughed and Lenore looked confused. "Maybe we should learn sign language."

Lenore tried to explain the danger of trying to watch and sign words while driving. Laughter ensued as they got in the car and continued their drive, while Leah attempted sign language, a Leah version.

"This could be fun, Lenore. What do you think of—"

"Who?" Lenore asked, glancing at the passenger.

Leah turned up her collar and shifted her eyes from side to side. Lenore laughed at the interpretation of an agent.

"I didn't like him at first. Now, I suppose he was just doing his job. By the way, I don't appreciate your accepting an invitation for me."

"What could it hurt? He seems nice and you could at least go for free food."

"That's not a good reason. It just wouldn't be nice."

Leah unfastened her seatbelt and leaned over to whisper in Lenore's ear. "Maybe he would be more inclined to tell you things, if you know what I mean."

She returned to her seat and fastened her seatbelt while Lenore pondered the possibilities.

"Well, since I've filed for divorce, and if I haven't heard from Gregor, I'd consider it."

The two women looked at one another and nodded.

"Sure, besides that, he's cute."

"You said that before. I don't see it."

A grimace covered Leah's face and she gave Lenore a light punch on the arm.

"Just think of that nice smile and those pretty blue eyes. You said you thought he was a really nice guy."

Lenore crossed her eyes at Leah. "Well, yes. Since I've gotten to know him a little better, I guess he does have pretty eyes. How about changing the subject?"

Leah gave a submissive shrug and launched into new subject matter.

"Do you and the boys want to come by the house for Christmas Eve? I know you want to have Christmas Day together at home, but we'd love it if you would spend an hour or so with us. We'll have a little nosh, a little nog. How 'bout it?"

"I'd love it, but that depends a little on how Grant feels when he gets here. I sure hope the weather cooperates."

"It's a little early to predict. They're saying we'll have a white Christmas."

"If it just holds off until my Grant gets here, I don't care how much it snows. We need this time together."

"I know you do. We'll just keep positive thoughts in our heads and a dog sled at the ready. You know Rusty has his four-wheel drive truck and would go for Grant in a heartbeat."

"I'll keep that in my mind."

＊ ＊ ＊ ＊ ＊

Leah left Lenore at the back of the store with hugs and laughter before heading for their respective destinations.

When Lenore walked through the front door, Joel had a fire going in the little stove and the house was filled with cozy warmth. Holiday music floated amid conversation and dinner preparations. Soon, Lenore would look across the table at both her sons. A smile was comfortably in place as she listened to her youngest relate the day's adventures and the evening's plans. She was at peace with her world.

＊ ＊ ＊ ＊ ＊

John Dixon walked into his Denver apartment and went straight to his living room to check his message machine. Pick up overdue dry cleaning; call the Director, whatever time he got in; then a message from his uncle. It was very matter of fact; his grandfather was dead, and he was to call for details on the funeral arrangements at his convenience.

Greg Parish and Lenore Appleby slipped to the back of his mind as he walked to the liquor cabinet and poured himself a good bourbon, neat. Then he sat down on a leather sofa, staring at the blinking light of his answering machine as it spewed messages to an audience of one, who wasn't listening.

When effects of the alcohol began to numb the jolt of emotions, he picked up the phone next to the answering machine and called the Director.

"It's Dixon, returning your call."

"I got your message about the meeting with the two women in Fort Collins. Anything enlightening come of it?"

"They both appear to be anxious to help. I learned Greg has a brother still in the Soviet Union. That's something we weren't aware of. I think it's something to follow up on."

"We'll have operatives in place as soon as I make a call or two. Anything else?"

"He didn't talk much to Lenore, unless it was of a personal nature, but Leah had some pretty interesting conversations with him. He's predicting the fall of communism and warning about gun control in this country. They talked about his childhood and hit men."

"Hit men?"

"Yeah, that one got my attention, too. He was never involved with any assassinations, was he?"

"Not that we're aware of, but then it seems there may be quite a bit we don't know about Parish. We need to find this guy, Dixon. Continue to keep in touch with these women. I can't help feeling if he's going to surface, one of them is going to know it first. I want you close. Can you pursue the Appleby woman?"

"Pursue?"

"Get involved. Earn her trust. Consider this a covert operation. Have an affair, if that's what it takes. We have to flush Parish out of hiding and that might do it."

John was silent for a minute as he thought about Lenore Appleby. It certainly wouldn't be unpleasant. He didn't mention the fact he had already asked her out on a date.

"I'll see what I can do." John drained the bourbon from his glass. "Oh, by the way, I'll be taking a few days to go back east. My grandfather just died and I owe it to the old guy to show up for the services."

"Not a problem, Dixon. Sorry for the loss. I know you were close to him. Let me know if there's anything I can do."

John found it interesting the Director made the offer as an individual, instead of an organization. He hung up the phone and poured another bourbon before he made the call to his uncle. He wrote down times and locations as the man on the other end of the line related them. The family was intent on getting it over with, so it didn't mess up the holidays.

There had been the same lack of emotion when, at the age of twelve, John had been informed his parents had been killed in a plane crash. He had been deposited at the doorstep of his grandfather's house, not knowing if it was because J. Milton Dixon wanted him there, or because no one else wanted the bother of a twelve-year-old boy. His answer came when the staunch old man had taken him into the living room, closed the door behind them and held him close as they both cried.

John had never been encouraged to get into the family business, but they had been horrified when he made the decision to join the Central Intelligence Agency. The exception had been his grandfather. Perhaps the old man had gotten a little enjoyment in seeing their reactions. He had encouraged John to follow his own instincts, and break away from the greed and corruption which had eclipsed the business, once a source of pride for J. Milton Dixon.

John swirled the last of the liquid in his glass. As far as he was concerned, his last ties with the Dixon family were cut. He would sell whatever stock he owned in the company and be finished with them all.

He had seen J. Milton in October and had known the eighty-seven-year-old man wasn't going to live much longer. They had spent two peaceful days together. Words had been said which needed saying, and he could feel good about that.

John Milton Dixon III sat down in the privacy of his living room and allowed tears to fall freely. No one would ever know.

CHAPTER 24

Christmas Eve at the store was a happy day. The customers were cheerful, if not a little frantic, in search of last-minute gifts. The employees were eager to assist, knowing occupied time passed more quickly than idle time. At two o'clock, the last customer was let out of the door and the lock secured. Three employees gathered in the office with JD for a celebratory glass of wine.

"Well gang, we got through the holiday season in good shape. No major scars I can see." JD poured and Lenore handed out the filled glasses. As eager as everyone was to get to family circles, this was a family time, too.

"I thank you for all your hard work. We still have another week but I thought I'd go ahead and give you your year-end bonus today. I've got the best team in the company, and I know it."

"It's because we have the best leader," Royce offered, with Rusty and Lenore chiming in. They held their glasses in a toast and took sips.

JD distributed each envelope, to be opened in privacy, with a handshake and a thank you. "I hope you all have a terrific Christmas. Lenore, I know yours is going to be a little different this year, but it's going to be a better one."

"It's going to be absolutely terrific." She smiled. "I just hope the snow holds off long enough for Grant to get here."

"You'd be a mess right now if it was snowing," Royce noted.

"No, she'd be just fine," Rusty interjected. "Because we'd just use my four-wheel-drive truck and go after him. We wouldn't let our Lenore worry for long." He gave her a wink, then a hug.

"You guys are the best. I'm so lucky to be where I am and have the friends I do. I don't know if I could have made it without you." She looked at each one and felt a lump in her throat.

"We'll always be here for you. We're family." JD was anxious to avert her tears. "Now, as much as I'm enjoying this great company and the wine, I'm going to chase you all out, so I can go home to my family and you can go to yours."

Glasses were emptied amid hugs and good wishes. JD confirmed plans with Lenore for later in the evening as Royce and Rusty left. He insisted she go home, leaving him with the daily report. She walked to her car still smiling, anxious to begin an evening with her boys.

The car door was locked, which it normally wasn't. She could see three packages in the passenger seat, brightly wrapped and topped with an envelope. She unlocked the door and took the envelope as she sat down behind the wheel. The contents of the note surprised her.

Lenore,
Please don't be offended with this gesture. I hope your holiday is the best.
Sincerely,
John M. Dixon III

She wasn't offended, but very much surprised. She picked up the packages and examined them. There was a gift for her and one each for Joel and Grant. She sat them in the seat beside her and started the engine.

"Bad move, John. How do I explain these?" She spoke aloud, hoping some unseen microphone would pick up her voice. After letting the engine warm a little, she pulled out of the parking lot and drove home. She carried the packages in the front door and Joel was there to assist.

"More packages!" He grinned. "Neat! From you?"

"No. I don't know who they're from. They were in the car when I left work."

"No kidding?"

"No kidding. Have you heard from Grant? His plane landed an hour ago." She hung her coat in the hall closet and kicked off her shoes, then carried the shoes and her purse to her bedroom.

"Not yet. Shouldn't he be here by now?" He yelled from the living room. "Wasn't there a card or anything?"

"No card." She hoped he would just drop the subject, because she really didn't want to lie anymore. "Grant will be here anytime. Let's not start worrying, okay? The airport is probably super busy with car rentals, and traffic is undoubtedly busy between here and the airport."

Lenore walked past the living room, where Joel was busily arranging the new gifts under the tree. He had already turned on the twinkling lights. She had smelled the wood smoke from the stove when she walked up to the house. It felt like a holiday house, and she smiled. Joel put a Christmas tape into the player while she changed into comfortable black jeans and a holiday sweater.

Joel was still sitting beside the tree when Lenore entered the room and sat down on the sofa. She sorted through the mail and opened two cards from distant relatives. She handed them to her son, who glanced at the names of unknown people and put them into a basket containing similar holiday greetings.

"Did you get your bonus?"

"Of course. JD always gives us our year-end bonus on Christmas Eve, then pretends it was a spur-of-the-moment idea. He's so funny."

"What are you going to use it on?"

She relaxed into the sofa. "I think I'll pay off the legal fees for the divorce. I think it's the best gift I could give us, don't you, Joel?"

"Sure, unless you want to use it to buy me a car." He smiled and wagged his eyebrows.

Lenore smiled back and leaned forward to rub his back. "It's not much, Joel. I'm afraid the car we could afford wouldn't be road-worthy. I wish I could buy you a car, but I just can't right now."

"Well, could I go to work and buy one myself?"

Lenore looked at her son and pondered his words. She knew the importance of a young man having his own car.

"Tell you what, if you can find a job that won't interfere with school work or your music, I'll consider it. If your grades start slipping, you'll have to give up the whole idea, okay? Is that fair enough?"

"Fair enough. Dad said if I earn half, he'll pay the other half."

"That's generous of him. I'll make you this deal; if you buy the car, I'll pay for your title and tags and the first insurance installment. If you manage to keep your license free of any tickets, I'll pay for the next insurance payment, too. After that, you're on your own."

"Now, this is a Christmas present! Thanks, Mom. You'd better start saving." He pulled Lenore off the sofa and hugged her, lifting her off the floor until she laughed. "How about some hot cocoa to celebrate?"

A few minutes later, they sat in the living room and talked about what kind of car Joel wanted while sipping steaming mugs of cocoa. The doorbell rang and they raced to answer it, expecting to see

Grant's smiling face on the other side of the door. They weren't expecting to see Nick. He had an armload of packages and was waiting for the door to be opened.

"Mom, what should we do?" Joel answered, frowning.

"I'll handle it." She opened the door a little, but didn't invite him in. "What's this, Nick?"

"I'm Santa Clause, let me in. These are getting heavy." He was smiling and Lenore let her guard down for a moment and let him into the house. Too late, she noticed the smell of alcohol. He handed the packages to Joel, and turned to Lenore.

"Nice fuckin' house."

Lenore continued to hold the door open. "I think you'd better leave now."

"Why? We're still married until things are final and Santa wants to give you something a little extra special." He grabbed his crotch and leered at her. She backed away from him and started for the living room when he caught her arm. His laugh made it all the more frightening.

"Let go of me! Don't you dare come in here and ruin our Christmas!" She slapped him, struggling to free herself.

Joel returned from the living room, packages still in his arms. He dropped them and managed to shove Nick away from Lenore.

"Mom, call the police. I'll take care of him."

Lenore ran for the kitchen phone with Nick in pursuit. Joel was knocked to the floor and scrambled to get back on his feet. He dove at Nick's back, letting years of pent-up anger and frustration surface into rage.

"You're not going to hurt her again. Not as long as I can draw a breath, you asshole!"

Lenore watched, horrified as Nick turned, grabbed Joel and raised his fist.

"I don't think you want to do that, Nick."

Grant's voice was quiet, as his presence filled the doorway of the kitchen. It was as if someone put the action into a freeze-frame.

"I'm only going to say this one time, Nick, so I think you'd better pay attention. I want you to leave. I don't want you to ever come back. I've been away a long time, and obviously there's been a lot of things going on I didn't know about."

Grant stepped further into the kitchen. "You're not going to hurt anyone, anymore. Not my mother. Not my brother. Certainly not me." Grant's laugh was sarcastic. "Now, we can call the police, and I promise you'll be here for their arrival, but I feel really generous. I'll let you walk out of here, but so help me God, if you ever set foot around here again, or if you ever try to bother my family again, there won't be a hole deep enough for you to hide in. I'll hunt you down and kill you, like the vermin you are."

Nick lowered his arm and Joel stepped aside to let him pass. Grant blocked his passage for a moment, to assure himself that Nick knew he was serious. He could see no doubting in Nick's bloodshot eyes.

Grant closed the door behind him and turned back to the kitchen, where Lenore and Joel were still frozen in place. A big smile softened his features.

"Well, Merry Christmas!"

Lenore sank to the floor where she had been standing, her legs unable to support her any longer. Joel ran to hug his big brother.

"Man, you came in just like the cavalry! I could have taken him, though."

"No doubt, little brother. Hey, I think you've grown six inches since I saw you." He turned to Lenore. "Mom, are you going to be okay?"

Lenore was laughing and crying at the same time as her two sons helped their mom to her feet. She hugged them both and spoke between tears and giggles.

"Grant, I'm so sorry. This wasn't supposed to be your homecoming. I wanted it to be perfect."

He hugged his mom. "How long has this been going on? You should have told me he's been hurting you."

"We didn't want to worry you. I really didn't think he'd try again."

"Well, let's not let it ruin everything. It's over. He won't bother you again." He grinned and winked at Joel. "I think I smelled the odor of shit as he passed me."

With the mood considerably lightened, they helped him retrieve suitcases and packages from his rented car, Joel finding it necessary to rearrange the bounty under the tree.

"Mom, do we keep the gifts from Nick?"

"I won't make that decision for you, Joel. I don't want anything from him."

Grant sat down on the sofa next to Lenore and handed her a glass of wine. "Let him keep whatever Nick bought. I think he's earned a gift or two for putting up with the asshole. Don't think of it as something from Nick. Think of it as compensation for your tolerance. I plan to keep mine."

"Suit yourselves. I'm going to drop mine off at the police station to be donated to the homeless or needy." She patted her oldest son on the knee. "That reminds me, Grant, do you want to go to JD and Leah's for an hour or so tonight?"

"Do I remind you of the homeless and needy, or do they?" He chuckled.

"Neither, silly. I just thought we could stop at the police station on the way. Want to go?"

"Sure, fine with me. I didn't bring any gifts for them."

"I have gifts; don't worry about it."

"Hey, Joel, let's go see if any stores are still open." He got up from the sofa and smiled at Lenore. "I want to at least get the little guys something."

"Great, I'll drive!" Joel announced, heading for the door.

"Boys, it isn't necessary," Lenore said, as she got up from the sofa and followed them to the front door.

"Mom, we need to take your car, because I can't drive his rental car ... okay with you?"

Seeing the situation hopelessly out of her control, she relented and smiled as they raced for the driver's seat of her car, laughing.

She loved her boys.

* * * * *

A block away from the house, an agent settled back into the seat of his pickup truck. He had started for the house with Nick's appearance, but backed off with the arrival of Grant Appleby. Though he stayed close enough to ensure the situation was under control, he did not intrude. He made a point of notifying the local police of an apparent drunk driver on the streets when Nick Carlson left the neighborhood.

As the two young men left, he remained vigilant in his duty. Lenore was safe and secure.

* * * * *

Lenore got busy baking pumpkin pie for their Christmas dinner and the boys returned as it was coming out of the oven.

"Smells like Christmas, Mom." Grant enveloped her in a hug and she nestled her nose into his coat, feeling the chill from outdoors.

"C'mon Grant, I'm not going to wrap for you, too," Joel called from the living room. "Pie smells great, Mom."

"Is it snowing yet?" Lenore asked, squinting her eyes, looking out the kitchen window.

"Not yet." Grant hung his coat in the closet. "Looks like it could start any minute. The clouds are hanging pretty low and it's gotten a lot colder. I hope we get a foot of it."

The two boys retreated to the living room and discussed snow and skiing, while Lenore cleaned the kitchen. She knew better than to fix dinner before going to the Chase house for Christmas Eve. Leah's idea of a little nosh was enough to feed a starving army.

* * * * *

At seven-thirty, Lenore knocked on the front door of JD and Leah's house. The sound of laughing children and Christmas music greeted them as Leah opened the door. She was resplendent in a long satin skirt of deep red, and a white cashmere sweater. A gold belt was snugged around Leah's small waist, matching her gold shoes. Red earrings and a necklace of red, green and gold beads completed the outfit.

"Merry Christmas! Come on in. Grant, you look wonderful. I know your mom and brother are so glad you're here, and we are too."

She hugged each one as they entered, taking their coats and directing them to the dining room. "Grab some nog and nosh. It's all on the table. Make yourselves at home." Leah was in her element.

The house was brimming with people. Lenore and her sons felt very much a part of the family, which was always the goal of JD and Leah. Dustin, their oldest grandson who had recently turned four, was anxious to examine the new packages, and Danny at a very busy two and a half, trailed behind his brother, trying to mimic and join the action.

After everyone had eaten their fill and gifts were exchanged, Leah and Lenore managed a quiet moment in the kitchen, wrapping and putting away leftovers. The events of Grant's homecoming were discussed and Leah laughed at the thought of Nick being bested by Grant.

"Grant looked eight feet tall standing there in the doorway." Lenore smiled proudly. "He had this dare-me look on his face, like he was just waiting for an opportunity to pound Nick into the floor. His voice was quiet, so Nick had to pay attention. It was something else."

"Well, I don't think you have to worry about Nick anymore. That guy's history!" Leah nibbled on a piece of celery. "So, you're going to pay off your divorce with your Christmas bonus?"

"Yes, first thing Monday morning." She thought a moment. "Well, I guess Friday afternoon. We'll be busy with after-Christmas exchanges and sales all week." Lenore put the last plate into the dishwasher and dried her hands. "We'd better be going. I know Grant has to be exhausted from traveling all day."

"And you need time alone on Christmas Eve. I'm so glad you decided to join us tonight." The two best friends hugged. "I feel like our family circle was complete with you three here. Thanks for the gifts, but you know it wasn't necessary."

"It was easier to manage this year than I thought it would be. Thanks for having us."

"I'm anxious to hear what your secret Santa gave."

"Anxious would pretty well cover my feelings, too."

Dustin and Danny howled, "Don't Go!" as their new-found friends began leaving. Joel was slow to stop playing with Dustin's little cars. Grant laughed when Danny latched onto one of his legs. It took hugs from the big boys, and restraint from JD and Leah before the little boys allowed them to leave. Joel promised he would play cars with Dustin again soon.

"It looked like you were having more fun with those little cars than Dustin," Grant teased.

"Hey, it wasn't all that long ago you and I played with cars like those," Joel replied.

"I know. Still got yours?"

"Sure. They're in a box up in my closet. I think I could find them pretty easily."

Lenore smiled as the two grown young men in the front seat discussed toy cars, and plans to play with them.

At home, they enjoyed the fire in the stove as Lenore and Grant sipped the wine he had brought and Joel sipped apple juice. The young men were in serious discussion about little cars. The twinkling lights of the tree were the only illumination and soft Christmas music soon lulled Lenore to sleep. Her boys were with her and life was good. It was close to midnight when they woke her.

"Mom, can we open just one gift tonight?" Joel whispered.

"Sure. What? How long have I been asleep?"

"Well, in about five minutes, it'll officially be Christmas morning," Grant said. "Can we open something?"

It took a minute for her to wake up and look at the eyes of her two sons, transformed into children once again at the prospect of opening gifts. She smiled and sat upright.

"Okay, you can pick out one gift each to open. Don't ask for more, because I will be unmoving on the subject."

They agreed in unison and went to the tree. It was a ritual that had been played out for years. As they searched through packages, Lenore noticed the neatly parked toy cars under the coffee table and smiled. After several minutes of discussion and much arranging, shaking and feeling of the assortment, they approached Lenore with their choices.

"We decided on these, the ones the mystery Santa gave us. Joel says you don't know who they're from."

"No, they were sitting in the front seat of the car when I left work this afternoon."

Grant frowned. "Mom, don't you lock your car?"

"Not normally." She yawned. "Not when it's here at home or at the store."

"What if these gifts were bombs or someone was hiding in the back seat? You have to start locking your car every time you leave it. Promise me, Mom?"

She started to smile at the scolding, but the seriousness on Grant's face prevented it.

"Okay, I'll start locking it. I promise! Now, go ahead and open the gifts."

"Lighten up Grant. If she had locked the doors today, we wouldn't have these packages to open. I'll make sure she starts locking them from now on." Joel handed Lenore the package from John. "Here, Mom. Open the one with your name on it."

"Oh, I'll wait until morning. I have self-control."

Joel and Grant smiled at each other as they watched their mom lifting and gently tipping the package back and forth. The contents shifted slightly.

"What do you think it is?" the boys asked in unison.

She looked up to see her sons with half opened packages sitting in their laps, smiling.

"Okay, I'm a little curious."

They all laughed and the festive paper was torn and boxes opened. Joel and Grant had sweaters in their packages, along with tickets for a Denver Nugget's game.

"Aw, these are for the middle of January. You won't be able to go." Joel pouted.

"I'll see what I can work out. Maybe I can still go." Grant patted his younger brother on the back.

As the boys compared gifts, Lenore lifted the lid off the box in her lap. White tissue paper was folded back to expose a teal colored sweater. It was beautiful. When she lifted it from the box, something fluttered to the floor at her feet. She held her breath for a second as Joel and Grant looked at the envelope and then at their mom. Joel reached for it.

"No!"

He stopped, and looked questioningly at his mom. Lenore let the sweater drop to her lap and picked up the envelope. She considered leaving the room before opening it, wondering how she would explain a note from John. What if it was news of Gregor? Surely, he wouldn't put anything in writing.

"Maybe I got tickets to the game, too." Lenore hoped her smile looked sincere as she slowly opened the envelope. There was no note concerning the Russian. What she found was a ticket for the Fort Collins Symphony. Relieved, she showed it to Joel and Grant.

Grant noted the symphony was the same night as their game. "Looks like someone didn't want you to sit here alone. Are you sure you don't know who this is from? It has to be a man."

"Why do you say that?" Lenore asked.

"Well, first of all, a woman wouldn't give basketball game tickets as a gift. I think it's someone who wants a date with you, and the only way to arrange it is to send you to this concert. I'd lay odds the guy will be sitting beside you at the concert."

"Maybe I shouldn't go." Lenore frowned and looked at the ticket.

"Why not, Mom?" Joel asked. "If Grant's right, and it is sort of a date, what could it hurt?"

"Maybe nothing," she conceded. "It would be a very public place and I've been wanting to go to the symphony. I guess I'm a little curious, too." She raised her eyebrows at the boys. "Maybe it's Robert Redford."

Lenore's ongoing infatuation with the famous actor/director was something they always teased her about, as if not actually meeting him was merely a matter of bad timing.

"That's got to be who it is. He probably stopped by the store while I was busy and had to rush off to catch a plane. He's always in such a hurry." She rolled her eyes in feigned exasperation, which made the boys laugh. "We'd better get to bed or Santa won't be able to come." She stood and offered a hand to each boy, pulling them up off the floor. "I wonder if it's snowed yet?"

The trio went to the patio door and Lenore opened the vertical blinds as Joel turned on the lights for the back yard. Lacy white flakes danced in the glow. They were coming down at a fairly good rate and the ground was already covered with a blanket of pristine softness. Three smiling faces reflected in the glass of the patio door as they watched the Christmas snow. Lenore had her arms around the waists of her sons, and their arms laced over her shoulders.

The world was at peace for a moment. Her thoughts were filled with happy times and smiling faces. The smile of a certain Russian settled in her thoughts, and a lump formed in her throat as a mist of tears blurred the view.

"It sure feels good for the three of us to be together again, doesn't it, Mom?"

"Yes, Grant, it does. We're so glad you could be here. It makes this Christmas so very special."

"I suppose if I lived closer, we probably wouldn't appreciate moments like this as much, would we?"

"Oh, I think we absolutely would. I'd love to find out," she said, staring out the glass door.

"Well, I was going to wait until morning to give you this gift, but it's essentially morning and this is definitely the moment." Grant turned Lenore toward him and put his hands on her shoulders. "This isn't entirely a holiday vacation. I've been offered a transfer to Denver, and I'm supposed to be finding a place to live and checking out the new job while I'm here. Merry Christmas, Mom. You, too, Joel."

"Grant! Really?" She hugged him tightly as he laughed and nodded. "That's the best gift you could have ever given us. We'll all be close again. Will you live here? We could make room, couldn't we, Joel?"

"Definitely!" Joel hugged his brother. "This is going to be terrific!"

"I'll need to live in Denver. I just don't want the commute, especially when the weather is like this. It's still better than having me in Chicago, isn't it?"

"Yes! I won't complain. I won't even expect you home for dinner every Sunday. To be honest, I'm not the Sunday dinner kind of mom anyway." She laughed.

"I think you're the best kind of mom. I'll come and take you out for dinner once in a while. You don't have time for all that cooking anyway, with the exception of your wonderful holiday dinners. You'll always have to take time to do that."

"Okay now boys, we really need to get to bed or this holiday dinner will be a midnight snack tomorrow."

They hugged their mom and closed the blinds. The tree lights were left on, following the tradition of Santa needing to be able to see what he was doing.

After the boys were in Joel's room and the door closed, Lenore crept quietly back into the living room and filled their stockings with candy canes, Hershey's Kisses and new little Match Box cars. The detailed little toy cars were an expected tradition, even though her sons were supposed to be too grown up. The imaginary garage under the coffee table, lined with Joel's collection, was evidence they would never outgrow them.

She smiled and walked to the patio door, pushing the slats aside to look out across the moonlit field to the foothills silhouetted against the sky. The snow as not as heavy now and the clouds were illuminated by reflected city lights. The blanketed ground shimmered with a bluish glow.

Lenore was thankful for where she was and for the new direction in her life. She was thankful for her sons and the prospect of Grant living closer. She tried to be thankful for the experience of Gregor, but it was cloaked with a feeling of sadness. She knew the brief memories would eventually fade, and he would not intrude her thoughts. She quietly whispered a prayer.

"God, you alone know where he is and what is in his heart. If he is in danger, protect him. If he is alone, comfort him. If it is meant to be, bring him back to me. If it isn't, please move him out of my heart and give me peace of mind about it."

She let the blinds swing quietly back into place and went to her room. A peaceful warmth enveloped her and she fell asleep quickly. Vivid dreams of the smiling Russian filled the night.

* * * * *

Bacon! Suddenly, she smelled bacon. Coffee, too. Why was Gregor drinking coffee and eating bacon? He didn't drink coffee.

The fog of sleep began to lift and Lenore had the uneasy feeling of being watched. Slowly she opened her eyes and nearly jumped off the opposite side of her bed. Grant and Joel had their chins resting on the bed and had mischievous grins fixed in place. They rolled back on the floor with laughter at their mom's reaction.

"You two nearly scared me to death!"

It took a minute before they caught enough breath to speak.

"We got tired of waiting for you to get up, so we went ahead and made breakfast. Hurry and get up, Mom. We want to open presents. Breakfast is served!"

"Yeah, Mom. Grant wouldn't let me bring you breakfast in bed. He said it would make you cry and we'd never get to open gifts."

"Okay, okay, I'm getting up. I'm going to make you two pitch in for the bottle of hair dye to cover all the gray hair you just gave me."

In a fleeting move, which defied her recent awakening, she grabbed a robe and jumped from the bed, messed up the hair of two startled young men sitting on the floor and bounded out of the room, calling over her shoulder from the hallway.

"Last one to the kitchen has to carry out the Christmas trash today!"

"How does she do that?" Grant asked his brother.

"I've never figured it out. I haven't seen her like this for months."

Two brothers got up off the floor and walked together to the kitchen, where Lenore was sipping coffee.

"What time did you two get up? It's only seven now."

"Five-thirty," Joel announced. "We couldn't go back to sleep. Are you mad?"

"Are you kidding? Seven is sleeping late on Christmas morning with you two." She laughed. "Let's eat!"

After breakfast, they settled in front of the Christmas tree. A warm fire in the little stove added to their comfort, and the brilliance of sunshine, reflecting on snow outside, competed with the twinkling lights of the tree. Joel distributed gifts and stockings into three neat piles. Although by most standards, the gifts were meager, the love filling the room was abundantly rich. Lenore had purchased slippers and pajamas for both sons. She had wrapped empty shoe boxes and put notes inside, promising each a pair of shoes of their choice, along with a pair good socks. She also gave them a new sweater and shirts and ties to coordinate. Lenore received a mountain painting Grant had painted and framed for her, along with a pair of warm gloves and a matching scarf. Joel had made a cassette tape of his jazz band group performance for his mom, and a sweet little heart pinky ring he had to have saved quite a while to purchase. She felt like the richest woman on earth.

Later that afternoon, the traditional Christmas feast was consumed from a festive table, amid laughter and conversation. Lenore was pleased when her sons offered to help with clean-up.

"Mom, I'm tired of Christmas music. Could I put a tape in the player?"

"Sounds like a great idea. You choose."

Joel disappeared for a few minutes and returned as Don McLean's "American Pie" began playing. The familiarity was too much to resist and one-by-one they began singing along. The dishwasher was filled and leftovers refrigerated with painless efficiency. They laughed when the song ended and noticed the chore was finished as well.

"Ed Sullivan, you quit too soon!" Lenore laughed.

"Who?" The boys asked in unison.

"Never mind. I think I'll catch a nap. You two can watch TV or whatever."

"I think we'll go for a drive, if that's okay. We'll take my rental car in case you decide to wake up and go somewhere."

"Try to get back before dark. The streets are pretty snowy. It could get a little slick after dark." She winced, realizing what a mommy thing she had just said.

Before Joel could protest, Grant graciously agreed and they picked new sweaters and leather gloves, gifts from JD and Leah, to wear for their outing.

Lenore waved from the door as they pulled out of the drive. Then she curled up on the sofa with a blanket and was soon asleep. She seldom took naps, but this was Christmas. She was still in her nightgown and robe and wouldn't be changing until morning, if possible. It felt wonderful.

A peaceful day. A peaceful end to a year of changes and challenges.

CHAPTER 25

By the third week of January, Lenore had paid for her divorce, Grant had moved to Denver and life seemed wonderfully mundane. Joel was delighted at having his brother to go on ski trips together and have overnight stays at Grant's apartment in Denver. January brought the usual business slow down, but Lenore had additional duties to busy herself with this year. JD and Leah would be leaving on their annual cruise and she would be in charge of the store in his absence. With Rusty and Royce to assist, she wasn't worried about the responsibility.

Her Friday afternoon off was less than an hour away. The best friends would go shopping for Leah's cruise clothes and Lenore's concert clothes. A perky blonde interrupted her thoughts.

"I'm early!"

"*I'm glad!* Lenore smiled at her best friend and put her pencil down. "This is going to be fun, isn't it?"

"Yes! Shall we go to Denver?"

"It's up to you; my need is fairly basic. You're the one who has to buy out a couple of stores."

Leah put her hands on her hips. "I'll have you know I have made a list and plan to stick to it. I'm just buying stuff to update what I already have. That way I'll have more money to spend on the cruise." She smiled, clearly proud of her plan. "There are always so many things I see and want to bring home. Can we go now?"

"Royce is still at lunch. It might leave the store shorthanded."

"As slow as it is? I'll ask my wonderful husband."

Lenore closed the ledger and took her purse out of a drawer. She knew Leah would have her way with JD about leaving early. They were out the back door in less than five minutes.

"Now we have time for lunch before we shop. You choose where we go."

"Chinese food," Lenore said with a smile.

"Really, you're suggesting it?"

"It's a new year and I'm a new woman. It sounds good, as long as you don't explain about your ancestors to the wait staff." They both enjoyed the memory with a laugh.

* * * * *

After a quick meal, they were soon driving south on I-25 toward Denver. Lenore handed Leah the fortune cookie she had brought from lunch.

"Here, read my fortune." She accepted the crumbs from the broken cookie and popped them into her mouth.

"Okay. It says: Answers come when questions are no longer asked. Do we see the wisdom in this?"

"No. Read yours." Lenore laughed.

Leah was more than willing to explain. "I think it means when you least expect it, you'll find out about Gregor."

Lenore put her finger to her lips and glanced at Leah, who put her hand over her mouth and winced.

"Sorry." She unfastened her seat belt and leaned over to Lenore. "I keep forgetting. Don't you think that's what it means, though?"

"Leah, it's just a slip of paper from a cookie. I could have gotten yours. You could have gotten mine. It's just a novelty."

"Right! I'll read mine." She sat back in her seat and re-fastened her seatbelt before opening her own cookie. "Ha! How about this one? Travel to warm places lightens winter darkness."

"Coincidence, that's all." She glanced at Leah. "What's on your shopping list?"

Her best friend's disappointment faded quickly at the prospect of shopping.

"Just a few necessities; a couple of tops and shorts, a new bathing suit or two and some spectacular things for the formal affairs. That's about it, except or a new scarf or belt to go with things I already have."

"Oh, hardly anything then." Lenore chuckled. "Where do we want to start?"

"Let's just stop at the first big mall and find a sports wear shop. My summer clothes are the most important. I can always make do with the rest. Well, except for the formal stuff."

Lenore laughed at Leah's version of paring it down. "I only want to find an outfit for the symphony concert. A little dressy, but not elaborate. It's still cold and I was thinking a nice pants outfit would be in order."

"No way!" Leah punctuated the remark with a wave of her hand. "We're going to find you a dress. A pretty one, too. You wear pants to work all the time. I think it's time the world found out Lenore Appleby has legs!"

Lenore smiled at her friend. "I'm just trying to be practical. I always need clothes for work, so this could do double duty. I don't have money to throw away."

"You wouldn't be throwing it away. Get something basic, preferably black, then you can get things to go with it to make it different every time you wear it. You'll enjoy it for years and no one will even suspect it's the same dress. Remember Lenore, you're a new woman. You might have all sorts of occasions to wear a dress from now on."

"We'll see."

It wasn't an outright commitment, but it satisfied Leah. A little smile settled on her lips. Lenore glanced over and knew she would be going home with a dress. Undoubtedly a black one.

"Are you excited about the concert?" Leah asked.

"Excited? No, just looking forward to it. It's going to be symphonic strings. Should be some beautiful music."

Leah struggled to release her seat belt and leaned over to Lenore's ear. "I mean, excited to see if John is going to be there? This will be your first actual date since being almost divorced."

Lenore frowned and whispered back. "This is not a date. I'm just going to a concert. If someone else happens to be there, fine."

Leah settled back into her seat and crossed her arms, still looking at Lenore.

"I don't know why you have that attitude." She fastened her seatbelt again. "He's nice and apparently interest in you. I just wish it wasn't going to be a week and a half before I hear about it. You have to go home afterward and write down all the details so you don't forget. Promise me!"

Neither woman was giving a potential listening device any regard.

"There won't be any details worth remembering other than the music, Leah. I don't want there to be. Besides, I'm trying to get on my feet with the job and past the divorce. I'm also trying to get past what happened before. My mind has to stay free of any more problems and I have to concentrate on my job and getting Joel through high school." She glanced at Leah, who was listening with concern in her eyes. "There's lots of responsibilities at work now and, to tell the truth, I don't think my heart can take being involved again. Not now. Maybe not ever."

"You're pretty sure you won't hear from *him* again, aren't you?"

Lenore thought about the possibility of their conversation being heard, then decided she didn't really care.

"Yes, Leah, I'm pretty sure. It still hurts to remember. It may hurt a long time, but it won't hurt forever. I know that. There are times when I'm all alone and start thinking about him. I cry, but I also smile sometimes. I'm getting closer to making him a memory. The less I have to do with someone like John, the easier it's going to be to put the memories into perspective and quit hoping for things that will never be."

Leah was quiet as Lenore continued to purge her thoughts.

"I'm setting new goals for myself. After Joel is in college, I may be offered a store of my own. I'm excited about that. It's something to work toward that is real, and I only have one person to count on to make it happen." She pointed a thumb at herself. "Me!"

"So, you plan to accomplish all this and never have another relationship with a man?"

"Ideally, yes," Lenore avowed, convinced she meant every word.

"It's unrealistic, but I respect your tenacity." Leah patted Lenore's arm. "You're too special to remain alone the rest of your life, though."

"Leah, what I felt for Gregor will never be duplicated. It would be like settling for an imitation. It may have been a total put-on by him, but my heart took it seriously. I don't think I want anyone to ever touch the special place I have in my heart for him." She put her hand on her chest. "It's precious and private. When I'm old, I'll look back on him as my one true love."

"I guess I understand. You know, I'll always be here for you if you ever need to talk about him."

"I appreciate it. Now, let's get back into a shopping state of mind!"

"Onward and upward!" Leah pointed first straight ahead, and then up in the air.

The first mall was in sight before they had gone much further.

"Shall we try this one?" Lenore asked.

"Sure. It'd be nice if we could find everything here, then we could just good off the rest of the day. You could show me where Grant lives and works."

"Let's see how long it takes to stimulate the economy. I'll show you where he lives and works, but we won't stop. I wouldn't want to embarrass him by showing up at his job."

"Okay, but I'll bet he's mad when he finds out you were here and didn't stop."

"Always easier to apologize for not doing something than to apologize for doing something wrong."

"That's Lenore logic! And an interesting theory." Leah patted her purse. "I have three little charge cards all ready to be maxed if necessary. Let's get started."

As they approached the door of the mall, three men in work clothes walked out and smiled at the two attractive women. Leah smiled back, but Lenore spoke, which was out of character for them both.

"Hello, gentlemen. How are you today?" A smile punctuating the greeting.

"Much better now!" The man in the middle answered.

As Lenore and Leah passed them and reached the glass doors, they could see the reflection of the action behind them. All three men had turned and were smiling. Two were holding onto the one who had spoken, to prevent his following. Once inside and out of sight, the ladies broke into laughter.

"Little do they know, they just flirted with a grandmother and a woman who's sworn abstinence."

"I didn't take an oath of abstinence," Lenore protested. "I just don't ever want to get involved again."

"How can you not get involved an have the other?"

"Use 'em and lose 'em." Lenore shrugged and giggled. "Sort of a catch and release program."

"You don't mean that!"

"Sounds like a good idea. Guys do it all the time."

"You're not a guy!"

"Sure would be easier if I was." Lenore steered her friend to the right. "Look, a sports wear shop."

Shopping became the focus as they entered the store. Leah found more than she expected, and Lenore found the will to refuse temptations. After touring several stores, and one trip to the car for depositing Leah's packages into the trunk, they found a dress shop with selections appealing to both their tastes and Lenore's budget. Though she normally hated shopping for clothes, Lenore was enjoying the experience. She narrowed her selection to two and tried the first for Leah.

"Very elegant." Leah smiled. "You could use a variety of accessories to make it look different each time you wore it. Put the other one on and let me see."

Dutifully, Lenore returned to the dressing room and changed into the second dress. It was basic black, as was the first, but the neckline was considerably lower. With a blush of embarrassment, she walked out to face Leah.

"That's the one! "Leah jumped from her chair and pointed. "No doubt about it. You look fantastic. Wow!"

"It's a little daring, don't you think?" She put a hand over her exposed cleavage.

"No, I don't. Sure, you can see a little cleavage, but you couldn't hide your bust line in a flower sack. Might as well be proud and show it off. This does it very tastefully. You're just not used to looking sexy."

"I don't know." Lenore frowned. "This isn't something I could wear to work."

"Wait a minute." Leah disappeared from behind displays of clothes and returned with a long, black scarf. Gold and silver threads were woven in a delicate pattern throughout and caught the light. She fussed and adjusted until she was satisfied, then turned Lenore to face the mirror.

The scarf draped across the expanse of previously exposed flesh. She turned and caught her reflection from several angles, agreeing it was just the touch needed. She found the price tag and her shoulders drooped.

"No way, Leah. This is way beyond my budget. See if there's something cheaper."

"This is the only one that will work." Leah whined, then smiled and winked. "I'm going to buy it for myself and just let you borrow it for the concert. Have you got shoes and a bag?"

"Of course I have shoes and a bag. I work in a shoe store." Lenore shook her head and started to take the scarf off. "I can't let you do this, Leah."

"You can't not let me. I'll get a lot of use out of it. You're just borrowing, remember?"

"Oh, I can't decide if I should hug you or just smack you!" A hug was the choice. "Now don't you think this will be a little too dressy for the concert?"

"No, people really dress up for symphony concerts, even in Fort Collins. Leave work a little early so you won't be rushed getting ready."

"Can't. Remember, you and JD will be boarding a plane tomorrow afternoon to take you to the ship. I'll have to close and do the daily and weekly."

"You might have to close, but you can do the books on Sunday. JD has done it when we had something planned." She adjusted the scarf on Lenore a little more. "We'll ask him tonight. I'm sure he'll tell you it's alright."

"I'm not too concerned anyway. The concert doesn't start until eight. I'll have time."

"I wish I could be there to see you. Ask Joel to take pictures before you leave the house."

"He won't be there. He and Grant have tickets for the game in Denver, and he's staying over." She frowned. "I just realized I have a problem. He needs to get to Denver, and I need to get to the concert. We only have one car."

"Use Baby. No!" Leah shouted, startling Lenore. "I mean, you can use Baby of course, but I think you should rent a limousine instead, to drop you off at the door and pick you up after."

Lenore laughed and rolled her eyes skyward. "For Heaven's sake, Leah. If I can't afford a scarf, I sure can't afford a limousine. Maybe I'll just take a taxi."

"Well, I guess it's the next best thing. I'm still leaving Baby with you. Something might come up while we're gone." She took a deep breath and blew it out. "Okay, we're all set. You have the perfect dress, the accessories and the transportation. Now all you need is the handsome prince."

"No thanks, I just want to ...." Lenore stopped mid-sentence and stared into the mirror. She could see the front of the store. A man was standing there, intent on watching her. She looked away, hoping he didn't know she had seen him.

"Leah, try to be discreet and go to the front of the store. Tell me what you think about the person standing there."

Lenore continued to turn and admire her own reflection, or so it seemed. She purposefully removed the wrap to expose the open neckline, hoping it would distract the man long enough for Leah to get closer. She smiled as the petite blonde inched her way toward the front of the store. She used her stature to hide behind racks and displays and got a good look at him before he noticed her. Startled, he quickly turned away and ran from the store bumping into several shoppers in the mall.

Leah stood for a moment watching his retreat before coming back to Lenore's side.

"Are you thinking what I'm thinking?"

"I hope we're wrong. Let's get out of here." Lenore hurried to the dressing room and changed into her own clothes. She paid for the dress. Leah paid for the scarf, along with a dress and blouse for herself.

They cautiously stepped from the store and looked around. No one seemed interested in their presence, and the man was nowhere in sight. With eyes sweeping, they walked deliberately to a different exit from than the one they had entered. They looked around the parking lot and then at each other.

"I don't like this," Lenore said.

"Maybe we're overreacting. Maybe it was just a guy looking for his wife and saw you. You look awfully sexy in that dress. You're going to attract stares."

"Leah, you saw him up close. Do you think that's the case?"

"Truth?"

"Truth!"

"He looked like someone who got caught doing something very wrong. If it was a man looking for his wife and got distracted by you, he might have been embarrassed, but he wouldn't have taken off like he did. He didn't slow down as long as I had him in sight." She looked at Lenore. "Do you think it's one of ours or one of theirs?"

"Ours, of course." She bit her lower lip. "I'll find out tomorrow night, one way or the other."

"You'll ask John?"

"If he's there. I'll also demand the surveillance be stopped. It's stupid and totally unnecessary. If Gregor was going to be in touch, he would have already done so. Don't they know that?" She ran her fingers through hair.

"Maybe they're watching you in case the other side is after you."

Lenore sat down on a bus bench and Leah sat down beside her.

"I'm going to remain calm. I'm not going to get upset." She stood and began pacing.

"Isn't it a little chilly out here?" Leah asked as she stood and began walking beside the brunette.

"So, I shiver a little. I just have to sort this out."

Leah clutched her shopping bag for warmth and took Lenore's, freeing her friend to pace more effectively. They looked out across the sea of cars in the parking lot.

"Wait until you talk to John. It's possible the guy we saw was just a pervert or something."

"Is that supposed to make me feel better?"

"Well, yes, unless you see him again. Then you get worried. How about asking the police to step in and protect you?"

Lenore shook her head and continued pacing. "Leah, I sure as hell don't need someone else following me around. Besides, if our own government's best is in on all this, what good are the police? They wouldn't think of interfering and possibly couldn't if they wanted to." She extended her arms in exasperation. "Then there's the fact that if the local police got into it everyone would know I was having a fling with a Soviet spy before Nick and I split up. JD would find out and he would never trust you and me to go anywhere together again. Nick could use it against me before the divorce is final. Just imagine what my two sons would think?"

"Whoa! Slow down." Leah stopped Lenore's pacing and held her by the shoulders. "You keep this up and you'll make yourself responsible for global warming just because you fell in love with someone."

"Oh, Leah. I'm just so frustrated!"

"I know you are." Leah said, smoothing a stray hair from Lenore's face. "I wish I wasn't leaving. I feel like you need me right now."

"I'll always need you." She rubbed where the hair had ticked her cheek. "It'll be okay. Just think of all we'll have to talk about when you get home. Speaking of home, I think I'm ready to go. Do you mind?"

"Not at all." Leah grinned. "How about having a little fun first?"

"Like what?" Lenore asked, eyeing her friend.

"Just in case we're being followed, let's leave here like we're going somewhere else, then turn and go home instead. I'll watch to see if we're followed and you can take evasive action." The petite blonde wagged her eyebrows and smiled; her eyes full of mischief.

"You're getting into this, aren't you?"

Leah nodded and continued to smile, which made the previously-vexed brunette laugh.

With their bounty safely stored in the trunk, they left the parking lot and headed for downtown Denver. After several detours, turns and lane changes, they headed north for home with assurance from Leah they were not being followed.

Their good-byes tonight would be for two weeks. There would be long conversations when they next saw each other.

* * * * *

A dark blue, mid-sized car blended into the traffic behind the duo on Interstate 25 north from Denver. The agent behind the wheel was talking on a car phone to John Dixon, who was trying to keep the frustrated agent from shooting the tires out on the car he was following.

CHAPTER 26

Saturday was an unusually busy day at the store for the end of January. Lenore had little time to think about her best friend leaving for two weeks, or of herself attending the concert later that evening. In fact, at five o'clock, she had to be told it was nearly closing time. After preparing the deposit and securing the alarm, she stood outside with Rusty and Royce, ready to go home.

"I just feel funny leaving without getting the books done."

"I've seen JD do it many times," Rusty replied. "Just come in tomorrow. You have big plans tonight?"

"Just a symphony at the Lincoln Center." She tried to sound casual. "I want some time to relax before I have to get ready to go."

"Sounds like a date to me," Royce teased.

"So, what if it is?" Rusty scolded the younger man. "It's none of our business."

"Guys, if it was a date, I'd tell you." She tried to restore calm. "I just got gifted a ticket to the concert and I'm looking forward to getting dressed in girl clothes for a change. I don't do this very often, so I need all the time I can get."

Satisfied, Royce smiled and Rusty nodded. They made sure her car had started before either pulled out of the parking lot; a winter time ritual. She appreciated their concern and waved as she put her own car in reverse.

The smell of cologne and increased humidity greeted Lenore as she walked into the house. She knew Joel was getting ready to leave for Denver. He would drive her car to his brother's and they would go to the Nuggets game. Baby was sitting in the garage, left by JD and Leah, for Lenore's use while they were gone.

"Mom, you're home. Good!" Joel was slipping a sweater over his head as he met her at the door. "I need to get going."

"Joel, your hair is still wet." She hung up her coat while he grabbed his from the closet. "Oh well, the car is warm and full of gas. You have plenty of time so don't drive like a maniac! Remember this is the only car we have. You stay with Grant tonight, right? I don't want you driving home that late."

He only rolled his eyes a little as he received her instructions. "That's the plan, Mom. Are you driving Leah's car tonight?"

"No, I'm wearing high heels and I'll get a taxi to drop me off at the door and pick me up, too. It'll save me from having to walk so far and from getting into a cold car after the concert."

Lenore kicked off her shoes as Joel was putting his on.

"Well, watch out for the drivers," he advised. "I've seen some real weirdos driving those things."

She smiled. When did he get so protective?

"I'll be fine. You have fun and be careful. Try to be home by early afternoon, okay? Give my love to Grant."

"No problem. Love you, Mom." With a quick hug and a peck on her cheek, he grabbed his travel bag and headed out the door.

Lenore walked to the bedroom and put her shoes away. She pulled the new dress and scarf from the closet and hung them on the back of the door. A new pair of pantyhose was opened with another pair ready in the event a thumbnail went through the sheer material; she was a little out of practice with pantyhose.

She took a little more care with her preparations than a normal workday routine. As she sprayed an errant hair into place, the taxi honked. She quickly stepped into shoes, grabbed the small black evening bag and made one final check in the mirror. The reflection was of someone Lenore didn't know. She was elegant and beautiful. With a little shift of the scarf around her shoulders, she assured herself it would provide enough warmth to get from the taxi to the door. Once inside she would make adjustments to be sure no one would see anything she didn't want them to see.

"I wonder why they call it a neckline, when it's nowhere near my neck!" She questioned the lady in the mirror who looked as clueless as she felt.

She grabbed her coat out of the closet, then put it back, locked the front door behind her and walked to the cab. The driver, seeing her exit the house, uncharacteristically got out to open her door. He smiled as she sat down and he closed her door. She was glad to see he was a clean-cut older man. When he had settled into the driver's seat and they had gone a few blocks, Lenore decided she wanted the same driver on her return trip.

"Sir, could I arrange for you to pick me up after the concert?"

"Sorry, Ma'am, I'm off duty in an hour. I could leave a message for someone to be there for you, if you'd like."

"I'll just call when it's over. I may get busy talking or something."

"Whatever you'd like Ma'am."

Lenore would have to take her chances. Right now, she didn't want to think of anything more than a concert.

As the car stopped in front of the Lincoln Center, her driver immediately got out and came around to open her door. She knew the gesture was not usual and gave him an extra two dollars. She wished it could have been more, but she had brought little more than enough to cover the fare both ways and buy for a beverage during intermission. She would forego the beverage now. He thanked her as if were much more.

A steady flow of people bustled toward the doors. Few took time to notice the attractive lady walking away from the taxi. Lenore found herself hurrying a little. The cold January night air was penetrating her scarf and dress as if she were naked. She wished there was something under the dress besides pantyhose and lacy black underwear. With a vision of red long johns gracing her body, and black material of the dress swishing in contrast, a smile settled on her lips. It was a favorite game of Lenore's—think absurd thoughts as the rest of the world went by, totally unsuspecting. A gentleman held the door for her and smiled back.

After mingling in the lobby for a few minutes, looking at various sculptures and paintings and nodding to an occasional familiar face, she decided to find her seat. An older lady took her ticket and directed Lenore to her destination with gracious manners perfected by years of practice. Lenore sat down and surveyed her surroundings.

Scattered throughout the large concert hall, mainly older couples collected in small groups amid the tiered seating. Lenore assumed they were the season ticket holders. Ladies admired one another's dresses or new hairdos. Gentlemen nodded an unspoken alliance of having to attend, when they would have much preferred a night in front of the tube watching a Nuggets game with a cold beer in hand.

Lenore shifted her knees to the side to allow a middle-aged couple to pass. The man received a punch in his ribs when his wife noticed he lingered a bit too long over Lenore. He smiled sheepishly as Lenore caught him shifting his gaze from her cleavage to her face. He moved on and his wife occupied the seat closest to the brunette. One empty seat was left on the aisle next to Lenore.

Two older ladies waved at Lenore as they took seats several rows in front of her. They were customers from the store, and Lenore tried to remember their shoe sizes and preferences. She was beginning to feel too young to be there. As the sound of instruments tuning-up filled the air, the crowd began to pattern into neat rows, fitting like pegs into a large pegboard.

As the house lights dimmed and lights went up on stage, Lenore was aware of someone sitting next to her. She turned to see John, dressed in a tuxedo and poorly tied bow tie, smiling at her. She smiled back, wondering if she was really glad to see him, or just someone who was closer to her own age. He opened his mouth to speak, but applause for the conductor's entrance took her attention to the stage.

At intermission, Lenore accompanied John to the lobby. The gathering was as diverse as the city of Fort Collins itself. Though the majority were older, elegantly dressed patrons, the spectrum ran from there to blue jeans and Birkenstock sandals. Colorado State University provided an interesting influx of ages and attitudes from around the world.

"I apologize for being a little late. I'm delighted you decided to attend; I wasn't sure you would." He smiled. "You look spectacular, by the way." His eyes never drifted from Lenore's eyes.

"Thank you for the ticket and the compliment. I'm enjoying the concert very much."

"I didn't see your car in the parking lot. How did you get here?"

She cocked her head. "Do you always check for my car? We need to have a talk."

"About?"

Lenore spoke as quietly as she could and let her eyes turn up the volume. "About precisely that, checking up on me. This isn't the time or place to discuss it. A taxi."

"I beg your pardon?"

"I came in a taxi tonight. I didn't want to walk very far. Joel took my car to Denver for the game with Grant."

"I see. If you would allow me to take you home, we could discuss whatever is on your mind."

The prospect of taxi driver roulette made her decision easy, but she hesitated.

"Tell you what, Lenore, after the concert, I'll get my car, let it warm up a bit and pick you up right at the door just like a taxi. You can even ride in the back seat, if it would make you more comfortable."

His affable manner brought a smile to Lenore's lips. She lowered her lashes, then looked back into John's eyes.

"I'll accept the ride because I need to talk to you."

There was a hit of resignation from John, then she continued.

"Quite honestly, I don't trust taxi drivers so late at night, either."

As the lights blinked, John escorted Lenore down the hallway with is hand on her elbow.

"I suppose I can feel good that you trust me more than a cabby."

Lenore laughed, then stopped and straightened his tie. As they continued down the aisle, he felt the tie and then shrugged, wondering what she had done.

At the end of the concert, John held Lenore's hand on his arm as they ascended the aisle to the lobby. She liked the gesture.

"Shall I get your coat?"

"No coat. Just the scarf."

"No coat? Well then, I'll get my car. It's a couple of blocks away. I'll let it warm up a bit and pick you up at the door." He told her as he retrieved his black wool dress coat from the check room.

"Wait!" She held his arm as he headed for the door. "What kind of car am I looking for?"

"That might be good to know." He laughed. "It's a Mercedes. A black one."

She was glad he turned away before her eyebrows went up.

It was almost ten minutes before he pulled up by the curb outside the main door. The lobby was slowly clearing of ladies awaiting husbands to rescue them as well. John got out and opened the door for Lenore as she exited the warmth of the Lincoln Center. The cold blast of air almost took her breath, and she gladly sank into the plush warmth of the luxurious car.

John closed her door and hurried over to the driver's side. He closed his door and looked at Lenore.

"You didn't wear a coat? Are you new in town or what?" He teased. "It gets cold here in January, you know."

As the last shiver convulsed throughout her body, she relaxed. The heater was performing its duty well, and she was comfortably aware of the heated leather seat.

"I don't dress up very often, and I suppose I wasn't really thinking about being cold tonight. I figured the scarf would be enough, given I wasn't going to walk very far. I was just looking forward to the symphony concert."

"You really look fantastic in that dress." He pulled away from the curb and onto the street. "Cold, but fantastic. Hope you don't take offense at voicing my observation."

"No, I bought it to look fantastic. Now, what I want to talk to you about—"

"You certainly get right to the point, don't you?"

Ignoring his question, Lenore continued.

"When Leah and I went to Denver yesterday to get this dress, we were followed. I don't want to be followed, John. Don't you people realize that if Gregor was going to contact me, he would have already done it?"

"Whoa! Back up a little. What makes you think you were followed?"

John knew they were followed, but the expertise of his agents in performing such a task undetected was something of a source of pride to him.

Lenore related the experience in the dress shop and waited for his reply. It didn't come. He drove to her house with his lips pressed together and drummed his fingers on the steering wheel. He couldn't tell her all of the truth. It would be too much. As they stopped in Lenore's driveway, she could take it no longer and verbally exploded.

"I don't understand any of this. I want to know why you're still following me, and I want it stopped. I am not going to keep looking over my shoulder everywhere I go, or worry I may say something out of place in a phone conversation. This has to do with my rights and I'm going to exercise them. If you don't want to handle it, I'll take the name of your superior and see what I can get done. Maybe I'll call the President of the United States and throw myself on his mercy for falling in love with a former Soviet spy."

He stared out the windshield, listening.

"I can get over Gregor, but not if you people won't let me. I feel invaded. I'm trying to make a living and raise my son. I left a train wreck of a marriage and feel like a failure for not making it work. This is what you call STRESS, John! I'm trying to handle it as well as I can, and if I can remove some of it, I will. Your following me is something I can change one way or the other." She waved her arms. "Talk to me, damn it!"

The silence was almost deafening. John turned to stare at Lenore and she realized she was taking out all her frustrations on him. He turned back to the windshield and took a deep breath, then let it out slowly.

"Lenore, I'd love to take all the stress out of your life, but I can't." He turned back to her. "Unfortunately, I'm about to add to it."

"I don't think I want to hear this." She settled back into the comfortable, warm leather seat and stared at the illuminated controls of the Mercedes. Was he going to tell her Gregor was dead? Or worse, he had gone back to Russia with secrets?

"Lenore, we stopped surveillance on you a week after Christmas. If you're being followed, it's not by us."

It was a lie he had to tell. She was going to be followed. She might as well accept it. If the knowledge of someone else following was what was needed, so be it.

She frowned and slowly looked at John, who was looking at her. "I don't understand."

"From everything we can find, or not find, I guess, it looks like Greg may have gone back. Whether he took anything with him, we may never know. He would have had to forge documents to do it, which is no big deal to someone in his line of work. We're checking on the brother aspect. They could be together. So far, we can't find either of them."

From the look on her face, he knew he had her attention. "I don't like the sound of your encounter. It's very possible Leah just disturbed a voyeur. Maybe your soon-to-be former spouse is having you followed."

"So… what are you saying?" Lenore asked quietly.

"I hate to suggest it, but would you mind so terribly if we followed you again for just a while, to make sure you're not in any danger? I promise we will be discreet and not get into anything personal."

"You're going to do it anyway, right?"

"Right." He smiled, apologetically.

She bit her lower lip, then turned toward him. "I don't know what to think. You're telling me Gregor has gone back to Russia, at least apparently, yet you're afraid I might be in danger? Why?"

"One may have nothing to do with the other. I'd just feel better if I knew for sure. I thought tonight would be good-bye. I was going to tell you about Greg and figured it would be the last time I saw you." Another necessary lie. "I can't say I'm unhappy it's not. Can I walk you to your door?"

"Yes, in fact, if you would also come in and check the house, I'd appreciate it." She hugged her arms around herself and looked at the house. "I suddenly feel a little nervous about being alone."

He turned off the car and escorted Lenore to her front door. She fumbled with her keys, dropping them twice before finally handing them to John. They stepped inside the house and he put his hands on her shoulders.

"Stay here. I'll check your house."

Lenore stepped into the kitchen and turned on the light. She took the scarf off and tossed it onto the clean counter, then picked it up and folded it neatly before laying it back down. She stepped out of the heels she was unaccustomed to wearing. The cold tile felt especially good on her feet.

"Everything looks fine." He called from the living room. "Can I start a fire for you? The house is pretty chilly."

"That would be great. Can I pour you a drink?"

"Sure. Whatever you're having will be fine."

Lenore took two small glasses from the cabinet and filled both with ice. From another cabinet, she took a bottle of fifteen-year-old scotch, a gift her boss had received from a sales representative. Fortunately for her, JD didn't like scotch and knew she did. She opened it and didn't measure, just pouring enough to add a splash of water. With a quick stir, she carried the glasses into the living room and sat them on the coffee table.

Flames were flickering behind the glass door of the little wood stove.

"It'll be warm in no time." He walked to the sofa and took the drink, sipping cautiously. "Scotch? I wasn't expecting it." He took another sip. "It's a good one, too."

"Don't I look like a scotch drinker?"

"Actually no. Champagne would have been my guess."

She wrinkled her nose. "I can't say I'm crazy about it. Had it a couple of times at New Year's Eve parties and wasn't impressed."

John sat at one end of the sofa and Lenore sat in the middle, pulling her feet under her and nestling into the full skirt of her dress, facing him.

"Sounds like you need to have some really good Champagne. I'm sure you'd like it."

Lenore sipped her drink, appreciating the smoothness as it warmed her. She noticed John's watch.

"That's beautiful! I don't think it's a Timex."

John unfastened the band and handed the watch to her.

"It was my grandfather's watch. I only wear it on very special occasions."

Lenore turned the watch over in her hand and noted the initials in the gold case. "J M D?" She handed the watch back to John. "That's a very expensive watch."

"John Milton Dixon. Yes, it is a very expensive watch." He fastened it back on his wrist and admired it himself for a few moments. "He recently passed away and I inherited this, along with everything else. I was the only heir to whom he left anything."

"Heir? Sounds like old money."

"Old and plenty of it. I didn't get the Mercedes with what the government pays." He laughed.

"If you're rich, why do you work?"

"I need challenges in my life."

"Like me?" Lenore asked, then sipped her drink.

"No. You're not the sort of challenge I'm used to. Meeting someone like you is a rarity. I wish we could have met under different circumstances."

Lenore watched John sip his drink, and wondered if he was carrying a gun tonight. No discernible bulges in his jacket to give her the answer. She tilted her head a little and watched his face as she asked her next question.

"John, is Gregor gone for good?"

"Looks that way, Lenore. There's just no way to prove it. I can't believe it, but I guess he had us all fooled. It's a little embarrassing for our side."

Lenore took another sip of her drink, hoping it would help her swallow the lump forming in her throat. A deep breath brought back momentary control.

"I guess embarrassed would be one way to put how I feel, too."

"Lenore, I know it hurts. We were fooled, but your heart got involved. I really thought I knew this guy. I can't believe he would walk away from you with no explanation. Something just doesn't fit right in this puzzle." He shook his head. "Maybe he didn't choose to go. Maybe he was taken back or went someplace entirely different. I'm going to keep working on the brother theory."

"Don't put in any extra effort on my account. I don't hold onto men very well, anyway. I now have two ex-husbands to go with a vanishing lover."

"I can't say anything about your first husband, but you can't blame yourself for Nick. He wanted to have his cake and eat it, too. That's why he got so violent. He knew you were on to him and he didn't want to lose you, but he had gotten trapped by knocking up his little side-dish. I don't think he ever intended it to happen."

John sipped his drink, then continued. "Your former husband has an addictive personality. Alcoholics do. He was trying to prove to his buddies he could be just like them and have little flings like they were having and bragging about. He just wasn't smart enough to protect himself. He's miserable right now. She's done this to two other guys. She gets a name and child support for each kid, then moves on to the next one. It'll last about a year after the kid gets here."

Lenore frowned. "You spent a lot of time checking into him. Was this part of the assignment?"

"Not really." John shook his head and shrugged his shoulders. "Just personal curiosity. I always wonder what makes people like him walk away from something so good."

"Will he come after me again?"

"No, I think he knows better. He put his foot in it good, and he knows you'll never take him back. As far as trying to hurt you again? I believe your sons have convinced him it's a bad idea."

Lenore nodded. "You mean the incident on Christmas Eve?"

"No, I mean the day of a ski trip later. They looked him up and beat the hell out of him." John smiled. "Don't worry, there were no charges filed."

Lenore stared at John, trying to recall the day they returned from the ski trip.

"So, my little boys didn't collide on the downhill and get those bruises on their knuckles?"

John shook his head and chuckled. "Let it be their secret. I'm kind of proud of them. You should have seen Nick."

She smiled, then tried to force a disapproving frown. It couldn't be done and they both laughed.

"Those little poops! They could have gotten hurt."

"I think the odds were on their side, Lenore. I'm sure it was something they felt they needed to do. I imagine they'll break down someday and tell you all about it."

Lenore had nearly finished her drink. She was warm and the scotch was taking effect. She was finally relaxed and comfortable with John.

"Every time I see you, it's an enlightening experience." She smiled. "I'm sorry I was so rude when I first met you, although you didn't really try to charm me."

"I wish I could have handled it differently. I had no idea of how you would react."

She shrugged. "Well, we got past it, didn't we?"

"Yes." He smiled. "This date was a bit contrived on my part. What would you say to a real date sometime in the future?"

"Oh, John, I don't know." She looked down at the glass in her hands. "I don't know that I'm ready for dates."

"Who better to take you out on one? I know you're in a healing stage now. But you need to get out and enjoy life. You need to find more excuses to wear dresses, too." He smiled. "We can just go out and have a good time, nothing more. I'm not saying I'll be around forever, but I won't make a promise I can't or don't intend to keep. I do promise you will know when I have to go and where. Fair enough?"

"Fair enough." Lenore wondered if the scotch had relaxed her too much. "I need to call it a night. I have to work a while tomorrow to finish the books." She sat her glass on the table. "I had a lovely time, John. Thank you. I'm sure the boys had a great time at the game. You've been very kind and generous."

As they stood, Lenore found her feet had become numb from sitting on them and nearly fell. John caught her.

"Whoa, my feet are asleep!" Their eyes met for a moment and Lenore was afraid he would kiss her. Instead, he simply held her in a comforting hug. Tears immediately brimmed her eyes and she hugged him back.

John made no attempt to let go. "Just stand here a minute and let me hold you until the tingling stops. I wondered how you were sitting like that."

"Thanks." She wiped the tears from her eyes and noticed mascara on her fingers. John pulled a handkerchief from his pocket and offered it.

"Oh, no, I'll ruin it. I'll get a tissue."

"Nonsense. It's what they're for." He smiled. "It's been a long time since a beautiful lady smudged my handkerchief with mascara."

She accepted the monogrammed cloth, dabbed at her eyes, and laughed a little. John tilted her chin upward and took the handkerchief from her hand.

"Now, let's see." Gently he touched her cheek and stared into her eyes. "Your eyes are incredible!" He spoke quietly. "I never realized how green they are, but then, I've never been this close to them before."

He released her from the hug and put both hands on her face, cupping it as if to study the phenomenon further. With the feeling completely back in her feet, Lenore stood still and allowed him to look. She didn't see passion in his eyes, just a sweet tenderness and curiosity.

"I'd better stop looking. I'm afraid I could get lost in them," he whispered.

He let go and stepped back, clearing his throat. "I'd better go and let you get to bed. Look, it's almost midnight."

Lenore smiled and looked at the watch on his wrist, though she couldn't see the time. With their gaze broken, she relaxed a little, relieved he hadn't tried to kiss her. She wouldn't have resisted and it wouldn't have been fair to him. What she needed he could not provide. He would have been a substitute, filling the emptiness. Perhaps he knew.

She walked with him to the front door and accepted a kiss on her cheek, then closed the door after him and secured the deadbolt, as he advised. She left the outside light on and walked back to the living room. It still felt cozy from the fire and the company. Her empty glass and John's half-full glass were carried to the kitchen, but instead of emptying John's glass down the drain, she emptied it into her mouth, having to swallow twice. A dribble of diluted scotch escaped her mouth and she wiped it off with the back of her hand. It was far too expensive to waste by pouring it down the drain, she rationalized. She also rationalized the extra dose of alcohol would help her sleep.

She carried her shoes and scarf to the bedroom and put the shoes into their designated spot on the floor of her closet. The scarf was left folded and laid on her night table. She unzipped her dress and stepped out of it, then draped it onto a padded hanger, which she hooked on the back of her bedroom door.

Pleased with her minor efforts toward neatness, she walked into the bathroom and looked into the mirror. He eyes were green and just a little red around the edges. She shook two ibuprofen tablets from a bottle on the counter, and swallowed them with cupped hands-full of water.

"Yuck! Bathroom water."

She made a face in the mirror, then took her toothbrush out of the holder, filled it with a generous dollop of Crest toothpaste and began brushing her teeth. She found her hairbrush and gave her long tresses a thorough brushing as well. With teeth and hair properly brushed, she washed her face and smiled at the face looking back at her.

Lenore walked back into the bedroom and stood before the full-length mirror. She teetered a bit as pantyhose were removed and tossed toward the closet. So much for neatness, she thought, and giggled.

Black lace panties and bra were left on as she slid her hands over her body. With sensual grace, she began moving to the beat of an unheard melody. She turned away and looked back over her shoulder at the mirror with a teasing smile, slid the straps from her shoulders and unfastened the lacy apparel, letting it drop to the floor.

After a long, sensual stretch, she lifted her hair and let it fall back to her shoulders in a dark, feathery shawl and performed a little pirouette in front of the mirror. Unfortunately, the effects of her last swallow of scotch sent her crashing into the wall. Lenore righted herself and looked at the mirror again.

"You silly bitch, go to bed! Gregor can't see you. He'll never see you again. You'll never wear sexy clothes for him. You'll never dance with him again. So, get over it!"

She turned away from the mirror and started crying as she slipped into a clean cotton T-shirt and nestled into the warmth of her waterbed. She clutched her pillow and sobbed into it ... but no one could hear her heart breaking.

CHAPTER 27

Cold.

Incredible cold.

He knew it was morning but it didn't matter. There was no sunrise to see. No job to go to.

The tray of food was slipped under the door. Again, no contact. No human voice. Just the scrape of a metal tray on the dirty wooden floor. He forced himself to reach for it, knowing the meager nutritional value would give him strength for another day. He had to endure. He had to get back to Lenore.

As dirty fingers fed broth-soaked bread to his mouth, Gregor's thoughts filled with her. He closed his eyes. Visions of her smile and her beautiful eyes fed his soul. He hoped his words of love had been enough for her to believe in his promise to return. He forced himself to believe he would once again hold his precious Lenore.

It had been nearly four months since his return to the Soviet Union. In the first few days he learned, because of his own defection, his brother was in prison. Old contacts proved to be unreliable, and he was lured into a trap by a former Soviet comrade.

Beatings and interrogation were a part of his life. He almost looked forward to it. It was the only human contact he had. There were always the same questions and the same answers. They had trained him well, and it was now a source of frustration.

It had only been four days since his last session, so the sound of a key in the lock surprised him. The heavy wooden door opened, and two guards motioned with Tokarev pistols. Gregor could overpower them, but he didn't know how many others he might encounter, nor exactly where he was.

Someone would slip. He would be ready.

The fate of his brother might remain a mystery. Twice, his plan to take Alexander to the United States had failed, and now they were both prisoners in a land he had once called home.

Plumes of vapor escaped the nostrils of his guards as they walked beside him to the now familiar interrogation room. It was warm there. He squinted to allow his eyes to adjust to the brightness. Natural light filled the room from steel mesh covered windows. It was a brief reprieve from his six by nine-foot cell, with its single bare light bulb.

Perhaps today he would think of the proper procedure for taking apart and reassembling the weapons being held on him. He never allowed thoughts of Lenore to enter his mind in this room, lest they could somehow invade those thoughts and know of her. She would be a useful tool for them. He would do anything they wanted in order to protect her. He must protect her, yet he knew it was impossible. His only hope was the American agent who had monitored his life in the United States. It was possible he knew of her and was close enough to ensure her safety.

"Prisoner Parishnikov, please be seated."

An uncharacteristic gesture for the usually obdurate Soviet officer. Gregor was immediately on guard.

"Perhaps we have been unfair to you. It is obvious our efforts in this room have been ineffectual. We are proud to have taught you so well how to withstand such interrogation. It is my belief other measures are necessary." He walked to the front of his desk, facing Gregor. "Perhaps the friends you have made in your new country would be of great value."

Gregor's eyes focused on the wall behind the simple wooden desk.

"We have operatives in the United States seeking out these friends."

There was no response from Gregor. He would not give any. He narrowed his focus to a water-stained crack, noting the discoloration bleeding away from it.

"The results have been most satisfying. There is a woman who would like to know what has become of you. Would you care to send her a message?"

His brain screamed. This could not be. He fought to control the surge of emotions; his eyes burning into the wall behind the smiling officer. Directly below the crack, the plaster was bubbled and darkened. The water was continuing to deface the wall. It was too late for repairs. It would fall.

"For what purpose did you return to the Soviet Union?"

Back to the usual line of questions.

"I am here to visit my brother."

A nod from the officer to one of his guards produced a blow to the side of Gregor's head. Recently healed tissue opened, bringing a flow of blood over the top of his ear and down into his beard.

"Lies! You are working for the CIA. You have come here to destroy the government. What is your mission?"

"I am here simply to visit my brother! I have missed him."

A blow to the ribs sent white-hot pain through his chest. This time, they had broken the already cracked rib. He drew in a slow, painful breath and continued to stare at the deteriorating wall.

"Your brother claims he has no wish to see you. He believes you are the enemy. You will see what your actions have done for your brother."

A new twist to the game. His focus was drawn from the plastered wall to the photograph held before him. He dare not smile, but the signal was there. The barely familiar face, swollen and bruised, was indeed his younger brother Alexander. His eyes were most definitely crossed. A renewed strength grew within Gregor. There was hope.

"Your brother will see you as well."

Gregor set a grim face for the camera. As he watched the finger tense on the button, he stuck his tongue out, as if wetting the parched flesh of his lips.

"Return him to his cell. When next we meet, perhaps there will be messages from your concerned friends in the United States. It would be a shame if some tragedy were to befall them."

Back in the cold, dark room, Gregor huddled in the corner, taking shallow breaths to minimize the movement of his broken rib. Friends. There was but one person he considered a friend in the United States. Their relationship had been mostly of a professional nature, but the necessity of having to be followed was tolerable with John. They knew nothing of the other's personal lives, yet Gregor hoped somehow John knew of Lenore. It was his only hope for her safety.

His thoughts turned to Alexander, his pesky younger brother, and their childhood. From the time they were very young, Alex had believed his big brother could do no wrong. With their father in the Soviet Army, they seldom had contact with him. Their mother had moved back to her childhood home, bringing her two small sons. When Alex was two and a half, and Gregor nearly five, their mother had died during childbirth. The infant had died soon after. There were no doctors or hospitals in the remote mountainous region. Even if there had been, technology was not advanced enough to prevent such tragedies.

Gregor and Alexander clung desperately to their gentle grandparents who cared for them. Love was abundant and they grew into healthy adolescents, learning the simple ways of life. They worked hard and respected the land and its people. Free to explore the surrounding forest, they learned to appreciate nature, and their grandparents taught them of the beauty and love of God.

When Gregor was eleven years old, and Alexander nine and a half, their father had shown up for one of his rare visits, a stranger to them. His manner was harsh and stern, and they were horrified to learn he was taking them away from the only home they had ever known. He had decided it was time for them to be educated in a State-run boarding school. Amid pleading and tears from their grandparents, and after futile struggling, the boys were removed from the emotionally nurturing environment and placed into a structured, ten-year school in Moscow. They were allowed to see their grandparents once a year for the first two years. After that, their father decided it was a childish need and they were denied visits.

When Gregor was seventeen, he graduated from school and was admitted to Moscow University. He was educated in electronics and excelled in his studies. He seemed very adept at learning foreign languages and became proficient in English, and German, and had a working knowledge of Chinese.

Alexander joined him two years later and they were allowed to have adjoining rooms in the dormitory. The precious few hours not spent studying were devoted to brotherly chats and reminiscing. It was during these private hours that the signal was chosen. If ever one needed to let the other know, despite any circumstance, they were still brothers and therefore a team, Alexander would cross his eyes and Gregor would stick out his tongue. It was a juvenile gesture and practically undetectable.

Gregor smiled. Even though Alexander had been in obvious pain, he had managed to let his brother know he was still part of the team. They would survive their ordeals. If only things had gone differently two years ago, none of this would have happened.

He had made careful arrangements for Alexander to escape with him. Somehow, the plans were detected, and the person he met on the darkened street was not his brother, but another agent. They had graduated from the university together. Gregor and Sergei had become a part of the KGB. Alexander's field of study had been in meteorology, and he was never chosen to be a part of the government elite.

Old school alliances had not been a factor. Sergei had put a gun to Gregor's throat and was going to use it if he did not accompany him back to KGB headquarters. Had it not been for the distraction provided by the American agent assisting in Gregor's apostasy, his fate would have been sealed. The split second he needed to turn the situation in his favor, was all it took.

Disarmed, Sergei had looked into the eyes of Gregor, knowing pleas would not save his life. First the gun was pointed to a spot between his eyes, then slowly lowered to the heart, then to Sergei's crotch, which brought tears to his eyes. Gregor had smiled and stepped back from his former schoolmate. A look of relief was short-lived as Gregor pulled the trigger on the silencer-equipped Makarov, successfully disintegrating the knee joint of Sergei's right leg. A calculated second shot had similar effects on the left. Sergei would live, in a manner of speaking.

Gregor had left the country, not knowing the fate of his brother. It had taken him two years to find a way back. Now, he had not only failed to find Alexander, but had been captured and imprisoned.

His mind, however, refused to accept his situation as totally hopeless.

CHAPTER 28

By the time Leah and JD returned from the cruise, Lenore was ready for a break. Instead of the Friday afternoon off she had missed for two weeks, she was given Friday afternoon, Saturday and her usual Sunday off. It felt like a vacation.

With so much to catch up on, Leah spent Friday afternoon with Lenore and would stay overnight as well. They rented movies, stocked up on Diet Coke and an assortment of treats, none of which would be found on any nutrition list. Not wanting to intrude on the ladies' time together, Joel decided to spend the night with Eric.

Leah regaled Lenore with stories of her cruise. Her dark-eyed friend laughed and nodded as the adventure was recounted. There was no envy, just a delighted interest in life as Leah saw it.

After Joel had made his escape, Leah breached the subject of Lenore's date.

"I want to hear about the concert!"

"Leah, it was lovely. The music was captivating and I was so impressed the selection of—"

"Will you stop that! You know what I want to hear about. Start at the beginning. You left work and ...?"

Lenore laughed. She knew Leah had spent the balance of her patience, waiting until they would be assured of no interruptions before asking about the event.

"Let's refill our Diet Cokes first. Want me to pop more popcorn?"

"No! If I eat anymore popcorn, I'm going to pop. You start talking and we'll go together and fix the drinks."

"Okay. Let's see ... I got home in time to get a kiss from Joel and hand him the car keys. He was still damp from the shower, so I had to wait to take mine." She turned to Leah and put her hands out, exasperated. "I don't see why he has to use up every drop of hot water when he takes a shower. I mean, this water heater has a really large capacity!"

Leah grabbed Lenore's arms. "I will absolutely get a blunt instrument and beat you unmercifully if you don't get on with the story!" Lenore was laughing. "How did you look in the dress?"

"Well, not to sound conceited." She smiled. "I think I looked really neat."

"Neat? You do go on, don't you?" Leah shook her head. "Did you drive Baby?"

"No, I took a taxi and the driver was wonderful. An older man, clean cut. He even opened my door!"

Lenore told of the older patrons and the beautiful artwork on display in the lobby at the risk of being beaten with a blunt instrument. When she told of the cold and how she envisioned long red underwear with the gorgeous black dress swishing over it, she paraded around the kitchen in a silly prance until Leah was laughing so hard, she couldn't breathe and asked her to stop. They took their freshly filled Diet Cokes to the living room and sat down on the floor.

"By the way, that scarf is not very warm in January temperatures. I should have worn a coat, but I didn't want an old coat to ruin the look. Silly me!"

"I'll remember that." Leah grinned. "Was John waiting for you?"

"No. He didn't get there until the conductor walked on stage. We didn't get a chance to talk until the break. I told him I had something I needed to discuss with him, so he gave me a ride home and came in for a while."

"And?"

"We talked for a while and had a drink. We had that scotch JD gave me. Good stuff, by the way. That's about it. I sat on my feet and they went to sleep, so when I got up, I nearly fell. He caught me, though."

"Did he kiss you?" Leah grinned.

"No. He just held onto me while I waited for the feeling to return in my feet. He certainly had the opportunity and stared into my green eyes for a long time, but no kiss." She shook her head. "He's really a nice guy."

"Were you driven in your standard undercover sedan?"

"No, you won't believe this. He drives a black Mercedes!" She allowed Leah a moment to let it sink-in and give an appreciative "Wow" before continuing. "He was wearing a beautiful gold watch from his grandfather. It really glinted in the light, so you couldn't miss it. He was the sole heir and has lots of money. He works because it's a challenge."

"Let's back up. Why were your eyes green? Were you mad or sad? Did he tell you something about Gregor?"

"Oh, just that he's gone. They think he may have un-defected." Lenore busied herself with smoothing out the edges of the blanket. "What made me cry was just being held. I guess I needed a hug." She shrugged.

"That's baloney!"

"No, really, the hug made me cry!"

"No Lenore! I mean, it's baloney if they think Gregor un-defected. I know he didn't. He went back for his brother." She pointed her finger into the air. "We need to call him. I know there's more I can tell him about the situation. Do you have his number handy?"

"No, I don't, and we're not going to call tonight. It won't make any difference."

Leah jumped up from the floor. "I have it in my purse. It might make a huge difference."

Lenore groaned and rolled back on the floor. "You've already told him about the brother."

"Yes, but they were planning to come together. His brother didn't make it. I'm telling you he's gone back for his brother and got caught." Leah took the business card from her purse, then went to the phone. "We have to do something!"

Lenore rolled her eyes and sat up, shaking her head at the excited blonde.

"Don't look at me in that tone of voice!" Leah scolded. "When are you going to trust my instincts?"

"Your instincts seem to get me in trouble. I don't trust your motives, either."

Leah made the call while Lenore rewound the tape from their last movie. She had no desire to be a part of Leah's project. In less than five minutes, her best friend returned with a smile on her face.

"He cut me short!"

"Is there any other way with you?"

"No short jokes, although that was a good one." She nodded. "No, he cut me off because he's going to be here in under an hour. He thinks I might have good information and didn't want to discuss it over the phone. I personally think it's an excuse to see you again."

"I don't want him to come here tonight!" Lenore whined. "Look at this place. It looks like a tornado hit." She gestured around the room. "And I look like a victim."

"You care, huh?"

Lenore frowned and picked up the blanket, making hurried efforts to fold it.

"Damn it, Leah! Let's get this place cleaned up."

"I'll tidy up in here. Go get out of those baggy sweats and put on some make-up and brush your hair." She took the blanket from Lenore. "You might not want to impress him, but you don't want to frighten him, either." She laughed.

Lenore slipped into comfortable jeans and a soft blue sweater, brushed her hair, checked her teeth for popcorn and brushed a fresh smile into place. She put on a minimum amount of make-up, and returned to the living room, where Leah had turned their junk food haven into its normal, orderly look. Leah only brushed her teeth. She was always meticulously dressed, even for casual sleep-overs. They both tackled the kitchen, and in just under an hour the bell rang.

Lenore held an air of detached interest as she opened the door.

"Hello, John. Come on in. Can I fix you a drink while you talk to Leah? Diet coke or juice? Scotch?"

"Juice will be fine." He removed his coat and Lenore hung it in the closet. He stood for a moment watching her walk into the kitchen, before joining Leah in the living room. Lenore didn't notice, but Leah did.

As they delved into possibilities and conjecture, Lenore took her time in the kitchen. By the time she served the juice, John was busily writing in his notebook and Leah was on the edge of her chair.

"Thanks, Lenore." John said, then turned his attention back to Leah. "So, this brother, Alexander, is a weather man? You're sure about this?"

"I know Gregor said his brother would love the weather in Colorado because weather was his field of study. I just know if you can find Alexander, you can find Gregor. They were extremely close. I also know Gregor is not there by choice."

John took a moment and sipped his juice. "Why do you insist he didn't leave by choice? Do you think he was abducted?"

"No. I think he left by choice, but I don't think it was his intention to stay there. I can't give you the logic or evidence you need." She shrugged petite shoulders. "It's just not my forte'. I do know people though, and I know this man would never give up what he found here. I believe he fell in love, but before he could accept happiness for himself, he needed to get his brother out of the Soviet Union."

Lenore had been thumbing through the TV Guide from her end of the sofa when the silence made her look up to see John and Leah looking at her.

"I want no part of this! I personally don't think I'm a factor in your theory. He's gone. Period." She stood up tossing the little magazine on the table. "If someone goes over there and tries to find him and he isn't wanting to be found, someone could be put in a dangerous situation. I think we should let sleeping dogs, or Russian bears, lie!"

Leah looked hurt. John looked surprised. Lenore stomped into the kitchen to forage for food she wasn't especially hungry for, and turned on the radio.

"She's as adamantly convinced he's gone by choice as you are, he's not." John frowned. "I don't get it."

"You would if you knew her better. She's the world champion at burying her feelings and this whole situation has kept her from admitting anything. If she can convince herself it's hopeless, she can put those thoughts and energies in a different direction. Her focus is trying to make it on her own and get Joel through high school. But the truth is, she's scared to death."

They were both quiet a moment before Leah continued.

"It took so much energy from her when Gregor disappeared. She let her guard down and he got right in her heart. Now he's gone, and she feels embarrassed and ashamed for letting him get that close. I know he was sincere, but all she knows is he's gone and it hurts."

John listened, as Leah told him about her friend listening to the music in the other room.

"There's never been a lot of stability in her life and she's learned love only results in pain. If he would have just explained everything before he left, it would have been so different."

Leah looked through tear-glazed eyes. "Please bring him back to her. If you can't, and you care for her at all, find a way to let her know. I don't know what's going to happen when Joel graduates and goes out on his own. It's her last goal."

John spoke softly to Lenore's very concerned friend. "You know, Leah, there are a lot of reasons the agency needs to find our missing Soviet friend. I have a reason to pursue it a little harder." He looked toward the kitchen where music comforted the brunette. "She's a beautiful woman. She deserves to be happy. I hope she knows what a valuable friend she has in you. Hang in there and keep her going." He gave her hand a squeeze. "I'll work with the new information, and I think I'll correspond with you concerning the case. You'll know what the status is and can decide what you feel she needs to know."

"Sounds like a plan." Leah nodded. "We'll just tell her you think she's probably right. She'll love that. Do you think you'll take her out again? She had a lovely time, you know."

"I'd love to if she would accept." John smiled. "But I may just be a painful reminder of Gregor."

"Try," Leah advised with a wink.

She excused herself for a visit to the bathroom. John walked to the kitchen to find Lenore leaning on the counter, munching an apple and moving to the beat of the music. She straightened, sat the apple down on the counter and turned off the radio.

"Looks like you're ready to leave. Sorry you made the trip for such a bunch of nonsense." She took the empty glass from his hand and rinsed it out before depositing it in the dishwasher.

"I'd never pass up the opportunity to see you again, Lenore." He smiled and was pleased to see a smile form on her lips as well. "Am I going to have to send a gift certificate for a restaurant, or could we dispense with my obvious ploys and let me pick you up and take you out to dinner?"

A small laugh and slight blush, was her answer. He was delighted.

"How about next Saturday night? We'll have dinner someplace nice. Maybe we'll even get some really good Champagne for you to try."

"Let me check with Joel. Sometimes he has concerts and doesn't let me know ahead of time. Call me on Monday." A little frown furrowed across her brow and she looked away. "On second thought, we'll call it a plan unless I call you." She looked back and smiled. "How's that?"

"Terrific. I'll pick you up at seven."

"How dressy?"

"Your beautiful black dress would work nicely." He laughed. "You might consider a coat, too."

"At least I know I don't have to go shopping for another dress; which reminds me, did you find out anything about the guy we saw?"

"No. Nothing. Just someone embarrassed to be caught watching you, I suppose." He shrugged his shoulders. "You might be right. We may just be wasting our time. I'm going to think about closing the case on Greg."

She looked relieved. "Good … Good!"

As Leah walked into the room, he saw Lenore's eyes glaze over before she was able to shake it off and tell Leah of their plans for Saturday night.

* * * * *

With a good-bye to Leah and a quick kiss on Lenore's cheek, he left. Once inside the Mercedes, he hit the steering wheel and cursed. He blinked his lights at the blue sedan parked down the street and received a blink in return as he drove out of the neighborhood. He was doing everything in his power to protect Lenore. Someone wanted her pretty bad, and they wouldn't stop just because one attempt failed.

She needed normalcy in her life, but what he knew would shatter it. They had successfully detained the man from the shopping trip; he had run smack into their own agent. John had laughed at the blundered attempt to track Lenore Appleby. She was a beauty by any standards, and the man had succumbed to temptation and got too close. He wasn't talking, but they had a pretty good idea who he was working for. The KGB and Greg Parish, a.k.a. Gregor Parishnikov, were factors.

"Parish, I could kick your Russian ass for what you've done. Why didn't you let us know what you wanted to do? Hell, we would have done it for you. Instead you go and get yourself in trouble and leave your lady wondering what she did to drive you away. You're a fool, Parish. I can't wait to tell you what a fool you are."

With frustrations vented, he settled back into the seat and mindlessly followed the interstate home. He would feed the additional information about Greg's brother to the right people and see what they could do with it. Their efforts, so far, had turned up nothing. It was as if Greg had fallen off the face of the earth. That meant he was either dead or in prison. They would check on Alexander's occupation.

There were a lot of people on both sides of the iron curtain working to find Gregor Parishnikov. John knew he had to press a little harder. Lenore was running out of hope.

* * * * *

"Do you want to watch another movie?" Leah asked.

"Sure, but I'm getting back into my sweats."

"I've got to whiz, then I'm putting on my silk pajamas."

They talked through the bathroom door as Lenore changed clothes. She hung up her jeans and folded her sweater to put back in the stack of similarly folded sweaters in the top of her closet.

"Aren't you excited about going to dinner next Saturday?"

"Not especially." Lenore replied, flatly. "I haven't decided if I'm going."

"What do you mean? You've accepted."

"Something could come up. You know how my life goes."

Leah pressed her lips together to keep from breaking into a lecture. "It would be fun if you go; he sure seems nice," she finally said.

Lenore walked out of the bedroom and into the bathroom, where Leah exited, heading for the bedroom to change into her own comfy clothes.

"He's nice enough. Great car." Lenore conceded.

"There you go. Just think of riding to Denver in a Mercedes. You'll look just like a movie star." Leah spoke louder to be heard from the bedroom. "You thrilled John, you know, by accepting. He's crazy about you."

"Don't start that," Lenore warned. "I think he just feels sorry for me."

"Well, he sure gets a silly grin on his face when he looks at you."

They met in the hallway again, and Leah was taken totally by surprise when Lenore took her by the shoulders, bringing them face to face.

"Leah, I love you, but don't do this to me. Don't make me start seeing things I don't want to see. I just can't take it." Her eyes were full of panic as she held onto Leah.

"Oh, my God, Lenore! I didn't mean to upset you. I didn't mean anything like that. I'm sorry ... I'm so sorry." She put her arms around Lenore and held tight, patting and rocking, as if comforting a child awakened by a nightmare. "It's okay, Lenore. It's going to be okay. I promise. I won't have it any other way for you. I'm here for you and I won't go away, ever! I'll never let anyone hurt you ever again. If you really don't want to go, you don't have to. He's just someone who cares about you as a friend. There's nothing more to it than that."

Lenore spoke quietly. "It's just too much right now. When I started thinking about having John call me, I started thinking about waiting for Gregor's call. He never called, Leah. He didn't come back." The brunette's tears were flowing freely. "He's never, ever coming back. Never, ever."

"I know, but it's going to be okay." She stroked Lenore's long, dark hair and held her close. "You got along fine before you met him, and you'll get along fine now. It's just going to take some time for the hurt to go away."

"I don't think so. He changed me, Leah. I'm not the same person I was before," She said between sobs. "I don't know who I am or where I'm going. I just wake up each day and try to think of a reason to keep on trying. I used to wake up every morning in celebration for having another chance at life." She shook her head. "I can't tell you the last time I saw a sunrise. I just don't care anymore."

"Sure you do. You're just healing right now. It's going to take a little time for the old Lenore to surface again, but I'll bet she does." Leah continued to soothe as Lenore continued to cry. "These dark, dreary days and cold weather don't help anyone's frame of mind, either. It'll be spring before you know it and we can get out and go for rides in Baby with her top down. We can go to the rock for picnics and sun bathing. You just need the seasons to hurry up and change." She leaned away slightly, and looked up at Lenore. "It's a whole new year, and it's going to be a good one, no matter what. We just have to wade through it together, right?"

The positive thoughts Leah planted seemed to lift the spirits of her friend, who managed a smile and nod between intermittent spasms of breath.

"That's better," Leah said. "Now, we're a team, aren't we?"

"Yes."

"We won't let anyone or anything change that, right?"

"Right!"

"Okay, now let's go watch the movie." Leah took Lenore by hand and led her to the living room.

"Leah, don't ever give up on me." Another spastic sob interrupted her words.

"Not a chance! We might be crazy, but we're crazy together, always!" Leah looked at Lenore and crossed her eyes. Lenore laughed and stuck out her tongue.

They went to the living room and resumed their slumber party. True to form, Lenore fell asleep shortly after the movie started.

* * * * *

"Lenore, wake up! You have to wake up now. We have someplace to go. Come on, that's right, sit up there."

Lenore sat up and looked around. She was in the living room and Leah was standing over her, dressed and offering a cup of coffee. She accepted the coffee and sipped carefully, then looked at Leah. First attempts to talk were done in an inaudible whisper. She cleared her throat and tried again.

"Where do we have to go? What time is it?"

"Don't worry about it. Here, put on your shoes and grab your coat. Hurry up!"

Like a mindless robot following orders, she put on her Nike's and laced them up. At Leah's urging, she sipped a little more coffee, then put on her coat.

The crisp pre-dawn Colorado air opened her eyes and she yawned and shivered. Baby was already running, and they quickly got in and closed the doors. Leah was at the wheel and Lenore was awake enough to question her sanity.

"What's going on? Is something wrong? Where are we going and what time is it?"

"There you go, worrying about the time. Nothing's wrong. I just had an incredible urge for breakfast. Aren't you hungry?"

Lenore sat for a moment and thought it over. There was the slightest grumble in her stomach.

"I guess I'm hungry. Couldn't we have waited until it was light?"

"I don't think I could have lasted that long."

Lenore shrugged her submission and they drove away from the house.

"See Lenore, we're not the only ones getting out this early." She gestured toward the car sitting near the end of the block. "That guy doesn't look very happy about having to go to work this morning."

* * * * *

The ladies' early morning adventure had taken the occupant of the blue sedan by surprise. He hoped they didn't notice him following. His relief was already in town and could take up the surveillance before they went very far, providing the occupants of the Chevelle didn't try to lose them. The usual break in routine had them all concerned.

John Dixon was awake and on the radio with three agents; one following, one about to take up the route and another on his way from Denver. He listened as the two agents in Fort Collins orchestrated the trade-off.

* * * * *

"Your neighbor just turned off," Leah noted. "I thought he was going to follow us all the way to the donut shop. Guess he had breakfast before he left home."

"We could have stayed home and had breakfast. I can't believe we're doing this." Lenore didn't bother to stifle a yawn.

The brightly lit shop welcomed them.

"Let's go in and get some pastries and coffee or whatever we want."

As they perused the selection and made choices, the driver of a black truck watched from across the street. He hoped they wouldn't notice.

With pastries and cups of coffee to go, they walked outside.

"Now, we're going home, right?"

"Wrong!"

"Where are we going now?" Lenore asked, exasperated.

"Look over to the east." Leah pointed before getting into the car. 'What do you see?"

Through the clutter of buildings and silhouetted trees, Lenore could see the faint glow of light on the horizon.

Climbing into the car, Lenore said, "It's almost sunrise."

"Exactly! We're going to catch it up on the dam by the lake. It'll be beautiful. You need this, Lenore."

"Think it'll help?"

"Can't hurt," Leah answered cheerfully. "Besides, when was the last time we saw a sunrise together?"

Lenore yawned again before answering. "Never, seems to come to mind."

"Really? Well, if it's a first, all the better."

They drove to the lake and parked on a hill facing the sunrise. Below them, the city lights twinkled like gems on a blanket of black velvet. As they sipped coffee and munched the sweet pastries, the eastern sky slowly grew brighter and the lights below succumbed to the glowing competition. They squinted their eyes when the first rays of sunlight burst over the horizon. Then Leah handed Lenore her sunglasses and donned her own.

"Lenore, this is beautiful! No wonder you're a morning person. This does something to your soul, doesn't it?"

"It used to. I suppose it still does. I know I like the light more than the dark." Lenore's voice was quiet as she watched the landscape brighten with the sun's rays.

"You don't get out much during the day in cold months. Maybe on your lunch hours you should sit out in your car or take a walk on the nicer days. Just get a little more time in the daylight."

"I could try," Lenore replied. "Have you seen enough? I'll bet you have to go to the bathroom."

"You know me well."

"Thank you, Leah." Lenore hugged her best friend. "I did need to see a sunrise. I feel better."

It was what Leah needed to hear and there was some truth to it. Lenore would try extra doses of sunshine during the week. Maybe it would lighten her outlook on life and she could get past the monotonous gloom.

* * * * *

John Dixon had watched the sunrise from his own window. When he got word the two ladies had returned home safe and sound, he sat down on the sofa and ran his fingers through his hair. The spontaneous morning adventure had been for nothing more than watching a sunrise.

He smiled and shook his head.

CHAPTER 29

It was a busy week. Lenore was mired in routine, but the extra doses of sunshine seemed to have a good effect on her attitude. The divorce had proceeded as expected and she simply waited for the final decree and she could forget, or try to forget, she had ever been married to Nick Carlson. Having never taken his name when they married, she wouldn't have to bother with a name change.

The five-thousand-dollar settlement was a pittance. She had wanted nothing, but her attorney had convinced her she was due. He suggested ten. She compromised with five. She knew more than anything, it would just be an irritant to Nick.

She received the check and planned to deposit it on Friday afternoon. She started making mental notes on what she should do with it. Joel would benefit from the settlement. If his dad would indeed match contributions, Lenore would donate a thousand toward a car. Joel's new part-time job as a dishwasher at the new Mexican restaurant in town would ensure the gas and maintenance. She wished he had a job that would let him get home earlier, but he was okay with it. He rode his bike there after school and Lenore picked him up after he was finished, normally about nine-thirty. The bike was carried home in the trunk of Lenore's car, ready for his next adventure. He was sure he would be promoted to wait staff any time. She would keep her promise of tags and insurance, and couldn't wait to tell him the good news.

When Leah arrived at the store for their Friday afternoon, Lenore was noticeably excited.

"I don't know if it's the money, the extra doses of sunshine or the prospect of your date tomorrow night, but I like the transformation. That looks like a genuine smile on your face," Leah noted.

"It is!" Lenore grinned. "It's not the date. In fact, I may cancel it."

"Why?"

"Well, Joel's going to want to car shop all weekend. The money from his dad should be here Monday or Tuesday. We're going to be busy!"

"Lenore, you can't shop for cars on Saturday night. You might as well go ahead and have your date. I think you're just using it for an excuse. Are you chicken?"

"No! I just figured Joel would want me to go with him to check out cars from the newspaper."

"Did you tell him you have a date?"

"I might have mentioned it." She grabbed her coat as they walked out the back door. "Leah, I haven't dated in years. I don't know how!"

"Don't be silly. It's not like a blind date, or going out with someone you don't really know. He's a sweet guy. You'll have fun and won't have to fight him off. He knows the situation and neither of you will have to pretend. How much safer could it get?"

"Okay, okay! I'll go." She was still hoping something would come up to change it. "Here, I circled ads in the paper. We can drive by and look at the cars before Joel gets out of school."

After two hours of categorizing cars into their lemon list, they were not feeling very good about the choices. If they had good bodies, they needed an engine. If they ran well, they looked like entries for the demolition derby.

"Poor Joel. He's not going to get much of a car. The reality check is going to be painful."

"Lenore, most boys are tickled to have something to get them from point A to point B as long as the radio works. He likes to work on cars, doesn't he?"

"I guess I'm the one who needs to lower their standards."

"You don't have to get something right now. You could wait a couple of weeks and see what turns up."

They got out to look at a '63 Chevy pickup. There was more rust than paint and when they noticed the bed of the truck would go down the road at a noticeably different angle than the cab, they got back in the car without bothering the owner.

"It's nearly two-thirty. Want to drop me off at my car? Joel will be waiting for you."

"I suppose." She checked the time for herself. "Are you sure you don't want to come along?"

"No, this an important time for you two. I'll stop by tomorrow evening to see you before John picks you up. I want to see you in that dress!"

"Okay. Come right after work and help me get ready."

"Great! Why don't I bring my silver fox jacket? Maybe you won't freeze to death this time."

"Seriously?" Lenore grinned. "I'd love it."

"Either that or we could go shopping for long red underwear."

With laughter, they parted ways.

When Lenore pulled into the driveway at home, Joel was out the door, and in the car before she had a chance to turn off the engine.

"Hi Sweetie! I wish you were a little more excited about car shopping," she teased.

"Are you kidding? It's all I could think about today." He bit into an apple and handed another to Lenore. "Do you think Dad has sent the money?"

"I'm sure he has." She accepted the offering and took a bite. "It'll get here the first of the week. You realize we won't actually buy something today, right?"

"Yes, but we could give them a down-payment if it's one we don't want to lose, right?"

"Absolutely. I also want you to think of another option; we aren't on a deadline here. We should take our time and be a little picky, don't you think? The ones I've see today left a lot to be desired."

"But Mom, just think; you won't have to pick me up after work. Besides, I'm about the only guy left in my class who doesn't have a car!"

Lenore knew it was probably an exaggeration, but she remembered the importance of having her own first car, and it had been missing a driver's window and the right front fender had a pretty big crunch, but it was all hers and she loved it. The radio worked!

"Well, Joel, let's see what we can find. If it's something you really think you can't live without, we'll give them a deposit."

A look of relief and gratitude settled on her son's face. However, an hour later, and looking at six different cars, he accepted the idea of shopping a little longer.

"I think I'm bummed!"

"I know. There's not much out there for two thousand." She looked over at Joel as she drove home. "Tell you what, I'll consider upping the amount, if you're willing to make payments to me. I'm donating a thousand and so is your dad. Anything over that, you have to pay back."

"Seriously, Mom?" He perked up. "You'll do that for me?"

"Yes, but only with the stipulation you pay me back. It won't be a lot more; say five or six hundred, tops."

"It has to make a difference. Mom, have I told you lately you're the best mom in the world?"

"No, and I was beginning to wonder if my standing had slipped." She laughed. "Maybe you and Eric can do some looking tomorrow. I'm ready to call it a day. You could also ask Grant to look in Denver." She patted Joel on the arm. "We'll have a car for you in a week or two at the most. It might just be worth the wait."

An impatient little groan signaled his resignation.

"If Eric and I find something tomorrow, can we go after you get off work and put a deposit on it?"

Lenore took a deep breath and glanced at Joel. "Well, I sort of have a date."

"A date?" Joel raised his brows. "You?"

"Is it that much of a stretch of the imagination?"

"I didn't mean it that way." He laughed. "Who with?"

"The same guy who gave me the ticket for the concert and your tickets for the game."

"I haven't met him. Where did you say you met?"

"I met him at the store. He bought boots from me. I told you that." She tried to sound casual.

"Right. I forgot. What does he do for a living?"

"What difference does that make? Are you screening my dates now?"

"Ha! You don't know, do you?" Joel replied, smirking.

Lenore's mind was racing to keep up with the inquisition. She thought over her options. She could lie and tell him she didn't know, but then she would seem careless. She could tell the truth, that he worked for the CIA and had been tailing her since she had the affair with a Soviet spy. A half-truth was in order.

"He's an investigator of some sort."

"Cool! Does he carry a gun?"

"Not that I've ever seen. I don't think he's that kind of investigator." She hoped it would satisfy Joel without getting too detailed.

He shrugged, then the subject returned to his search for a car.

"Can I call Grant tonight and ask him to check the Denver papers for cars?"

"Yes, but don't expect him to devote all his time to the task. He has his own life and schedule."

With Porsche expectations on a second-hand Ford budget, Joel promised patience. They drove home where Joel glued himself to the phone and Lenore busied herself with preparing dinner. Salad was on the table. Rice pilaf was cooked and she was taking chicken breasts out of the oven when Joel interrupted her.

"You've got a call. I think it's the guy you're going out with. I've got Eric on call waiting, so could you make it quick?"

"No, you can call Eric back if you need to." She removed her oven mitt and accepted the phone.

"Sounds like I'm interrupting an important phone call. I'll try to make it brief."

The sound of John's voice made her smile. "It's fine, really."

An impatient Joel went to the table, took a cherry tomato from the salad and popped it into his mouth on his way to the living room.

"I didn't hear from you. Are we still on for tomorrow night?"

"I'll be ready." She wondered why she was smiling and tried to stop.

"Great! I'll see you at seven."

"Okay. I'd better give the phone back to Joel. He's car shopping."

"Oh? Maybe I can help. We'll talk tomorrow night."

With brief good-byes, Lenore handed the receiver back to Joel, and told him his dinner was ready. She was still smiling and convinced herself that she was only looking forward to the event, not in seeing John.

* * * * *

John was preparing to leave his office when a co-worker happened to note the end of the conversation.

"Will your date need a taxi tomorrow night?"

"No, Frank, your services won't be needed. I'm just taking her out to dinner. I thought you guys could use a night off from surveillance."

"Your generosity is overwhelming. I wonder if Parish would think you were being kind? I think he would see it as you moving in on his territory."

"Seems to me he shouldn't have left the territory. I'd like nothing more than to have him surface long enough to punch me in the nose. The big boys still think she's a factor in his returning. He should be grateful I'm the one taking up her time. It's taking a lot of restraint to not get emotionally involved."

"What if she gets emotionally involved with you?"

"Won't happen." John shook his head. "No, this one's a lost cause. Greg made sure of it. I don't know what he did to her, but he's ruined her for any other man. Believe me, if I thought there was a chance, I'd try."

"You're a brave man, Dixon." The older agent slapped John on the back. "Maybe we should get you a commendation for going above and beyond."

"I'd rather you take up a collection for a nose job. He could get a little nasty over this."

John stopped on the way home and ordered flowers.

CHAPTER 30

It had been weeks since Gregor had heard the sound of another voice. He busied himself with isometric exercises, taking care to prevent further injury to his healing rib. He had found a broken sliver of concrete and used it to scratch various mathematics problems into the dirt of his cell one day, and spent the next day finding answers. He drew detailed sketches of an assortment of firearms, both together and dismantled. He recited childhood rhymes and stories in four languages. He worked hard to keep his mind alert and prevent his physical condition from deteriorating.

The filth Gregor was forced to tolerate was taking the most from him. His hair was matted and straggly, and the neatly trimmed beard had grown into an unruly mass. Though he made attempts to stay as clean as possible, he was resigned to his present fate. The bi-monthly hosing down of his cell provided little relief, and the cold water left him chilled for hours afterward. It was with total surprise he found himself being taken to a shower.

"Prisoner Parishnikov, you are to clean yourself. Be quick in your efforts."

The guard took his filthy clothes and replaced them with a gray, one-piece uniform. Gregor stood under the steamy hot water as long as he dared, scrubbing deliberately with harsh soap. The uniform, though baggy and stiff, was clean and welcomed.

He was ushered, with impatient jabs from a rifle barrel, to a clean room, devoid of furnishing, except for one lone chair. Soon, a portly man entered with the guard, carrying a razor and scissors. Gregor's hands were tied before the barber began.

Liberal amounts of hair were crudely trimmed from his head and beard before he was taken to another room. It was clean and warm. There was a flimsy bed with a mattress and clean blankets. A window provided a view of the wintry landscape, though wire mesh and bars prevented any hope of escape.

Before Gregor could examine his new quarters in detail, food was brought to him. Instead of the watery broth and stale bread he had tolerated for months, before him was a thick, beefy stew. It was hot and the aroma made his mouth water. Two generous slices of fresh bread and an apple accompanied the fare. Hot tea was poured from a vessel and left on the tray for him to finish.

"We trust you will find this to your liking, prisoner Parishnikov." The guards had never spoken kindly to him before. "Please enjoy your meal. Would you care for an after-dinner cigarette?"

Dumb struck, Gregor shook his head and continued to stare at the meal before him. The door to his new cell was closed, and he heard the lock engage before he picked up a spoon and dipped it cautiously into the stew. Perhaps he was dreaming. He tasted the stew carefully, then smiled as he closed his mouth around the delicious, hearty food. He would worry about the motives later. For now, every sense was involved in the task at hand.

With enormous restraint, Gregor limited his intake to a very small portion of what was before him. Having gone so long without substantial food, he knew his body would not tolerate it well. He hid the apple under a corner of the covers, and settled on the lumpy mattress, slowly sipping the strong, hot tea. However, he didn't have long to ponder the situation; his interrogator and the ever-present guard stepped into the room.

"Did you not find the meal to your liking?"

Gregor sat up straighter. "Let's say my body is having trouble getting over the shock."

The officer nodded. "I see. You are wondering about all of this, yes?"

"I am curious."

"Your curiosity will be satisfied. We are having visitors. There will be a film crew coming to document life in the Soviet prison system. We want to impress them."

"You want to lie to them." Gregor did not flinch as the guard poised for a blow.

Instead, the well-groomed officer plucked an imaginary piece of lint from his uniform.

"If you cooperate, we may let you get used to these quarters. If they ask you to describe your imprisonment, you are to tell them you are made very comfortable. You will tell them only that you are a prisoner of the Soviet State for crimes against the government."

Gregor settled back onto the cot. "And if I tell them the truth?"

"You will be shot five minutes after they depart." It was not an idle threat. "We have some interesting news from America. You would miss the details of that information. I think it will be worth your cooperation."

With a sardonic smile, the officer and guard left the room. The tray of food and tea was removed, and the door once again locked. Gregor knew he must cooperate, though the chance to alert someone of the situation was a temptation. He could only hope the film would be seen by American CIA agents. Perhaps the situation was not hopeless.

Stretching out on the mattress, he slept peacefully, for the first time in many months. He slept for nearly eighteen hours and attempts to awaken him for meals brought little or no response.

* * * * *

"Prisoner Parishnikov, it is getting late. You will awaken!"

Gregor opened his eyes as he was pulled from the cot and dragged from his cell, stripped and thrown into the shower. The warm water eased him into a state of awareness, and he realized they must be getting ready for the visitors. He quickly washed and dried himself, then was given another clean uniform. This one fit better than the last. Once again, a hot meal was served shortly after he returned to his room. Thick strips of meat and chunks of potatoes were covered in a rich, dark gravy, accompanied again by fresh bread and another apple. He ate slowly, savoring each bite. Before he had finished, he heard voices outside his door. They were speaking English!

"Could we interview this prisoner without a guard present?"

"We feel, for your protection of course, it is not possible. We will assure you the guard's presence will have no bearing on the interview. We have nothing to hide."

The door opened and Gregor watched as the journalist and a man carrying a video camera were ushered into the tidy room. Two chairs were brought in and they sat down as if awaiting a friendly chat with a neighbor.

"Hello. We are members of the International Press Magazine. We understand you speak some English. Could we ask you a few questions?"

Gregor caught a warning glare from the guard, and smiled at his visitors. "Yes, I will answer your questions."

"You speak very good English. Could you tell us your name and why you are here?"

"I am Gregor Parishnikov. I have committed a crime against the Soviet State. That is why I am here."

The guard smiled, but the interviewer would not accept the answer.

"Exactly what did you do? Why are you here?"

"Perhaps you should ask others. I am not at liberty to discuss the situation."

The guard frowned and adjusted his rifle. It didn't go unnoticed by the journalist, who changed the subject.

"How long have you been here, Mr. Parishnikov? Your room looks very clean and comfortable."

"Any amount of time is too long, is it not, when one loses his freedom? Yes, these quarters are most comfortable. Far better than what one would expect. It would almost make one think they were trying to impress you, wouldn't it?"

A murderous look from the guard assured Gregor, he would pay for the remark. He would endure the punishment. It was worth the risk.

"Tell us, Mr. Parishnikov, where did you learn to speak the English language so well?"

"It was part of my schooling at the University."

The guard smiled. The journalist glanced at the guard and frowned. He looked back at Gregor and raised his eyebrows.

"Is there anyone you would like to send a message to—a family member or friend who could be assured of your well-being?"

It was the ultimate temptation, but the risk was far too great. Gregor simply smiled and shook his head.

They thanked him for his time and prepared to leave. The camera man lowered his equipment and winked at Gregor as he left the room.

Did he know this man? After they left, Gregor sat on his cot and tried to remember the face. No, he could not recall ever seeing the face, yet he had winked. Was it a signal? Perhaps simply an assurance he was not to be forgotten. He lay back on the bed and closed his eyes. He would enjoy the comforts of his new room for as long as he could. The wink was dismissed as he settled into a nap.

CHAPTER 31

Lenore stood in the shower and let tears run down her face. It was one of the few places she allowed thoughts of Gregor to fill her mind. She prayed for his safety and his return. In the middle of the night, she often got out of bed and down on her knees in a childhood posture of prayer, asking for miracles.

As the water washed the last of her tears down the drain, she took a deep breath and turned off the water. She could hear Leah's voice through the door.

"I was beginning to think you had fallen asleep in there."

Lenore stepped out of the shower and wrapped a towel around herself. She opened the door and found the rush of cooler, drier air refreshing.

"I was trying to wake up. I'm so tired from working all day, and I'm supposed to go out to dinner? I'll fall asleep in my salad."

"Just don't get any croutons up your nose. Look, I remembered the jacket." Leah held up the elegant wrap.

"Are you sure you want me to borrow it? I'll be scared to death I'll ruin it or that someone will take it."

"Oh, you're being silly! It's had everything from champagne to chocolate pie dripped on it and it cleans just fine. I got this when we lived it Texas." She stroked the luxurious fur as if it were a favorite pet. "It was a wise investment. I've enjoyed it so much."

"I'll take very good care of it." Lenore promised.

Leah hung up the jacket and held the dryer for Lenore, who turned her hair upside down to dry it from underneath. A few minutes later, Lenore flipped it back and brushed until there were no tangles. It's satiny texture and shine hung perfectly straight.

"What do you think?" Lenore asked.

"Gorgeous, but I thought you were going to wear it up."

"Still could." Lenore shrugged. She plugged in the curling iron before going to her bedroom to start dressing.

Leah was convinced Lenore should wear stockings and a bustier, but Lenore's practical side won out; she didn't own a bustier. Matching black lace panties and bra would suffice.

With a terrycloth robe covering the ensemble, they returned to the bathroom. Lenore curled and lifted and pinned with help from Leah. Soon, her hair was up and feminine, but still reflected the soft, easy style of Lenore. She carefully applied what little makeup she wore and they went back into the bedroom. She slipped into the dress and into high heels, recently purchased. After all, she did work in a shoe store. She stood in front of the full-length mirror.

"Look at me. I'm all grown-up!" She had seen herself in the dress, but Leah hadn't.

"I sure hope John is wearing garters on his socks."

"What?" Lenore laughed. "Why?"

"You're going to knock his socks off!"

They were filling a small dress purse with necessities when the doorbell rang. She could hear Joel answering as she ran back into the bathroom for last minute checks.

"Hello, I'm John Dixon. You must be Joel."

"Hi. I think Mom's about ready. I smell hair spray and perfume. Have a seat."

Leah joined the two gentlemen in the living room to watch reactions, and when Lenore entered, they both stood to greet her.

"Wow, Mom!"

"My sentiments exactly, Joel. Wow!"

Lenore blushed and turned as if to leave the room. Leah grabbed her arm and whispered, "No way, Lenore. I don't think John would let you back out now!"

"I forgot something," John said and dashed out the door, leaving Lenore, Leah and Joel wondering if he was the one backing out. He returned with a bouquet of yellow rose buds and white daisies that he presented after removing a protective bag.

"John, they're beautiful! Thank you." She drank-in the aroma of the bouquet. "I need to put them in water."

"I'll do it if Joel will find a vase," Leah offered. "You two get going."

John held the silver fox jacket as Lenore slipped into it. Joel couldn't resist a last-minute repartee.

"Now, don't be late!" He gave his mom a kiss on the cheek, then shook John's hand firmly and smiled.

Leah and Joel watched the handsome couple walk away. The young man turned to Leah.

"I can't believe that was Mom! I've never seen her look so beautiful. He'd better be good to her."

"I'm sure she'll be fine." Leah laughed and gave Joel a hug, making him smile back. "You go find a vase and I'll trim the flowers. She'll have a beautiful reminder of her evening."

* * * * *

As the couple walked away from the house John flexed his hand and laughed. "I think your son was trying to convey a warning." He opened her door and she sat down, then he closed her door and went around the car to get in behind the wheel.

"What do you mean?"

"He nearly cut off the blood supply when he shook my hand." He started the Mercedes and backed out of the drive.

Lenore laughed and apologized at the same time. "I'm really sorry, John."

"Hey, you might think it's funny, but I've seen what he and his brother do to men who hurt their mom."

"Are you planning to hurt me?"

"Lenore, I never want to hurt you or see you hurt." He smiled. "It's not just because your sons would beat the hell out of me, either."

Lenore wanted to steer the conversation a different direction. "I sure hope the service is fast where we're going. I'm starved!"

"If it isn't, I'll personally go into the kitchen and raid their refrigerator for you."

"You're a prince!" She giggled.

"I know." He looked at Lenore. "Have to be. I'm with a princess."

"Enough flattery! I'm curious about something. Why did you buy those expensive hiking boots? Do you do a lot of hiking?"

"I had to with Greg. I decided I'd better get into it if I was going to follow him. He loves being outdoors, and taught me what little I know about being outdoors. He also taught me to ski."

"He knew you were following?"

"He used to be a spy, remember? He realized what and why we were doing it and accepted it quite graciously. We spent a lot of time together. You could say we are, or were friends ... sort of."

"Why just sort of?"

"I guess in the back of our minds, we knew it was a forced relationship." He smiled at Lenore. "I still hope we find him. You always hope your trust hasn't been violated."

Lenore fell silent and John wished he had kept the last statement to himself.

"I'm sorry, Lenore. Let's try to get past that last one, okay? We're out to have a nice evening and we're not going to let the unexplained absence or the mental presence of Mr. Parish ruin it. I think he's taken enough from both of us already."

"You're right, John. He's taken enough." She slid a little closer, tucked her hand through his arm and smiled. He returned the smile, admiring the beauty at his side. Maybe he was wrong about her.

* * * * *

John bribed the waiter to bring shrimp cocktail shortly after they were seated. Lenore thanked him profusely, and used the tiny fork to capture her prey and dip it into the sauce. She chewed slowly, savoring every bite. With half the shrimp devoured, she dabbed at the corners of her mouth with the linen napkin.

"Thanks! Now I won't be tempted to eat the flowers or swipe food from a passing server. I'd like for you to order my dinner. I'll trust you."

Dinner went well. The food was delicious and the service excellent. The atmosphere was relaxing as they drank an after-dinner coffee.

"This has been lovely." Lenore sighed.

"You talk like the evening's over."

"Isn't it?"

"I was hoping we could go to the other room and dance a little before I had to take you home. It's still pretty early." He checked his watch.

"Early for you, maybe." Lenore could only touch her bracelet. Leah had forbidden her to wear a watch. "I can stay a while longer." She smiled. "It sounds nice."

John smiled and handed the waiter a gold card. When it was returned, he signed the receipt and they walked into the other room, where lights were a little more subdued and elegantly dressed couples swayed to soft music. They were quickly escorted to an open table. It only took a few minutes for their eyes to adjust to the different lighting.

"Shall we?" John stood and held his hand out to Lenore. As they turned around the floor, she found him an easy partner to follow. He didn't try to dazzle her with fancy steps and they were able to converse. They sat through a couple of songs and danced to another.

"Lenore, I hope you're having a good time."

"Actually, I'm having a really great time." She smiled up at John.

"You sound surprised."

"I am, a little. I nearly turned you down. I'm glad I didn't."

"Me, too." He smiled and looked at the lovely lady in his arms, smiling up at him. "Why were you going to turn me down?"

"I was afraid of trying to go out on a date. I wasn't sure what to expect."

"Afraid I was going to try something?"

"Maybe. I don't really know." She shrugged slightly. "You never have."

"No." He sighed. "Believe me, there have been times it took a great deal of restraint."

"Oh?"

"Like when I got lost in your eyes following the concert."

"Tell me, John, what stopped you?" She looked up at him with raised eyebrows.

"I suppose you could say it was out of respect for you and someone we both know. There's always the possibility he'll discover I'm taking you out and show up just to punch me in the nose." He felt her stiffen. "I've said something wrong, haven't I?"

"It's time to go. I'm very, very tired!"

She walked back to their table long enough to retrieve her purse, then made her way through the crowd to the front door. John secured their wraps from the check-in and met her at the door. He put the silver fox jacket on her shoulders and she stepped away when his hands lingered a bit.

As they waited for the car to be brought around, he attempted to break through the wall quickly building between them.

"Lenore, I'm at a loss here. I'm not sure what I said that offended you, but if you could tell me, perhaps I could understand and—"

A cold glare from her eyes silenced him. He would wait until they were in the car. The valet handed John the key and the doorman opened Lenore's door. When they were encased in the plush interior of the Mercedes and had gone a few blocks, he tried again.

"Lenore, tell me what's going on here? Please! What did I say?"

Lenore bit her lower lip in an effort to keep tears in check. She wasn't sad. She was infuriated, and was about to unleash it on an unsuspecting CIA agent.

"Pull over!"

Not sure if she was going to walk away or was about to get sick, John pulled into an empty parking lot and stopped. She turned in the seat and faced him.

"I suppose I should thank you for making things a little clearer," she said quietly. "Maybe if you would have let me in on the rules of the game, or the objective, we could have been putting on quite a show." She smiled, but there was no humor in it. The sentiment behind it was not conciliation. "I'm bait, aren't I? You're using me to try to lure Gregor out from wherever he is."

"Lenore, that's not—"

"What? Not true?" The quiet voice was getting steadily louder. "I'm tired of being lied to. I hate lies! I hate 'em! I hate 'em! I hate 'em! And guess what? I'm out of the game!" She jabbed a finger at her chest. "I've had it." She wagged a finger at John. "You and your little CIA buddies can find some other way to win back your little prize." She laughed. "He's become quite an embarrassment for you, hasn't he?"

John sat quietly and looked at Lenore. She wasn't going to relent.

"I am quite the fool. Here I am, a middle-aged shoe clerk with a teenager to raise, thinking someone like Gregor found me to be the woman of his dreams." She spoke in a whisper. "What a joke!" She flashed dark green eyes back into at John. "He doesn't want me, John. I'm not worth the trouble."

There were tears, but her voice never wavered. "Then, you walk into my life. You make me think my life is in danger. You make me think Gregor's life could be in danger, when all you want to do is keep me on a line and see if he's interested enough to be jealous. News flash, John! He isn't!" She shook her head and raised her voice another decibel. "He's gone! I don't know where and I don't care either. He's probably found someone with far fewer complications. I hope he's right under your noses, holed-up with some bimbo making you all look like the hopeless asses you are, just like Nick did to me. Now, point this car north and take me home!"

John obligingly put the car in gear and pulled back onto the street. Lenore had turned in the seat and faced forward. She was shaking from a rush of adrenaline the outburst had triggered.

They were half-way home before John spoke.

"Lenore, I know you don't believe it, but I've never used you."

She looked out her side window at the blackness. Patterns of light defined the communities and houses in the distance. She tried to tune out his voice.

"Maybe I'm the fool. Remember, I believed in Greg, too, although a different set of emotions were involved. I thought I knew the guy, then I met your friend Leah, and realized I only knew what was on the surface." He glanced at Lenore and sighed. "You do have one thing right; the company thinks you're a factor in his returning. They'll continue to watch you off and on for a long time. They want someone close. Out of respect for the friendship I had with Greg, I'd rather it was me than a stranger."

She continued to stare out the side window.

"The date was my idea; not because I want to make Greg jealous and force him out into the open. I asked you out because I enjoy your company, although you can be challenging at times." He shook his head. "I don't want to see you sit and wait for him to show up. You should be going out and enjoying your life. I want to be the one taking you out and showing you as good a time as I can manage. That's out of respect for the lovely lady you are."

Lenore turned her head from the side window, and although she didn't look at John, it was an acknowledgment she had heard him. He continued.

"It did take a lot of willpower to keep from kissing you when I had you in my arms and your lips were so close. Maybe someone else would have taken advantage of the situation. I know better than to let myself get emotionally involved with you, because if Greg does show up again, it would be over for me."

"You're pretty sure of that, aren't you?" Her voice was very quiet.

"Shouldn't I be?" He found her hand and she didn't pull away from him.

"How do you know I'm not over him already? I told you, I don't think he's coming back. At least not for me."

The blue luminous sign indicated the rest area, and John slowed to exit. He pulled into a parking spot, away from the clutter of cars near the facilities and turned off the engine. The faint whine of traffic on the interstate seemed to magnify the silence in the car. John released the seatbelt and turned to face Lenore. She was nestled down into the fur jacket and stared straight ahead. He held her hand to his lips and softly kissed her fingertips.

"Lenore, I wish I could believe you're over him. I wish I knew he was never coming back for you."

"What would be different, John?"

"I would become totally selfish. Instead of being your protector, I would try with all my heart to make you forget him."

"Are you my protector?"

"I'm trying to be. Right now, I want you to have someone you can turn to if you feel threatened, or even if you just need a break from routines and want to have a date. I'll never ask for more than you're ready to give."

"What if I only need a hug?"

"Especially if you need a hug." He smiled and kissed her fingertips again. "Sometimes even crusty old CIA agents need hugs, too."

She slipped out of the jacket and into his arms. "Hold me, John. I need a hug right now. I'm so sorry I yelled at you. You didn't deserve it. I'm sorry."

He held her close and drank in the perfume of her hair. His hands softly caressed her back, soothing her. Every nerve in his body was electrified. When she turned her face to him, he didn't refuse the soft moist lips and covered them with his own. She kissed him back and their kisses were deep and heartbeats were racing. John wanted nothing more than to make love to Lenore, but once again, held himself in check.

He stopped kissing Lenore and held her for a moment until he felt control return. He held her back and touched her lips softly with his thumb as he looked into her eyes. He took a handkerchief from his pocket and dabbed at the tears on her cheeks, then handed it to her. She smiled and touched it to the corners of her eyes, then noted the black mascara.

"I either need to use waterproof mascara or buy you a box of handkerchiefs if I keep ruining them like this."

"I always have a good supply on hand, but I'd like to believe I can take you out at some point and not make you cry." He raised his eyebrows and smiled.

"You're a very kind person, John."

"Don't let that get around. It could ruin my career." He chuckled.

She smiled. "I needed the hug and I enjoyed the kiss."

"You're a very passionate woman, Lenore Appleby."

She smiled, then looked out the window.

"I'd love to get inside that mind of yours right now."

"Ah, you're wondering if I was thinking of you or Gregor, right? Maybe I was just satisfying my curiosity."

"I'll never know, will I?"

"Probably not. I don't know if I have the answer, either. Maybe I'll wake up tomorrow and wonder why I kissed you." She looked at him. "Maybe I'll want more than a kiss someday. Maybe I'll never see you again." She frowned and looked away from him.

"I appreciate your honesty. Just remember, Lenore, I'll never go away and not let you know. My job can take me anywhere in the world, but this is home. I hope our friendship grows, and if I'm lucky enough for it to turn into something more, all the better."

He started the car and put on his seatbelt. Lenore settled back into the nest of fur. He merged the Mercedes into northbound traffic and set the cruise control, continuing to hold Lenore's hand.

"John, will you be truthful if I ask you something?"

"As truthful as I can be. Promise!" He smiled at her.

"You haven't recorded all of this, have you?"

He laughed and kissed her hand. "No! I don't take recording equipment on dates. I think it's tacky."

"Good!" She moved closer and put her head on his shoulder.

They rode the rest of the way in silence. When they pulled into her driveway, John was surprised to find Lenore still awake. He squeezed her hand and kissed it again.

"Thank you, Lenore."

"For what?"

"For letting me take you on a date tonight." He brushed a stray hair form her cheek. "I hope it's not our last."

He looked into her eyes, but she looked down, not allowing him to look further.

"We'll play it by ear. I might just need a friend sometime."

"I want that above all else. Just remember, I'm as close as a phone call."

She adjusted the jacket around her shoulders as John got out of the car and escorted her to the front door.

"I hope you don't mind, but I'm awfully tired. Maybe it's best if you don't come in tonight."

"I understand completely."

After she had unlocked the door, she turned and kissed John fully, deeply. She slowly backed away from his lips and looked into his eyes.

"Good-bye, John."

Before he could recover from her kiss and find his voice, she had closed the door. He returned to the car, started it and pulled out of the drive. The stirring in his groin affirmed the fact he would find it difficult to consider Lenore Appleby just a friend. As much as he wanted her, he knew there was someone who wanted her just as much. Someone who had known the passion of this woman. He also knew the passion she let him taste tonight was meant for someone else.

"Greg, old buddy, you're either dead or in prison. That's the only possible answer. I may be the biggest fool in the world, but I'm going to find you and bring you back to her. If she doesn't want you anymore, then maybe I'll have a chance."

* * * * *

As the Mercedes pulled onto the southbound interstate highway heading for Denver, a film cassette was being sealed in an envelope and addressed to a bogus foreign film company. If it somehow managed to get out of the country without being confiscated, there were plenty of people waiting to analyze its story.

The agent handed the package to a clerk sitting behind a desk at the Swiss Consulate. He was assured it would reach its destination, though the agent didn't know what good it would do. Other than an all-out raid of the prison, he didn't see how they could help the man sitting, smiling and talking on the tape.

He turned his collar up against the cold Moscow winter and walked out of the building. His job was finished. He would be assigned a new task. The diplomats could fight this one out.

CHAPTER 32

Gregor was surprised to awaken in the same room. He was hungry and remembered the apple lying under the corner of his mattress. Surely it was only a matter of time before he would be sent back to his previous cell. He sat on the edge of the bed and ate the apple, savoring the taste of fresh fruit in his mouth.

He got up from his bed, munching thoughtfully, and walked to the window. Peering at the endless landscape of white gave him no clues as to his location. It was the first unobstructed view he had enjoyed since his arrival. There were no visible signs of civilization, but he knew it was not a gulag in Siberia. While winter had encased the area in snow and ice, directly below his window were signs of dormant vegetation. Such bushes did not grow in the tundra-like climate of Siberia. Gregor felt a little relieved. If such bushes grew, then there would be signs of spring in the coming months, and perhaps a chance to escape. He had only to survive the inevitable coldness and solitude.

The sound of footsteps and the rattle of keys interrupted his thoughts. He quickly put the apple core back under his mattress. Accompanied by the guard, a young man brought in his tray of food. He was obviously a fellow prisoner and avoided eye contact. Gregor thanked him but received no response. He wondered what one so young could have done to be imprisoned. Possibly a parent or brother had committed an actual crime, and the family members were destined to endure punishment as well. It was a common occurrence, and something he knew personally to be true.

Gregor ate the thick potato soup. There were bits of carrots that had apparently been added as an afterthought, because they retained their raw texture. He didn't mind. Every morsel of nutrition he could put into his body was important. The fact he had maintained a rigorously nutritious diet and exercise lifestyle prior to his incarceration had aided in the swift healing of his broken rib. Though the break had not healed correctly, it caused no pain.

Soon after Gregor had finished his meal, the somber young man was again let into his room. Lenore's son, Joel, was probably near the same age. Would he ever actually get to meet Joel? He thought about the photograph Lenore had so proudly shown of the smiling young man and his brother. He wanted to be with Lenore, helping her make a good life for her younger son. There were probably those who wished the same for this young prisoner. Gregor turned to stare at the brilliant landscape outside his window. He would not succumb to the hopeless feeling in the pit of his stomach.

The empty tray was removed, and the bucket used as a toilet was replaced with a clean one. Small scraps of stiff paper were provided for necessary cleansing. It was not sanitary, by any means, but compared to the lack of even a bucket in his solitary confinement, Gregor was grateful.

A bowl of fresh, hot water was brought into his room next, along with a towel stiffened and gray from numerous washes with harsh soap. When he was left alone, he stripped and washed from head to toe. It was a luxury he vowed to never take for granted.

When Gregor had dressed, the guard unlocked the door and stepped inside the room once again. With his military issued rifle at the ready, he ordered Gregor out the door. The doors to the familiar interrogation room were opened and he walked mechanically to the wooden chair. The officer smiled, and Gregor, feeling somewhat assuaged from the influx of a few good meals and cleanliness, smiled back.

"I'm glad to see you in such high spirits, prisoner Parishnikov. You conducted yourself well with the journalist, therefore you were allowed to stay in your comfortable quarters." He gestured toward Gregor. "It appears to agree with you. I imagine you would like to remain there, yes?"

"No!" Gregor detected a flush of anger and surprise in the face of his interrogator.

"You prefer the filth and isolation?"

"Of course not. I would prefer to be allowed to visit my brother and return to the United States, as was my plan before I became your guest."

"Tell me, what would you return to in the United States? Why can you not find it in your own country?"

"I will be returning to the life I have chosen, instead of one chosen for me by the Soviet Union."

"Our sources revealed you indeed had employment and a residence." He laughed. "Do you believe these things still await you?"

"This I could not say. If not, other employment and other residences will be arranged." Gregor smiled. "It is the American way. You should try it."

"Unlike you, I am loyal to the Soviet Union. I have a job and residence. I am pleased with my situation." The conversation was remaining amicable. "Though we cannot directly connect your activities with the operations of the CIA, you associate yourself closely with an agent of the CIA. Can you explain this?"

The prisoner decided to answer the questions, though he was alert for entrapments.

"The association is not of my choice. I have refused offers to be involved in their operations. The person you speak of is assigned to monitor my life. They fear I am still working for the Soviet Union in some capacity."

"I see." The officer opened a drawer. "This must also be the reason for him to so closely monitor the life of your other friend."

Gregor was immediately on guard. A large envelope was being opened on the desk before him. He was determined to keep emotions in check; he would not betray Lenore.

"As you can see, your friends spend a great deal of time together. The woman is very beautiful. I can understand the attraction."

A series of black and white photographs were laid out before Gregor, with the intent of making him jealous.

The first was of John and Lenore sitting in a café with Leah. In the second, Lenore was straightening John's tie. She was wearing a black dress and looked so beautiful. She did not smile in either picture.

Another picture showed Lenore in the company of two men. Though they had changed a bit from their picture, Gregor recognized Lenore's two sons. Several other photographs appeared to show Lenore with an assortment of men. The background invariably included shelving or store fronts, and he knew they were fellow workers or customers.

"Your beautiful friend has many suitors." The officer smiled. "She is a whore?"

"It would appear so." He dared not show any offense.

Next was a picture of Gregor's home. Marushka and Nikolai were sitting on the porch with the couple who took care of the large white dogs and his home when he was away.

"Even your home is no longer yours. It would appear you have nothing to return to. Your new country has forgotten you."

"Perhaps you are right, but my decision to return would not be affected by these matters." He pushed the pictures away. "I choose to live there because of the freedom to begin again. Freedom is not bound by a small circle of acquaintances or a house. I will make other friends. I will have the freedom to choose other housing."

The pictures were stacked neatly, leaving the picture of Lenore and John on top.

"You speak as though you are returning. That will not be possible, of course. We wanted you to see the pictures in hopes you would give up the idea of returning and accept repatriation in the country of your birth. Your brother would benefit from this decision as well."

"And if I do not accept repatriation?"

"You will remain in prison."

"What of my brother? He has done nothing to deserve imprisonment."

"He conspired to defect. You set a very poor example for your younger brother. Because of your actions, he has been without freedom." The voice was filled with disgust. "While you sated yourself on the luxuries of Capitalism, he was deprived. It is little wonder he detests the very mention of your name."

Gregor knew this was not true. The suffering of his brother had been great, but they were still brothers. They were a team. That would not change.

"If what you say of my brother is true, why do you continue to punish him? He is obviously a loyal Communist who has seen the error of his ways. That is the only reason for a brother to turn against a brother. What better torture could there be than to know you have freed him because of his hatred for me?"

The influx of logic quieted the officer. Gregor used the opportunity to let his eyes fill with the picture of Lenore, though he appeared to be disinterested.

"We are getting nowhere with this conversation. Perhaps you need further inspiration."

The pictures were returned to the envelope, with the exception of the top photograph.

"You will return to your room. Unfortunately, it will not be the warm, clean room you have enjoyed these past few days."

With a nod to the guard and a sadistic smile from the officer, Gregor was ushered from the room.

* * * * *

The darkness and stench of his cell added to the chill. He would endure. He had to endure. The vision of Lenore so fresh in his mind would warm his soul, though the interest they showed in her troubled him. Knowing John Dixon was in contact eased the worries Gregor had for her safety. He huddled into a corner and closed his eyes. Soon a smile settled gently on his face.

CHAPTER 33

"Mom, can I borrow the car?"

Lenore opened her eyes and saw Joel standing beside her bed, a cup of coffee held out like a ritualistic offering. She raised on one elbow and accepted the coffee, taking a sip before answering.

"Where do you need to go?"

"Grant said if I can get to Denver, he would take me around to look for cars. Eric has plans today and so does Kim, so no one can take me. Can I use the car?"

Lenore sat up and swung her legs over the edge of the bed. She sipped a little more coffee and looked around the room. Her dress was in a heap beside the closet door. Somehow, she had managed to hang up the fox jacket and put her shoes away.

"How long do you plan to be gone?"

"I'll be back whenever you want, I promise." He was smiling his most sincere little boy smile.

"What if you find a car?"

"Grant said he could make a down-payment and we can pay him back." He patted his mom on the back. "Don't worry, he won't let me get into anything bad."

His maturity amazed Lenore. "If you promise to be home by dark and not argue with your brother if you disagree on a car, then you can take my car."

"Deal. Can I go now?"

"Don't you need to call Grant and tell him you're coming?"

"Well, no." He grinned. "We figured you'd agree, so I'm supposed to be there by ten."

"I'm getting far too predictable!"

"Only when it comes to logic, Mom. Thanks. By the way, you looked great last night. Did you have a good time?"

She got out of bed, put on her robe, and followed Joel to the hall. "Yes, except I was tired. I'm too old for dates."

Joel slipped into his jacket and kissed his mom on the cheek. "You will never be too old for anything!"

Lenore returned his wave as he walked out the door. Then she padded into the kitchen, where she refilled her coffee cup and noticed the radio was tuned to the oldies station. She wondered if it had been Joel's choice or a gesture for her benefit.

She perused the refrigerator and sang along with James Taylor until they got to the part where he always thought he'd see her one more time again. She rolled her eyes, quit singing and resumed her search. She pulled a bag of bagels from the refrigerator, and she was pleased to see they hadn't been there long enough to mold.

"Great! No green bagels today."

As soon as the bagel popped from the toaster, she spread cream cheese on one half and peanut butter on the other. She took her breakfast to the living room, stopping long enough in the dining room to admire the bouquet of flowers. She sat her bagel down and opened the vertical blinds, then positioned the rocking chair in front of the glass doors.

It was a clear morning. Chinook winds had taken away the last traces of snow from the immediate landscape. Far to the west, snowy peaks glistened in the sunlight, a reminder that winter was not over. Lenore opened the patio door and let fresh air flood the room. Spot ran through the open portal and straight for the kitchen, mewing loudly. Lenore closed the door and went to the kitchen to feed her feline pal before returning to her chair, breakfast and the beautiful view.

She sipped hot coffee and nibbled on the bagel halves, rocking and watching the puffy clouds appear and disperse as they traversed the altitude change. The view blurred from time to time from tears forming and falling down her cheeks.

Just before noon, Lenore took a shower, standing in the stream until the hot water ran out. It felt grand and she realized why Joel was always lingering in the shower. As she dried, the phone rang. She walked over to it, still towel drying her hair.

"I hope I wasn't interrupting anything," John said.

"I just got out of the shower."

"I forgot to tell you last night, one of the guys at work has a car he wants to sell. He's asking eighteen hundred."

"Thanks, but I've seen what eighteen hundred buys. We probably aren't interested. I want Joel to have a reliable car."

"Well, this is sort of a special deal. He only owes eighteen hundred on it and wants to get out from under the payment. It's probably worth well over five thousand. It might be worth looking at."

Lenore found a pen and paper and took down the information. She assured John she would have Joel and Grant get in touch with the owner, if she was able to get in touch with them.

"Are you recovered from last night?"

"Sure. I had a great time. Thanks." She opened the refrigerator and grabbed a Diet Coke.

"I'm not sure how your mind works, so I didn't want you to have regrets about anything … I don't."

"That's good, John. Now, I really have to go put some clothes on. It's a little chilly in here. Thanks for the tip on the car. I hope it turns out to be what he wants. Thanks for calling."

Lenore didn't know why she was short with John. Perhaps she was trying to get comfortable about the necessity of him in her life, and he was crowding. She called Grant's number and was surprised to find the guys there. She conveyed the information.

"You don't know what kind of car it is?" Grant relayed the question from Joel.

"No, I forgot to ask. It sounds like a deal though, so go have a look." She tossed the note into the trash. "When are you going to come for a visit?"

"Soon, Mom, I promise. I've been trying to get settled into the new place and the new job. You know how it is. How about next Sunday? I really miss you."

"Sounds good to me. You two have a good day together. I know Joel really appreciates your help. I hope he's showing it. It's a blessing to have you close, Grant."

With assurances they were having a great time, Lenore ended the conversation.

She walked to the patio doors, not afraid of being seen. There were no houses or streets between her and the foothills. She opened the doors and stepped out onto the sun-warmed surface. The air had warmed considerably and she stretched as the sun warmed her naked body.

She stepped back into the house long enough to pour her Diet Coke into a glass and retrieve her comb and towel. Using the towel to cushion the concrete, she sat down in the sun and combed through the tangles in her hair. It felt free and relaxing to sit naked in the fresh air. The lack of sunshine on her body had long faded the tan she had worked so hard to build the summer before. She lay back on the towel and closed her eyes against the glare. It was a perfect day.

The sixty-degree temperature and lack of a breeze made her drowsy, and until the doorbell rang, she wasn't aware she had actually fallen asleep. Draping the towel around her, she walked to the door and peeked through the view port. She opened the door to greet Leah.

"Were you sleeping?"

"I think I was. Come on out to the patio. Want a Diet Coke?" She asked, knowing the answer. She took a glass from the cabinet and filled it with ice as Leah retrieved the beverage from the refrigerator.

"Thanks. Were you out there in just a towel?"

"No, I was laying on the towel."

Lenore removed the towel and stood naked in front of her friend.

"You were out there naked?"

"Sure!" Lenore shrugged. "No one can see me."

"Oh, okay." Leah poured her diet Coke over the ice and followed Lenore to the patio. "JD was watching a basketball game, so I thought I'd come over and see how things went. When we were putting your flowers in the vase last night, Joel said he was hoping to go to Grant's today."

Lenore offered Leah a section of the towel as they both sat down. Neither seemed concerned with Lenore's nakedness.

"Joel and Grant know me pretty well. Those little stinkers knew I'd let him go before they even asked. Maybe I'm too easy."

"No. They just know you will fairly judge a reasonable request. That's all." Leah turned to Lenore. "Now, tell me about last night."

"We had a nice dinner, danced a little." She patted Leah's leg. "By the way, I didn't spill anything on the jacket."

"It was never a concern. Go on."

"Let's see." She acted like she was trying to recall. "We got into a fight, then we made out and then he brought me home. Ta-dah!"

"Okay, details! Especially the one about making out." Leah's eyes were big. "Did you really?"

Lenore sipped her drink. "Yes, really!"

"But what about—"

"What about who?" Lenore frowned. "There's no one else to consider, Leah. We made out and I enjoyed it. We could actually start having a relationship. We may even make love at some point if I decide I want to." She ran her fingers through her hair. "Why is it so hard to believe and what does anyone else have to do with it?"

"Easy, easy, Lenore. I think it's wonderful."

Lenore stood and paced the length of the small patio.

"Wonderful. I'm not quite at the wonderful part yet. I feel like I've betrayed Gregor and it's preposterous to feel that way." She waved her arms. "It absolutely infuriates me!"

"You'll get past it, Lenore. Tell me about the rest of the evening. Tell me about your dinner and dancing."

Lenore finally quit pacing and settled back onto the towel. She relayed the information to her friend, but avoided discussing the argument. She even managed a smile as she told of the emergency shrimp cocktail.

"It was a fun time, and John's a really nice guy. I want to see him again. I think he'll be a good friend, and most certainly knows how to show me a good time."

"That's what you need most of all. You deserve it, Lenore."

She smiled and nodded submission. It was what Leah needed to hear, whether or not Lenore really felt it.

CHAPTER 34

The next few weeks brought warmer weather and more sunshine. Lenore seemed to smile a little more, which made Leah feel like a crisis was over. There was a stubborn sadness in her eyes and the only time Leah saw it fade, was at one of Joel's concerts. He was highlighted with a trombone solo, much to Lenore's surprise. His performance was nothing short of spectacular and he received a standing ovation. Lenore cheered and even whistled. When the fuss was over and the performance continued, Leah saw tears brimming in her friend's dark green eyes.

After the concert, Joel drove several of his friends to their favorite restaurant for a late dinner. He rarely ate before a concert, and was always starved afterward. Grant had joined them for the concert, but had to get back to Denver. She would catch a ride with Leah, but declined when offered the keys to Baby.

"You don't want to drive? You always want to drive Baby."

"I feel like passenger material tonight. Thanks anyway." She smiled and got in the car. "I was sure proud of my baby boy. He's good, isn't he?"

"He's very talented. I imagine he'll have a scholarship because of it. Won't that be great?"

Lenore nodded. "We're counting on it. It will be the only way he can go to college. His dad and I don't have much saved. I wish I could do more for him."

Leah pulled out of the parking lot, joining a line of cars.

"He's doing just great. And that new car of his is in better shape than yours. He really got a good deal on it."

"I have my suspicions about that whole deal." Lenore said, staring out the window.

"Like what?"

"I imagine John had a lot to do with the price being so good. He probably paid the guy five grand to knock it down to eighteen hundred."

"If he did, fine! He can afford it or he wouldn't have done it. Joel benefitted. That's what counts."

"I suppose."

The traffic started moving slowly. "What made you cry at the concert?"

"Oh, just pride, I suppose." She smiled. "And wishing someone could have met him and seen what a wonderfully talented young man he is. It's been five months since he left."

Leah was surprised Lenore brought up the Russian.

"They would have been fast friends."

"I think so, too."

"It's been a long, hard winter, hasn't it?"

Lenore nodded.

"Spring is finally in the air. It's the new beginning of everything. It's supposed to be in the seventies on Friday. We'll put the top down on Baby and go for a ride. Let's plan a picnic on the rock, too. Okay?"

Lenore's agreement wasn't full of enthusiasm, but it gave Lenore something to look forward to, in spite of herself.

* * * * *

The phone rang in John's apartment at two in the morning. He let the answering machine take the call, though the noise had him fully alert.

"Dixon, if you're there, pick up. It's important."

He groaned and picked up the receiver, recognizing the Director's voice.

"What's up?" He held the phone away from his mouth to yawn.

"We have something here you need to take a look at. How soon can you get here?"

"I'll call the airlines." He sat up, rubbing his eyes and stifling another yawn. "Do I get a clue?"

"We found your buddy."

"Parish?"

"Right."

John was standing beside the bed, fully awake, adrenaline pumping through his body.

"Where is he?"

"There's the problem. He's the guest in a rather confined environment. Don't know if there's much we can do, but get your ass here and let's get to work on it."

"I'll catch the first flight. Have a car ready at the airport."

"You realize it won't be a Mercedes?"

"Hell, I'd take a bus for this one." He hung up the phone and immediately called the airline. He could catch a direct flight early enough to get there before evening, local time.

As he threw clothes in a bag and headed for the shower, he thought about calling Lenore. No, it wasn't good news. Maybe he would call from the airport, just to tell her he would be out of town, though he doubted if she would care.

He had received a most gracious thank you card from Joel, and a polite call from Lenore, regarding Joel's car. If she knew he had contributed to the purchase price of the car, she hadn't let it keep Joel from getting it. Joel was a good kid. He deserved a break. She had turned down two dates, so he had decided to back off for a while, though surveillance did not.

It was nearly six a.m. when he called Lenore. Joel answered the phone and after another thank you for helping him find the car, he called his mom to the phone. A barely audible "hello" made John regret the early call.

"Sorry to wake you, but I'm trying to keep a promise. I told you once I'd let you know if I had to leave for any length of time."

"Okay. Where?"

"I got a call early this morning and I have to go back east for a while. I don't know how long I'll be, but I can call you and keep in touch if you'd like.

"That would be okay. Is there anything wrong?"

He could tell sleep was slowly leaving Lenore, because her sentences were getting longer.

"No, strictly routine. They just get an urge to see me once in a while, and I have to go. I think they worry I'm sitting here in Colorado having fun and not working hard enough."

"I see. I really appreciate the call, John. I'm sorry I haven't called you. It's been busy at the store with inventory and sales."

"I hoped that was it. Maybe we can go have dinner when I get back."

"We'll see. Have a good trip."

"Sorry again that I woke you."

"It's okay. My alarm is going off right now. I'd better get it before it wakes Joel again."

"Bye, Lenore. Take care of yourself, okay?"

She didn't reply. He hung up the phone and left for the airport.

By the time she walked back to her bedroom, Joel was standing in the doorway and the alarm had been turned off.

"Why did he call so early?"

"To tell me he was going out of town for a while. I'm sorry the phone woke you." She grimaced. "Guess the alarm did, too."

"It's okay. I'm going to try to sleep a while longer if I can. I don't think I'm fully awake."

"No, your eyes are still closed." She giggled. "Go back to bed."

He shuffled back to his room and closed the door as Lenore started her morning routine. Meanwhile, John boarded a jet, hoping to get some sleep before landing in DC. It was going to be a very long day.

* * * * *

When Leah walked in the back door of the store on Friday, Lenore had already changed into casual clothes and worn Nikes. She allowed Leah to give JD a quick kiss before dragging her back out the door.

"You're excited." Leah noted.

"It's seventy-four degrees, there's not a cloud in the sky and we're going to the rock. Can I drive?"

Leah tossed her the keys. They lowered the top on Baby and Leah gave her hair an additional coat of hair spray. Lenore secured her long tresses with a ribbon before putting the car in gear and backing out of the parking lot.

"We're off!" She yelled.

"And we're leaving, too!"

There was a smile on her face and Leah knew the old Lenore had surfaced. It was going to be a fun day, and they stopped for deli sandwiches and snacks and drove to the lake.

"Good! No one's here." Lenore said.

"They wouldn't dare! I think the rock would shake them off. It knew we were coming today." Leah pointed. "See, there are even little tiny flowers growing at the base. We've got a pretty special rock."

315

"Yeah, what a great rock!"

It took a few minutes to get settled and start digging into the sack for their lunches. Lenore pulled an envelope out of a pocket and laid it on the blanket between them.

"What's that?" Leah asked.

"A letter."

"From?"

"From me!" Lenore grinned.

Leah looked from Lenore to the letter, and back to Lenore. "A letter from you?"

"Yep!"

"To?"

"Gregor!"

"You got an address to send a letter to Gregor?" Leah grabbed Lenore's shoulders. "This happened and you didn't tell me? Did John get it for you?"

"Nope!"

"Nope to what?"

"All of the above." Lenore laughed. "I just sat down and wrote a letter as if I could actually send it. It's sort of a letting go thing. I thought I'd let you read it. Then we can tear it up into little teeny, tiny pieces and feed it to the wind. Maybe the fingers of God will carry my words to wherever Gregor is." She tilted her head and looked at Leah. "Think I'm nuts?"

"No! It's probably one of the sanest things you've done in a long time. It's a catharsis. You needed a way to get it out of your system."

Lenore looked out across the lake and took the ribbon from her hair, letting gentle breezes blow through the unconfined tresses and settle the tangles.

"I've had so many words building up for Gregor. I just had to release them. I let out my anger and my passion, my worries and my regrets, and my prayers. I know he'll never see these words, but I just had to get them out."

Leah pulled the paper from the envelope and began reading aloud. Lenore stared at the spot beside the lake where she had sat with Gregor, listening to his promises and feeling so loved. It seemed like a lifetime ago. Smiles and tears came with the words. When she finished, Leah handed the letter back to Lenore.

"Sure you don't want to save it?"

"I'm sure. There's no reason to."

Using the envelope as a receptacle, the paper was torn again and again until the pieces could not render a single word. Lenore stirred through the paper with her finger and smiled.

"What's the smile for?" Leah asked.

"Oh, for memories. I really hope I never forget how special it was. It changed my whole life. I know I'll probably always wonder what it would have been like to share my life with him, or just to introduce him to my sons or meet his dogs." She laughed. "It's time to say good-bye. I have to go on. Life is too sweet to waste away, like I've been doing for the past five months. I'm ashamed of myself. I even thought about ending it all a couple of times. That's not me, Leah."

She shook her head and continued. "Life is a celebration. If what I felt for Gregor was love, then I'm not sure I want to ever feel it again, because I don't think I could survive it a second time."

Leah patted Lenore's hand. "I guess it's different when you've shared a lifetime with someone and have a family together. You have all the memories to comfort you and children and grandchildren to help you remember just by looking at their faces. You weren't given the memories of a lifetime, but you were given the love of one. You were entitled to mourn and you've done well to get past it. There's a life full of adventure out there, and now you can embrace it again. I'm proud of you, Lenore. I knew you were on the edge, but all I could do was hold on as best I could and hope it was enough. It scared the hell out of me, because I never want to lose you. Ours is the friendship of a lifetime, and I'm not full enough of memories to let you go."

"Well, you won't have to. I can't promise I won't stumble a time or two, but I won't ever get so low again. I may have grandchildren to look forward to one of these years, and I want to be around to enjoy them."

Before they released the contents of the envelope, they prayed, asking God to take the words from Lenore's heart and give them to Gregor, wherever he was. They asked for His love and protection for Gregor, and strength for Lenore. They raised the envelope together and the wind lightly plucked and carried the offering, as though an invisible hand was accepting the request.

"Let's walk down by the water," Leah suggested. "The lake's going to begin filling with the spring thaw and we won't be able to walk there. I'll bet we can find all kinds of driftwood and treasures."

"If I know you, we'd better take a sack for all the rocks you'll find."

With the blanket and food wrappers put into the trunk, Lenore stuffed an empty sack into her pocket. She caught up with Leah further down the path from the rock. It was steep and washed out, but their matching footwear enabled them to traverse the terrain with sure-footed, though somewhat slow, progress. As the trail opened onto the level area of exposed lake bottom, they were able to walk together and talk.

"Look at these trees!" Leah said. "It amazes me they can grow when most of the time they're sitting in water. Guess it's why they grow so weird."

"The water washes the sand and dirt from the roots. They're so smooth. Hey, a chair!" Lenore clamored over the combined root system of two trees and found a spot where the twisted growth joined together and took on the shape of a primitive arm chair. She sat down and nestled-in.

"I've heard of hugging a tree, but this is the first one I've seen that could actually hug you back!" She giggled. "Here, try it."

She jumped up and offered the seat to her best friend, who took her place. Although her feet dangled where Lenore's had been able to rest comfortably on the ground, Leah agreed it was a hugging tree.

"This is great, but I think I need a foot stool."

Lenore searched the immediate area and found a piece of driftwood. She situated it under Leah's feet, then took a seat on a nearby exposed root. It wasn't as comfortable as the tree chair, but she didn't mind.

"What a perfectly gorgeous day, Leah!"

"Know what makes it perfect?"

Lenore shook her head and smiled at Leah.

"That!"

"What?"

"Your smile. I've missed it."

Lenore looked down as if embarrassed. "I just misplaced it for a while." She got up and walked over, on and around the smooth root system. "Let's go walk along the edge of the water."

They abandoned the ground-level tree house and walked north along the lake's edge. With eyes focused on sand, earth and water, they collected a vast selection of man-made junk in the sack and used pockets for Leah's growing collection of rocks.

Rounding an outcropping of rocks, they came upon a man who was fishing. Lenore frowned as she tried to remember the face. Leah was surprised when Lenore approached him.

"Hello!" She waved and walked straight to him. "You gave me a ride in your cab one night, and I wanted to tell you how much I appreciated your courtesy. I didn't think you guys normally opened doors."

The gentleman looked a little uncomfortable at first, then smiled back at the two ladies.

"Normally we don't, but it looked like a special occasion and I thought you might appreciate it. Hope you got home okay."

Lenore was surprised he remembered her, and even more surprised he remembered her concern over getting home. She looked at Leah, who was not looking at her or the cabby, but at the fishing equipment laying neatly around him.

"I think it's time we got back, don't you, Leah?" She started walking backward. "Thanks again for your courtesy. I hope you catch something."

"I beg your pardon?" He frowned, then looked at the pole in his hands. "Oh, you mean the fishing, of course. Well, I'm kind of new at this fishing thing. I just like being outside on such a nice day."

"Us, too. Well good-bye."

She waved and turned away, grabbing Leah's arm. They walked until out of sight, then increased their pace, though neither spoke a word. Back at the chair tree, they sat down after making sure they weren't followed. They spoke quietly.

"What are you thinking?" Lenore asked.

"Same as you. He's no fisherman, and I doubt he's a real cabby. Lenore, he wouldn't remember you, would he?"

"I wouldn't think so. I sure don't look the same as I did that night." She held out the front of her T-shirt.

"Exactly! Besides, most of that fishing gear was still in plastic packaging." Leah looked back toward where they had left the fisherman. "He also had on wing-tips for crying out loud! Who goes fishing in wing-tips?"

"I noticed them, too. Has to be CIA. Shit! Now they know where our hide-out is."

Leah picked up a small piece of driftwood and, using her best Russian accent, held it out to Lenore. "Speak into the microphone. We want to know all your secrets."

"I am Lenore Appleby. I don't know where you have misplaced your Russian. I do not have him."

They both laughed. Leah held the driftwood to her own mouth. "I am Leah Chase. I haven't got him either."

They laughed again, then looked around to make sure they were still alone. Lenore stood up and began pacing.

"Those bastards! You know, I'm getting pissed!"

"More pissed!" Leah corrected. "You were already pretty hot about it."

"I wish I could mess with them." Her eyes were dark and full of mischief. "I have an idea."

She grabbed Leah's arm and began climbing the hill toward the car. Before they got inside, she saw a pickup truck parked about a half-mile down the road. They knew the cab driver was already inside.

They buckled their seatbelts and Lenore smiled at Leah, who gave a thumbs up to the lady behind the wheel. As the engine rumbled to life, Lenore put the car in gear and pulled onto the narrow two-lane. Instead of heading back toward town, they continued around the lake.

"Is he back there?" Leah asked.

Lenore looked in the rearview mirror and smiled.

"Yes, a nice respectable distance. Are you ready?"

"You bet!"

"Let's see how fast that old truck will go. I'm going to try to lose him."

Baby's powerful 350 small block responded efficiently as Lenore let familiarity and skill take the convertible well past the posted speed limits. The winding road and steep grades soon provided a considerable space between them and their pursuer. It was enough time for Lenore to ease the car into a driveway partially obscured by trees and brush and turn around. They turned off the engine and listened for the sound of the approaching truck. When it had passed, she started the engine.

"Now, let's follow him!"

They laughed and pulled back onto the road, easing back up to speed. It didn't take long for the truck to come into view. He apparently saw the convertible and began to slow. That gave Lenore an opportunity to catch up with him, pass and wave, as once again they distanced themselves from the truck and the frustrated agent.

The back-road continued to State Highway 34 coming out of Loveland to follow the Big Thompson Canyon to Estes park. They turned east toward the Sweetheart City of Loveland, and once inside the city limits, they pulled into a restaurant parking lot, making sure the car was visible from several hundred yards down the highway. A few minutes later the truck came into view and pulled into the parking lot beside them. Lenore got out of the car.

The agent turned off his truck and got out. "Fancy meeting you here," he said, smiling.

"Fancy, my ass!" Lenore was not to be humored. "Does the CIA think I'm stupid, or what? I want to see some ID."

"What gave me away?" He reached into a pocket and retrieved his ID case, then handed it to Lenore.

"Your memory and your wing-tips." Lenore studied the badge. "Look, Frank Gillespie, when I have a day off, I don't want to have to be looking over my shoulder. I realize I may have no choice in the matter, but you'd better believe I'll try to lose you every chance I get." She handed the badge back to the agent.

"That might not be such a good idea." He seemed unruffled by Lenore's outburst.

"Why, because you're protecting me? I think you guys are all paranoid or voyeuristic." She dismissed him with a wave of her hand. "I can take care of myself just fine!"

"No doubt you could out-drive just about anyone on the road. How'd you learn to do that?"

Ignoring the compliment, Lenore opened the door of the Chevelle and turned back to Frank before she got in.

"Just remember, if I know you're there, I'll make sure you have just about the toughest job in the world. Now, we're going home. You remember where that is, I'm sure. I don't think we need an escort." She reached into her pocket and produced two quarters, tossing them at his feet. "There. Now, go sit down and buy yourself a cup of coffee and relax. You could have a heart attack at your age."

Lenore sat down behind the wheel of Baby, started the car and drove out of the parking lot, away from the man staring at the quarters, wondering how he was going to explain this to Dixon.

After the surge of adrenaline had leveled off, Lenore relaxed her shoulders and smiled at Leah.

"How'd I do, my little cohort?"

"Lenore, if that didn't get the message across, I don't know what would. He was sure impressed with your driving."

"Oh, he could have done better in a car. You recognized the truck, didn't you?

Leah thought for a minute, then her eyes opened wide and do did her mouth. "That's the truck Gregor was driving when he met us in Denver. Do you suppose that's the agent Gregor poisoned?"

"Possibly." Lenore grinned. "He should be about ready for retirement, don't you think?"

"You probably hurt his feelings when you tossed the quarters down and made a crack about his age."

"Don't try to make me feel guilty about it. He's too old to be chasing people. They need to put him behind a desk or something."

"He's probably older than Rusty!" Leah noted. "Rusty could out-maneuver that guy any day." She laughed. "And I'll bet he's never even been on a horse."

They drove a while, with ear-to-ear grins.

"Would you and Joel like to come over and have dinner. Maybe we'll just watch a movie and order a pizza."

"If he has plans with Kim, can I come alone?"

"Of course, silly girl!"

* * * * *

When they stopped in front of the store, Lenore gave the driver's seat up to Leah and got in her own car. It was after five.

The phone was ringing when Leah got home. She dropped everything at the door and sprinted for the phone before the answering machine could engage.

"Hello, Chase residence. This is Leah."

"Leah, this is John Dixon. I've been trying to reach you all day. Is this a bad time?"

"No, it's fine. It's Friday, you know. Lenore and I went to the lake. We sort of had an encounter with one of your agents."

"An encounter?"

"I'm sure he'll explain it to you." She took the new cordless phone with her as she retrieved her deposits near the door. "What's up? Why are you calling?"

"I wanted to let you know, we found Greg."

Leah dropped her packages again, then walked over to the sofa, the phone glued to her ear. She sat down and pulled her legs up, sitting cross-legged. "He isn't dead … is he?"

"Worse, he's in a Soviet prison. They took him just after he got into the country. We found his brother, too. They have him in a different prison. There might be a chance of getting the brother out, but it's going to take some doing to get Greg. They want him back to work for the KGB pretty bad, or they would have shot him by now."

Leah winced. "I don't think Lenore needs to know all of this, John. She's starting to do so well. I don't want to get her hopes up."

"Understandable." There was a pause. "Do you think she still loves him?"

"Oh, I think she always will, in a way. But she's managing to put it in the form of a memory." Leah stood up and walked back to the door to pick up the dropped items once again. "I think we should keep it like that until Gregor comes back, if he comes back. And I'm not sure he would be welcomed, to tell you the truth."

"Not welcomed? But if she loves him—"

"It's hard to explain. I know she'll always love him, but she doesn't want to be in love anymore. It makes her feel out of control. She doesn't handle it well. Does that make any sense to you, John?"

"More than you know."

"You're in love with her, aren't you?"

The voice on the line was quiet. "Pretty hopeless, isn't it?"

"I'm so sorry, John. You two could be so good together. I know she likes you. I wish it could have come at a different time and circumstance." Leah settled back on the sofa with her bags beside her. "I don't understand why you want to bring him back to her."

"Initially, it was my job to retrieve him. But if I bring him back to her and she's truly over him, maybe there's a chance for me. I'd try very hard to make her happy."

"I know you would. Right now, could you arrange for her to have some freedom?"

"You mean slack off the surveillance?"

"Exactly. No more wing-tipped shadows."

"It's a done deal. Thanks for the ear, Leah. I'll let you know if there's anything more positive to report."

"I appreciate it, John. Take care of yourself."

As she hung up the phone, Leah felt a little surge of pride in persuading John to get rid of the agents tailing Lenore.

* * * * *

John had no intention of letting Lenore face the world on her own. He would ensure she would not be made aware of their presence again. Maybe it was time for Frank to be assigned to a nice comfortable desk job.

CHAPTER 35

Gregor became aware of warmer weather as water from thawing snow began to seep under the outside wall of his cell. Though it left almost a fourth of his floor space wet, he adjusted to the inconvenience. The temperature within his confines would surely reflect the warmer weather soon. He was relieved to have any change in the monotonous solitude. He had not heard another human voice for over a month. The sound of his own voice was becoming an unfamiliar noise.

When he heard the door of his cell being opened, he assumed it was again time for the room to be hosed down. Instead, he was motioned into the dark hallway. The lone guard jabbed Gregor between the shoulder blades with his rifle barrel and was surprised when he suddenly found the weapon in the hands of his prisoner.

"I would appreciate it greatly if you did not use this in such a manner against me again. I have no desire to kill you, but as you can imagine, I am just a little irritable." Nose to nose, Gregor smiled and handed the weapon back to the guard. "Shall we continue our walk?"

The guard, visibly shaken from the experience, accepted the weapon back, and gestured with his hand to the doorway at the end of the hall. A respect for his prisoner took root, in spite of their opposed positions.

"Prisoner Parishnikov, sit."

Gregor took the familiar seat, impatiently awaiting the latest efforts to persuade him to give secrets he did not have, or agree to repatriation into a country he no longer desired. He looked around the room and finally focused on the wall behind his interrogator. The crack had grown since he was last there. The crack was noticeably enlarged, and the water stains bled several inches away from the edge. The entire wall would crumble with the slightest disturbance. Gregor wondered if he would be able to see outside, if it fell.

"The stench of you fills the room Parishnikov." The officer held a handkerchief to his nose, in an attempt to block the intrusive odor.

Aware of his appearance and the obvious odor, Gregor smiled at the officer. "You must forgive me. You see, I have missed my morning toilette." He expected a blow from the gun barrel for his facetious remark. It didn't come.

"Perhaps we could remedy the situation. Are you ready to cooperate?"

"I do not know how I could further cooperate." Gregor shook his head. "I have no secrets. I was on no mission other than to visit my brother."

Surprisingly, the officer chuckled. "You make us proud of our work. We trained you well. It is unfortunate you now choose to use it against us. I believe we will soon have your cooperation. We will return you to the comfortable quarters. We would not want her to see you in this state. "

Gregor's eyes burned into the eyes of the officer. He could feel his heartbeat accelerating. This could not be possible! They would not take his Lenore from her home.

The officer clapped his hands together. "At last we have a reaction! We have aroused your curiosity. As we sit here, three of our most competent people are making preparations to bring the beautiful Lenore to your side. If you have her here, you have no reason to return to the United States. Perhaps then, you will repatriate!" He motioned to the guard. "Take him to the shower. Please, prisoner Parishnikov, take your time, and do not be stingy with the soap."

As Gregor was escorted from the room, the officer opened a window. It gave the prisoner an opportunity to smell fresh air for the first time in nearly six months. It stirred his senses, though his mind was reeling from the possibility of Lenore being kidnaped. He ached for her, but never at the expense of her own freedom.

The guard, sensing the effect of the words, did not force Gregor to the shower. He made sure there was a comfortable distance between the prisoner and his weapon, not knowing if Gregor would return it or use it now.

As the steamy water pelted its stinging spray on Gregor, his mind raced. Had he been away so long they would no longer be watching Lenore? Surely John would not give up so easily. Perhaps they had decided he was not returning by choice. There was no way to get word to her, or to John.

He had been trained to create his own solutions, but he didn't need a solution; he needed a miracle. Somehow, through the layers of fact and logic, he knew the only thing he could do was pray to the God his grandparents had taught him of so many years ago. Would this God remember the small child who once believed so strongly? Would He recognize that child, in the man who would speak to Him now? Gregor had to try. Soon the rudiments of prayer was to become a constant part of his daily routine.

* * * * *

"Lenore, could you come to the office for a minute? There's something I need to talk to you about."

"Sure!" Lenore stepped down from the window and over the clutter of shoes she was trying to work into a display. Royce walked back to the office with her.

"You must be in trouble," he teased. "Did you screw up the books or something?"

"Give me a break, will ya Royce? Maybe you're in trouble when the boss calls you into the office, but it doesn't mean everyone else is."

"Ouch!" He flinched at her words.

"I'm sorry. I just want to get the window display done before I leave tonight, and I'm running out of time."

"What can I do to help?" Royce was sincere in his offer.

"How about bringing more plexi heel risers. Three more singles and a double or two. Oh, and a couple of handbag props, too." She patted him on the back. "Thanks!"

Lenore walked into the office, then closed the door behind her. "What's up, Boss Man?" She sat down with an expression of anticipation.

"I just got off the phone with the home office. They're pretty impressed with your work here, and they want you to attend a management training session in Kansas City." JD smiled at Lenore. "Think Joel could get along without you for a few of days?"

"I don't think it would be a problem. When?"

"Next week. You fly out on Sunday morning and come back Wednesday night."

"Wow!" She ran her fingers through her hair. "They sure don't give you much time to think about it, do they?"

"Not this time. They were filled up, then one of the guys had to cancel. You normally wouldn't be going to one of these for another year, but I've done some bragging and they think you're advanced enough. At this rate, you might have your own store within a year. What do you say?"

"Can I have the rest of the day off to get some laundry done and get things settled with Joel?" She stood and started to pace. "Shit! I've got the window display torn apart!"

"Don't worry about it. I'll get in there with the guys and we'll get it done." JD smiled at the pacing brunette. "I think I can still dress a window."

"Okay. Plane reservations?"

"Taken care of. You'll pick up your ticket at the airport." He laughed. "I knew you'd want to go. Want Leah and me to take you?"

"No, I'll take the shuttle and close my eyes when we get to the airport traffic." She held her hands over her eyes.

He laughed and handed Lenore two checks. "Here's your paycheck and another check to help with expenses. You'll need a briefcase, so I picked this one up at lunch."

JD handed a handsome leather case to Lenore. She opened the shiny latches and lifted the top. The rich smell of fine leather greeted her senses. An assortment of pens, pencils and notebooks were inside.

"Mine? How much?"

"It's a gift from Leah and me."

"Wow! This reminds me of the first day of school. I never had anything this nice though. Thank you so much!"

She gave him a hug, then a handshake. She walked out of the office, then came back in.

"Where do I stay? What do I wear to these sessions?"

"Bosworth will pick you and several other up at the airport and take you to where you're staying." He handed Lenore a piece of paper. "Here's the contact number of where you'll be for Joel. Tell him to call us if it's an emergency." He thought for a moment. "As far as what you wear, the guys usually wear suits or sport coats. I think what you normally wear to work will be fine. If you throw in a dress, it's okay, but it'll put them into shock. You're entering an almost exclusively male world."

With hugs and congratulations from Rusty and Royce, Lenore left the store and headed home.

* * * * *

Joel immediately called his brother upon learning the news. The phone was finally handed to Lenore, but only after Joel felt he had worked Grant into a state of excitement equal to his own.

Mom, this is fantastic! We're so proud of you. How's it feeling to become an executive? Joel says you have a great looking briefcase."

"It feels really good and a little exciting. You should see the briefcase. It's leather and smells so rich. That must be the secret to successful people; they have leather briefcases."

"Don't worry about Joel while you're gone. He'll do fine. I'll call and check up on him. I told him to play by the rules while you're gone, because if he screws up, it could cost you a career. I think he believes me."

"He's got plenty of people to call if there's a problem, and I'll let the neighbors know I'll be gone, too. I'm not worried. He's earned my trust."

Joel smiled as he looked up from the briefcase. When the phone call ended, she hugged her baby boy.

Joel hugged her back. "I'll be fine while you're gone. Maybe Eric can stay with me. You'd trust us here together, wouldn't you?"

"Any other mom in the universe would have second thoughts, but I know you two would be fine. Call him and I'll talk to his parents. I'm going to change clothes, then we'll go to the grocery store." She walked toward the hall. "I want to make sure you're stocked up while I'm away."

Arrangements were confirmed for Eric's temporary change of residence, with assurances from his parents they would be as close as a phone call if they were needed. Groceries were bought and laundry was done. It was nearly ten when the phone rang.

"Lenore, it's John. I haven't talked to you for a while and thought I'd let you know I'm still in Virginia. I've been thinking about you a great deal."

"You must be bored there, John." She chuckled, while trying to sort through her purse and put necessary things into the briefcase to eliminate the need of a purse. "You've been there quite a while. Is it going to be a permanent move?"

"No, just taking one class and teaching another." It was the truth, just not the whole truth. "I always wish you were here when I get a day off. There's so much I'd enjoy showing you. I hope we can go out when I get back to Denver. Anything new going on in your life?"

She knew if he found out about the trip, he would have her followed. She decided against an escort. "No, same old routine. The weather is warming up and I guess that's putting me in a better mood these days. I hate to cut this short, but I'm really tired tonight. Why don't you give me a call when you get back? I'd enjoy a night out. Take care of yourself, John. Thanks for the call. It meant a lot."

She hung up the phone and walked to her bedroom. Joel was standing in his doorway.

"I wasn't really eavesdropping, but why didn't you tell him about your trip?"

The question surprised her. She stared at Joel for a minute before answering. "I don't know. I guess I just didn't feel like having a lengthy conversation."

The answer seemed to satisfy her son. He went to the living room to finish a movie and she went to her room. She closed the door and stared at the empty suitcase on the bed. She would take her time and choose carefully. She wanted to look efficient, but not at the sacrifice of looking feminine. She wished Leah could be there to help and offer advice.

* * * * *

"You're up kind of late. Anything wrong, Dixon?"

He turned to see the Director standing at his door. "Not sure. That was Lenore."

"I gathered as much."

"She's never really chatty on the phone, but she seemed especially eager to get off the line tonight. I'd like to see if there's anything on the phone taps. It may be nothing, but maybe we could double surveillance for a couple of days."

"Dixon, I think you might be a little too personally involved to think clearly about this situation." John's boss leaned against the door and crossed his arms.

"Possibly, but indulge me. If they've still got Parish in a prison, it means they're doing everything in their power to break him and it isn't working. We know they're aware of Lenore. She could be the one key they need to force his cooperation. They'll take her if they can."

"Other than sidestepping Frank, she's been predictable," said the Director.

"Only because she's mired in routine. My gut instinct is telling me something is off. What if her routine is broken?"

"How?"

"Say a trip; vacation or business. Stapleton would be an ideal place to grab someone."

"John, I'm going to let you fly with this one, but I may clip your wings if it turns out to be nothing. I have a lot of respect for your instincts; that's why you've gotten where you are, but I won't allow your personal feelings to conflict with duty."

A half hour later, two phone calls and confirmation with a wiretap, John smiled and handed the boss a print-out of the passenger list for United flight 423 departing Denver at 10:20 Sunday morning. L. Appleby was going to Kansas City.

"Okay, you called this one right. We'll have agents in place at the airport and on the flight. The Kansas City bureau can take it from there. For her sake, I hope it's an uneventful trip."

The call he had made to Leah had confirmed his suspicions, and provided her projected schedule and location in Kansas City. He had a lot more calls to make to get operatives in place before 10:20 Sunday morning.

* * * * *

Lenore left Joel and Eric amid hugs and assurances they would give her no reason to regret her plans as she boarded the shuttle. A quick glance at her fellow passengers brought a smile to her face. It looked like she had successfully managed to leave town without the knowledge, or company, of CIA agents.

The clutter of traffic thickened near the airport, and Lenore closed her eyes, placing her confidence in the driver. As she departed the shuttle at the United Airlines door, she tipped the driver. The din of passengers inside the terminal clamored for space, and Lenore eventually made her way to the ticket counter, relieved to be free of her suitcase.

With the ticket tucked into her briefcase, she meandered to the concourse, stopping to browse windows filled with travel brochures and souvenirs. Her flight didn't leave for an hour and she was in no particular hurry to get to the gate. It also gave her opportunity to see if she was being followed.

Satisfied she would be leaving Colorado undetected, Lenore went through security screening, located her gate, then backtracked to a crowded bar. Flying always made her a little nervous, so she ordered a scotch and water, and sat at the bar. The flight wouldn't be long, but sitting there with nothing to do for an hour would make her want to pace. She smiled at the thought of driving passengers crazy with her pacing. Maybe she would buy a crossword puzzle book.

* * * * *

Keeping Lenore Appleby in sight was no problem in the crowded airport. The assigned agents were a man and woman who appeared to be distressed at the prospect of being apart. They cuddled and argued playfully, constantly aware of the brunette in the kelly-green sweater. Lenore never gave it a second thought as the man boarded the flight without the woman. His partner confirmed departure with John Dixon in Virginia, and went back to the office in Denver.

* * * * *

Lenore was very relaxed by the time she landed in Kansas City. The pre-flight drink and the two consumed in-flight had installed a seemingly permanent grin on her face. Grover Cleveland Bosworth, Personnel Director and major board member of the home office, touched her on the elbow as she started down the concourse toward the baggage claim. She was startled.

"Hi Lenore. I'm here to pick you up."

Shocked at hearing her name, Lenore turned around, then smiled. She gave the man a generous hug and a slap on the back.

"Hello Boz! I made it. I need to get my suitcase though."

"Right. Well, let's go down here and pick up another passenger. His flight will be arriving in just a few minutes, then we can all go together to the baggage claim area. Are you feeling alright?"

"To tell you the truth, I feel a little too relaxed. I guess it was the drink I had on the plane."

She failed to mention the two additional drinks contributing to her inebriation, but the scotch-induced smile looked sincere enough to fool Bosworth.

"I've experienced that effect myself." He nodded. "I'm sure it has something to do with all the altitude changes as well." He smiled at her. "Here we are. Why don't you have a seat. I'll watch for Clint."

Lenore sat down and clutched the briefcase tightly as she watched Bosworth walk toward the passenger arrival gate. He was a tall, trim man with thinning hair. Though she was sure he was nearing sixty, he walked with the stride of a much younger man. She had never seen him wear anything less than expensive tailored suits. Today he was sporting sweats. No doubt expensive sweats, but sweats just the same. She smiled. He had a nice-looking butt in those high-dollar britches. A trickle of logic seeped through her clouded senses and she decided against informing him of her observation.

Before long, a stream of passengers flowed past Lenore. Some were joyously greeting loved ones. Others strode purposefully toward the baggage claim area. She remembered her own suitcase. It would be twirling like a lone passenger on a carousel. Her thoughts were interrupted when Bosworth returned with a young man at his side.

"Lenore Appleby, this is Clint Zachary. Clint is from Indiana. Clint, Lenore is from Colorado."

"Nice to meet you. Call me Zach."

She smiled and shook his extended hand.

"Shall we go get your luggage?" Bosworth suggested.

Like dutiful participants on a museum tour, Lenore and Zach followed Bosworth to the claim area. Bosworth started to carry Lenore's suitcase, then sat it down and took another grip.

"Lenore, what have you got in here?"

"Necessary equipment, Boz. I prefer to use the wheels and pull most of the time." He laughed as she unfastened the strap and offered it. The trio exited and walked to Bosworth's station wagon.

The fresh air, though somewhat tainted with the odor of exhaust fumes, seemed to clear Lenore's head a little. They drove into the city and were treated to a little sightseeing tour on the way. Lenore appreciated the city skyline, but felt a little insecure without the mountains.

After they were checked into the hotel and briefed on the next day's schedule, Bosworth left them standing in the lobby, still burdened with their luggage.

"Lenore, would you like to get something to eat? I'm starved. And I must confess that I had a little too much to drink on the plane."

"You? I couldn't tell." Lenore giggled. "I thought I was the only one half-blitzed."

"No, I think it's part of the training. You get drunk before you get here, and wish you were drunk until you leave. We're on the same floor. Let's put our suitcases away and go forage for food!"

On the elevator, Lenore told him he would have to be the designated driver, and therefore responsible for pushing the right button. He made sure she was safely in her room, then went to his own. The huge bed looked inviting, but hunger was a great motivation for staying away from it. She brushed her hair and checked her make-up. She had just opened the suitcase when Zach knocked on her door.

"Ready?"

"Should I change clothes?"

"You look great."

"You really are starved, aren't you? Let's go."

Lenore was pleased when he smiled. He was a handsome young man, probably not much older than her son, Grant. She wondered if she was going to feel like a den mother at their training sessions.

The hotel lounge was dark and smelled of whiskey and polished wood. Lenore liked it. They chose to sit at the bar. By the time their sandwiches arrived, several company employees had introduced themselves and the group moved to tables to accommodate it's growing numbers. Lenore was sure the influx of alcohol was a factor, but she was feeling like one of the guys. It was a position she preferred in the business world, and the training seminar would go well.

CHAPTER 36

With certificate in hand, Lenore waited for her flight in the noisy din of the Kansas City Airport. She had made good friends and valuable allies throughout her training. Her briefcase was brimming with notes and information, as well as phone numbers. Zach sat beside her as they watched travelers arrive and depart. They were both relaxed for their flights, as they sat at the bar for a quick drink.

"Lenore, when we were first introduced, I thought you would be like a mom or something. Boy, was I wrong."

"How's that, Zach?" She laughed.

"You don't act like a mom. You're intelligent and fun and silly."

Lenore sipped her drink, then said, "Just because you give birth doesn't mean you're no longer a person with dreams and desires."

"I can see that now. I think I'll look at my own mom a little differently from now on. You're going to be a great manager. You're a leader!"

"It's the same reason you're here, Zach." They clinked their glasses in a toast. "We'll see one another at a manager's meeting someday."

"I look forward to it." He checked his watch. "Looks like I'd better get to my gate. Take care and keep in touch."

Lenore offered her hand, but Zach kissed her on the cheek instead. With a final wave, he disappeared down the concourse. It was still a half hour before her flight. She refused another drink from the bartender and walked slowly toward her gate. Even with a stop at the restroom, she was still going to wait twenty minutes for her flight to begin boarding.

She looked at the assortment of passengers. Seasoned travelers looked at watches or dozed. Couples nuzzled one another at the prospect of separation and several novice fliers nervously adjusted carry-on baggage and rechecked tickets.

A scream startled her. She craned her neck to see past the crowd to where a man was sprawled on the floor, in obvious medical distress. Having had CPR training, she started toward the melee, when a man took her by the elbow.

"Lenore Appleby, I need you to come with me—quietly."

He steered her to a door and quickly orchestrated a code into the security panel. In a matter of seconds, they stood in a stairwell.

"What's going on? That guy probably needed CPR. I can help." She frowned. "Am I being protected or about to get a lecture for not letting you guys know I was going somewhere?" She was sarcastic. "Make it quick. I have a flight to catch."

The man reached inside his jacket and produced a stainless steel, two-inch barrel revolver. Lenore's eyes widened as she wondered how he got it through security, then remembered he was CIA.

"You don't need to worry about your flight. Let's go." He gestured with a nod of his head toward the descending stairs.

Good old CIA! A real gun! She shook her head and smiled at the incredulous situation. She turned toward the door leading back to the terminal. "This is not happening to me," she mumbled.

His warm breath on her hair was in stark contrast to the icy coldness of the gun barrel on her cheek. "I assure you it's happening. Now, you will go down those stairs and out the door without incident. There's a van waiting for us."

"Are you guys really this upset I didn't let you know I was going?" She tried the handle, finding it an unyielding force. "I'm sorry, okay? Now let me back in the door."

"You will not be going back into the terminal." He pulled her arm from the door, twisting it painfully behind her back. The gun barrel was still on her cheek. "I do not wish to use this, but I assure you I can."

"I could scream, you know." She turned toward the stairs.

He laughed. "I don't think you're a screamer myself, but if you want, go ahead. No one will hear."

She should have been afraid, but fear was held in check by mounting anger. How dare John allow this to happen? A real gun! And, the son-of-a-bitch had actually put it to her cheek.

Lenore stomped down the metal stairs and out the door, jerking her arm free of the hold. The noise on the tarmac was deafening, further assuring the uselessness of a scream. She walked to the dark blue van emblazoned with AIRPORT SECURITY and got in. Her seat was facing the rear seat.

She was sitting beside a man dressed similarly to her abductor, who had closed the door and went around to get behind the wheel. The roar of air traffic was somewhat abated inside the warm vehicle. She sat the briefcase between her knees on the floor and glared at the third man facing her.

"This is positively the most absurd situation I've ever been in. I want to talk to John, right now! You people are in big, and I mean really big trouble!"

"I am pleased to finally meet you, Ms. Lenore Appleby."

"Oh shit!" she whispered. She stared at the huge man facing her. His nose and eyes glowed as he puffed on the pipe. His accent was much stronger than Gregor's.

"You're not CIA."

He smiled and a chuckle could be heard from the other two men. "No, Ms. Appleby, we are not CIA."

"What do you want from me?" Her palms began perspiring and a spasm of pain shot through her abdomen.

"I believe it is what you would be wanting from us." The huge man casually tamped the contents of his pipe with a fleshy finger as he spoke. "There is someone who would very much like to see you, and you would be wanting to see him as well. Am I correct?"

"No, you are not correct. I'll be leaving now." She moved toward the door and was re-seated, somewhat abruptly, by the man beside her.

A laugh erupted from the man with the pipe. "I do not believe you. Why would you not want to see your lover?"

Lenore glared first at the man who had forced her back into the seat, then at the man who addressed her. "If you're speaking of Gregor, I don't care if he wants to see me. I don't want to see him! Now, may I go?"

She eyed the door but didn't move.

"I have a plane to catch."

The airport buildings seemed to move as she realized the van was slowly pulling away.

"Aw, please don't do this."

* * * * *

"What do you mean she's gone?" John ran his fingers through his hair and closed his eyes against the voice coming through the receiver.

337

"All you had to do was keep one person in your sight at all times. Are you absolutely sure she did not get on the flight? Did you check the restrooms? The bar?"

He took the phone away from his ear and looked around the room, shaking his head. He put the receiver back to his ear, though he wasn't ready to listen to any more excuses.

"You'd better hope she's found soon or the only thing you're going to be watching is ice forming at the north pole and your retirement going up in smoke!"

Slamming the receiver down onto the cradle didn't give the satisfaction that slamming the inept agent against a wall could give, but it was all he had. He looked at his watch and picked up the phone.

John paced as he spoke to the Director. "Now you understand why I thought it was important to follow her? She's gone! Vanished! I want the company jet to fly me to KC—now! I want all flights from there and surrounding airports monitored, and if anyone even looks like Lenore Appleby, I want the plane delayed. If we don't act quickly on this one, she'll wake-up in the Soviet Union."

"John, I never doubted your instincts. Just doubted their audacity. Take the company jet. I'll scramble KC and any airports within a 500-mile radius. If she slips through our fingers there, we'll monitor all overseas flights that could end up in the Soviet Union. Get going. I'll get busy here."

John Dixon had one more call to make. It was going to be a tough one.

* * * * *

Leah was chopping carrots when the phone rang. She dried her hands and picked up on the third ring. John's voice interrupted her greeting.

"Thank God you're home. Can you talk?"

"John? What's going on? You're upset!"

"Leah, we've lost Lenore." He waited for her reply, but there was only silence. "We had an agent tailing her in Kansas City, but we lost track of her at the airport. We were trying to be as discreet as possible, given her reluctance of being followed. Looks like we got careless. We know she didn't get on the flight, but we can't find her."

Leah sank to the floor and sat against the cabinet. "John, you're not saying she's lost in the airport. You're saying someone took her."

"That's what I'm saying. Yes."

Tears rimmed Leah's eyes, then she sniffed and stood up, control wavering. "What are you doing to find her? What can I do from here? What do I tell her son?"

"Leah, I'm heading to Kansas City as soon as I get off the phone. With any luck, I'll have her on a flight home by morning. For now, tell Joel she ran into me and I talked her into staying another night. If we don't go into details, it could save her problems later on."

"Pull all the plugs, John. I don't care if she likes it or not. Keep me informed. Please!"

"As best I can. If she contacts you, call my number and they'll transfer the call to me."

Leah hung up the phone without saying good-bye. She paced around the kitchen and nibbled on a carrot stick before returning to the phone. It would be no problem to tell people of the change of plans, for now. Tears fell freely when she thought about what she would have to tell them, if Lenore could not be found. JD walked into the kitchen to find Leah crying beside the phone.

"Who was on the phone?" He put his arms around his wife and she buried her face in his chest. "Why the tears?"

"It was Lenore. She's staying another night in Kansas City and wanted to let us know." The lie was hard, but she had to sound convincing. "She ran into John, and he talked her into staying. I'm just happy she's found someone she's interested in, who takes such an interest in her."

JD chuckled and hugged Leah. "Well, I'm happy for her, too, but I'm sure not going to cry about it. Royce might when he finds out he's losing his day off tomorrow to cover for her."

He kissed the top of his wife's head, grabbed a carrot stick and went back into the living room to watch the ball game, as Leah picked up the phone to call Joel.

* * * * *

The jet was waiting for John at the company airfield, fueled and ready for take-off. He took a seat and buckled his seatbelt before noticing a fellow passenger across the aisle.

"Thought you might want some help in KC. Heard what happened and since I know what Lenore looks like, I could be useful. Might make up for my blunder at the lake."

"Thanks, Frank. She's going to need all the help we can give her right now. I appreciate it." He looked out the window at the lights penetrating the blackness. "I never considered it a blunder, you know."

"Thanks, John. That means a lot to me."

The two men fell silent as the sleek craft maneuvered down the runway and the sudden lack of vibration accentuated takeoff. They would land in Kansas City in less than an hour to begin a search for someone they feared could already be on her way to Moscow.

* * * * *

Lenore shifted the briefcase between her knees to steady it, as the van cut in and out of traffic. She strained to see her watch as they passed under the lights of the freeway. Her flight had already departed.

"Yes, Ms. Appleby, you have missed your flight. Perhaps we can arrange another, if you cooperate."

"As if I have a choice." She glared at the man sitting across from her. The interspersed lighting provided little illumination inside the van, but she was able to detect leg braces and a set of crutches. He made no effort to avoid her stares. He was bearded, with light hair, maybe blond. No, definitely white. He took the pipe from his mouth and once again tamped the contents, making Lenore wonder why it didn't burn his fingers.

She pretended to look out the window to her right, but used the position to study the man next to her. Thirty-ish, dark hair, mustache. The bulbous appendage on his face produced a startling snork sound every few minutes. She didn't see a gun, but knew it was probably within easy reach. He returned her stare for a minute, then looked back out the window.

She was in a van with three men. One, whom she knew had a gun, was driving. A second, who probably had a gun and suffered with a disgusting sinus condition, was sitting on her right. Across from her was an obese crippled man, who probably didn't need a gun, with two able-bodied aids. Maybe not a hopeless situation.

Who was she kidding? She didn't have a gun, just a briefcase full of information she would probably never get to use. Cramps racked through her abdomen as she thought about her luggage arriving at Stapleton in an hour or less. How long would it ride on the carousel before some attendant took it to a room with other orphaned pieces? How long before Joel knew she wasn't coming home?"

She looked at the mass of flesh propped in the seat opposite her. "Is Gregor here in Kansas City?"

No response.

She tried again. "Can't you at least tell me if he's here in Kansas City?"

Again, no response.

"Look, asshole, you could at least tell me where this joy ride is going!"

Lenore watched as he re-lit his pipe and puffed, as if considering an answer. He removed the pipe from his mouth and spoke to the man next to her, who turned in his seat and slapped her with the back of his hand.

Tears stung her eyes and genuine fear shot electric pain throughout her body.

The huge man spoke quietly. "You will be careful in your words, yes? It seems you are anxious to see your lover after all."

The word *lover* struck a harsh chord. "I just want to see him to clear up the misconception he must have." She flinched as the man beside her sneezed and followed it with the annoying snork. "That's the only reason I want to see him."

"I do not believe you. You will enjoy a sweet reunion in a few days." He smiled. "You will be made comfortable until that time, if you cooperate."

Lenore's voice was louder than she expected. "A few says? I don't have a few days!" Another slap. This time she wet herself a little. "Please, I have a son at home and a job to get back to. I have responsibilities." She was shaking and crying. "Why can't he call me if he wants to talk?"

His voice was quiet. "That is not possible. Perhaps we will arrange for your son to join you."

"No. Not my Joel!"

The slaps had been humiliating and painful, but when they threatened her son, survival instincts keened. The guns didn't matter anymore.

Traffic on the off-ramp had slowed to a crawl. She leaned forward and gripped the handle of her briefcase. Such fine leather. Such sturdy construction. Such an unlikely weapon.

She quickly lowered her right leg and swung the rich, full-grained leather case as hard as she could, making contact with the nose of a very surprised Soviet agent, just as he made that infernal sound once again.

One down. Two to go.

She landed a blow with the heel of her hand in the mouth of the fat man before he had a chance to remove the pipe. A gurgling noise was the only sound he could produce, as fleshy hands struggled to pull the smoldering appendage from his mouth and blood spurted profusely.

The driver stopped the van and turned in his seat, trying to assess the situation. Lenore didn't wait to see if a gun was pointed at her when she rammed the briefcase through the opening between the seats, hoping it would make contact with something. She heard an exclamation of profanity, as the driver fought the seatbelt to retrieve the weapon from the floor of the passenger side. It provided her enough time to open the door and bound out of the van.

She ran behind the van and slid down the embankment toward the busy interstate. Traffic continued to feed onto the exit ramp and horns blared at her.

She stood at the edge of the pavement and watched for an opening, glancing nervously over her shoulder. The driver stood outside the van and pointed at her.

No! He wasn't pointing, he was aiming.

Tires squealed and horns honked and Lenore ran.

When she reached the grassy median, she wasn't prepared for such a transition from smooth pavement. She tripped over a piece of shredded tire and landed, face down, amid broken glass and ancient remnants of discarded food wrappers and wax coated cups.

Cautiously, she raised her head and looked back at the exit ramp. The driver looked toward Lenore, then at the traffic surging noisily behind the stopped vehicle. He lowered the gun and got back into the van. Maybe he thought he had shot her. My God! Maybe he had! She watched the van move forward and out of sight before she began to check for injuries, or worse, bullet wounds.

There were no more horns sounding, just the roar of traffic as it passed on either side of her self-made safety zone. She raised herself to hands and knees.

"Ouch!" Lenore yelled as she rolled into a sitting position, then pushed her hair away from her face and pulled a piece of wet paper off her cheek. Oncoming traffic illuminated her sporadically, like a cheap light show, but it was enough to see the blood. Her hand was cut, but not shot. She picked flecks of mud from the wound and continued her assessment. The sleeve of her suit jacket was torn at the shoulder seam and hanging by just a few threads. Both knees of her pants were still intact, though caked with mud and grass. She pulled the material up to expose bruised and bloodied flesh. The cut on her right knee could probably benefit from a few stitches.

"How in the hell can you get a cut like this and not tear your pants?" No one answered. "I've gotta get out of here." She reached for the briefcase. "There I go, talking to myself again."

The sound of horns honking brought her attention back to the interstate. The van had taken the on-ramp and was now attempting to back up on the shoulder.

"Shit!"

She tried to stand, but pain dropped her back to the ground. A quick check found the flesh around her ankle swollen, but no wound. She looked back at the road. The van was nearly opposite her now. She had to run.

A surge of adrenaline, fueled by genuine fear, pushed her back to her feet. "Oh, God, give me wings!" She took a deep breath and limped across traffic to the northbound shoulder as cars and trucks swerved and honked to avoid her.

From the relative safety of the northbound shoulder, Lenore began to frantically wave at oncoming traffic, keeping an eye on the driver of the van, who had gotten out and was looking for a break in traffic. No one even slowed down. She got to the northbound on-ramp where headlights from an oncoming eighteen-wheeler caught her like the spotlight on the center ring of a circus. She waved her arm, put a hand out and closed her eyes. It would either stop, or run her down. The deceleration assured her she had a ride.

Across the interstate, a very frustrated driver was running back to his van. Now, all she had to do was take her chances with a trucker. It sounded like a safe alternative to any other option.

With determined effort and a great deal of pain, Lenore managed to haul her sorry looking self into the cab of the tractor-trailer rig. She closed the door, suddenly aware of just how cold she had been when the warmth of the vehicle enveloped her. She looked at her rescuer, who stared as she spoke.

"Hi. I'm Lenore. Thanks for the lift. Could you take me as far as the airport exit?" She tried to catch her breath. "I can make it from there."

"Ma'am, if you don't mind me sayin' so, you look like you need to go to the hospital instead of the airport." His soft, slow voice was full of southern politeness and concern. "But, if that's where you're headed, that's where you'll go. Anything I can do to help besides the ride?"

He was a young man with large brown eyes set in a too-thin face. The thick, black mustache he sported, moved to accommodate the smile he offered, revealing a set of good teeth. Lenore was almost surprised.

"Please, just drive. I realize I look a mess, but I have to get to the airport."

Lenore clutched the briefcase to her chest as she watched practiced hands shift gears and maneuver the truck into traffic. Shifting to a cruising gear, he glanced toward Lenore.

"Name's Jerry. Where ya flyin' to?"

"Nice to meet you, Jerry." She offered her hand, and he shook it before she realized it was her injured hand. She winced with the pain. "Sorry, I think I got blood on you."

He glanced at his palm and wiped it on the leg of his jeans. "Don't worry about it. There's a first aid kit in the back." He nodded toward the sleeper. "How'd you get hurt and wind up hitchhiking? Have a wreck?"

"You could say that." She smiled. "How far to the airport?"

He shifted a gear and looked into the side mirror. "Not far. Ten, fifteen minutes." He was frowning.

"Is there something wrong?" She was trying to see what he was seeing out his side mirror.

"Oh, there's some fool back there trying to pass everyone. He drove across the median to get onto the northbound. Must be in a hell of a hurry."

Lenore felt sick. Had she just put this polite young man in danger?

"Jerry, is it a dark blue airport van?"

He watched the mirror for a minute. "Yep, I believe it is. He's gonna cause a wreck. Someone you know?"

"I'm afraid so." She leaned over the center console to get a better look. "Jerry, they're trying to kill me. They have guns."

He looked at her, wide-eyed. "They know you're in this truck?"

"I think so." She looked into his face. "I'm so sorry I got you into this."

A low whistle was his only reaction as he shifted into another gear and Lenore felt the truck slow down.

"What are you doing?" She yelled as she grabbed the dashboard to keep from sliding to the floor. "Are you going to make me get out?"

The mustache revealed the smile again. "No, ma'am, but maybe we should let them catch up."

"Didn't you understand? They have guns!"

He glanced at Lenore, and back at the mirror. "Well, they may have guns, and we make a pretty big target, but this target can sure put a world of hurt on that van. We've got a pretty good-sized weapon under our asses, if you'll pardon the expression."

Traffic slowed away from the radically moving van, as it pulled up closer to the truck.

"How many in the van?"

"Three." She hesitated. "Two may not be conscious, though"

He glanced quickly at Lenore. "Did you shoot them?"

"No. I hit them with my briefcase."

"That briefcase?" He nodded to the object clutched in Lenore's arms.

"Yes."

He frowned. "Hey, this isn't some kind of drug deal gone bad, is it?"

"No. Actually they're Soviet agents."

He shook his head. "So, that makes you an American agent?"

"No, I work in a shoe store. It's a long story." She hoped he didn't ask her to elaborate. He did.

"What the hell did you do, fit 'em in the wrong size?" He laughed. It was more like a giggle, which made Lenore laugh, too.

"I'll tell you what, if we get out of this, I'll try to expl—" The glass in the driver's window shattered and the bullet tore through the head-liner.

"Hang-on! It's time to play freeway bump-em cars."

Lenore felt the cab sway slightly to the left as he turned the large steering wheel toward the center lane. It was no contest. The shower of sparks was visible in the side mirror as contact was made. A slight jolt could be felt as the eighteen-wheeled weapon pushed the van toward the median and an upcoming overpass support pillar.

"Damn, I don't think they hit hard enough." He lifted his cap and wiped perspiration off his brow, replaced the cap, pulling it down, then back up to its original position. "You okay?" He glanced at his passenger.

She was bleeding, bruised, swollen and shaking so hard she could scarcely hold onto the briefcase. "Yes, I'm okay."

"I don't think they'll follow. That van can't be in very good shape." He tried to reassure Lenore, but she noticed he kept checking the mirror through the nearly opaque remnant of safety glass.

"Jerry, I'll find a way to pay for the damages to your truck. You could have been killed."

"Ma'am, it gave me a chance to be a hero. I couldn't pass that up, now could I?"

He laughed his giggle laugh again. It made her smile, but she couldn't quite manage a laugh.

They rode in silence until the brightly lit green signs indicated the approaching turn. Lenore opened her briefcase, knocking a piece of dried, muddy paper off one of the latches. She found a stack of business cards and offered one to him. He glanced at the card.

"You really do work for a shoe store!"

"Yes, Jerry, I really do. You keep that card. If you ever get to Colorado, I'll buy you a pair of the best boots we carry and a good dinner, too. You saved my life tonight!"

"Aw, it'll give me something to tell my buddies at the truck stop." He signaled for the turn.

"Just drop me here and I'll get to the terminal."

He shook his head. "Ma'am, I'm not going to let the good go bad now. I'll drop you at the terminal. I don't imagine you could walk that far anyway." He smiled.

She wrote down his name, address and phone number, as well as the name of his company. She hoped John could prevent any problems for Jerry, as far as damages to his truck or possible traffic citations resulting from the incident.

The terminal was bustling with activity as she carefully climbed down from the cab of the truck. The sight of an eighteen-wheeler cruising away from the terminal was soon forgotten as people stared at the woman waving at the departing vehicle.

Inside the brightly lit facility, Lenore was able to take stock of her appearance. The front of her jacket and pants were filthy. She picked off a stray piece of mud-caked grass from her lapel and examined the torn sleeve. She tried to push it back in place, without much luck. Blood from her hand was mixed with the filth from her jacket, and the cut on her knee had yielded enough blood to soak the top of her right shoe, which not long ago had been a great fitting tan, suede loafer. The tassels from her left shoe had joined myriad objects in the median.

She limped to the United Airlines ticket counter amid stares from passengers and the airport personnel. She attempted to smooth the tangles from her hair and brush off the unyielding filth from her clothes. Drawing herself up and squaring her shoulders, she spoke to the ticket agent and smiled.

"Hello. My name is Lenore Appleby. I need to see if I can get a plane to Denver tonight." She retrieved her unused ticket from the briefcase and handed it to the agent. "I missed my earlier flight."

The agent nodded and smiled her most professional smile as she turned from the counter to a phone. Lenore resumed trying to straighten her appearance when she noticed a uniformed security officer walking her way, speaking into a hand-held radio. She turned away from him, as if it would disguise her appearance.

"Ms. Appleby, would you please come with me?"

She turned pleading eyes toward the man. "What now? I just want to get on a plane and go home. I can pay more if I have to."

"It's not that ma'am. Please just come with me."

He gently took her by the elbow and she jerked it away from his grasp. "No way, buster! I don't go anywhere until I see some identification." Her eyes flashed with anger. "How do I know you're who you say you are?"

The officer sighed and reached into his pocket. "You're causing a very unnecessary scene here. I'm airport security and we've been looking for you since you missed your flight over two hours ago." He handed her the leather-bound badge. "Here's my ID, and if you open it up, you can also see pictures of my family. Now, please, come with me."

She looked from the badge to the face of Clarence Johnson, Security, KC International Airport. She looked at the ticket agent, who nodded and mouthed, "It's okay." The man then led her to a courtesy cart.

* * * * *

"Mr. Dixon, you have a call." The voice of the pilot informed over the intercom. John unbuckled his seatbelt and walked to the front of the jet, where an in-flight phone blinked. With a push of the button, he was connected to someone on the ground.

"Dixon here." He listened for a minute, then turned to Frank, who watched from his seat. John gave a thumbs-up as he spoke. "You found her where?" He listened again and frowned. "No don't take her anywhere. We're about five minutes out. Make her comfortable. Get her anything she wants." He listened for another minute. "Then get her the best scotch you have!"

John hung up the phone as the pilot reminded him to sit down and get buckled-in for landing. Frank waited until he was settled before asking questions.

"Where'd they find her?"

"At the United Airlines ticket counter." He pointed to the no-smoking sign as Frank fished a pack from his jacket, frowned and put it back. "She walked in the front doors and right up to the ticket counter."

"Just like that?"

"Not exactly. She's hurt. They didn't say how bad, but evidently bad enough they want to take her to the hospital. I told them to wait. We'll take her to the hospital. I don't want anyone to take her anywhere."

"Must not be too awfully bad."

John frowned. "What makes you say that?"

"She asked for scotch, didn't she?"

"Good point. She can talk and drink."

* * * * *

John and Frank ran from the jet to the VIP lounge. As they walked through the doors, two security matrons and a guard, gun ready, turned their attention to the two men entering.

"CIA! Back off!" Frank flashed a badge as John walked past them to Lenore. The authority in his voice discouraged any question from the guards. Lenore attempted to stand, but instead fell back onto the sofa.

"My God, Lenore. What happened to you?" John helped her stand, holding her close.

"John, I've had a really bad day!" She tried to smile, but her bravery and adrenaline were all used up. She clutched his jacket and started crying.

"Frank, take her briefcase. Let's get you to a hospital, Lenore. You can tell me about it on the way." He started to help her walk, but when he noticed the limp, he lifted her into his arms and walked out the door.

In front of the terminal, a four-door sedan waited in the red zone. Three radio equipped agents stood, poised for action near the car. A fourth sat behind the wheel. As John gently eased Lenore into the back seat, Frank motioned for the driver to get out, taking his place. John sat beside Lenore and closed the door.

"I need to call Joel. He'll wonder why I'm not there."

John patted her gently. "It's okay. I called Leah as soon as you missed your flight. She called Joel and told him you were staying another night, with me, as a matter of fact. I'll call her again from the hospital to let her know you're okay."

She frowned. "How did you know so soon?"

"Well, at the risk of making you very angry, I have to admit we've never stopped following you. In trying to be discreet, someone got sloppy. How'd you disappear so fast?"

Lenore began to unfold the story of the man falling with the heart attack, the man with the gun and the men in the van. As she described the crippled man, John and Frank spoke simultaneously. "Sergei!"

"What the hell is that?"

"Not what. Who! Used to be an acquaintance of Greg's," John said.

Frank filled in the details. "They were friends until Sergei tried to prevent Greg from leaving. That's how he wound up like he is. Greg blew away both his knee caps."

Lenore shuddered. "Gregor did that?" She looked at John, then at Frank.

John took Lenore's hand and frowned at the back of Frank's head. "Believe me, Lenore, it was deserved. Sergei was ready to kill Greg, and Greg could have killed him. I imagine Sergei wished he would have, in a way."

"Is he trying to hurt Gregor?" She looked from John to Frank.

"We really don't know." John couldn't tell her the truth. "It may be why Greg's gone deep. Maybe he knows Sergei is after him, but I can't believe he would intentionally allow you to be put in harm's way." He pulled her closer and kissed the top of her head. For the first time in several hours, Lenore felt safe.

* * * * *

Bandaged and stitched, examined and slightly drugged, Lenore was holding onto Frank and John as they walked through the lobby of the hotel. They attracted a few curious stares. Lenore didn't know if she was more embarrassed by her filthy appearance or the fact that she was going to a hotel room with two men. In the elevator, a disapproving stare from an older couple provoked the sedated Lenore to respond.

"This is my brother." She gestured toward John. "This is my daddy." She gestured to Frank. "Got a problem with that?"

The two seasoned CIA agents nodded at the couple and quickly moved Lenore off the elevator when they reached their floor. She giggled when the doors eased shut.

"Sorry, I just couldn't take them staring at me any longer."

Frank still looked a little grim, but John smiled.

"Oh, I think they'll survive. I think it's time for you to clean up and get into bed. Your pain pills have kicked-in, haven't they?"

"I actually couldn't say for sure. I still hurt all over." She giggled again. "But I don't care anymore."

"They're working." Frank mumbled as he took the keys from John and opened the door. John helped Lenore to a chair as Frank continued down the hall to the adjoining room.

"Where's my briefcase?" Lenore asked. She was up off the chair.

"It's right here." John retrieved it from near the door. "What's so important in there you don't want it out of sight?"

"It's not the contents, it's the case itself." She accepted it from John. "It's my weapon of choice."

"Your what?"

Lenore looked down at the filthy clothes she was wearing.

"Could you run bath water for me? I've never felt so grungy in my life." She looked in a large, black framed mirror. "I look like hell!"

"I'll start the bath, but what's this about your briefcase?"

Lenore limped back to the chair and slid the briefcase between her knees as she sat down. "I need clothes. Do you have a T-shirt I could sleep in?"

"I'll get you something to wear. Now, about the briefcase."

Lenore told of the conversation with Sergei and the painful slaps. She explained how they threatened to get Joel and the anger she had felt. At the point where she had swung the briefcase into the face of the Soviet agent, she once again swung with all her might. This time, however, instead of coming into contact with a face, she shattered a lamp sitting on the table beside her.

Frank burst into the room, weapon drawn, staring first at a wide-eyed Lenore, then at John, who's hand was covering his eyes, massaging his temples.

"What's going on? Is someone hurt?"

"No Frank, Lenore was just showing me how she managed to escape from Sergei. The lamp was just an innocent bystander." John gently took the briefcase from Lenore and handed it to Frank. "Would you please take this to our room? I'm going to get Superwoman here into the bathroom, then go to the lobby and get her some clothes. Keep the door open, just in case she decides to attack a towel rack or something."

Frank holstered his weapon and took the briefcase back to the adjoining room.

"John, I'm so sorry! I'll pay for the lamp." Lenore grimaced.

"Don't worry about it." He took a deep breath and smiled at her. "You just sit here and I'll run the bath water. Don't touch anything and for God's sake, don't try to get up and move. I'll only be a minute."

John disappeared and Lenore was sure she heard laughter along with the sound of running water. In minutes he returned to help her into the bathroom.

"They had complimentary bubble-bath and I thought you might enjoy it. Now, I'm going to help you undress and get into the water. I promise to avert my eyes."

As Lenore eased into the water, making sure her injured leg was propped on the edge of the tub, she giggled.

"John."

"Yes, Lenore?"

"Didn't work, did it?"

"What didn't work?"

"Averting your eyes."

They both looked at the obvious bulge in John's trousers.

"No, I guess it didn't." He sighed and shook his head at the lady nestled into the mound of bubbles, grinning. "If I can get this thing to go away, I'll go the lobby for your clothes. Please, don't drown while I'm gone."

John left the room and it was a few minutes before she heard the outside door close. She sank as far into the bath as her injured leg would allow and played with the bubbles. With some effort, she was able to submerge her head completely and swished her hair in the warm water. She came up with bubbles blurring her vision and managed to find the stark white washcloth to wipe them away.

She scrubbed herself from head to toe, careful to keep her knee out of the water and her bandage dry. The water was beginning to cool and she was getting very sleepy. She used the toes of her uninjured foot to push the drain lever and carefully stepped out the depleting bubbles to dry herself with a plush white towel. Just then, she heard the door and John's voice.

"It's only me. Are you ready to get out of the tub?"

"Already out."

John walked into the bathroom and found Lenore wrapped in a towel and drying her hair. He handed her a T-shirt nightgown, with KANSAS CITY ROYALS printed across the front.

"You should be able to sleep in this. I also bought an assortment of toiletries and something I hope is suitable for your flight home tomorrow. Not a lot of choices in a hotel gift shop." He walked to the bed as Lenore slipped the shirt over her head and allowed the towel to drop to the floor. "We had your luggage picked up at Stapleton. We can get it tomorrow."

Lenore limped to the bed and sat on the edge to look through the items John had procured.

"You're certainly thorough. Let's see: toothbrush and toothpaste, mouthwash, lotion, shampoo and conditioner, comb, hair brush, baby powder, mascara, lipstick, perfume, tampons. Tampons?"

Lenore looked at John, who shrugged. "I just asked for anything a woman might need who had her luggage take a different flight."

"How thoughtful! Thank you so much."

"I hope the outfit is okay." He pulled an emerald green wind suit from a bag. "If not, I'll have them open the gift shop again and find something else."

Lenore ran her fingers over the silky material. "It's beautiful. It's perfect." She stood and planted a kiss on John's cheek. "Thank you again."

"Your welcome, but you need to get off your ankle."

Lenore grabbed the toothbrush and toothpaste and the comb, then limped into the bathroom. "I have to do this first."

John pulled back the covers of the bed. "I'm going to call room service."

"Nothing for me unless it's a Diet Coke."

"Lenore, you need to eat something with the medication. I'll get you a club sandwich."

"Whatever," she said, with a mouthful of toothpaste.

When room service arrived, Lenore was snuggled into bed. John and Frank sat at the table talking. She couldn't hear what they were saying, but the low murmuring was like a lullaby. Ten minutes later, with half of the sandwich and another pain pill in her belly, she fell asleep.

* * * * *

As her eyes began to focus, she was startled to see John standing beside her bed, soothing her hair.

"You were crying. Do you need another pain pill?"

Lenore sat up in bed, trying to orient herself. Her ankle was indeed throbbing with pain, but it wasn't why she had been crying.

"I guess I could use another. I just had a bad dream. Can you sit here and talk to me for a while?" She accepted the pain pill and the glass of water he offered. "Have you slept at all, John?"

He sat on the edge of the bed. "I dozed a little. Don't worry about me. I can sleep tomorrow after you're safely home. Want to tell me about the dream?"

She took a sip of water with the pill and shook her head. "I just wonder if I'm going to have to look over my shoulder the rest of my life. Should I worry about Joel and Grant? Will someone try to take them next?"

John remembered Leah's warning about telling Lenore of Greg's imprisonment. Now was certainly not the time to add to her worries.

"Lenore, I wish I had easy answers for your questions. I really don't think Greg had anything to do with what happened. He wouldn't put you thorough it. My theory is that Sergei was trying to flush Greg out of hiding." He took her hands, careful of the bandage on her right. "As to the boys, unless you really see a problem, I've already assigned surveillance for both of them. I told our men to be discreet, but extra cautious, considering what's happened. Just go on with your life. We'll do the looking for you. I promise we won't get in the way."

Lenore sighed. "Right now, I don't think I'd mind how obvious they were, if it weren't for having to make explanations to Joel and Grant. Maybe I should just sit them down and tell them the whole story. Then again, it might cause them more worry than necessary."

She ran her fingers through her hair, then slipped them back into John's hands. "I'm so confused and frightened. I wish I'd never met Gregor." A tear slid down her cheek and she bit her lower lip. "Then again, I wouldn't have missed it for the world." She took a deep breath and slowly exhaled. "John, would you just hold me?"

Lenore shifted in the bed, allowing room for John to lay down. He stayed on top of the covers and cradled her in his arms, soothing and stroking her hair until she slept.

Sometime later, John slept, too, still holding Lenore in his arms.

CHAPTER 37

Lenore awoke alone in the bed, but she could hear voices from the adjoining room. Every muscle in her body rebelled against movement as she got up, and with determined effort, made it to the bathroom and closed the door. The assortment of toiletries was arranged conveniently on the counter. She smiled.

She stepped carefully into the bathtub and pulled the curtain, managing to keep her injured leg as free from the spray as she could, but lingering in the warm shower until she felt refreshed. She towel-dried, then brushed and combed and rolled-on until her ritual was complete. Using the complimentary hair dryer, she managed to dry her hair, though bending over to dry from underneath, produced dizziness. The perfume was a delightful uplift. She exited the steamy bathroom, clad once again in the KC Royals T-shirt nightgown and snuggled into the complimentary white terry-cloth robe provided by the hotel.

"Good morning, Lenore. I took the liberty of ordering breakfast for you. Bacon, English muffin, juice, coffee and—"

"Coffee, please! Thank you, Frank. Where's John?"

"He's on the phone with the boss. We need to ask you a few more question about your adventure yesterday, if you don't mind." He handed her the coffee. "Do you need a pain pill?"

Lenore was trying to ease into a chair with her coffee and grimacing with the effort, making sure her robe stayed closed. "Yes, a pain pill would probably help. What do I need to tell you about yesterday? I don't remember what I told you and what I left out. I was a little foggy last night."

"Maybe just a little." Frank chuckled. "Here's your pill. I'll let John know you're out of the bathroom. Can I get you anything else?"

Savoring her first sip of coffee, she shook her head, then caught Frank by the arm.

"Frank, I owe you a huge apology for the way I behaved in Colorado. I realize now how important you job is, and I took it entirely too lightly."

"No apology needed. Maybe you taught me a thing or two. I'm just glad things turned out okay yesterday."

Frank patted Lenore's hand before leaving the room and returned in a few minutes with John. At John's insistence, Lenore ate the bacon and half of the English muffin as they quizzed her for details.

"I know the man who took me to the van in the first place was the driver and came after me when I ran. I think he aimed a gun at me but didn't fire it. You don't suppose I killed the others, do you? I hit the one guy pretty hard and shoved that pipe down the fat guy's throat."

"Probably not, but there's something I want to show you. I didn't think you needed to be made aware of it last night."

John retrieved the briefcase and turned it around to show Lenore the bottom. A hole, about the size of her finger, showed the path of the bullet from one corner of the briefcase through the bottom.

Lenore looked, touched, then withdrew her hand and looked up at John. "He did fire the gun."

"I'm afraid so."

Tears came to her eyes and John was prepared to comfort her through the attempt on her life. Instead, he was shocked at her reaction.

"That bastard! JD and Leah bought this briefcase for me. Now, it's ruined because of the stupid bullet hole." She sobbed and the tears began to flow freely. "He didn't have to shoot my briefcase!"

John took her by the shoulders. "Lenore, that bullet hole could just as easily been through you instead of the briefcase. Doesn't that bother you?"

She frowned and nodded her head. "Well, of course, but you don't understand; this was the symbol of my getting somewhere in the management program. It meant a lot!" She sniffled and rubbed her nose with the heel of her hand. "It smelled so good and besides, Grant hasn't even seen it yet."

Frank shook his head and walked to the other side of the room, as John patted her back and reached for a tissue.

"We can get you another briefcase."

She blew her nose and looked up at John. "But it won't be this one. This is the special one."

John looked at Frank, who threw his hands in the air and turned to the window. She continued looking at the perplexed agent for an answer to the dilemma.

"Okay, why don't you keep the briefcase, tell people you fell and something poked the hole in it." He smiled and raised his eyebrows.

"Okay." She sniffed. "What?"

"What?"

"What could have made this hole?"

John ran his fingers through his hair. Frank turned back from the window.

"Lenore, you don't have to know. Just tell everyone you found it later and don't know what made the hole."

She nodded and smiled. "That'll work, I guess."

John smiled gratefully at Frank, then looked at Lenore. "Sure, you could have it repaired if you want. I'll even pay to have it repaired."

"Thanks." She smiled at the two agents. "I guess I'm pretty lucky it was the briefcase and not me, huh?"

"That pretty well sums up our feelings on the matter. Now, I had some pictures faxed to the hotel. Look through them and see if you recognize anyone."

With a fresh cup of coffee in hand, Lenore perused the pictures slowly, contemplating each face before turning them face down on the table. Two pictures were left face-up.

"Okay, this is the fat guy and this is the one who shot my briefcase. I don't see the guy who made such a horrible noise with his nose. He had a huge, red, pickle-looking nose." She gestured with her hand the generous size. "Do you know these two?"

"Yes, this is Sergei, whom I can't believe they are using in any official capacity. The other is a young KGB operative. He had been gaining a reputation for himself, but you may have tarnished it a bit."

"I know the fat guy was Russian or Soviet or whatever, but this guy couldn't be." She tapped her finger on the photograph. "He didn't have the slightest accent. That's why I figured he was one of you guys." She frowned, recalling Gregor's cautioning about people who are not what they pretend to be. She looked up from the photograph. "How did he know what buttons to push to get us through that door?"

"All minor details in their line of work." Frank explained. "Accents can be lost and codes can be de-coded, as simply as watching someone orchestrate the buttons in the course of a day."

"So, you're telling me nothing is secure?"

"Very little in this world, I'm afraid."

John put the two photographs into an envelope and the rest in a folder. "Whenever you're ready to go home, we can leave. You'll have a pair of replacement loafers here any minute, too, courtesy of your shoe company. Frank is going to stay here in KC to see if he can track down your abductors. I get the honor of seeing you to your door. Have you decided what you're going to tell everyone about your condition?"

"Oh, yeah, my condition." She grimaced. "I'll have to work on that story. If you two gentlemen will leave the room, I'll get dressed."

The two agents discussed the situation in the adjoining room, with the door closed.

"This could be a big break for everyone. Think you have enough information to find these guys?" John asked.

"I doubt they're in much condition to have gotten too far. In fact, I think I'll check the morgues first. If she hit anyone in the face as hard as she clobbered that lamp, they might be dead." He sipped his coffee. "Speaking of dead people, did you mention the heart attack victim at the airport died of lead poisoning?"

"For God's sake, don't tell her they shot the guy." John glanced toward the closed door. "Just do your best, Frank. If we can get Sergei, maybe we can use him as a pawn to get Greg back."

"Sure you want him back, Dixon? I've seen how you look at her. You're in love."

"That's why I have to do it. I owe it to both of them. At this point, I'd be a concession, not first prize. She'd always have him somewhere inside that beautiful head of hers; always wondering if he's going to show up again or what might have been if he did. I couldn't handle that." He paced a few steps and turned back to Frank. "No, she has to see him again, to either end it, which I hope is the case, or live happily ever after with the guy. I can't make the choice for her."

Frank nodded, then shook his head.

Two hours later, as the CIA jet left Kansas City, Frank was briefing an eager and capable investigating team.

The two injured Soviet agents were soon found at a hospital emergency room. The one Lenore hit in the face had a broken nose, cheekbone and jaw, and had swallowed several teeth.

Sergei had a punctured esophagus from having the pipe shoved into his throat. He would live with the aid of tubes and ventilators for a while longer. The third kidnapper became the focus of a massive manhunt.

* * * * *

"I couldn't get here fast enough! My God, Lenore, you look like you've been run over by a bus! What did Joel say when he saw you?"

Leah fussed and fluttered around Lenore, who was stretched out on her couch, until the patient could take no more. "Please, sit down! I'm fine. Really!"

Leah sat down next to Lenore and awaited details. After she heard the story, she sat quietly for a minute before speaking.

"So, did you have to pay for the lamp?"

"After all that, you ask about the stupid lamp?"

"Well, I don't know where to begin!"

"No, I didn't pay for the lamp. I assume John paid for it or the CIA picked up the tab."

"Weren't you scared to death to be out there on the interstate? What if the trucker had been a murderer or rapist? ... Or your ex-husband?"

"Leah, the way I looked, I don't think he would have bothered. Besides, it was either flag down a ride or keep trying to run with a bum ankle. I knew I couldn't do that."

"Guess not. What have you told Joel?"

"I told him I fell down an embankment when John took me to dinner. I went into great detail. He laughed pretty hard at the vision of his mom, trying to be such a lady, rolling into the ditch, ass over teakettle."

"I'd have bought that one, myself."

"Are you calling me a klutz?" Lenore looked offended.

"Well, except for minor details, like running for your life, you did, after all, fall flat on your face."

"I'll have you know, except for a little dirt and a bruise or two from the slaps, my face came away totally unscathed." She closed her eyes and raised her nose in the air. They both laughed.

"I'd love to have seen the look you got when you walked into the airport all bloodied and dirty, trying to look inconspicuous and innocent. They won't soon forget you."

"Probably not."

The two women sat quietly for a minute, then as if sharing a vision, laughed. Leah jumped up and began her imitation of Lenore walking into the airport, but rendered a version closer to the Hunchback of Notre Dame on a bad day. They laughed until Leah collapsed on the chair next to Lenore. It was several minutes before they could talk.

"What's John got to say about all this?"

She had held her own conversation with John and knew exactly what his thoughts were, and what he had assured Lenore. She had even been told of the murder at the airport.

"He thinks they were trying to get me as a way to flush Gregor out of hiding. I tried to tell the kidnappers I absolutely had no desire to see him, but they were convinced otherwise." Lenore touched her bandaged knee. "I'm satisfied it's over. Why can't everyone else be?"

"But what if he really did show up?"

"What if? What if! I can't live on what ifs. Joel will graduate in two and a half months. That's all that counts. Maybe, if I can ever walk again, I can keep training and get my own store in another year. That's reality. That's something to hold onto." She took a deep breath and let it out slowly.

Leah nodded and started to speak, but Lenore continued. "Here's something else to think about; look what I went through. Can you imagine having to wonder whether he was going to come home at night or if someone was going to kidnap me or kill us both? I couldn't handle that, no matter how much I love him."

"You said that in the present tense."

"What?" Lenore looked confused.

"You said love, not loved."

"Stop it, Leah! You know what I mean."

A simple "uh-huh" was Leah's response. She took their half-empty glasses to the kitchen for refills of Diet Coke, while Lenore drummed her fingers on the sofa and stared into space.

*****

It was weeks before Lenore could walk without a noticeable limp. Work was challenging with her new responsibilities, and graduation grew closer every day. Joel's activities increased, and there were times they didn't see one another, except in passing, for days.

John was in touch several times a week and took Lenore to an occasional movie or dinner. She was able to spot her surveillance from time to time, but she didn't mind. She had become circumspect with strangers, which was proving to be a detriment in sales. She relished the monotony of stock work when office work didn't demand her time.

*****

It was the middle of May when Leah received a call from John.

"Why are you calling? What's wrong?"

Leah, I feel really bad I can't call without your thinking there's a problem."

"I'll always be a little wary hearing your voice after receiving your call the night of Lenore's great Kansas City adventure."

He chuckled. "I think this time, it's good news. We have negotiations going back and forth between the United States and the Soviet Union, and there's a chance we'll at least get confirmation they have Greg. Since we're holding two of their agents, it's a little political blackmail on our part. They've assured us the third man is back in the Soviet Union being severely reprimanded. We're waiting for confirmation on that from our own operatives. Also, they released Greg's brother last week. We had nothing to do with it."

"Is Sergei still alive? You said he was in really bad shape."

"He'll live long enough for negotiations. Both men were in critical condition. She really hit hard. Who else would have thought to shove the pipe down Sergei's throat?"

"Their mistake was threatening Joel. I can only imagine the rage fueling those blows. Where's Gregor's brother? Is he here?"

"Still in the USSR for now. He knows better than to try and leave. The government there is in a transition, and they're trying to build relations with the West. They're releasing a lot of political prisoners. Alexander, fortunately, was one of the first. With any luck, they'll see the futility in keeping Greg and release him as well. We just have to tread carefully. If they think the CIA is behind it, they'll lock him so far away we'll never get him … or simply kill him." He thought about what he had just said, then continued. "Right now, all they know is our government is holding two of their people for what they did to Lenore. We'll hope for the best."

"What you're telling me is, don't get excited, but there could be hope on the horizon."

"Basically, yes. Do we tell Lenore or not?"

"No!"

"Are you sure? She's been through a lot over this guy, thinking he just disappeared for no reason. Don't you think it's time to tell her everything?"

"And get her hopes up he's coming back? Think what it would do to her if he isn't released? I think the best approach is to wait and see if Gregor wants to come back to her. He might not, you know."

"I guess that's hard for me to believe, but you're right. Do we wait until he's back in town, or what?"

"Maybe. I just don't want her to see her hurt anymore. It's going to be hard enough for her if he does show up. I don't know if she'll even give him a chance to talk to her."

"Just keep briefcases away from her if he shows up."

CHAPTER 38

Two weeks after Gregor had been settled into the comfortable room to await Lenore's arrival, he had been taken back to the barren, cold, isolation cell, where he now paced and performed whatever exercises he could manage. There had been no explanation, but he knew they had been unsuccessful in their attempt to take his precious Lenore.

He spent many hours trying to imagine how close they might have come, and wondered if they had merely frightened her or if she had been injured. He assumed if it was worse, they would have found a way to use it against him. Surely his friend John had been a factor in their failure, and he made a vow to thank him someday.

Gregor sat down on the damp floor and closed his eyes, trying to bring a vision of Lenore to mind. Would she still remember him? How would he ever be able to make amends for leaving for so long? Perhaps he was fooling himself for thinking such a beautiful woman would wait for him. He had worked so hard to gain her trust and convince her of his love. He would find a way to reach her. If he did nothing else in his life, he would tell her once again, he loved her.

Her lovely face filled his thoughts. The eyes so full of love for him. A smile settled on his gaunt features.

The vision disappeared with the sound of keys unlocking his door. He stood and backed against the wall, expecting the washing down of his cell. Instead, the guard motioned for him to leave the filthy confines. Warily, he stepped into the hall and walked down the corridor. The guard stopped him and gestured toward the showers.

"You have been asked to clean yourself. Be thorough."

Gregor stepped out of the filthy clothes. He adjusted the water until it was almost uncomfortably hot, then began scrubbing with the harsh soap. He was thin. His hands felt bones with very little flesh covering them as he washed the meager lather over his body. The location of open sores was evident with soapy contact. The hair on his head and face was long and matted, but seemed free of vermin. It took much effort to feel the effects of his washing.

A dingy uniform was given to Gregor. It was stiff but clean. He was taken to the interrogation room, but the only one there was the man who had given him a haircut several months earlier.

His hands were not tied. Perhaps it was because they were aware of his weakened state. Escape was not a threat.

Gregor dozed off and on as the robust barber cut and trimmed. He didn't care about the hair falling down the neck of his clothing. He could see where the wall had been crudely patched with plaster, then painted.

After his haircut, Gregor was taken to the clean room, but took little notice of the view from the window before lying down on the cot and falling asleep. He was roused shortly, as food was brought in and he was forced to eat. His hunger was abated with a few sips of broth. Returning to the cot, he was asleep almost immediately, and slept without interruption for more than a day.

* * * * *

The smell of food stirred his senses, but he was having difficulty coming to full consciousness.

"You must eat something, Gregor. You have slept long enough."

He opened his eyes to see where the quiet voice had come from. It had not called him Prisoner Parishnikov. A smiling face came into focus. Gregor sat up, not taking his eyes off the white-haired man.

"Much better! Please, come to the table and eat."

Another strange word. Please. With concerted effort, Gregor moved from the cot to the table and sat before the fare. Broth, thick buttered bread and a small pot of strong tea were waiting. He ignored the spoon and lifted the bowl of broth to his lips, taking a mouthful of the salty, clear liquid. It tasted of beef and was very good. He swallowed and took another mouthful. The influx of warm broth on Gregor's empty stomach momentarily nauseated him, and he sat the bowl down.

"You must eat more."

"I have to wait." He rubbed his face and looked again at the stranger. "Who are you?"

"I am a doctor, Gregor."

Gregor's eyes shifted from the face to the stethoscope in the doctor's pocket. A glance around the room showed they were alone.

"There is no guard."

"Do we need one, Gregor?"

With only a moment's hesitation, he shook his head. He was too weak to consider escape. He took a bite of the bread, savoring the feel and texture of its freshness.

"Good. Now we will talk. Please continue to eat." The doctor gestured to the food before Gregor. "Do you know why you were imprisoned?"

Confusion registered on Gregor's face. Was this just another attempt to make him admit to things he did not do? Was this, after all, just another interrogation? He felt anger toward the man who, only moments before, had put him at ease.

"What do you want me to say?" He pushed away from the table. "I came back to visit my brother only to find they had imprisoned him. They have punished him for my defection. I did not come bearing secrets, nor do I have plans to gather them. I do not wish to destroy your country. I wish only to go home."

"This country you used to call your home, Gregor, is not the same as it once was." The doctor took a seat on the bed. "There are many changes coming forth. It has caused great fear and stress among loyal Communists. It is out of that fear you were imprisoned. Because of great efforts being made to normalize relations with the West, those who fight this direction see you as their greatest threat. You bring visions of freedoms they cannot imagine, nor care to." He leaned forward, speaking quietly. "Tell me something, Gregor. Would you have tried to take your brother back to the United States had he not been in prison?"

Gregor considered the impact of his answer. "Yes."

The doctor chuckled. "They presumed as much."

"If they have me, why do they still hold Alexander? It is obvious I cannot carry out my plans."

"Your brother is no longer in prison. He was released several weeks ago. With the changes coming, those who were in charge have been replaced, and many political prisoners have been released."

Gregor felt elated. His younger brother was free; as free as could be allowed in the Soviet Union. Whatever was going to happen now would be more endurable. He considered his own fate as the doctor continued.

"You are the exception. At least, you were. Because no one knew you were here, there were no advocates for your plight. You were lost in what little system is left, but your new government is very persistent. They know where you are and are trying to affect your release. I do not want to give you too much encouragement." He smiled. "If it is possible, it could take months. You will be made comfortable until that time."

"Why do you give me this information? Why would it be allowed?" Suspicion filled his thoughts. "And who are you?"

The man with white hair lifted himself off of the edge of the bed, then walked to the door and knocked, signaling the guard to open it.

"Gregor, I am simply a doctor. Because of a documentary done regarding Soviet prisons, they have assigned new directors and doctors to every facility. Humane treatment is a requirement. It would appear our government is trying to assure the West of our efforts." The doctor pointed to the food before Gregor. "Now please, eat! You would not want me to get into trouble for not doing my job, would you?"

Gregor smiled and shook his head. As an afterthought, he called out as the door was closing.

"Could you tell me one thing more?"

The doctor turned to face his patient.

"Is it possible to get word to someone?"

The white-haired man shook his head. "I'm afraid it is not possible at this time. I assure you, however, your brother is aware you are being held."

Gregor nodded his thanks, but Alexander was not the one he had in mind.

CHAPTER 39

Guests began arriving minutes after Lenore and John returned from the ceremony. The eclectic group included family, friends and co-workers, and Lenore's first husband Craig with his wife Donna. She found no reason to exclude Craig from his son's important milestone.

With the attention shifted from the graduate's mother to the graduate, Lenore busied herself with preparations for the cookout. Leah and Gertie assisted, as did Donna. It was far more comfortable than she had envisioned. Knowing John was in the other room conversing easily with the guests brought a smile to her lips.

"What are you smiling about?" Leah asked. "I figured you'd be in tears."

"I don't know. I suppose pride in Joel and a little pride in myself, too. I've reached a goal in my life, you know? I'm sure there will be plenty of tears later when it all sinks in."

"Craig and I feel you've done a wonderful job raising Joel," Donna said. "We know you've worked hard. I appreciate it probably more than their dad at times. You've taught Joel and Grant values and responsibility, manners and respect. It's made being a step-mom a breeze."

"That's a kind thing to say. I appreciate it."

Gertie filled a bowl with potato chips. "I figured you two would hate one another."

Lenore and Donna both laughed. "Donna wasn't the cause of Craig and me divorcing. We had just grown up and grown apart. She came into his life long after I was gone. She's been a great step-mom."

Donna looked relieved and grateful for Lenore's comments. They smiled at each other, respectful of the other's contributions. John walked into the kitchen, breaking the mood and the comradery.

"Ladies, we're ready for the burgers!"

Lenore watched John as he gathered the platter of meat and juggled an assortment of utensils. With his coat discarded somewhere in the house, he had rolled up the sleeves of his white shirt and taken off his tie. He was a handsome man and so eager to please her. She wondered why she could not be in love with him.

Donna and Gertie followed John to the patio with condiments and buns. Leah remained and leaned against the counter beside Lenore.

"It's going well, don't you think?"

"Thankfully, yes." Lenore smiled and nodded. "It could really have been an uncomfortable situation."

"John's a good host." Aren't you glad he's here?"

"Very!" She smiled while putting a jar of pickles back into the refrigerator and pulling two Diet Cokes out.

"Bet you're glad he's incredibly handsome, intelligent and personable, too," Leah teased, accepting the can.

Lenore sat her own Diet Coke down and took two glasses from the cabinet. "You make it sound like I picked him just to impress everyone. John's a good friend."

"I know, but it doesn't hurt that he's all of the above, does it?"

"Absolutely not." They laughed and filled large glasses with ice to be filled with their beverage of choice. Leah carried their drinks while Lenore carried plates, flatware and napkins to the backyard and joined the others.

The graduate, his friends and brother Grant had changed into shorts and T-shirts, and were tossing a plastic disc back and forth, eventually coaxing Royce into the game. Lenore watched the assortment of personalities in friendly conversation. John and Craig seemed comfortable with sharing the cooking duties. JD had brought his video camera and captured moments on tape, to be viewed in years to come.

It was a relief when the last guest left. Joel had been gone for nearly an hour, making his rounds to an assortment of post-graduation parties with Kim and his friends. Grant had gone back to Denver. Leah, Gertie and Donna had done a majority of the clean-up. Only John stayed.

A few remaining glasses and plates were loaded into the dishwasher, and as it was started, John took Lenore's hand and led her to the patio.

"It's going to be a beautiful sunset. I think you should relax and enjoy it."

It was cooler outside and Lenore took a deep breath. "Thanks. I'm glad you were here today."

He smiled at her, his tanned face bathed in the sunset's colorful glow.

"Because I'm such a good cook, and I can clean, too?"

She smiled and put her arms around his waist. "No! I mean yes, but other things."

"What other things?" His arms surrounded her and he kissed the top of her head.

"Oh, your smiles and the occasional wink. You kept me from getting weepy."

"Good!" He tilted her chin up. "Those beautiful eyes have nothing to cry about. You've reached a major goal in your life, and you did it well. Joel's on his way."

"Yes, he really is. So many times, I didn't know if we'd make it to this day. Now that it's here and gone, I'm feeling a little empty."

He hugged her close. "Well, he still has to get through college, and you have your own career to work on now. You still have goals and, if it's any help, I'll still be here for an occasional wink." He held her back and gave her one. "How's that?"

Lenore smiled as she looked into the handsome face. He kissed her lightly and hugged her again.

As she spoke, a lump came into her throat. "You've helped me through the most traumatic time in my life, John, and I'll never forget it. I don't know if there can ever be anything more with us or not. I don't want you to hang around expecting something which might never happen. You may just want to walk away and get on with your life, too."

He held her back and looked into her eyes. "Lenore, I can't say I don't want more, but I also know why there may never be more. I'm happy to be whatever you'll let me be: a friend, a companion, an escort or even a chef at your cookouts. I'm satisfied."

Lenore put her arms around John's neck and kissed him with clear-minded passion. He was surprised and looked into her eyes. If Greg Parish was there, he was well hidden. He returned her kiss and felt her body press against his.

As sunset colors deepened to shades of purple and fiery crimson, two bodies melded into one. John lifted Lenore into his arms and carried her to the bedroom where fervent desire was guided tenderly by true affection. As breathing returned to normal, Lenore looked into John's eyes and ran her fingers through his hair.

"And an occasional lover, if it's okay?"

John looked at her, smiled and shook his head. "What?"

"Along with being a friend, a companion, an escort and a chef, I would like for you to be an occasional lover."

He laughed and kissed her softly. "I think I can manage it. You surprise me. I never know what to expect from you, Lenore."

"Do you mind?"

He smiled. "No, I'll never tire of your surprises."

He wanted to tell her how much he was in love with her, but they were words she had heard before. No, he would simply have to be there for her. He would show her his love in whatever capacity she would allow.

They showered together, washing each other and talking comfortably.

"So, was it my cooking you couldn't resist?" John teased, as he washed her back.

She turned and took the soap from him, making him turn away from her so she could wash his back. "You just looked so handsome. You were cooking and laughing and so comfortable with everyone. I felt urges I hadn't felt in a long time."

"Mmm, maybe I should cook more often." He turned around, but before things could get out of control, they realized the water was cooling considerably. It didn't take long to rinse and get dried.

They were dressed, sitting on the couch and watching television when Joel came home. He never suspected their smiles were fueled by anything more than his presence.

"Thanks for the great party, Mom. You too, John. If it's okay, I'm going to the after-graduation dance. I'm supposed to pick Kim up in a half hour." He started to leave the room, then turned back. "John, thanks for the gift certificate. I'll get some good clothes for college."

Lenore smiled as he left the room. John laughed. "I hope the hot water has recovered. I noticed he didn't wait for an answer when he asked about going to the dance."

"He knows better than to ask questions I'll say no to. We sort of read minds that way or something."

371

"You've got a healthy relationship with your son. Do you think you'll ever tell him about Greg?"

The question surprised her and she turned to him. "There's no reason to. Why did you ask that question, John?"

"I don't know." He shrugged. "There's always the chance ...."

"Of what? That he'll suddenly appear and I'll run into his arms and forget the hell I've gone through just for meeting him?" Lenore could hear the shower and was glad Joel would not be interrupting the conversation.

"For the first time tonight, I was able to put him so far in the back of my mind, I could only see you when we made love. I can't believe you would bring him up."

He wanted to take her by the shoulders and tell her Greg was in a prison. He wanted to tell her that one day Greg would be free to come back to her, and it was going to break his heart when she chose the Russian over him. Instead, he stroked her hair.

"He'll always be there, in the back of your mind. Until you know what happened, and why, it'll be in the back of both our minds. It might have been something beyond his control. You can't tell me you don't want to know."

"No, I don't!" Lenore folded her arms across her chest. "Can't we just put him behind us? I don't want to think about it because the whole situation scares the hell out of me. I need to get over it."

Lenore was shaking and tears were brimming. John reached out and drew her to him.

"I'm sorry. It's okay. I'll never bring him up again."

She leaned into him and cried softly. Joel entered the room and looked first at his mom crying, then questioningly at John. Before he could ask, John shook his head and motioned for him to go ahead and leave. Joel nodded and waved as he exited the room and then the front door. He would always assume his mom had succumbed to the realization of a son graduating from high school.

* * * * *

Demonstrations in the Soviet Union were something Lenore appeared to take little notice of, though Leah would bring it to her attention.

372

"Do you ever wonder if Gregor is over there helping them toward a new government?"

It was mid-July. Lenore had to finish putting laundry away before they could have the afternoon off together.

"No. Don't care if he is."

Leah followed Lenore around the house. "I find myself watching the newscasts and looking for him or his brother. I guess I don't know what his brother looks like, but I imagine he looks like Gregor … don't you?"

"I simply turn the television off when they start talking about it. I don't care." She put all but two towels away and slid the empty basket into the closet with her toe. She closed the door, then turned to Leah. "Look, I'm glad those people are making changes, but I certainly don't look for him. I don't care for the reminder, and I'm tired of talking about it." She smiled, taking the bite out of her words. "Change the subject, please."

"Okay!" Leah bounced back, un-offended. "When are you going to take your vacation?"

Lenore walked to the bathroom, Leah following, and hung fresh towels on the racks. "I haven't thought that far. I can't really afford to go anywhere with getting Joel ready for college. I may just take a day or two here or there and stick around home."

"That makes sense, as long as you save the last weekend of September for our annual trip to Glenwood Springs."

Lenore frowned. "I'm not so sure I want to go there again. Let's go somewhere different. How about Steamboat?"

"It just wouldn't be the same. Glenwood Springs is our special place, and we haven't hiked to the Maroon Bells!"

"It's just a little too special, Leah. There are plenty of fantastic places to see in Colorado."

Leah breathed out a loud, heavy sigh. "He has changed you in so many ways." She knew it would light up the brunette's defenses.

"What do you mean, he changed me?"

"Well, he has! You're too serious and you don't smile or laugh as easily. Now, you're taking something that was so special to you and me and letting him ruin it, too."

"Leah, I'm more serious because of the responsibilities I have. I worry whether I'm doing my job well enough to ever get my own store. I worry about Joel going off to college. It has nothing to do with ... him."

"Then why can't we go back to Glenwood Springs?" Leah whined.

Lenore turned and walked into the bedroom, pulling open drawers and getting her bathing suit and shorts. "That's almost two months away. Let's just wait and see if I can afford to go at all. We'll think about it, okay?"

"Hmmm, okay. How's John doing?"

"Okay, I guess. We've both been too busy to get together. He calls though." She tossed her work clothes into the hamper.

Leah knew what was keeping John busy. She had her own conversations with him from time to time. Though he was not directly involved with negotiations, he was apprised of situations as they occurred.

"You two need to go out more often. You're both workaholics."

"If that means I do little more than work, you're right." She said as she pulled on her bathing suit.

"You look tired, too," Leah added.

"Thanks! Any more compliments?"

"Seriously, Lenore, are you sleeping well?"

Lenore groaned and pulled on a pair of shorts over her suit, then stepped into sandals. Leah was determined to get an answer. "You're not, are you?"

"Not very well, no." She walked out of the bedroom and Leah followed. "I still have nightmares about the abduction. I woke Joel last night, as a matter of fact, screaming." She paused and looked blankly at the wall. "I got away and I know they caught the men who did it, but I just can't let go of the fear."

"John told you they were caught?"

"Yes." She turned and looked at Leah. "Why do you act surprised? He's telling me the truth, isn't he?" Panic edged into her voice.

"Of course, it's the truth." *A partial truth,* Leah thought. "I was just surprised he discussed it with you."

"I was afraid you were going to tell me they were still out there somewhere." Lenore chuckled nervously, picked up the cooler and walked to the front door. "I wouldn't exactly say we had a discussion on the subject. He just said the three men were caught when I asked about it." She tilted her head a little. "Why does John call you?"

"Oh, he just calls when he can't get in touch with you or to see how you're doing. He worries about you." She handed Lenore the keys to Baby and took the cooler. "So, if you know they aren't out there lurking around, why are you still having nightmares?"

Closing the door and locking it, they stepped into the hot Colorado summer day. Lenore pointed to her head. "I guess I don't have any control over this mind of mine at night."

＊＊＊＊＊

In half an hour they were laying prone on their rock, soaking up the sun's rays into already tanned bodies. Then Leah abruptly interrupted their bliss.

"I don't think anyone else will come after you, if that's what's bothering you."

Lenore raised herself on one elbow and looked over the top of her sunglasses at Leah, who continued to lay quietly with her eyes closed.

"What?"

Leah didn't stir, except for her mouth, which was rarely still.

"If you're worried someone will try and abduct you again or hurt the boys, I don't think you should."

Lenore thought back to their hour-old conversation and settled back onto the blanket.

"You don't, huh? Why?"

"According to John, the Soviet Union is so embarrassed about the whole situation, they've sent a formal apology to our government."

Lenore was silent for a minute. "Why haven't they sent an apology to me? I'm the one who went through it."

"Oh, they probably will, eventually. You know, red tape and all. It could take a while."

"Imagine that! Lenore Appleby gets a formal apology from the Soviet Union." She contemplated the idea for a few seconds. "Oh, shit! How would I explain that to the boys?"

"John would make certain to be discreet, I'm sure. Maybe they'll even send a special messenger." Leah smiled to herself, knowing the messenger would be Gregor Parishnikov.

"I sincerely hope not!" Lenore said with a chuckle.

This time it was Leah who raised on one elbow and looked at Lenore. "Why not?"

"Because if I see one more Russian, I'll lose it!"

"Even if it was Gregor himself?"

Lenore raised up and they were facing one another.

"Especially if it was him. I'm talking sanity and life itself here." She laid back on the blanket. "How did we get onto this subject anyway?"

"You aren't sleeping."

"If I promise to start sleeping, will you promise to stop talking about him?"

"Who?" Leah asked with feigned innocence.

"Gregor!" The brunette shouted. "Are you satisfied? I said his name."

"It didn't hurt a thing to actually say his name, now did it?"

Before the last words were out of Leah's mouth, Lenore had moved to the edge of the rock and started vomiting. A frantic Leah reached to keep her best friend from plummeting over the edge. It was several minutes before the retching subsided and Lenore sat back on the blanket.

Leah handed her a tissue, then soaked a napkin in ice water from the cooler and wiped Lenore's brow.

"My God, Lenore, I had no idea it would upset you so much to talk about him."

"I didn't either." Her voice was raspy and quiet.

"What gets you so upset?"

"Not knowing the answer and the prospect of having one. I do pretty good pushing it in the back of my mind." She coughed, then turned to face Leah. "The incident in Kansas City just added to my confusion. Maybe if I would have cooperated, I could at least have seen him again and asked why he left. When they threatened Joel, I just lost it. I lost the chance to ask why."

She took a sip of Diet Coke. "Please understand, Leah, I have to put him away for good. I've accepted the fact there's always going to be a cloud covering the answer. I don't know why John keeps talking to you about it, but just don't relate any of it to me. I'll eventually stop having the dreams." She shrugged. "Maybe I should get some sleeping pills. I used to have some, but I can't find them since I moved."

Leah knew where the pills were, but she didn't feel it was time to give them back. Lenore could always buy more, but Leah hoped she wouldn't.

"Do you want to go home, Lenore?"

"No way! Just let me relax here and think about something else. I'll be fine. I'm not going to waste our afternoon off together."

* * * * *

As the month of July passed and August came to a close, Leah continued to monitor the situation through John, but never mentioned the Russian again to her best friend. If Gregor had any hopes of reuniting with Lenore, he would have to be far more efficacious than the flirtatious dance of their first meeting.

CHAPTER 40

Gregor sat in the airport terminal and smiled as he listened to his brother. They had spoken only once since his release from prison a month earlier, and he had been able to ask very few questions. Finally, they were united at the US embassy and had been together for the last two days. Now they were both preparing to fly to the United States.

Gregor could have flown back immediately upon his release, but the paperwork for his brother's departure had been nearly impossible to process. He had chosen to remain until he could take Alexander with him; he would not leave his brother again. Gregor looked at the young man, so different from himself. He was clean-shaven and his hair light brown. The tortures in prison had left scars, not all of which were physical, but the life Alexander had led prior to prison was benign. The stresses of Gregor's chosen field had aged him more than the two-and-a-half-years difference would infer, as did the physical tortures Gregor endured in his own prison. They both had dark brown eyes, though the normal spark of mischief was missing. It would take a while to return to either of them.

"Gregor, will you still have the beautiful home you spoke of?"

"Perhaps not, but we will find another." Gregor patted Alexander on the shoulder.

"Will the American woman live with us?"

Gregor ran his fingers over his neatly trimmed beard. "It has been a very long time, Alex. It is possible she no longer remembers who I am."

Alexander frowned. "But you spoke of love to her and she to you, yes?"

"It was nearly a year ago."

"If she loved you once, she will love you still." He smiled at his older brother. "I could speak to her for you."

"My brother, I will speak for myself, if she will listen."

The plane was boarding. The only people to see them off were a secretary and an official from the US Embassy. They settled into the seats of the nearly vacant jet and were prepared for a long flight, neither quite sure what to expect when they reached their destination.

*****

John drummed his fingers on the desk as he listened to the phone ring. He was ready to hang up when he heard Leah answer.

"Leah, I was about to give up. Can you talk?"

"Sure. What's up?"

"I just got word Greg and his brother left the Soviet Union about two hours ago. You might want to let Lenore know."

"I can't believe he's finally coming home. Thank God! I don't think we should tell her yet."

John frowned. "Why not?"

"There's still the chance he won't want to see her. Have you talked to him?"

"Not yet. The Company thought if I tried, it could jeopardize the whole operation."

Leah was quiet for a few moments. "Well, first you have to find out if he still wants to see her. We'll make arrangements from there."

"I'll meet his plane in New York, then we'll head to Langley. They'll want to do some serious questioning, and check out Alexander as well. Don't know how long it could take."

"This is going to be a tough one on you, isn't it?"

John leaned back in his chair. "Leah, until she sees Greg and decides for herself whether or not she wants him, I just have to do my job. But, yes, it's about the toughest thing I've ever had to do."

"I don't know if it will make you feel any better, but the last time I talked to her about Gregor, she threw up."

John cleared his throat and smiled. "Thanks for the encouragement. I need to make a few calls now. I'll be in touch. You can figure out how to break the news to Lenore."

John hung up the phone, knowing he would escort the two Russians to Langley, and eventually to Colorado. He then picked up the phone to make reservations for the New York flight, then sat it back down. He walked across the room and sat in a chair, stared at the phone, then got up and walked back to his desk. Once again, he picked up the phone, then looked at his watch and put the phone back down. He walked across the room, switched off the light and closed the door behind him.

* * * * *

Lenore was walking to her car when the black Mercedes pulled into the parking lot. She went to the passenger door and opened it.

"This is a pleasant surprise. What are you doing in town?"

"Just had the urge to see you. I didn't call first." He offered a smile. "Can I take you out to dinner, or do you have plans?"

"No plans. I need to take the deposit to the bank and let Joel know I won't be home."

"Great! You can call Joel from the car on the way to the bank."

Lenore settled into the passenger seat after giving John a quick peck on his cheek.

Half-an-hour later, they were seated at a restaurant, when John took Lenore's hands.

"I wanted to talk to you before I fly to New York tonight."

"That sounds ominous." She peered at his face. There was no smile. "What's in New York?"

"Not what… who. I have to meet someone there. I wanted to see you and tell you how much I've enjoyed getting to know you." John smiled, stroking her soft hands. "We got off to a pretty rocky start, and now I'm finding it hard to say good-bye."

"John, this isn't good-bye for tonight, is it? You're saying good-bye for a long time." She pulled her hands away and put them around the glass of ice water in front of her. "I take it this person you're meeting in New York is someone pretty special." She stared at the glass in front of her.

"You could say that," John answered quietly.

Lenore sipped her water, suddenly wishing they weren't in such a public place.

"I'm glad you have the decency to say good-bye. I honestly do appreciate it, John." She swallowed hard to suppress the lump forming in her throat. "This person you're meeting, it's someone you haven't seen in a while?"

"That's correct."

"I'm not surprised you have an old lover. You're a pretty terrific guy." She tried hard to sound casual and happy for him.

"Lenore, this is going all wrong." He reached for her hands, but she put them in her lap.

"No. Really it isn't. I understand completely." She smiled her most phony, professional smile. "Listen, I'm not really hungry right now. Would you be horribly embarrassed if we just got up and left before ordering? I'd really like to go home."

She stood up before John could answer and walked outside. He left a twenty on the table and met her at the car.

"Lenore, I need to explain something." He put his arms around her and she turned away, not wanting to give into the emotions welling-up inside.

"Oh John, we both knew from the start what we had could never be anything more. My heart is in no shape for a relationship, and I suppose this is for the best. Let's not talk about it anymore. I should be really happy for you, but I'm going to miss you terribly." She forced cheerfulness into her voice. "You've become such a dear friend. Please tell her she'd better hang on to you. She's getting a pretty wonderful guy."

John took Lenore by the shoulders and turned her to face him, wrapping his arms around her.

"Lenore, there's so much you don't know and so much I need to tell you. For now, just don't write me off, okay? If things don't go well, there may be a chance for us."

She stood stiffly, not returning his embrace. "Please, don't confuse me anymore."

"Lenore, I love you." His eyes were filling with tears and he kissed the top of her head. "No matter what happens in the next few days, remember that, please!"

"Just take me back to my car now." Her eyes were dry, her voice quiet and steady. "You have a plane to catch. I'll be fine, John."

He opened the car door and she got in. When they pulled into the lot beside her car, Lenore turned and gave John a hug, then pulled away before the quick kiss could become anything more. She managed a smile and waved as her car pulled out of the lot, past the Mercedes.

The drive to Denver was too long and too lonely. By the time John boarded his flight, Lenore had cried herself to sleep.

* * * * *

Years of training were put to use as John watched the transatlantic flight taxi toward the terminal. Under different circumstances, he would have greeted the Russian in a friendly embrace, welcoming him back from a torturous experience. Under different circumstances, John would not have the emotional surges threatening to undermine his sworn duty. Theirs had always been a professional friendship. Two men, thrown together out of necessity. There had been little common ground, and the common ground they now shared was love for Lenore Appleby. Only one was aware of it.

Greg Parish was not hard to pick out from the small group of passengers arriving. Though he was noticeably thinner, the smile flashed with familiarity when he saw the CIA agent. The younger man at Greg's side was, John assumed, Alexander. He looked nervously at his surroundings, then back to his brother. The three men approached one another, with John extending a hand to Greg.

"Welcome back to the United States, Parish."

Russian words were quickly exchanged between the two brothers. John could understand most of it.

"You will have to excuse Alex. His English is not very good. I have tried to explain the Americanized version of our family name."

Introductions were completed, and John urged the duo toward another gate, where they would board a Company jet headed for an airfield in Virginia. Accommodations had been prepared. A battery of intelligence personnel was ready to question the two Russians. One was allegedly returning from a foiled attempt to remove his sibling from their homeland. The other man, the object of the attempt, was now asking to remain in a country his brother had chosen for him. The CIA's job was to be sure it was a warranted move for the American government.

John spent very little time with Greg and Alex over their first three days. He was relieved at not having to discuss Lenore or why the Russian had chosen to leave the way he did.

The reprieve was not to last.

* * * * *

The flight to Denver would be long and without the luxury of space to avoid confrontation. They had turned off the seat belt sign only seconds before Greg crossed the aisle and seated himself next to John.

"There is much we need to talk about before we get back to Colorado. You know what it is I wish to discuss."

"Lenore." John stared out the window, frowning.

"You have protected her, yes?"

John turned to look at the Russian. "I did my job."

"They were planning to bring her to the prison. I owe you so much for preventing this."

John shook his head. "No, you don't. Lenore prevented her own abduction."

Greg frowned. "You must explain this to me."

John related the story of Lenore's experience in Kansas City. He told of the murder of an innocent bystander in the airport, and the eventual death of Sergei from injuries Lenore had inflicted. He told of her injuries and hitchhiking with the trucker. He gave all the details, right down to the smashing of the lamp. All the details, that is, except of being so terrified of losing her. John watched the Russian's eyes go from interest, to anger, to tender concern as the story unfolded. There was no doubt this man was in love with Lenore.

"My Lenore, she is a brave woman, yes?"

John did not answer immediately. The word *my* stung sharply. He wanted to say Lenore had been his own on more than one occasion, but it wasn't a complete truth.

"It's been a difficult year for Lenore. She's been through a lot because of you. She didn't understand your leaving, and quite frankly, neither did I." He frowned and gestured with his hand. "What in the hell possessed you to attempt going back for your brother? You know we could have accomplished it for you."

Greg looked away from John and sat quietly for a moment before answering.

"It was not something I wished to ask of my new government. I feared it would put someone in great peril, and I could not ask this of anyone on my behalf. I felt I had received so much in being given the opportunities and freedoms I had only dreamed of. When Lenore came into my life, plans had already been made. It was tempting to stay with her, but I could never have enjoyed a life with her, when my brother was still in the Soviet Union." They both looked at the younger man dozing in the seat across the aisle.

"I had been out of the game too long and was not alert for entrapments. In all those many months, the only reason to resist repatriation or insanity, was the thought that Lenore would someday understand, and I would have both her and my brother to finally start living a life my heart was so very ready for." Gregor looked at John. "Tell me of her."

John began talking as though reading a dossier. He related her move and the divorce. He told of her oldest son moving to Denver and of Joel graduating from high school. He told of Joel's music scholarship and acceptance to Colorado State University. He told of Lenore's acceptance and training in management.

"John, what of Lenore? Are her eyes as beautiful?"

John thought for a moment, staring at the wall in front of them.

"Yes, Greg, Lenore's eyes are still beautiful. There's a sadness in them I believe you are responsible for. I don't know if you can take it away or not."

"What does she know of my absence?"

"Nothing, except you left with very little explanation and did not return. Her friend Leah thought it best. I agreed for a while, until I saw how much it tore her up." John rubbed his forehead and frowned. "She should have been told everything, but Leah was afraid it would be harder on her to know, in case we couldn't get you back."

Greg was quiet for a while.

"Will she want to see me?"

"It'll be tough trying to approach her. I know you're still in her thoughts, but she manages to cope by denying it."

"If she will only give me the opportunity to speak, I will tell her everything."

John shook his head. "You're on your own, Greg. You might enlist Leah, but I'm out of the game."

"John, do you understand my love for Lenore?"

"Yes, I do."

"This is because you love her also?"

John didn't have to answer.

"Is she in love with you?"

John looked out the window. "She hasn't room in her heart to be in love with both of us."

Greg moved back to the set next to his brother for the remainder of the flight. Each man was deep in thought; thoughts of Lenore.

* * * * *

When the Company jet landed in Denver, John took the two Russians to his apartment for the night. Greg and Alex were settled into the guest room, and John sat in the den, sipping scotch and water. Greg waited until Alex slept, then came into the den to join the only friend he knew for a drink. He sat on a chair opposite the agent.

"John, I understand how you must feel. It would be difficult to look into the eyes of Lenore and not fall in love with her. I do not feel betrayed."

"Rest assured, Greg, it was never my intention to fall for her. She was an assignment. I couldn't stand to see the pain in those eyes… the questions." John got up and poured more scotch into his glass, skipping the water. "I don't know, I guess I wanted to protect her. I wanted to take the pain away, but I couldn't. You were always there."

"If I am given the opportunity, I will spend the rest of my life trying to remove the pain I have caused."

"If you don't, I will"

They toasted one another and finished their drinks in silence.

* * * * *

It was just after midnight, and Lenore was pacing in her living room, restless and sleepless again. She was glad it was Friday and she would have the afternoon off. Hopefully, she could get through four hours of work. She would cancel her usual plans with Leah and try to come home and sleep. She finished her scotch and water and went back to her bedroom, hoping the alcohol would help her drift into a dreamless sleep.

She opened the jewelry box beside her bed and took out a heart-shaped locket. Inside was a small piece of paper. It was tattered from repeated folding and unfolding, the words barely legible.

Tears filled her eyes, further blurring the already faint letters, but she knew them well. She whispered, "For your safety. See you soon."

The paper finally succumbed to the stress of age and handling, tearing apart in her hands. She tried frantically to press the halves together, tears flowing down her cheeks. As she realized the futility of her efforts, she folded them together and tore again, and again, and again. Exhausted, she collapsed on her bed amid the scattered pieces of Gregor's last communication.

CHAPTER 41

At nine o'clock in the morning, Leah answered the phone. It was John.

"Leah, I have someone who wants to talk to you. Can you talk?"

"Certainly." She smiled. "Is it who I think it is?"

Before she got an answer from John, the soft accent answered her question.

"Hello, Leah. It is Gregor!"

"Gregor, thank God you're finally home. Are you in Denver?"

"Yes. Please tell me, how is my precious Lenore? Can I see her?"

"Well, you can try. I'll be honest with you, the last time we talked about you at all, she became physically ill. She got very upset. I don't know how she will react."

"Please, help me with this. I have to see her and talk to her."

They discussed at great length, how best to approach Lenore. Since it was a scheduled afternoon off together, Leah assured Gregor he could meet them at the lake. She was sure a more public encounter was not a good idea, and not completely sure Lenore would be receptive anywhere. The lake seemed to put her most at peace, making it the logical choice.

Leah smiled with tears in her eyes as she picked up the phone to call Lenore.

* * * * *

Lenore finished with her customer and went to the phone.

"Thanks for holding. What's up?"

"Just confirming our Friday afternoon. Let's go to the lake for a picnic."

"Would you be upset if I told you I'd rather not today? I didn't get much sleep and I want to go home and see if I can take a nap."

"But this is our only time off together." Leah whined. "You can nap at the lake."

Leah was confident Lenore wouldn't refuse. Not only did Lenore have trouble refusing her best friend most anything, but the lure of fresh air and sunshine was like offering a hit to a drug addict.

"Okay." Lenore agreed, dispiritedly. "Could you run by the house and get my jeans, a clean shirt and my Nikes?

"I'll be happy to. See you about twelve thirty."

Lenore groaned just a little when she hung up the phone, while Leah danced around the house, giggling like a child who had discovered her Christmas gifts and didn't get caught. She dressed, then drove Baby to Lenore's place, where she retrieved Lenore's clothes. After a quick trip to the deli to pick up sandwiches, she was at the back door of the store before noon. With gentle urging, Leah convince JD to let Lenore leave early. The two women left in Baby, heading for their favorite rock at the lake.

* * * * *

John handed the keys of his Mercedes to Greg. He did not wish him well on his journey; his heart wouldn't allow it. As the tail lights receded, his feelings confounded him. Would she, or wouldn't she? Should he have told her the truth or not? He cursed the air. Now that the time had finally come, how could he just step aside and watch his whole life drive away? As he walked back into the apartment, he knew he could and would. The choice was never his.

* * * * *

The drive from Denver to Fort Collins was long. Months of rehearsals for this day grew more ambiguous with each mile. How would he approach his beloved Lenore? He only knew he must find a way to make her understand the absence was not entirely his choice.

He had survived his ordeal and had managed to reach the goal of bringing his brother to the freedom he loved. The success would be hollow if he were not able to share his life with the woman he loved. The only woman he had ever loved. The woman who had penetrated his feelings and made him believe his life could have normalcy.

He slowed and pulled into the parking area. The convertible was there and its occupants somewhere near. He got out of the car and closed the door. He looked over the top of the Mercedes and saw Leah and Lenore atop a large boulder.

Gregor drew in a deep breath, preparing himself to answer questions as he watched Lenore climb down from the huge rock. He smiled and called her name, preparing for a sweet reunion. When she turned toward the lake instead of toward him, he furrowed his brow. Then he heard Leah yelling for him to stop Lenore. He ran down the trail past Leah, who urged, "Hurry, Gregor." His muscles soon screamed at the test after so many months of little more than isometric exercises in the small confinement of his cell. Silently, he prayed for the strength and agility he had once taken for granted.

He reached the shore of the lake seconds after Lenore had plunged into the frigid water. He jumped in after her and took her arm, stopping attempts to swim away. The haunting scream from his captive echoed off the lake. She tried to hit him, but he held fast to both arms until he felt her struggling subside. Slowly, gently, he moved her to the shore, where Leah helped him bring Lenore to solid ground.

He had not prepared for the hurt and anger he found, and was not quite sure what to do next. Leah was there trying to soothe.

The words from Lenore stabbed his heart as she spoke. "Why are you here? Why are you starting this again? I was getting over it. Over you!" Fists clinched in anger, pressed to her temples. She spat out words between sobs. "Just go away. Don't make me go through this again." Then in a whisper. "I won't survive it."

How would he ever be able to take the pain away from this beautiful woman? After so many months, this was the greatest suffering he had felt. He knew he had to try to make her understand. He had to ask for one chance to explain what his absence had been for and what he knew it had cost him. He hoped the love he felt for Lenore would get through to her. He prayed the love she had felt for him at one time would soften her heart, and she would hear his words.

"I'm not here to hurt you, Lenore. After I tell you what I've come to say, if you still want me to leave, I will go and not return. Please hear my words."

She sat quietly for a moment as if absorbing what he had said. Using the heel of her hand, she wiped the remnant of a tear from her cheek and looked skyward, taking a deep breath before she answered.

"Apparently, I have no choice but to listen to you; but before I do, you're going to listen to me!" She stood, shrugging off Gregor's attempts to assist her, and stepped back from him and Leah.

"You know, I had doubts for a while you even existed anywhere but in my mind. I thought you were just someone I dreamed up because my life was in such turmoil with Nick. I managed to get out of my marriage with your monetary guilt contribution. I managed without you to turn to for comfort and reassurance. I did it alone, Gregor, while you were off on your little escapade or vacation or your seclusion." She gestured with her arms. "Or wherever in the hell you took off to."

Lenore began to pace. "Reality really smacked me in the face hard when I started having to dodge CIA agents for privacy. Then some fat asshole Russian, who was pissed at you for blowing away his kneecaps, tried to kidnap me at the Kansas City airport. I think he thought that if he had me, you'd show up like a white knight to rescue me and he could have revenge or something, but you know what?"

Gregor and Leah were both standing. They watched the green-eyed brunette pace and rave, knowing she was not waiting for a reply.

"I got out of that one all by myself. I did it without the CIA and I did it without you. I imagine you knew all about it, and you still didn't come back because you didn't care!"

"Lenore, please!" Leah interjected.

Lenore turned to Leah, shook her head and ran her fingers through her hair. "I'm not finished."

Leah looked at Gregor, wishing he would scream out the truth. Instead, his mouth was set in a firm line as he watched and listened. Lenore continued to spit the words at Gregor like a poisonous viper.

"All those months, Gregor, I waited and prayed for your return. I watched my son graduate from high school and start college. I started a career with the store. There were so many times I wanted to share what was going on in my life, but you weren't there. I actually felt good about myself, when I noticed I could go most of a day without thinking about you or seeing something to remind me of you. I dated your friend John and had a lovely time. He told me he loves me, but I knew I couldn't return his love, because I still love you …."

Lenore stopped pacing and stood, facing Gregor. She ran the fingers of her right hand through her hair and looked momentarily confused.

"My God! Why did I say that? Why would I still love you? You've made me question my sanity and my reason for living for nearly a year. If it hadn't been for Leah pulling me and pushing me to go on, I wouldn't have survived. She convinced me there was purpose in my life, Gregor. I don't know whether I should have believed her or not. I don't know who to trust. I don't understand why you're here or why she allowed it to happen."

Lenore looked at Leah. Both ladies' cheeks glistened with tears, and Lenore and finally relented.

"I think it's time you did some listening," Leah said quietly. "You've gotten your point across very well. Now it's Gregor's turn."

Lenore took a defiant stance and glared into Gregor's eyes, challenging him to convince her of his innocence. He met her stare and began.

"When last we talked, Lenore, I told you I was going away. I could not tell you more, because I was going back to the Soviet Union to free my brother and bring him to live in the United States. I did not tell you more because I did not want you to worry. I did not tell John because I did not want my new government to do something for which I believed I was capable of handling."

Lenore looked from Gregor to Leah, who closed her eyes and nodded. Gregor continued, drawing back Lenore's attention.

"Since I was a former citizen who had defected, I was a valuable catch. They tried to repatriate me. There were beatings and threats, the most disturbing of which was when they were going to bring you to the Soviet Union, hoping I would no longer have reason to fight their attempts. I was relieved when I knew their efforts had not succeeded." He looked away for a moment, then back into Lenore's eyes.

"Of those many months in a small cell, there were times I went for weeks without hearing the sound of another human voice. My meals were pushed under the door of my cell. I had no bed to sleep on, no blanket to cover myself with. I was unaware of the changes taking place in my former homeland. I was completely isolated from news of any kind, and had no ability to send word to anyone.

Lenore's arms were hugged around herself and tears were flowing down her cheeks. She finally noticed his thinness and the influx of white in his dark hair. She wanted to hold him and comfort him. But she couldn't move.

"Only one thing kept me alive and sane. My thoughts of you. They could not take you from me. I feared for your safety, but I had to trust the God my grandparents had taught me about and prayed He would take care of you, and somehow bring me back to you. It would have infuriated my captors to know a man they had spent a lifetime training and brainwashing, could choose to trust and believe in God."

He was quiet for a moment, watching a softness come into the eyes of the beautiful lady before him.

"Also, Lenore, I believed in you. I believed you would somehow understand, if I was ever to see you again. I never wanted to leave you. I will never leave you again."

He put his hand to his chest, tears flowing down the handsome, haggard cheeks.

"You are my life, Lenore." He held his arms open to her. "You are my precious lady. I love you."

Lenore could no longer resist. She rushed to his open arms and they embraced, crying. They cried for the time lost and for the time they now had. Gregor kissed and caressed and finally held her at arm's length, gazing into her eyes.

"I promise, I will never be so foolish as to leave you again. I will spend the rest of my life protecting and loving you. I want to bring happiness back into those beautiful eyes. I am so very sorry for bringing you so much pain."

Lenore touched his face and smoothed his hair, smiling as her chin wavered and tears continued to fall.

"If I had only known. God in Heaven, if I had only known, Gregor."

Leah stepped toward the couple. "Lenore, I was the one who decided against telling you. I didn't know he was actually released until a very short time ago. I didn't want to upset you or raise your hopes, in case he couldn't be brought back to the United States. At the time, I thought it best." She stared at the ground. "You had been through so much. I didn't know if you could handle the fact they knew where he was, but not how to bring him back." She looked up at Lenore. "Can you ever forgive me?"

Lenore turned to Leah and encircled her with an arm, still holding fast to her Gregor.

"You know, if it was anyone else, I don't think I could understand. You did what you thought best for me. You were here for me during some pretty rough times, and you knew what I was capable of handling. Of course, you're forgiven." She hugged Leah. "What you did, or didn't do, was out of love for me."

Gregor hugged Leah as well. "I believe what you did was wise. I would not have wanted Lenore to know what I was going through. Though not knowing was difficult in so many ways, you made the right decision."

The three stood in an embrace for a few moments, then Leah stepped away and patted Lenore on the back.

"I told you the clouds would all be blown away, didn't I?" She grinned at the two reunited lovers. "You two were just meant to be together. I knew it the moment I saw you look into each other's eyes the first time. It took God and a few diplomatic miracles between two countries to achieve it, but you're finally together." She giggled and hugged them both. "When do we get to meet your brother?"

Gregor laughed and smoothed Lenore's hair, kissing her again, before answering Leah.

"There will be time for meeting my brother. Alex is anxious to meet you both. You will have to help him learn the language. He does not speak English as well as I." He laughed. "For the present, you will not be meeting him." He looked back at Lenore and kissed her softly. "I want you all to myself. There is much to catch up on, and we need to discuss broccoli."

Lenore and Gregor laughed at the confusion registered on Leah's face. The three friends ascended the steep hill and climbed up on the huge rock. They stood and looked at their surroundings and held onto one another.

And the winds of September were quiet.

THE END

CPSIA information can be obtained
at www.ICGtesting.com
Printed in the USA
LVHW090725070221
678564LV00006B/394